The Poet's Wife

The Poet's Wife

REBECCA STONEHILL

bookouture

Published by Bookouture

An imprint of StoryFire Ltd.
23 Sussex Road, Ickenham, UB10 8PN
United Kingdom

www.bookouture.com

ISBN: 978-1-909490-51-2
eBook ISBN: 978-1-909490-52-9

In loving memory of my father, Harry Stonehill,
who always drummed into me that nothing happens
unless you make it happen.

Carve, friends, from stone and dream,
in the Alhambra, a barrow for the poet,
on the water of fountains that weep
and whisper, for eternity:
'the crime was in Granada,
in his Granada!'

Antonio Machado

PROLOGUE

He thinks we can't see him, but I know he's watching us, drawing us. We don't mind. We are so used to his silent presence observing from the shadows. Father and I sit on a faded rug, shaded by the leafy, fragrant canopy of my orange tree. In that yellowing, high heat of the day, I feel drowsy and lie back on the rug, my eyelids drooping and my head against the comforting dip of Father's waist. I don't know how long we've been here for, and I don't know how many poems I've been read, but García Lorca's words continue to wash over me. '*In the green morning I wanted to be a heart. A heart. And in the ripe evening I wanted to be a nightingale. A nightingale.*'

I hear movement from the corner of the courtyard and slowly lift my head and turn it. Pablo has shifted to find a more comfortable position from which to draw. As I look behind, he catches my eye and a small smile creeps onto his face. I smile back at him slowly, lazily. Then I turn back to rest my head on the rug and stare up at the patterns the leaves make against the sapphire patch of Granada sky.

CHAPTER ONE
LUISA

Summer 1920

My daughter Isabel is born on a day of fire-breathing wind that gusts in hot, furious eddies through Granada. Rather than the heat dissipating by seven in the evening, it has gathered enough momentum and strength to power a steam engine and thus, my first labour is long and arduous. I fix my eyes upon the soaring cypresses and parched mountains through the open window whilst trying to control my breathing, loud exhalations punctuated by the sound of Eduardo thumping up and down the stairs.

'Eduardo, *por el amor de Dios*, stay still!' I scream between contractions, horrified to hear my profane use of the Lord's name but powerless to prevent it.

'I'm trying! What can I do?' he cries through the closed door as his voice crescendos with panic. 'Just tell me, *por favor*, what can I do?'

'I should like you to stop your pacing for a start and – *Jesús*!' A shaft of pain tears through my body and as I double over the midwife mutters something about never before having heard such obscene language and, brushing her hands together announces the baby is on its way out. As I push and scream the name of every saint I can remember and strain my child into the world, I envisage the green-grey eyes of my husband on the other side of the door, the only man I have ever loved.

As I lie back on the bed in deep, grateful exhaustion, the door is finally opened for Eduardo, tears staining his cheeks. The midwife hands our baby to him and I listen to both child and father crying as my husband kisses my eyelids and neck and each of our baby's tiny fingertips and dusting of hair, the colour of roasted *castañas*. There is something deeply comforting about hearing Eduardo cry, for he only ever sheds tears of happiness. Such a trait I admire in him, for men do not cry. Men *never* cry, particularly these machismo *hombres* of Andalucía who cannot bear to show even the slightest sign of weakness. Not my Eduardo. He is not afraid to feel emotion, nor show it. And whilst he suffers ridicule for this, particularly at the hands of his brothers and parents, I love him all the more for it.

Eduardo Torres Ortega is an aficionado of the arts, a most unusual trait in his family. During his student years at the Universidad de Granada, he enjoyed nothing more than sitting in a quiet corner of a *biblioteca* or café, poring over volumes of Quintana and Machado, scribbling notes down in his spidery hand. It was not until his studies had finished, however, that a daring young poet became known in the city. Federico García Lorca is the other great love of my husband's life and this I never question, I must confess. To know García Lorca's work and to witness him perform in public is to feel the stirrings of strong emotion for the man. He possesses the deftest touch with words I have ever known and weaves his tales of passion, destiny and revolution around us all. But Eduardo scarcely misses a single event, attending each poetry reading, discussion and gathering humanly possible.

It is at one of these poetry readings that we are first acquainted; at least, it's where we first make contact. My parents are displeased I should attend such soirées but I am the youngest of six daughters and their energy, I suspect, has been exhausted on raising well-bred young ladies by the time I come of age, thus practising a form of blind tolerance. I am permitted to leave the house under the condition I am accompanied everywhere by Conchi, our youngest maid, who is not much older than myself. Silent and taller than anyone I have ever met, with vast, ugly, calloused hands that take me by surprise each time I see them, at first I find Conchi's presence irksome. 'Conchi,' I beseech her, 'if it is necessary you accompany me, at the least could you walk beside me rather than behind? I feel as though I am being pursued.'

'No, Señorita, I shall not,' she replies, her jaw set in a hard line. In time, I grow accustomed to her immense shadow flung against the wall when we leave the house for our evening *paseo*. I scarcely succeed in encouraging her to talk, which is a pity, because conversing is a great pleasure to me. But these irritations aside, I cannot fault her work and I do respect her. Her view of *me*, however, is far less apparent, for I read disapproval in her face with equal measure as concern.

One evening, García Lorca is reading from his latest collection. His eyes are closed and his thick black eyebrows touch in the middle in concentration. Conchi insists we sit at the back of the hall (in the event, she tells me, the content of the poetry becomes shameless and the need arise to remove me). It is an airless evening and, as I slip my white gloves off, Conchi glares at me, fanning herself furiously with her *abanico*. We are sitting behind a young man with a full head of dark, shiny curls I cannot help but admire. Though I have not yet seen Eduardo's face, I sense he is agitated as his shoulders are tensed up around his ears and he is grasping the sides of his chair with tremendous force.

After he has finished speaking, García Lorca opens his eyes and fixes his dark gaze upon the audience, inviting us to share our thoughts. Not a word is spoken; I suppose we are all so much in awe of the great poet we are afraid we might seem ignorant. He tweaks at his bow tie, looks around the room and then calls 'You, yes you in the corner.' García Lorca is pointing towards the man with the curls and the most excruciating silence ensues with every pair of eyes in the room upon him. Yet the poor man is such a bundle of nerves that he can't get his words out, can only manage a stutter and then, to my great shame, I find a laugh escaping my lips. Eventually, the poet calls upon someone else and the poor man's chance has completely vanished.

I continue to attend García Lorca's readings but it is not until several months later that I next see the man with the curls. We both attend an impromptu poetry reading on the edge of Sacromonte, a *barrio* of Granada with narrow alleys and whitewashed, tumble-down buildings hugging steep hills. Only the first fifty arrivals are allowed in, and both of us arrive too late and are turned away. Upon remembering that the other unfortunate soul is none other than the man I cruelly laughed at, I become curious and, from our banished positions outside, we begin to talk. At least, I am the one to initiate conversation for Eduardo is both furious at his inability to cajole his way in and a bundle of stuttering nerves when it comes to addressing me, doubtless not helped by the fact I am un-chaperoned. For I have persuaded Conchi for the very first time to let me out alone, arranging to meet her at a certain place a little later. She was reluctant and crossed herself several times with those huge, calloused hands of hers before relenting. Eduardo walks me home through the narrow streets as we listen to the urgent peeps of birds in their wooden cages, hung up outside houses. He is too timid to make conversation and thus I am compelled to do so on his behalf.

When we reach the place I am to meet Conchi, he asks if he might see me again. I see no reason why this cannot be so and when I reply in the affirmative, he beams at me, his eyes crinkling into fine slivers. '*Gracias*,' he whispers.

'We live not far from here. If you should wait some-where…' I wave a hand through the air '…somewhere not *here*, then you can presently see.'

I hardly wish to spell out to the fellow I am inviting him to follow me, but he is none too quick to understand my meaning, for he continues to look at me with that pained, bewildered expression on his face.

'Ah!' he remarks finally. 'Well. *Buenas noches*, Señorita.'

'*Buenas noches*,' I reply firmly and watch as he picks his way through the plaza, casting one final glance backwards before he rounds a corner.

Eduardo stands outside for at least an hour. Conchi has pulled the brocaded drapery shut as she does every night, but there is the slightest gap and I can see him through it, leaning against an olive tree with his cap in his hand. I have not the slightest idea what he is doing stand-ing there, but he seems quite content. Every so often, I push back the eiderdown from my bed, lean forwards and peer through the crack. There he still is, rooted to the same spot, simply gazing up at the window.

Very odd, I think for the umpteenth time, but he has character and I like that, particularly as my parents are going through a phase of introducing me to various eli-gible bachelors. I am required to sit through one dinner after another being bored to tears by pompous oafs who believe I ought to be impressed by how much money they have or their endless round of socialising with equally dull friends of theirs. My parents desire that I marry into money; that is their main concern and thus, when Eduardo and his father call at our house the following week, my parents are so delighted by the wealth and charm (but most notably the wealth) of Eduardo's father, that Eduardo himself scarcely comes into the picture. We officially begin courting a few weeks later and it is not until that stage that my parents are forced to take notice of my new beau, the result being somewhat of a shock. Father in particular thinks Eduardo the biggest fool he has come across and cannot comprehend why anyone from such a good family should waste his time with poetry. I cannot deny that to begin with I persist with our courtship partly because he could not be more different from those dreadful young men who send me to sleep in my *tarta de manzana*, and also partly to vex my parents. But it does not take long for us to recognise in one another that we are the black sheep of our families. Just as gentle Eduardo was raised amongst arrogant and aggressive brothers, my sisters painted the perfect picture of decorum, while I, on the other hand, far preferred scrambling up the branches of a fig tree to needlework and, even more shockingly, love poems to lessons.

'That damned silly stuttering poet of yours will be your undoing, young lady,' my father growls on more than one occasion over the dinner table, whilst my sisters raise their superior eyebrows at me. I simply shrug and smile at them all as I run my fingers over Eduardo's latest letter on my lap with secret delight. Besides, I know the truth of it is that my parents are relieved I am courting at all, having assumed that no man in their right mind would want me.

True, he would not be their first choice, but he is at least studying law and comes from a respectable family.

As well as meeting on the occasional afternoon in Plaza Bib Rambla under the watchful eye of Conchi (who has been thundery ever since my single night of freedom), Eduardo and I adhere to the staunch courting tradition of talking through an iron grille that separates our house from the street. Reluctant as we are to partake in this, we can at least converse without Conchi's hawk-like presence.

'What did you eat for *cena* this evening?' Eduardo whispers through the grille as he crouches awkwardly on the cobbles.

'*Gazpacho manchego*,' I whisper back, 'and I nearly drowned in it with boredom.' As he laughs, his teeth gleam white in the dusky half-light of evening. Blushing, he glances nervously around him before producing a scroll of paper from his waistcoat pocket, tied up with a stalk of esparto grass and hands it to me through the grille. As he does so, my hand brushes his and his cheeks burn as he gazes at me with his wide green-grey eyes.

Eduardo's letters are filled with verses, eulogising my beauty, intelligence and wit which at first I find rather silly. But as the months pass, I find myself anticipating our meetings, surprised by the disappointment I feel should he be kept away.

One evening when Eduardo comes to visit me, he seems particularly agitated. He is wearing a navy blue bow tie that he persists in tugging at, as though it is too tight.

'Could you come and meet me tonight?'

'My parents have guests for dinner. We are having a huge *paella de marisco* and it shall be one of those affairs that go on for ever—'

'But can you not get away? Try! *¡Por favor!* I must talk to you.'

He clasps my hand through the grille and leans in close so that our faces are barely an inch apart and I can detect the faint smell of sherry on his breath and woodsmoke in his hair.

'I shall try,' I laugh, releasing his grasp slightly, 'though Conchi has returned home today so I am not sure how I shall manage it. What is so important? Could you not tell me now?'

His face clenches up and he drops my hand as suddenly as he grasped it.

'Now? Tell you now?'

I smile encouragingly at him. 'Yes, *por qué no?*'

Eduardo looks behind him, to each side and then stares up at the clouds moving overhead. He eases his head one way then the other and rubs his neck.

'Well...' he begins, seeming to address the sky more than me. 'You see, Señorita Ramirez Castillo, it is something I must ask more than tell; that is to say, if you do not desire this, then I should quite understand. And I am aware I must ask your parents as well, but I wished to ask you first, to save the possible humiliation...' He pauses and takes a deep breath, scratching beneath his chin. 'Because really, it is quite presumptuous of me to even think that you should, well...that you might...' Eduardo sighs and runs a hand through his curls as he frowns and looks back at me.

'*¿Sí?*' I ask softly as I reach as far through the grille as I can manage and take his hand, which trembles like a leaf in mine.

'Would you…would you do me the honour of becoming my wife?' Tears are running down his cheeks before I even have a chance to reply. This is the first time I have seen him cry and I rest my head against the grille and smile at him.

'*Sí,* Señor Torres Ortega. I should like to marry you.'

His eyes dance, two watery pools of green and as he brings his head towards mine and we kiss through the grille, our cheeks against metal, I taste salt and a hint of our happiness to come.

I know that Eduardo's parents feel much the same way about me as my own parents do about my new fiancé, content enough that somebody has accepted his hand that they are prepared to overlook the fact that I am neither as polite nor pretty as my sisters. Eduardo's grandparents died several years earlier, leaving a beautiful villa by the name of Carmen de las Estrellas. It is located in Granada's Albaicín, the old Moorish quarter with centuries-old white houses perched like clouds on a hilltop before tumbling down a slope towards the Río Darro. I have walked through this district on occasion and found it enchanting with its labyrinthine maze of narrow alleyways and ice-cold rivulets that descend directly from the sierras and stream over mossy cobblestones. The house has been neglected and fallen into disrepair, so as a wedding present, Eduardo's parents pay a large sum for the house to be restored to its former glory. The gardens are weeded, the fruit trees pruned, the floors polished, the large rooms aired and dusted, the gramophone cranked, the fountain and sapphire-coloured stars on the inner patio floor retouched, the columns re-plastered, the walls painted and, on a balmy afternoon in May, we are married in the nearby *iglesia* before Eduardo and I step over the threshold of our new home into its jasmine-filled courtyard.

A few days after Isabel's baptism in the small *iglesia* near our house, Eduardo proudly rushes out and buys an orange tree seedling. He spends the entire day on his hands and knees in the garden planting the seedling and patting down the soil around it, only to dig it up minutes later and re-home it in a new spot because the insects may get at it here, or the wind may be too strong for it there. He eventually settles upon the inner courtyard, heaving a plant to one side and placing the seedling in an huge earthenware pot over the top of a ceramic blue star. The same evening, Eduardo organises a little ceremony. The three of us gather around the seedling, Isabel's face peering out of an embroidered shawl. Eduardo clears his throat and stares deep into his daughter's eyes. 'Isabel María Torres Ramirez, this orange tree has been planted the same year as your birth. It shall grow as you grow. It shall breathe the air that you breathe.' I smile as I listen to my husband.

'And it shall bear fruit just as you will bear fruit. *You*, my daughter,' Eduardo continues as he brings his face down so that the tips of their noses are touching, 'are a child of the world.' And as the sky reddens above the courtyard, Eduardo takes Isabel from my arms, kneels down with her and gently stretches her chubby hand out to help smooth down the earth on either side of the seedling.

The year that Isabel is born is one of high emotion for my husband. He delights in watching the tiny being he has helped to create grow before his very eyes and then a telegram arrives which flings him into a state of un-controlled excitement. For years, Eduardo has been send-ing his poetry to various publishing houses, but he either hears nothing from them or receives curt, scribbled notes, thanking him for his time but explaining that his work is not in line with their ethos. Though he graduated in law in order to please his parents and uphold the family tradi-tion, I know and he knows and almost everybody knows that he is ill-suited to this profession. Yet money must be forthcoming and thus each morning Eduardo trudges down the hill to the city like a petulant schoolboy where he sits in his office and counts down the hours until his twice-daily escape, the first being his return home for *al-muerzo* and the second upon finishing his working day around nine in the evening. That is until one cool, bright morning when a letter is delivered whilst we are having breakfast.

Eduardo is sipping his *café con leche* when the telegram arrives and, upon noticing the sender's stamp, his hand starts to tremble so violently he places the coffee cup back in its saucer.

'What is it, Edu? Who is it from?'

'Brocches Baco publishing house,' he whispers, so quietly I can scarcely hear him. 'I must be alone.' Pushing his chair back hurriedly, he leaves Isabel and I as he slips from the room. But only moments later, I hear a door banging and noisy footsteps tripping down the corridor as he sweeps back into the breakfast room. His cheeks are flushed and, to my relief, I can see tears forming in the corners of his eyes as he takes me in his arms and squeezes me so hard I find it hard to breathe.

'Tell me! Quickly, what did they say?' I demand. Eduardo pushes me away and takes up the telegram, puffing out his chest like a peacock.

'*Estimado Señor Torres Ortega,*' he reads. 'We are delighted to inform you that we find great merit in your poetry volume, *Granadino Musings*, and would like to publish it in two months henceforth.'

I can see that Eduardo is having difficulty breathing and I try to coax him back into the chair to take some water, but there is no calming him.

'Luisa, do you know what this means? Do you *know* what this means?' Isabel is now squealing in delight at her father's enthusiasm and he turns and stares at her, as though suddenly remembering her existence, before dashing round to her side of the table, drawing her up and dancing around the table with her. She claps her hands and excitedly shrieks again, particularly when he knocks a half-eaten *torta alajú* to the floor, crumbs and broken shards of crockery splintering out across the floor.

'I am a poet! I am a poet!' he calls as he spins our daughter round and round. I perch on the edge of the table, shake my head and laugh happily. I know I can do nothing to stop him, and my heart sings for him.

Within twenty-four hours of receiving this telegram, Eduardo does three things in uncharacteristically flamboyant style. Firstly, he walks into the office of his superior in the middle of a meeting and announces to the room of bemused lawyers that he has a far higher calling than that of jaded notary, adding that one evening he saw the vice-president stealing money from the company safe. Secondly, he visits his parents and tells them that his is the life of a poet from thereon. Eduardo later recounts to me how the horrified Señor Torres clutched at the arm of his chair whilst his mother declared she was going to faint, demanding the smelling salts. He decided to leave them in this predicament, dashing out before they could discuss the matter further. Thirdly, he comes home three sheets to the wind for the first time in his life after spending seven solid hours in various *tapas* bars drinking strong red wine and spirits with his friends. When he eventually returns, I am obliged to virtually drag my husband up the stairs like a sack of *patatas* and heave him into bed. As I smooth his curls over his sweaty forehead and try to pour water down his throat, his last words are 'I'm a poet, *cariña*, I'm a poet,' before he falls into a comatose sleep that lasts a full day.

Eduardo experiences the sweet taste of fame and savours it in his mouth as a child relishes peppermint. Friends and neighbours rush out to the bookshop to buy that first edition, forming a queue for his autograph that snakes down the hill outside Carmen de las Estrellas. He is invited to be a member of the city's prestigious Literary Association whose meetings his hero García Lorca frequents. He buys fine dresses and hats with elaborate feathers for Isabel and myself. And he walks about town with a newly acquired swagger and sense of pride in himself.

The extreme euphoria lasts a year, a milder version perhaps two. Eduardo continues to write fiendishly, locking himself in his room for hours upon end, or sitting beside Isabel's orange tree sapling or out in the garden, gazing broodingly up at the mountains. Whilst I have lost Eduardo to the tempestuous seas of keeping his name in that bright place of stardom, I long for a new diversion, and I find it in walking. At first, I do not stray far from the house, taking Isabel down the hill of the Albaicín in her perambulator and strolling alongside the *río* into the sun-chequered plazas and narrow streets of Granada. In time though, I wish to explore more of the countryside that I see each day from the top windows of Carmen de las Estrellas. My upbringing has been so confined to the city, save the occasional trip out to a *huerta* to visit an uncle, that I find myself yearning more and more for wide open spaces and sky. Besides, though the landscape itself is dissimilar, being out in the hills around Granada remind me fondly of my summer spent in rural England.

One day, I attempt to push the perambulator off the main street into the fields, but return home shortly after, hot and furious; these contraptions are *not* devised with the uneven hillocks of the sierras in mind. And neither are these stiff skirts I must endure! Neither loose enough to be truly comfortable, nor close-fitting enough to look becoming, it is during my walks more than ever that I should like to wear a pair of Eduardo's trousers, or at the very least a skirt that constricts me less. The most comfortable footwear I am able to find are my lace-up boots, far from ideal but preferable to my court shoes. I know my mother, who bought me these fashionable boots, would be horrified to see all the delicate embroidery on the toes worn away and faded by the fields and the sun. *But*, I think resolutely as I pull a straw hat over my head, my mother, *gracias a Dios*, is not here and I am a grown woman.

Conchi has come with me to Carmen de las Estrellas but, now that I am married, she has been relieved of her duties as chaperone, much to our shared relief. She cooks and cleans in our new home and, after my unfruitful attempt of walking with the perambulator in the countryside, also proves very helpful in tying Isabel to my back with a length of long material. Conchi's ample hands secure a tight knot as she tuts under her breath. I know I must look peculiar, but with Isabel attached to me in this way, it enables me to walk across the *vega*, the fertile watered valley around Granada, through the Darro valley into the mountains, following streams through sugar beet fields and gently sloping olive groves.

One late afternoon in September, when Isabel is one week short of turning two years old, we set off to explore after the intense heat of the day has subsided. On my recent walks, I have been edging towards a settlement in the sierras not much more than an hour from our home, curiosity pulling me a little closer on each occasion. For I know that gypsies live in caves in these hills, and if one should ever find a person fascinated by the *gitanos*, it is I. For years, these people with skin the colour of Granada's *tierra* that sell prickly pear fruit or baskets and chairs made from esparto grass in the city's plazas have intrigued me. How I love seeing the women in their full skirts and bangles and bright tasselled shawls with their coal-black hair and jangling earrings and bold, proud faces. But I am probably most drawn to them because my parents have always told me to stay well away, and if they offer me a sprig of rosemary in the streets around the *catedral*, I ought to run a mile because they shall cast a spell on me.

All I desire is to observe these people from afar, but as I skirt around the periphery of the settlement, I am able only to see threads of black smoke trailing from the chimneys of the caves and the occasional figure moving around. I do not have the courage to move closer and can think of no reason why I should need to talk to anybody.

But on this particular occasion, Isabel and I have walked well beyond the settlement when I first notice the changes around me. I have learnt to read the signs of nature: the river flowing slower than normal means a period of drought is on its way; a flock of birds flying overhead southwards signals snow; and when the wind moves amongst the leaves with a certain rustling melody and the noise of the cicadas becomes headier this indicates rain. I know that it shall take almost an hour to get home, yet the rain I determine to be only fifteen minutes away. Remembering a cliff face we can shelter under, I quicken my pace.

But the rain comes sooner than I anticipate and within five minutes we are caught in a fierce downpour. We are in the middle of the open countryside with scarcely a tree in sight to provide shelter and I curse myself for not heeding the signs earlier. The dry *tierra* has been waiting for this for weeks and I sense it drinking in the water joyfully, a moment I should have savoured were it not for Isabel on my back. At first, she seems to welcome the few friendly drops. But with this sudden onslaught, she finds it not so desirable and begins to howl. I know I must keep my wits about me and hurry along the dirt track that is becoming more blurred by the minute.

Eventually, we reach the hill honeycombed with cave dwellings. I hesitate. What am I doing? I imagine Conchi crossing herself in horror and recall some of the unsavoury tales my sisters used to tell of *gitano* infamy. I am about to turn away when Isabel lets out a terrible scream. I bite my lip – if this child gets pneumonia I shall never forgive myself, I think. Taking a deep breath, I pick a door at random. I have to stoop to push aside the cloth hanging in front to pound against the low door with a horseshoe nailed onto it. For some time, my knock remains unanswered and I am about to try the next one along. But it creaks open and a large hand clasps my wrist and pulls me in. It all happens so rapidly that I am shocked to suddenly find myself in a warm, dry place. It is quite dark inside and I blink as my eyes grow accustomed to the dim glow of the room. The first thing I observe is a stove in the corner and a crackling wood fire. There are a few children seated around it, staring up at me with black eyes as wide as Conchi's copper pots. I then turn to look at the owner of the huge hand that still holds my wrist in a strong grasp. I stare into a pair of dark eyes framed by thick, black eyebrows. Around the eyes are dozens of tiny wrinkles, leading down to a small, but full mouth. The ancient lips part and I am astonished to see a row of dazzling white teeth within her weathered face.

'*Bienvenida*,' rasps a husky voice.

'G...*gracias*. I am sorry to intrude but it began to rain heavily outside and I feared...'

The old lady waves a wrinkled hand full of rings through the air disdainfully and tilts her head up to gaze at my daughter. And Isabel, I know, is gazing back at her for what feels like an eternity. I suddenly feel uncomfortable at this power the old lady, with her full green skirt and long silver hair twisted into a plait, seems to have over my daughter. I bring Isabel down from my back.

'Hungry?' the old *gitana* asks, but before waiting for a reply, she has muttered something to one of the children who scampers off and soon returns with a large pan of half-eaten *tomates y pimientos*, struggling under the

weight of it. The child then brings me a hunk of bread
and the gypsy nods at me. Tentatively, I tear off a piece
and dip it into the pan, allowing it to soak up the olive
oil and herbs before placing it in Isabel's mouth. Ravenously, she gobbles it up and opens her mouth for more
like a little bird and the old gypsy throws back her head
and lets out a shrill laugh. The smell is so divine it makes
my stomach turn with longing and after Isabel has eaten a
few mouthfuls, I can contain myself no longer and scoop
a dripping red pepper into the fold of my bread and place
it in my mouth. I close my eyes in pleasure; never has
food tasted so good. When I open them again, I see that
the old woman is staring at me, one thick eyebrow raised.
Isabel and I continue eating under her gaze and, when
we have finished, she silently hands me a tumbler of red
wine. It is delicious, heavily spiced with cloves and nut-
meg, and the gypsy watches me as I sip at it whilst the
children clamour round, marvelling at the fairness and
smoothness of Isabel's skin.

The old woman pushes the remains of the pan towards
me. I protest, but she merely grunts.

'You've been traipsing all over the countryside,' she
growls. 'You need to eat well, for you and your child.'
Isabel's eyes are starting to droop and the old lady picks
her up and, with surprising strength and agility, carries
her over to the far side of the cave where she lays her onto
a pile of blankets. Returning to me, she points her chin
towards the pan, motioning once again that I should eat.

She is silent for a long time and just as I think I shall hear nothing more from her, she says '*Me llamo Aurelia.*'

'Aurelia,' I repeat. '*Encantada.* My name is Luisa. I am terribly grateful to you.'

'These little ones are my grandchildren,' she continues. 'Each and every one of them.' She has a peculiar expression of pride and sadness in her eyes that I cannot quite fathom. 'Their mother's gone on a trip,' she adds. As she says this, Aurelia fixes me with an intense stare, almost as though she is searching my face for a reaction of some kind. Remembering the effect the old *gitana*'s gaze had on Isabel, I stare defiantly back. I soon realise, however, that I am in the presence of a greater obstinacy of spirit than my own and feel myself blushing under Aurelia's scrutiny.

The children flit around us like moths, sweeping the floor, clearing away the dishes and laying out blankets, and as I watch their slight figures, entranced, Aurelia walks over to the stove, pours something into a cup and then returns to the table.

'*Té* de menta.' She points to the cup. 'Drink.'

'*No, gracias*, Aurelia.'

'Drink!' she rasps and watches as I pick up the cup and sip at the tea. 'Every meal should end with *té* de menta. It helps digestion.' She nods. 'And increases sexual potency,' she adds, laughing so suddenly and loudly that I splutter into my cup, only making her laugh even more. I cannot help but be amused.

'And now,' Aurelia continues, once she has composed herself. 'I am going to read your palm.'

I feel the smile fade from my lips as the same clutch that drew me into the cave pulls my hand into her lap with one swift movement. Out of nowhere she produces a tiny wooden ruler and for a long while she takes measurements between one line and another, grunting occasionally. While she is doing this, I have the opportunity to look around the room that serves as kitchen, main living and eating area, as well as bedroom for the children, who are starting to sprawl out in front of the fire on rugs. Red peppers, dried corn on the cob, chillies and garlic are strung up from hooks and all kinds of copper pots and pans and ladles hang from every section of the fossilised walls moulded from rocks and mud. Several geckos scurry around, their tails flicking behind them and I watch as one relishes a meal of spider followed by moth, expertly reeling the creatures in with whips of its tongue.

Aurelia breathes out deeply and heavily, a sigh that seems to reach the very roots of the earth. She proceeds to tell my fortune, whilst I sit listening, scarcely breathing. She describes my past, reaching into the deepest caverns of my mind and extracting memories that I myself have forgotten. Then she dwells on my life at present and how fortunate I am to have the love of a good man. Finally she talks about the future: how many children I shall bear, the changes the course of my life shall take, the joy I shall feel and the great suffering I shall endure. Finally, Aurelia tells me the age I shall live to.

As she draws to an abrupt end, I feel more alarmed than I ever have done in my life. As a young girl I read tea leaves with my friends, inventing all kinds of wild fancies. But never has my palm been read like this, and most certainly not in such an authoritative manner which leaves no room whatsoever for the speaker to be challenged. Aurelia sighs deeply, the spell of her flow broken.

'I am tired, we should go,' I say weakly. Aurelia's face breaks into a broad smile. Picking up the hand she has drawn so much information from, she strokes it gently.

'You must not be afraid of your future, *mi querida*,' she says. 'And don't ever try to change it. It simply won't work.'

I swallow and stare into Aurelia's impossibly deep, black eyes. She heaves herself up from the table and fetches warm woollen blankets, motioning for me to follow. 'It's still raining outside, child. You must stay here.'

The prospect of sleeping in a *gitano* cave unnerves me, but the truth of it is I am deeply exhausted, more so after my fortune has been told. Gratefully, I stretch out with Isabel snuggled contentedly at my side. Minutes later, I feel the pull of sleep tugging at my eyelids and in a gentle delirium I think of Eduardo, remembering how anxious he shall be. My Eduardo, the poet, I think. How I love him. I watch Aurelia at the table reaching into her mouth and yanking around. Pulling out her perfect set of teeth, she cleans them thoroughly with a brush and drops them into a liquid-filled glass. The last thing I remember before falling into a deep sleep is the old *gitana* turning around and smiling a gummy grin whilst the false teeth smirk at me from their glass.

❊ ❊ ❊

On our return to Carmen de Las Estrellas, I find Eduardo
in his musty study in the exact spot I left him the previous day. His elbows are on the desk and his palms pressed
deeply into both sides of his head. One of his braces has
slipped down over his shoulder and I notice his straw
boater carelessly flung beneath the desk. In front of him
lies a blank sheet and strewn around the floor are dozens
of crumpled pieces of paper. It is not a promising sight.

'¡Dios mío!' I cry and fling open the window. 'Esposo,
you must shave that stubble from your chin at once.'

The fresh air hits Eduardo with a start and he looks
at me, stunned. He squints through the shaft of bright
sunlight pouring in through the window, exposing the
myriad dust mites that dance around him.

'Eduardo!' I say sharply. 'Will you please get up and
put on a clean shirt? You look dreadful.'

'Where have you been, Luisa?'

'Never mind about that now. Eduardo, por favor,' I implore, 'do this for me.'

It is a cheap trick and we both know it, but it is for
my husband's own good and it works every time. I have
become well accustomed to Eduardo's bouts of unpro-
ductive melancholia. He is simply unable to reconcile the
recent image he held of himself – of a man bursting with
pride and success – with the stale inertia he experiences
when he starts to write. During such spells, he forgets to
wash or change his clothes or even run a little brilliantine

through his hair. I know he would even forget to eat were it not for my insistence we sit down together for three meals each day. It is only when Eduardo actually forgets to sleep, which has clearly been the case in our absence, that I insist upon a change of scenery.

The following day, we lock up Carmen de las Estrellas and travel south to spend a week with Vicente, one of Eduardo's brothers, who has moved from Granada down to the coast. Vicente's wife is of a nervous disposition and cannot abide the noise and clamour of the city, preferring the gentle murmur of waves. Of all the Torres Ortegas, Vicente showers the least scorn upon his youngest brother's sensitive shoulders and Eduardo concedes that the sea air may do him some good.

On the train journey down, I look at Eduardo who stares out of the window, hunched and distracted. A boy passes along the carriage selling cigarettes and I shake my head at him and turn to face my husband.

'Do you not want to know, *cariño*, where Isabel and I spent our night away?' I ask.

He frowns. 'Were you not with your parents?'

'No. Why should you assume such a thing?'

He stares from me to Isabel, who is pressing her nose against the window and blowing hot round clouds on the glass.

'Well?'

I cannot keep the smile from my face, so excited am I about our adventure and, as the landscape outside changes from rolling hills to gentle slopes and olive groves, I recount the events of the previous day down to the smallest detail. Eduardo listens in silence, lips parted and his green-grey eyes wide.

'*¡Por Dios!*' is all he can think to remark after my story has ended.

I clap my hands together. 'Is it not marvellous? To have actually been inside a *gitano* cave!'

'*¡Por Dios!*' he repeats. 'I have been neglecting you and Isabel, Luisa.'

'Well—'

'No.' He puts a hand firmly out to stop me from speaking. 'No, I have. I see that quite clearly now. Whilst I have been wasting precious time, attempting to recreate *Granadino Musings* which,' he winces, 'I shall probably never be able, I have failed to notice what the two people closest to my heart have been doing. I knew that you had been walking a bit here and there but not in a hundred years did I imagine you were gallivanting around the countryside quite so…quite so *widely*.' He scratches beneath his chin.

'It's been splendid, Edu, *really*—'

'And what's more,' he cries, pulling Isabel down from the window pane and rubbing vigorously on the marks she has made with his sleeve, 'being entertained by all kinds of insalubrious characters. *¡Dios!* I forbid you to return to those caves, Luisa!'

'That is absurd, Edu,' I reply, and that is the end of that. I know Eduardo feels it his duty to utter such words, but I have little doubt he thinks me quite plucky for venturing into a gypsy's lair.

'I shall be more attentive from now on, *cariña*,' Eduardo says quietly and he reaches out and takes my hand.

'I know you shall.' I run a finger down his cheek. 'And do *not* give up on the poetry, Eduardo Torres Ortega, you have a talent for words.'

He smiles gratefully at me, nods slightly and turns to look out of the window.

So attentive does my husband become following our conversation on the train that the heady smell of bougainvillea, combined with glasses of chilled *vino de la costa* we drink each night, lead to a few romantic evening walks down to the ocean. One night, we come across a deserted old fisherman's shack on a cliff top and make it our own, rediscovering one another's bodies whilst listening to the crash and heave of the waves below us. I am overjoyed to see that not only is some colour reappearing in my husband's pale cheeks, but a spring has returned to his step.

One evening following *cena*, Vicente suggests to Eduardo that they leave their wives alone to tittle-tattle (which makes my blood boil; should I feel inclined to indulge in so-called 'tittle tattle', Vicente's dreary wife is the last person I should choose to spend time with). I have already retired by the time they return a few hours later, but I am aware of my husband tossing and turning in the bed and his occasional sighs.

I stretch out an arm and rub his back. 'What is it?' I murmur.

'Can't sleep,' he mumbles.

'Shall we open the window more?'

'No, it's not that. I've just had an unsettling conversation with Vicente.'

I wait. 'Do you want to tell me?'

'No,' he replies. 'In the morning.' Eduardo turns round to face me and squeezes his eyes shut, willing sleep to come. But moments later, his eyes are open again and in the dim light of the bedroom, I see a frown draw lines across his forehead.

'*Bueno*, here it is,' he sighs, propping himself up on his elbows. 'First of all, Miguel has become entangled in a messy new love affair.' Miguel is Eduardo's eldest brother, an unkind, hard bully of a man with a fast, spiteful tongue and an eye for the ladies. To find two more different brothers would be impossible. Miguel married a local beauty ten years previously then set about destroying her by barely allowing her to leave the house, and treating her as his personal slave whilst he gads about town, openly taking mistresses whenever he fancies. His long-suffering wife accepts all his indiscretions because she has no alternative. The law *never* falls in favour of mistreated women.

I do not know how he does it, but Miguel always manages to emerge unscathed and with that steadfast, arrogant smirk painted upon his lips. He is a wealthy and successful lawyer, covering up his tracks and ensuring his trousers are firmly buttoned up when propriety calls for it. Eduardo can scarcely bear to be in the same room as him, and I cannot blame him. Miguel was his greatest childhood tormentor, burning a stack of his poetry books when he was still a small boy and forcing his arm into a lock so tight one time that he almost broke it. Though we live in the same city, we see mercifully little of him.

'There is no novelty there, Edu,' I reply.

'Except it's a little more complicated this time. This new girl is with child.'

I raise an eyebrow but I am hardly surprised. His love affairs are so prolific, I am amazed this has not happened already.

'His poor, poor wife,' I murmur.

'Poor wife, and poor stupid girl he's got pregnant,' Eduardo mutters. 'And what's more, Miguel's not owning up to it and he's in danger of causing a scandal because this girl keeps appearing at his house, demanding to see him. Apparently she's of the lower classes, so the poor damned girl probably has next to no money to raise this child.'

I sigh. 'Edu, of course it is quite dreadful what Miguel has done. But this is not our problem, *cariño*.'

Eduardo smiles tightly and nods, a lock of dark hair falling over one eye.

'You're right, Luisa. Somehow that brother of mine still manages to torment me whilst having nothing to do with me.'

'We must sleep,' I whisper. 'It is late.'

❊ ❊ ❊

At the end of the week we return to Granada and life resumes its gentle course. If the weather permits, when the sun is high overhead we take our *almuerzo* on the patio under the overhanging wisteria, and these meals sometimes

stretch for hours, particularly over the course of the weekend, as we enjoy food from the fertile *campo* of Andalucía
and fruit from our own garden. When we finish eating,
Eduardo often carries Isabel through to the inner courtyard to the orange tree sapling and the two of them inspect its growth, water it and even talk to it, imploring
it to grow. We spend long evenings in the conservatory
as Eduardo writes, I read and Isabel sleeps. I meet with
friends who are also starting families, comparing first
smiles, first steps, first words, and I continue to walk into
the open fields beneath the relentless sun until my boots
are positively threadbare. It is on one of these walks I feel
faint and sit down hurriedly under the shade of a *mimbre*.
Little Isabel peers at me with concern.

I attempt to reassure her but find myself being violently sick into the willow's roots.

'*¿Mamá, mamá, estás bien?*' Isabel cries.

I smile and shrug. There can be no doubt: I am expecting.

❄ ❄ ❄

Exactly nine months after our trip to the coast, we welcome our second child into the family. I consent to a
more traditional name on this occasion and our baby is
christened with Eduardo's longed-for name, María. Isabel is not delighted to have a new sister. She stands over
the crib and peers down her nose at María, her pretty
face twisted into a scowl. When she takes to wheeling
her around the garden in the perambulator, I imagine
she is beginning to accept her sister's presence, but then

on one occasion, Isabel leaves her in the furthest hidden corner from the house, later claiming that María herself wanted to be there. I know I can do little, save wait patiently for the green-eyed monster to release its hold on my first-born.

But this year, due to a strange sequence of events, our family grows not by just a single child. Around three months before the birth of María, we receive a visit from Vicente at Carmen de las Estrellas. We are sitting in the garden, the sinking sun catching against the bright yellow of the lemons hanging from the nearby tree. Even with the large glass of sherry Eduardo has poured him, Vicente is nervous and fidgety, which is quite unlike him,. He asks polite questions about Isabel and our health and how my pregnancy is progressing, all matters we know he is not terribly interested in.

'*Venga*, Vicente,' Eduardo says jovially. 'Let's hear it.' My husband has been in good spirits lately; he is looking forward to the arrival of our second child and is enthused by some new poems he is working on.

Vicente shifts in his seat and clears his throat. 'Yes, well. Eduardo. Luisa. The truth is that there *is* something else I must talk to you about. We need to discuss something extremely important.'

'*¿Sí?*' Eduardo asks, smiling.

'Do you remember when you came to visit several months ago and I told you about a complicated situation that Miguel had got himself into with a girl?'

Eduardo's smile crumples into a frown. 'Yes, but what business is that of ours?'

Vicente takes a deep breath. '*Pues…*' he falters.

Eduardo and I exchange a glance.

'Something terrible has happened.' Vicente stares into his tumbler of sherry. 'You see, last week, Miguel returned home one evening to find a box on his doorstep and inside the box was a baby.'

I let out a loud gasp.

'*His* baby, you mean,' Eduardo snorts.

'*Bueno*, his baby.'

I glance at Eduardo and can see a small purple vein on his forehead that is only visible when he is angry. I place a hand on his arm and look at Vicente expectantly.

'And?'

'And because Miguel doesn't know where the child's mother lives, he's had to bring the baby into his house.'

'How very noble of him,' Eduardo mutters.

'And what else?' I push.

'And…and what Miguel wants to know is if you will have the baby,' he blurts out.

This time it is Eduardo's turn to gasp. His face turns very pale and he stares at his brother, aghast.

'*Por favor*, what do you mean, Vicente?' I ask. 'How can we possibly take in another child, particularly the child of Miguel?'

Vicente takes a large gulp of his sherry and his eyes flick from me to Eduardo, who has been shocked into silence, and then back to me again.

'He's prepared to give you money if you agree,' he says very quietly. 'A great deal. I told him to come here and talk to you himself, but he knows how much you dislike him and…well, he's being a coward. I said that I'd talk it over with you. See what you both thought. So there it is.'

Vicente suddenly looks enormously relieved. He drains his tumbler and helps himself to more sherry. I look at Eduardo, who is gazing out over the mountains, a strange expression of hatred and pity etched into his face. The Alhambra has been cast into shadow and the garden is losing its warmth and I am about to suggest we all go inside when my husband, still staring at the mountains, starts to speak.

'Do you understand what you are asking, Vicente? I mean, do you…or *Miguel*,' he scoffs, 'truly understand? How, for a start, would we be able to explain to people where this child came from—'

'Yes, but Luisa's going to give birth soon. Of course that's one of the main reasons he thought of you. You could tell everyone they're twins.' Vicente stares at his brother imploringly. 'I agree with you that Miguel has behaved outrageously. But he seems to be repentant and he's going to stop all this messing around with women. Like I said, he would provide you with a handsome sum of money. If you say no…I must be honest with you, I fear for the fate of that child.'

'Why can't *you* take the infant, Vicente?' Eduardo snaps.

'My wife? Looking after a baby?' He shakes his head. 'We decided a long time ago not to have a family and nothing, I fear, shall change that. You and Luisa are mar-vellous with children, we saw how you were with Isabel when you came to stay with us.' He draws a hand through his hair and looks at me. 'Luisa, at least tell me you'll think about it.'

I glance back at Eduardo, the small purple vein on his forehead pulsating.

'Let's go inside,' I say again. 'Eduardo and I will need some time alone to talk about this, Vicente.'

'*Claro*, I quite understand.'

I squeeze Eduardo's shoulders and he pushes back his chair to stand up. 'I cannot take in the child of Miguel,' Eduardo says, staring defiantly at his brother.

'Edu,' I press. 'Oughtn't we discuss this after Vicente has left?'

'We can talk all you like,' his face is ashen, 'but my answer shan't change.' I sigh and pull my shawl around me. I know it shall be a long night for both of us.

❋ ❋ ❋

Miguel and Vicente bring the tiny dark bundle late one night to Carmen de las Estrellas. Miguel holds the baby, entering the courtyard awkwardly and handing him over to my outstretched arms since Eduardo says he cannot bear to see his brother for fear of what he may do to him. I take one look at the child and realise immediately we have made the right decision. He stares up at me with bright, inquisitive eyes and grasps my thumb. I must say it is the first time I have ever seen Miguel acting sheepishly. His eyes dart nervously around the room and he digs his hands deep into his pockets before pulling them out again.

'I know Vicente mentioned money to you, Luisa. How much do you and Eduardo want? Name your price.'

Money? I have completely forgotten about all that. I continue gazing at the enchanting child in my arms and am about to speak when we hear a creak of the door behind us and turn to see Eduardo standing there.

'We don't want your money.' His voice is quiet but confident and I feel a surge of pride. For the first time in his life, Eduardo holds an incredible power over his brother.

'We want nothing from you. You disgust me.' Vicente and I watch in astonishment as Miguel stares at his feet, cowed. 'I never want you to darken this house again, do you hear me? I want nothing from you towards the upkeep of this child, not now and not while he's growing up.'

'Eduardo,' interjects Vicente. 'Why don't you accept some money? For the boy's future? Tell him, Luisa—'

'I don't want your money!' Eduardo barks so loudly that it makes us all jump.

I rush to my husband's side and lay a hand on his arm. 'Edu! Isabel will wake up!'

Eduardo pushes his hair away from his face and stands upright. 'We don't *want* your money,' he says more quietly through his teeth.

'Well, if you change your mind, you know where to find me. And...I am extremely grateful, you know.'

'I don't want your gratitude either. I'm doing it for this poor creature, not you.'

Miguel nods briskly and makes for the door. 'Are you going to come now, Vicente?'

'No, I may stay here a little while.'

As Miguel is about to close the door behind him, Eduardo suddenly remembers something.

'Oh, d…does he have a name?'

Miguel merely shrugs his shoulders and with that, he is gone.

❋ ❋ ❋

Isabel is puzzled by the origins of this baby and frequently points to my rounded stomach and then to the baby with a bewildered look upon her face. I am pleased that she understands this; after all, I have taught her to be curious of the world around her. But all the same, I do not wish to confuse the child and decide that as soon as she is old enough to explain the situation to her, I shall do. Curiously, Isabel's aversion to being presented with a younger sibling never extends to her new brother, whom we decide to name Joaquín . She can be equally unkind and spiteful with María as she is loving and gentle with our new child and I can only hope that this shall not always be the case. María is as fair as Joaquín is dark and as timid as he is curious. A less likely pair of twins could never be found, but to our great relief, nobody thinks to question it. Not my parents, nor Eduardo's, not the postman, the butcher or the stream of visitors that flood through the gates of Carmen de las Estrellas three months after the birth of María. Up until that point, Eduardo and I decide it unwise to allow anyone into our home, as most likely they will discern the difference in age. Thus the story sent out to the world is that I suffered a trying pregnancy and labour and feel terribly fatigued. Joaquín is, naturally, much bigger than María but we explain this is due to the fact he is the first-born and thus more strapping. It is far-fetched, but it works.

I have scarcely a moment to sit and breathe with three small children. Conchi, whom I know will keep our secret, helps enormously in her customary stoical manner. Yet even with the two of us, there seems an inordinate amount of work. I must confess I should be quite lost without her during these days. Eduardo, meanwhile, reluctantly concedes that he is not receiving the financial returns that his poetry merits, and returns to the city to work in the only law firm prepared to accept him after his previous dramatic resignation.

My new role as mother of three consumes me so entirely that it is not until some six months later I feel able to resume my walks across the sierras. Isabel is old enough to walk alone by then, and although Conchi wishes to accompany me and help carry the children, I know her disapproval would be all too predictable should I make my way back to the gypsy settlement, particularly if she discovers we spent a night there. Her older sister still works for my parents and word is likely to reach their disparaging ears through this channel. Anxious that I am embarking on such a walk alone with three children, Conchi helps to attach one baby to my front and the other to my back, furiously pulling at the knots till I am quite winded. María and Joaquín are heavy, but I know if I walk at a slow, steady pace, I can manage it.

We wind our way through the whispering fountains and graceful cypress trees of the Albaicín, along grassy banks by the Río Darro until we reach the *montañas*. It is a day in early autumn and as I breathe the sharp, silvery air into my lungs, I feel utterly free and exhilarated.

I have not been close to the cave at all since the night Isabel and I slept there, though I have thought about it on many occasions and I know that my curiosity is too great to resist walking in that direction. It is intriguing approaching the settlement in daylight, for everything was cloaked in darkness on my first visit. Just beyond the cluster of caves I notice the remains of Moorish walls, crumbling forlornly into the hillside. Children play on the ruins and shout to one another as they balance precariously on the sunken bricks. I can see a number of people, some of them lost in their tasks, and I watch as *gitanos* pick through olives covering large sheets, throwing the bad ones aside. Others sit in small groups between the clumps of sharp-spiked agave plants, weaving baskets from beige strands of esparto grass and I can hear the distant banging of hammers against metal. Most of them heed me no attention, but one woman stands on top of a cave, staring at me with open hostility. Her hands are placed on her hips, belly thrust out, and she glares at me as I nod and carry along the path.

From around the back of the dwelling's blinding white façade, a wisp of smoke curls upwards and I can hear the crackle and spit of logs being placed on a fire to stoke it. The door is half open and I call into the gloom. Two young children come out, both of whom I recognise from the previous visit.

'Is your abuela here?' I ask. They stare solemnly up at me with huge dark eyes before scurrying off around the outside of the cave to the backyard where they call excitedly to their grandmother. A noise startles me and I look up to see that a swallow is building a nest from mud and twigs on the cave and a piece of the wall has dislodged, rattling noisily to the ground. I stare, transfixed, until the children return, beckoning me to follow.

'*Ven! Ven!*' they call, their black eyes shining like coal. Aurelia is burning leaves, a musky scent spicing the air. Her hair is drawn straight back and caught up with a clasp at the back of her head, falling down into a tress which rests below her shoulders. Beneath her brightly coloured skirt, she is barefooted and as she moves, her bangles clash noisily against one another. In the sunlight, she looks not as old as I recall; it must have been the cave's dark shadows throwing lines onto her face that did not truly exist. She looks at us and smiles that same, knowing smile I remember so well from the previous occasion. Scattered around the yard are baskets filled with esparto grass and several half-started woven baskets. How I should love to learn weaving, I think.

'*Pañí?*' she asks. I look at her questioningly, for it is a word I am unfamiliar with. She performs a mime of drinking from a glass and I nod. 'You should learn some Caló, child. Your first word: *pañí*.'

Aurelia disappears round the back of the cave and a few moments later returns with a vessel filled with water.

She pours out a cup for me. 'Take it,' she says. '*Es un pañi muy puro.*'

'*Gracias,*' I reply and gratefully tip the cold water down my throat. Aurelia motions to follow her round one side of the cave where amongst the prickly pears and cacti there is a rusty old table and a few stools lying on their sides. She turns them upright, brushes off the dirt and nods at us to sit down. Gratefully, I heave the weight of the babies off my front and back and look around for Isabel, who is sidling up to the two small children in curiosity.

I sit down and wait for Aurelia to say something. When no words are forthcoming, I clear my throat.

'*¿Cómo estás, Aurelia?*'

She grunts indifferently as she beckons for one of the children to come to her. The little girl has a mass of black tangled curls and I think wistfully how I should like to take a comb to them, for her hair would doubtless look quite pretty if given a chance. Reluctantly she approaches and raises her hands above her head. Aurelia peels the child's grubby vest from her body, picks up a pot beside her and scoops out a handful of what resembles thick grease and begins spreading it all over her granddaughter's back and shoulders, pummelling it in with her callused hands.

'*Manteca pal cuerpo,*' Aurelia says as the little girl squirms. She turns the child round to face her so that she can repeat the same lathering on her chest and then once she has finished, does the same with each of the children who begrudgingly come forward.

'What is it?' I ask.

'It's lard. I put this on their bodies every day for health and luck.'

'And…does it work?' I ask hesitantly.

Aurelia turns round and stares at me, her eyes wide and defiant. 'What do my grandchildren look like to you? They're healthy as fleas, each one of them.' I avert my eyes from her gaze and look down.

'And you, child?' Aurelia continues. 'I see that you have your hands full.' She gestures towards the babies. María is sleeping and Joaquín has just woken up, rubbing his eyes groggily with his small fists.

'*Sí.* I…I…had twins.'

Aurelia looks at me long and hard, then stands up and shuffles under the overhanging cloth protecting the mouth of the cave. A few minutes later she returns with a bowl of peeled *higochumbres*, the prickly pears that liberally dot the *vega*. As she pushes the bowl towards me, she looks me directly in the eye.

'We both know you didn't have twins.'

I gulp. That same sensation I experienced the last time I was here tugs at me: unnerving yet enticing. Aurelia knows things about me that she oughtn't logically know.

The children have spotted the prickly pears and are approaching the table. Isabel returns to my side and gawks up at Aurelia who is smiling down upon her like an indulgent grandmother. Nudging me, Isabel points at the old *gitana*.

'*Sí*, little one,' Aurelia intones. 'You remember me, do you not?'

My daughter beams and starts swinging on my skirt. Aurelia hands out *higochumbres* to the children and then places a large one in my hand. I cannot bring myself to eat; I am still reeling in shock from her earlier comment whilst she noisily sucks the juice from the fruit. Finally, I can contain my curiosity not a moment longer.

'Do you know who this child is?'

Aurelia emits a deep, throaty laugh that makes all the children titter and even produces an enormous smile in Joaquín's little face.

'Why, *claro que sí*. This is my grandson.'

I feel all the blood slowly draining from my face. The *higochumbre* falls with a gentle thud to the floor and two dogs immediately hurry over and battle one another for the fruit. Isabel and the small children stare up at me as I push it aside with my foot to move the dogs away.

'Sorry,' I mumble. Aurelia looks unaffected by my reaction. When she has finished eating, she licks the juice from her fingers, a thin trickle dribbling down her chin.

'In fact,' Aurelia continues, once she has finished, 'you shall meet his mother. She'll be back any minute.'

I stare at the old *gitana*, eyes wide open. 'But…I don't understand.'

Aurelia kicks at the dogs then leans forwards in her seat. 'Come now, child. What is there to understand?'

Suddenly, I feel afraid. Afraid of Aurelia's powers and afraid of what I have just been told. But what alarms me most is that Joaquín's mother may want to reclaim him. I jump up from my seat and hurriedly begin preparing the makeshift length of material to re-attach the babies. 'I really ought to get going. It must be late and I—'

'Sit!' barks Aurelia.

I stop what I am doing and sink back onto the stool.

'You have nothing to be afraid of,' Aurelia says. 'My daughter does not want the child back any more than you want to give him up. You did a great kindness taking him in, and Mar will be the first to thank you.' She pulls one of the children onto her lap and absently pats his tousled head with her huge hand. 'You see how simply we live here. Look at this poor *chaboró*. We can barely feed these children, let alone any more that come along.' The child nestles into her frame and begins to play with strands of Aurelia's long silver hair. 'My daughter falls in love far too easily. Look at these little ones. They are the result.' Aurelia's features soften. 'But for all that, she's not a bad girl.'

'How did you know that we took Joaquín in?'

'Joaquín?' Aurelia grunts. 'Is that his name? *Pues*, how do I know the difference between black and white? How do I know that winter is on its way? Don't ask silly questions, child.'

With that, we hear a rustling of leaves from the front of the cave. Turning away from the table, there she is. Mar. Against my will, I gasp. Never in my life have I seen such a striking woman. She is dressed in a simple long skirt and loose blouse, but this cannot detract from her beauty or the pride she exudes. It is not difficult to see what my brother-in-law was attracted to. Her long black hair hangs to her waist in curls and she has a bold green sash wound around her head, framing beautiful dark-lashed eyes that flash boldly. Her face is stern and haughty and as she stands there at the gate, hands on hips, I see that she is looking towards her son. *Our* son.

Ever since the extraordinary day that Joaquín arrived at Carmen de las Estrellas, I have thought a great deal about the identity and whereabouts of his mother but did not know how to search for her. I knew that she had given her child up, yet was aware this was an act of desperation and that she had possibly regretted it. On several occasions, I had attempted to contact Miguel without the knowledge of Eduardo, but he remained silent and elusive. At the same time, I found myself growing more and more attached to this mysterious child with his heart-melting smile and dark, intense eyes. I suckled him at my breast and loved him as much as if he were my own. And now, to be confronted with his mother in flesh and blood, and discover that she is the daughter of Aurelia of all people, is almost more than I can comprehend. Surely she shall take one look at Joaquín and wish to reclaim him? The thought of this causes a physical pain to wrench its way through my body and I find myself fighting back tears.

Mar approaches us. She reaches into my lap and holds Joaquín up at a distance, as though inspecting him. The tiny boy peers solemnly at her, his legs dangling in their cotton trousers.

'Well, *buenas tardes.*'

She immediately hands him back to me and smiles, her features softening.

'He looks well. You've been taking good care of him.'

I know at that moment, with all certainty, that Mar does not want Joaquín back. I feel sick with relief and smile at Mar, who then turns and walks into the cave, the small children scampering after her. A chill has crept into the air and, allowing my breathing to return to normal, I turn to look at Isabel as she chases dancing leaves around the yard.

'We really ought to return before it starts getting dark. *Gracias*, Aurelia. For your understanding.'

Aurelia rises, smiling with her pearly whites and reaching for a broom. 'Don't thank me, child. Thank Mar.'

I breathe deeply and walk towards the cave where I enter through the low door to see Mar at the stove with her back to me.

'Mar...'

She spins round, a trace of a faint but cheerless smile upon her lips.

'You know that you can come and visit any time you want? Truly, I mean that. Eduardo and I have not yet made a decision what we ought to tell him when he is older. But... I know should feel so much happier if you were to be a part of his life.'

Mar half turns, her eyes cast downwards. '*Gracias*,' she whispers, almost inaudibly.

We stand there in silence for several moments. Eventually I turn, organise the children with Aurelia's help and, as the warmth of the day leaves the valley, bid her farewell as I begin to walk along the jagged path strewn with rusty nails and cacti.

❀ ❀ ❀

That winter is ruthless. The cold creeps under the door
cracks of Carmen de las Estrellas and tiny icicles hang
from the ceilings. Bitter winds whip through the corridors of the house, causing heavy doors to bang and the
neighbourhood dogs to howl. We all spend most of the
time huddled in the kitchen around the fire whilst icy
gusts batter against the windows. I desperately long to visit Aurelia and Mar and take Eduardo with me to meet the
mother of our son, but a fierce snow flurry has rendered
the mountain paths impassable. Nor has Mar taken up
the offer of visiting Joaquín. In order to keep my hands
warm and my mind lively, it is during these cold winter
nights I commence with my new pursuit of making and
selling fortune cookies.

As a child, I read in a book about the Far East that
it was common to eat such snacks, breaking open their
crunchy shells to reveal wise words written on small
scrolls of paper. I have no idea whatsoever of the recipe,
but invent my own. I mix almond butter, orange water,
molasses, oats, vanilla and mulberry essence, cinnamon
and crushed cloves in a huge pot on the stove, thickening
the mixture with the most essential ingredient: generous
helpings of compressed figs. I then leave the mixture outside in the cold yard to harden a little before moulding it
around the fortune. I spend hours upon end writing these
out in black fountain pen, inventing un-extraordinary
words of advice to the reader, for I am no diviner of the

future. But my new pastime keeps me busy and warm and the aroma of spices from my cooking lingers in the air, often sending my children into an agitation of hunger and longing.

By the time winter begins to thaw out and spring is breathing her temperate brightness over the frosted river and slated roofs, I am with child again. I do so enjoy being pregnant; it makes me feel more alive and vital than ever and brings a healthy glow to my cheeks and gloss to my hair.

When I go into labour one month prematurely in the dead of night, I roll over and pinch Eduardo awake. 'Edu! The baby is coming!'

He moans in his sleep and turns away from me before resuming his snoring.

'Edu!' I cry, pinching him harder. 'Wake up!'

He heaves himself up in the bed. '¿Qué pasa, Luisa?' he grumbles, rubbing his arm.

'He is coming, the baby is coming.'

'Impossible,' he replies. 'We have a whole month—'

'Te prometo, Eduardo, he is on his way. Now go and fetch the midwife and bring plenty of warm water and blankets. And hurry!'

Comprehending at last that my words are in earnest, Eduardo is thrown into a frenzy as he runs to and fro trying to organise everything.

'He's coming! He's coming!' he cries as he darts along the corridors, his thin white legs flailing out from under his nightshirt. At one point, he stops in his tracks. 'How do

you know it's a *he?*' he calls, but I am in mid-contraction
and cannot answer. It is a good question, however. I have in
fact known for some time; sometimes a mother just knows
such things. In the weeks following the birth of our son,
Eduardo comments that it was probably due to the manly
kicks he gave whilst still wrapped up inside me. I say not a
word, but this is certainly not the case. One can say many
things about my darling Juan, but he should be the last of
our children to be giving great kicks, manly or otherwise.

Delicate as an orchid, Juan is the spitting image of
his father. He wails at the slightest provocation, suffers
chronically from asthma and is allergic to a multitude of
things, from dust to dogs. But for all this, he is the most
sweet-natured child imaginable.

I am busier than ever dealing with the ups and downs
and caprices of four children. Of course it is no surprise
that Joaquín's appearance is something of an anomaly, for
as he grows his entire countenance turns darker. But the
dissimilarities between the other children only help to as-
similate Joaquín smoothly into our brood.

Eduardo continues his work at the law firm, devoid
of enthusiasm. He has little choice, considering the pace
at which our family is growing. Nevertheless, not once
have I heard him admit he practises law. 'Poet,' he utters,
his bottom lip quivering with pride. '*Granadino Musings*,
1920, Brocches Publishing House.'

Amidst the whirlwind of feeding, bathing, dressing,
changing, mopping up and generally raising children, I
never cease hoping I shall receive a visit from my friends

on the other side of the valley, but as the months pass, I have to acknowledge it is becoming less likely. Any spare time I find, I spend in the kitchen stirring my pot of fig flesh and fortune with a wooden spoon, humming happily as the breeze carries the aroma out of the open kitchen windows.

In September our family begins to make preparations for Isabel's fourth birthday. Eduardo suggests a quiet family tea-party in the courtyard beside her orange tree. Señor and Señora Torres, however, are calling for a far more ostentatious affair in one of the city's finest tea-houses, modelled on a French patisserie with balloons, tartlets and cousins one and all. Frankly, it is dreadfully pretentious but just the kind of place that my parents-in-law adore. The notion fills Eduardo with horror as no doubt it shall involve the presence of Miguel. Ever since the fateful day on which his brother handed the sleeping Joaquín into our arms, Eduardo has managed to avoid his brother entirely. Miguel's eyes have never fallen upon his son and Eduardo tries to avoid the impending tea-party in every conceivable manner.

'I'm certain I have signs of influenza,' he tells me one morning, clutching one hand to his forehead whilst looking fit as a fiddle. 'See how pale Isabel is!' he gasps the following day.

'Eduardo,' I say firmly. 'We *have* to go to this party.'

'But…why don't we all go to the coast to celebrate? I'm sure the sea air would do us some…good?' He raises an eyebrow and cocks his head to one side. I know that look so well and it makes me smile, for it helps me imagine my husband as a young boy.

I hug him. 'Edu, it shall be fine, honestly. We need only spend an hour or two at Café Royal and then we can come home again. Miguel may not even come. I am sure he has no desire to be there.'

Eduardo snorts. 'What kind of nonsensical family tradition is it anyway, to cart the entire Torres clan to some pompous patisserie for a child's fourth birthday just so we all eat far too much and feel sick?'

I laugh and smooth a curl away from Edu's eyes. 'Really, it shan't be so terrible. And think how much Isabel shall adore it.' He grimaces, looking more like a sulky schoolboy than ever and my heart fills with love for him.

The day soon arrives and the six of us set off down the hillside from Carmen de las Estrellas towards the city, the children jumping from one long-fingered shadow of a cypress tree to another as the distant church bells chime. At Café Royal, waiters in tuxedos whip around the black and white lacquered floor, noses held high and strong, taut fingers holding up shimmering trays covered with hot chocolate served with rich fruitcakes and cream whipped sky-high. About two-thirds of the café has been taken over by our party and at the end of the table dozens of garish, sparkling balloons are tied to Isabel's birthday chair of honour. I exchange an eye-rolling glance with Eduardo and, with that, we paint smiles upon our faces and make our way into the throng of family members.

Miguel has the good sense to arrive late and by then Eduardo has started to relax, thinking that perhaps his brother shall stay away. Isabel sits on puffed-up cushions, devouring an enormous chocolate cake whilst my other children and their cousins smear sugary icing all over the pristine upholstery. The waiters hover, staring down their noses in horror at the children. I am unable to resist smirking, thinking that it serves this toffee-nosed place right. Señora Torres, seated to the right of Eduardo and dressed in a plum-coloured chiffon gown which looks more suited to the opera than a child's birthday party, is interrogating Eduardo about Juan's allergies, prescribing all sorts of nonsense to deal with them.

Quite suddenly, she says in a loud voice 'I've just realised Migé hasn't arrived yet. Does anyone know where he is?' Instinctively, Eduardo pulls Joaquín, who is covered in chocolate, closer towards him.

'Poor boy, he works too hard, does he not?'

I can see Eduardo gritting his teeth, yet no sooner has Señora Torres uttered these words than Miguel materialises in the doorway of Café Royal with his three bad-tempered children and wife with all her broken prettiness. There is space for them at the end of the table and Eduardo does not take his eyes from Miguel as he slides into his seat gratefully and begins conversing with his father.

'No kiss for your mother, Migé?' Señora Torres bellows down the length of the table, causing all the cousins to fall about laughing. Abashed, Miguel slowly rises and walks the length of the café, his polished black shoes clicking with each stride. Stooping down, he kisses his mother briskly on both cheeks. 'Eduardo,' he says tersely, nodding his head. Eduardo unsmilingly nods in return and both of us notice the swift glance Miguel shoots at Joaquín. And then, head held high, he marches back down to the other end of the table.

'He doesn't seem at all himself,' Señora Torres remarks as she helps herself to her fourth *pionono*, a small, sweet pastry. 'He must be working too hard, *pobrecito*.'

Eduardo grimaces and turns his attention to a feud that has broken out between the twins. Whilst I have always found Señora Torres to lack depth, she is not a dimwit and thus it astonishes me how unobservant she is when it comes to simmering tensions between her sons. She is so proud of her large brood of handsome boys that I suppose she failed to notice that Miguel's merciless bullying of Eduardo when they were children was anything more than harmless teasing. She proceeds to spend the rest of the birthday tea lamenting the deplorable hours her first-born must work, whilst Eduardo does a laudable job of ignoring her and I am left to listen and nod in the appropriate places.

When we finally leave the café, much to the relief of the waiters, it is starting to grow dark. Burdened down beneath the weight of Isabel's gifts, we are about to start making our way home when I suddenly see something that makes me stop in my tracks. I grasp Eduardo's coat sleeve.

'Look!' Eduardo follows my line of vision and then turns to look at me questioningly. There, in front of the portals of the cathedral, stands Mar. Although she is turned away from us, it is unmistakably her. She is clasping a bunch of rosemary, trying to press sprigs into the hands of passers-by.

'What am I looking at?' Eduardo asks.

'That girl,' I whisper, 'the one with the shawl and her back to us. It's Mar!'

'Mar?'

I nod and we stand in silence for a few moments, watching her. I desperately want to talk to her and instinctively begin to move towards her but Eduardo pulls me back. 'You can't,' he hisses. 'Miguel is standing five metres from us. It shan't be helpful for either of them to see each other, particularly not like this. And besides,' he continues, his voice even lower, 'if my parents see you talking to her, they're bound to ask questions. Come on, let's go.'

We bid our farewells to everyone and after Isabel is smothered in more kisses by aunts, uncles and grandparents, we begin to make our way towards the path that leads up to the Albaicín. I walk at a reluctant pace as I keep looking back, willing Mar to turn. Whether this longing reaches her or it is pure coincidence, Mar suddenly catches sight of me. Our eyes lock for an instant before she takes in the scene. Miguel...Joaquín. We stare intently at one another, then at the same time, smile. We continue to smile until, eventually, I am forced to turn and continue my journey home.

It is not until two weeks following this incident that I have the opportunity to visit the caves. Seeing Mar again after all this time has rekindled my curiosity and I know, without doubt, that I must see her. I go alone this time, leaving the children scrambling over Eduardo as he sits in his study endeavouring to write. As I walk along the arid, cacti-fringed trails, swallows swooping in front of my path, I think about that auspicious day three years previously when I knocked on Aurelia's door. How much has changed since then.

Aurelia is in the yard, hanging clothes out to dry over rusted, battered chairs. Upon seeing me, she scarcely nods. One of her granddaughters, the girl with the matted curls, lies stretched out on a tasselled rug above the cave, sucking her thumb intently and staring at me with wide eyes. I sit quietly on a grassy verge near the cave entrance, waiting for Aurelia to finish. Why must I always feel so infuriatingly cowed and tongue-tied in her presence? Glancing around, I pull back the tasselled cloth hanging over the cave door to see if Mar is inside, but the interior is dark and still. I can feel the child's eyes boring into the back of my head and turn round to face her.

'What is your name?'

'Beatriz.' The little girl rises from the rug and jumps as nimbly as a cat from the roof of the cave. 'Do you want to see my doll?'

I nod and the child scampers inside to fetch it. She returns and thrusts a tattered rag doll with stringy yellow hair and blue button eyes into my hands. I wince. I have always gone to great pains to not spoil my children, yet looking at the grubby doll now in my lap, I realise how much they have in comparison.

'Her name's Candelaria. I love her.' The child brings the doll to her chest and hugs her fiercely, her thumb going back into her mouth. Looking at the little girl, it is clear this is Mar's daughter. Despite her youth, she has the same wave of tight, dark curls crowning her head and proud, discerning face. And the resemblance she holds to Joaquín is undeniable. Her oversized, thin cotton dress slides off one shoulder and around her neck hangs a length of black cord with a tiny bag attached to it.

'What do you have in your little bag?' I ask her gently.

Beatriz pulls her thumb out of her mouth. 'A *trozo* of bread,' she replies, 'and some snake skin.'

'*Snake* skin?'

'*Sí*. The skin is to protect against snake bites and the bread is to protect against ghosts and evil spirits.'

I cup my chin in my hand. 'Are there many ghosts around here?'

'*¡Claro que sí!*' Beatriz's dark eyes open wide. 'Mamá and Abuela are scared of them, but I'm not. I'm not scared of snakes either. There are ladder snakes everywhere.' I find myself eyeing the ground and shifting a little. 'They put a curse on you. But Candelaria keeps me safe.'

'Has…has anyone in your family ever been bitten?'

She looks at me in surprise and smiles, almost sympathetically. 'Of course not, because we all wear our *bolsillos* all the time. We can't get bitten if we wear these.'

I nod and smile back at her as Beatriz begins to sing softly as she plaits the doll's grimy hair. I remember the packet of fortune cookies I have brought and, reaching into my knapsack, pull one out and offer it to the child. Squealing with delight, Beatriz grasps the sugary treat and holds it out like a trophy for her grandmother to see. Aurelia grunts and the little girl calls towards the entrance of the cave.

'Pablo! Pablo!'

A boy, whom I recognise from both of my previous visits, appears in the doorway, notebook and pencil in hand.

'Look what the lady gave me!'

Thrusting her hand out under the nose of her elder brother, he arches one eyebrow and stares at me suspiciously.

'Would you like one?'

He glances hesitantly at his grandmother and, after receiving a nod from her, edges his way slowly towards my outstretched palm then swipes the cookie from it in one swift motion. Dropping what he holds in his hands, he darts towards the gate as Beatriz chases after him.

Left alone, Aurelia comes and sits down. I am shocked to see yet another transformation in her dignified face. This time she seems neither aged nor youthful, but tired and despondent. Dark, bulbous folds of skin hang heavily beneath her eyes and her long, grey hair is pulled tightly back from her face.

'Will you tell me what it is?'

I am shocked by the words that have escaped my lips. Aurelia has said not a word, yet it is clearer than the cloudless sky that she is troubled.

'Mar has gone.'

I feel a bolt of pure fear rush through my body.

'Gone? Gone where?'

Aurelia shakes her head dejectedly and gestures towards the mountains. 'Out there. To the sea. North, west, another country… I don't know.'

'But I only saw her a couple of weeks ago. I tried to talk to her…I couldn't…I—'

'Hush, child, I know.' Aurelia rises from her seat and begins to sweep the yard. For a while she is silent, lost in her task. Eventually, she speaks again. 'After she returned that day from seeing you all, she wasn't herself. Early the next morning she was gone. No message. Nothing.' She shakes her head again. 'She's done this before. Taken off without so much as a word. I know she'll be back, I just don't know when. And with all these children…' she breaks off '…*pues, es difícil.*'

'But why did she go? Was it because of Joaquín? Does she regret the decision she made? Is she angry with me? Does she…'

Aurelia starts making tutting noises and stops sweeping, looking at me long and hard.

'Child, she sees you as far more of a mother to Joaquín than herself. You are the one who has nurtured him. You are the one who will provide him with far more opportunities than the poor little mites here who do nothing but run around in the dirt all day.'

'Well, what then?'

'She's still in love with that fool of a man.'

I pause and frown.

'You mean Miguel?' I am stunned, desperately trying to picture my husband's most detestable brother as a man who could possibly evoke such strong sentiment. Yes, I must concede he is handsome. But he is so cold. And Mar is so enchanting.

'*Claro que sí*,' Aurelia grunts. 'Who else?'

Try as hard as I might, I simply cannot imagine the two of them together and I most certainly cannot understand how Mar has failed to break an emotional attachment to such a callous creature.

'I know what you're thinking. It astounds me as much as it does you.'

'I suppose love is blind,' I offer.

'No, it's damned dimwitted, that's what it is,' Aurelia snaps. 'I brought that girl up to be cautious of her emotions. To never fall in love. But look what she does, she runs all over Andalucía handing her heart over on a silver platter to any man that asks for it. And now she has all these little ones to show for it.'

'How many children does she have?'

'Eight,' replies Aurelia tersely.

'*Eight?*'

'Three of them never made it past the age of two, they died of *mal de ojo*.' I frown, not understanding, but Aurelia continues. 'So there are four left here. But you can see why Mar gave up Joaquín. Just look at this place.'

Aurelia walks up to the gate and picks up the notebook that the little boy dropped, handing it to me.

'Pablo's the eldest. He's mute. Locked inside his own world.'

I open the book and flick through page after page of intricate drawings of life going on around him: Aurelia plaiting her long mane of hair; Beatriz playing with her doll; Mar weaving esparto grass into the seat of a chair.

'I wouldn't mind so much, if only he'd smile,' Aurelia continues.

I look up from the book. 'These are good.'

Aurelia nods. 'I know. That's all he does all day: helps with the chores and sits in the shadows drawing. Half the time I don't even realise he's there, drawing me. I have no doubt the boy can talk, he's just chosen not to. My daughter tells me I'm crazy, but in my opinion he's frustrated.'

'Can he not go to school?'

'School?' Aurelia scoffs. 'How many schools have you seen around here?' Shaking her head, she resumes sweeping. 'No, education's not our lot. We're scum of the earth, us *gitanos*. That's what the *payos* think of us.'

I open my mouth to contradict her but am immediately silenced. 'I'm not talking about *you*, child. But you're not exactly like all the rest, are you?' Aurelia stares at me and I feel myself blushing. 'No, we're to be seen and not heard. If the government really had its way, we would be burnt, buried and forgotten within days.'

I feel angry and deeply ashamed, not only of the snobbery so rife amongst my class but also because I know that Aurelia speaks the truth. On countless occasions I have heard my parents or sisters pour scorn on the *gitanos*, calling them pilfering thieves and murderers. I know that there is an element of truth to some of the stories that circulate of their crimes, yet the majority are pure fiction, invented by bored and malicious tongues. People see what they wish to, and all that I perceive at this moment is an honest woman minding her own business and trying to eke out a living for her daughter and grandchildren. As I study Aurelia's face, I am shocked to see stout tears form in the corners of her eyes and steal down her cheek. Instinctively, I stand up and move towards her.

'Aurelia. *¿Estás bien?*'

She pauses. 'I'm not crying because I care what people think of us. I don't care, believe me, I don't.'

I hold up a hand and stroke the old *gitana*'s arm. Aurelia stands there, rooted to the spot as she weeps. Taking my hand in hers, she looks at me directly; that same forceful look that has stunned me into silence on several occasions and that right now is racing with demons and clouds. 'I am crying because of what is to come. I would give anything to change it. But the fact is I cannot.' And with that, she pulls her hand away sharply and walks towards the cave.

CHAPTER TWO
ISABEL

Winter 1927

'Isabel *cariña*, come here.'

I wander over to Mother and let myself be turned around so that my hair can be arranged. Leaning back into the warmth of her familiar chest, I reach up behind me to pull her long, sleek mane of hair over my shoulders, running my fingers through the dark threads before bringing the ends to my nose. I can smell cloves and figs and stare at her hair slipping like sand through my fingers. I decide that, if not black, it's very close to it. The man who cuts Mother's hair at the salon told her recently that the fashion is now for short bobs. He's right, for we can see them everywhere; not up here so much, but down in the city, in the fashionable shopping streets. But Mother isn't interested in short hair, and I'm relieved. I think ladies with short hair look peculiar.

'Stop that,' Mother says gently as she pulls back her hair and resumes her plaiting.

'Why don't I have the same hair as you, Mother?' I ask.

'Because we are all different, and that is what makes us special,' Mother replies as she ties a large white bow in my hair. She turns me around and brushes away escaped strands from my forehead. '*Bueno*,' she says and kisses the tip of my nose. 'Now it is my turn.' I love this early morning ritual of neatening our hair in front of the looking glass and then putting on our clothes together. It's Conchi's job really to dress me and my brothers and sister, but if I get up early enough, which I always do, I can slip into Mother's room so we can be alone as even Father has left for work by this hour. For a short while I can pretend it's just Mother and I, that I am her only child.

Mother lets me brush her hair out with a tortoiseshell comb, so long it almost reaches her waist, and I linger over this job, finding imaginary knots as I tug through the strands, seamless as silk. Then she gathers up a top layer and expertly plaits it, the tendons in her dark, sinewy hands tensing and relaxing before she scoops it into a chignon at the back of her neck. *When I grow up*, I think, *I shall grow my hair that long.* But so far, it has stubbornly refused to grow much beyond my shoulders before it curls up in revolt and the plait Mother forces it into is more stubby than sleek.

I sit on the counterpane and swing my legs over the side of the bed, my hands resting on my pinafore as I survey Mother. She steps into a cream petticoat and then pulls a yellow dress gracefully over her head. It falls to just above the ankle, hugging her slender frame that bulges out around the waist. Even after giving birth to four children, her bump is still small and neat. I would like to have another sister, a better sister than María, who I find terribly prissy. She's the least likely of us all to get her hands dirty and the only one who can't climb up the garden wall without being given a leg-up. She is also maddeningly rosy and beautiful and on top of that has a sweet nature. Sickeningly sweet, in my opinion. There's one day that Mother takes the two of us for a walk. María looks such a picture of perfect prettiness with her blonde hair and dark eyes that, since I am her sister, I assume I look the same until I catch sight of my reflection and realise that with my dishevelled chestnut hair and broad features I'll never be what's regarded as classically pretty.

Walking to the wardrobe, Mother crouches down and pushes through shoes before settling on the gold pair. These are my favourite; they have stars on them and are narrow at the toe with a small, dainty heel and a strap over the top. Not long ago I tried them on and stood before the full-length looking glass, squinting my eyes and imagining myself to have long, dark hair and narrow eyes, the shape of almonds and the colour of olives. Mother pats her hands over the top of her dress and then turns to the side to look at her back in the looking glass, lifting the toe of one shoe up. As she does so, she catches my eye and smiles at me, and her smile is warm and open and mine.

My mother has lean but muscular arms that are always active with us children, the kitchen or garden. She never stops, not for a minute, and when she does, her hands still

seem to be busy. I love the way she challenges convention
with such easy and good-humoured grace. I love the way
dark strands of hair work their way free from her chignon
around her forehead and neck as the day wears on. I love
the way she always pushes her sleeves back up over the
elbows, as if preparing her hands for work. Her arms are
dark from the elbows downwards and white and smooth
as paper above. I love the freckles that are flickered over
the bridge of her thin nose, making her look younger
than she is. What I would give for people to exclaim 'Oh
Isabel, you are so like your mother!' But, *claro*, they never
do. Because I know I'm not like her, not physically at
least, and I must content myself with the fact that my
smile is, apparently, Mother's.

After breakfast, Conchi pulls a cloak on to us all and
we walk into the city together for it is market day.

'You shouldn't be going to the market, Señora, not in
your condition,' Conchi says, her black eyebrows knitted
together as her frame fills the doorway.

'*¿Qué dices?* I am quite alright. In fact,' she says as she
ties the ribbon under María's straw hat, 'I always feel as
though my energy increases when I am carrying a child.'
She pauses, as though taking in this reality afresh and
then shrugs and laughs.

Down in the city, it is a frenzy of activity and commerce
with peasants flocking in from the villages to sell their
fruit and vegetables. Away from the main market square
though, ladies with fancy hats and dressed in the latest
fashions saunter elegantly from one shop window to the

next with their parasols, staring through the glass at delicate hosiery on waxed legs, waves of silk and ribbon and costly headwear shipped in from Paris or London. Mother does no more than give these displays a cursory glance and I feel a surge of affection for her; in her simple dress and golden shoes offset by her dark fountain of hair, she is far lovelier than any of the other flamboyant ladies I see.

We are about to cross the street when we hear the ring of a tram and Mother, instinctively, throws both her arms out to keep us all back, flattening us with the baskets she holds in each hand. The tram is followed by a horse-drawn omnibus and my youngest brother Fernando, just four years old, stands with his mouth agape as the horses trot dutifully by, swishing their tails this way and that. The street clears again; Mother waves the baskets over our heads to our backs and pushes us gently across.

The market stalls are filled to bursting and Mother picks through gleaming red tomatoes and finely spiked artichokes whilst I push my nose into the fragrant green leaves of bright oranges which spill down the trellises of stalls, smiling as I think of my orange tree back home. Mother buys saffron-scented soap and small, gnarled *garbanzo* beans tied up in a muslin square with string. The fruit vendor with crooked eyes hands each of us a shiny red grape and I bite into it, savouring the nectar as sweet as honey. Once Mother's baskets and mine are filled – for I am seven years old and the others are too little to carry this load all the way home – we thread our way through the cobbled streets and begin our ascent back to Carmen de las Estrellas.

❋ ❋ ❋

As soon as Alejandro is born, I forgive him for being a boy. For he is a beautiful, tiny black-haired creature who opens his mouth and squawks like a little bird for mother's milk. This same year, I feel the softness of snow for the very first time. I have grown up with a view of the Sierra Nevadas, liberally cloaked in whiteness for five or more months of the year. When I sit in the garden and stretch my arm out I pretend I'm touching the mountains. I turn my hand upside down and use my fingers as legs to climb the craggy peaks. But until now, the reality of snow, how it must feel, taste, smell has always been out of my reach.

Then one evening, my family and I are eating dinner when strange white shapes begin to drift silently past the window. We all jump up from our seats and gather noisily, impatiently pushing one another out of the way. I can't bear to fall asleep that night I'm so excited and the very next day we wake up to an entirely different world. Mother stays at home with Alejandro, and Father bundles the rest of us up in our warmest coats, mittens, woollen hats and thick scarves tied so tight and so high that we can barely breathe or see. We make our way down the slopes of the Albaicín in single file, one hand holding onto the shoulder of the person in front to prevent slipping. Father walks at the back, and when I turn I see him struggling under the weight of Mother's best skillet pans we have decided will serve best as sledges.

At the foot of the Albaicín we walk out to a wooded slope on the other side of the Río Darro where we spend hours hurtling down hills at top speed. On one of my descents, during which I go so fast that all the breath is punched from me, Father stands in my path to prevent me careering into the ditch beyond. I don't know if it's Father or I who is more terrified and thrilled as I plunge towards him and before the pan and I crest the next ridge, he pulls me free and we laugh with cold and with joy. Moments later, I show him the pattern of a snowflake which has lodged on my mitten and Father stares at it, his eyes widening in amazement and then he picks me up and holds me under my arms as he spins me round and round.

I bottle up a handful of snow in one of Conchi's pickling jars, leaving it beside the icy draught beneath my bedroom window in the hope it remains intact. When it melts, I am bereft. Not only does all the snow vanish as quickly as it settled, but this year spring seems almost forgotten as a thick blanket of heat descends upon us as early as May. By July, the heat is unbearable and my face turns pink and bothered. On one of these breezeless days, most of my family are inside trying to nap after a heavy lunch, but the combination of a large meal and the high temperature, rather than encouraging sleep, just makes me restless. Mother has insisted I attempt a short siesta, but it's no use. Instead, I lay a rug out in the inner courtyard in the shade of my orange tree, as I so often do, imagining shapes in the clouds through the leafy fingers of its canopy. All my family call it 'Isabel's tree', and it's as though there is a metre circumference around it that nobody may enter. Do I appear that unwilling to share the tree that Father planted at my birth, I wonder, or is nobody else interested in coming near? Even when it begins to bear fruit, those scaly, dimpled Seville oranges that are far too bitter to eat but which Mother sometimes adds to her fortune cookies, it's my unspoken task to collect them in a basket and hand them to her. Nobody in my family ever talks about it but somehow the orange tree remains, quite indisputably, mine.

Lying under it this breezeless summer day, I hear the sound of footsteps approaching the main door. I wait for the knock, but when it doesn't come, I stand up and listen to the pacing back and forth. Conchi must have heard the footsteps too as she has made her way out of the kitchen, her apron and hands bloodied from the meat she's preparing.

'*Está bien*, Conchi, I'll see who it is,' I tell her. I leave the courtyard through the kitchen and run out into the garden. From as early as I can remember, along with my younger brothers and sister, I'd haul myself up onto the ivy-covered wall surrounding the house and garden and lie flat on top of it, peering down into the alleyway below to see who is visiting us. Father always panics when he sees us up on the wall, convinced we will fall and break our necks, whereas Mother just says that if we're stupid enough to go up there, it will be our own faults if anything happens.

On this occasion, I pull myself up and lie on the wall's surface, sucking my breath in and studying the woman below. She is clearly upset, but she's the most beautiful woman I've ever seen, with long night-black curls and an expressive face. As I lie there gazing at her, a small pebble dislodges itself from the wall and rattles down noisily. I'm not sure who is more startled, because we both stare at each other, shocked, for some time.

After a while, she clears her throat. 'Are you Luisa's daughter?'

I nod.

'Is your mamá here?'

'She's having her siesta.'

The woman looks disappointed. I can see her biting her bottom lip then she turns her head up towards me. The fix of her stare alarms me; it is so dark and so bottom-less and so full of a pain I can't understand.

'I'll come back another time,' she says quietly, and quick-ly turns and starts to make her way back down the alley.

'No, no, wait!' I spring down from the wall and race round through the inner patio, heaving at the door and beckoning for her to come in. 'I'll get her. She won't mind.'

After a few moments of faltering, the woman walks in and, satisfied I've trapped her, I turn round. Conchi is standing there, her hands cleaned. She gives me a strange look as I pass her to run up the stairs and stands there in silence, staring at the visitor.

'*¡Mamá, ven rápido!*' I cry, hurling myself into her bed-room. 'Somebody is here to visit you!'

Mother stirs, the imprint of pillow against her smooth cheek. 'Who is it?'

'*No lo sé*, but you must hurry, before she leaves again!'

Mother is out of bed in a flash and I race down the stairs behind her as she takes the mysterious woman into the conservatory, closing the door behind her. Disappointed, I peer through the keyhole and watch, puzzled, as Mother draws the lovely lady into her arms and her body shakes with loud sobs.

'Come away, Señorita,' Conchi chides as she tugs at the sleeve of my blouse.

'Who is it, Conchi?'

'I have no idea,' she replies, pursing her lips, 'but no doubt your mother will tell you when she wants to.'

And she does, that very evening, explain to me that this is Abuela Aurelia's daughter who has been away for a long while but has now decided to go home to her mamá and little ones. It all seems very odd, but in our following visits to the caves, Mar is nearly always there and I think little of the fact that this mysterious woman has been curiously absent for so long.

After the birth of Alejandro, Conchi does most of the shopping for our family. But occasionally, if he is calm and sleeping, Mother hands my baby brother over to Conchi and takes my sister María and I to the city to shop. Less frequently, she takes me alone and I love these snatched moments of intimacy with Mother more than anything. They mean more to me even than when we dress in the morning, for I have her out of the house, all to myself, where she doesn't need to worry about María's questioning, Alejandro's crying or Father's fussing. We buy sweetmeats from the Santa Catalina de Zafra Convent and at the market Mother shows me where to buy the best *chorizo* and how to tell if it is good quality flour by how quickly it runs through your fingers. One thing I notice, however, is that these trips to the convent to buy sweet delicacies are becoming more infrequent and that Mother is buying less flour, eggs and coffee than before. I don't know much about Primo de Rivera who rules the country, except that I don't like the look of him one bit from the posters I see everywhere; he has cold eyes and dark bags underneath them running into sagging cheeks. But what I do know is that everything seems far more costly. On one occasion when Mother and I are in the city, we see young people marching and shouting outside the government buildings, waving banners.

'Who are they, Mother?' I ask breathlessly as the young people march past us.

'Students,' she replies.

'But what are they shouting about?' I turn to look at Mother and I can see excitement in her face too, though the face she turns back to me is far more serious.

'They're calling for democracy. Away with Primo de Rivera. Quite right.' A small smile dances on her lips. 'Come, let us hurry to the market before all the best fruit goes.'

'But what exactly is wrong with him?' I persist as I hurry behind her. I always have difficulty keeping up with Mother; with her long legs she walks far too fast for me.

'The rich are suffering. The poor are suffering. What's right with him!' she calls back over her shoulder and I laugh happily, understanding nothing.

✱ ✱ ✱

When I am ten years old, the king dismisses Primo de Rivera. But this is the extent of my political understanding; my world revolves around games in the courtyards and garden of Carmen de las Estrellas, meals with my family, lessons in the attic and hours spent reading and dreaming in the shade of my orange tree.

Every so often Mother takes us to visit Aurelia and her family. I long for these excursions because they are so alien to our everyday activities. My family must be such a curious sight, winding our way over the mountain paths with Mother at the helm and an assortment of youngsters trailing behind. We spend a few hours there in the yard of Abuela Aurelia's cave, playing with her grandchildren and helping her to collect bits of twine and esparto grass she crafts chairs from.

Pablo is a few years older than me. He is the most serious boy I've ever met but he intrigues me. He has a clear talent for drawing, but I'm also fascinated by the walls of silence he's pencilled around himself and forbidden anyone to enter. Whilst the little ones noisily race around the yard after the chickens, I like to sit beside Pablo on the roof of the cave watching him draw. I always sit at a slight distance so he's not uncomfortable, and I never feel he objects to my presence.

On the way home from visiting our friends, we pass a small chapel on a lonely mountain pass. Mother's hand instinctively flickers up to cross herself and we all follow suit, a fumble of fingers. My parents are officially Catholic, yet they both strongly feel we shouldn't receive our worldly education in an institution that Mother describes as being riddled with Catholic dogma and disease. So several years ago Father converted the attic into a schoolroom with wooden desks and chairs and a blackboard, convinced that without the distraction of windows to gaze through, we'd daydream less. His plan failed of course, because when a child doesn't want to listen to their teacher, the setting is irrelevant.

We've had tutor after tutor, a number of them cracking under the pressure. Fernando constantly clowns about, rarely taking lessons seriously at all, and what with Alejandro forever staring into space and Juan looking like he'll break into a hundred pieces if asked a question, I'm frankly unsurprised that several of our tutors barely last a month.

One morning, Fernando manages to squeeze himself into the back cupboard filled with notebooks and chalk sticks. Giggling away, the rest of us close the door on him and return to our seats to wait for the tutor to arrive. When he does appear, he eyes us all suspiciously because we're seated so quietly at our desks staring up at him. The poor man's downfall is his failure to notice that one child is absent and he proceeds with the lesson whilst we bend our heads over our arithmetic. Moments later, the soft mewing sound of a kitten comes from the back cupboard. The tutor glances round, but as the noise stops, he continues writing sums on the blackboard. After a while, the mewing resumes. Bewildered, the tutor pulls dust-laden boxes away from the wall, searching for a lost cat. María flicks her hair and innocently suggests that perhaps it has become trapped in the back cupboard.

Bending down, the tutor unlatches the door and as it swings open on its hinges, a skinny boy jumps out, chuckling like a little ghoul. The tutor is given such a fright that he lets out the most high-pitched scream I've ever heard from a man in my life, leaving him mortified and blushing the shade of ripe tomatoes. Mother hears the commotion, *claro* – she hears *everything* – and flies up the stairs as fast as her long legs can take her. The tutor takes the rest of the day off with a migraine and Mother sits at the front of the classroom, taking his place, demanding complete silence. The glint of humour in her eye is, however, unmistakable. After this, in order to instil some kind of discipline into Fernando, he is assigned with menial household tasks for each misdemeanour reported, no matter how small. But my brother takes to these duties with the same energy he does to his classroom pranks, quite unexpectedly delighting in weeding the garden and dusting the skirting boards, and we must all concede that he is, simply, a law unto himself.

One day, Fernando even offers to polish the guitar that my brother Joaquín was given for his eighth birthday and has not been separated from ever since. Joaquín looks at Fernando suspiciously before agreeing to part with it and stands over him as he sits on the patio step shining the rich ochre body with a rag. When he hands it back, Joaquín smiles, tucks it under his arm and begins to play a tune that he has been learning. María and I are helping Conchi to hang clothes out to dry in the garden but the minute we hear the music, we both stop pegging; I to listen to the wonderful sounds my brother is capable of making and María to pout. My sister, you see, dislikes nothing more than attention being diverted away from her and feels that Joaquín should be devoting all his time to her and not his guitar.

She flings the pegs petulantly to the floor and marches over to Joaquín, hands on her hips. 'Joaquín,' she says. 'You know Mother doesn't like you playing your guitar too early in the morning.'

Fernando scrunches his face up to her. '*No*, María. It's you who doesn't like it, not Mother. At any time, for that matter.'

I stifle a snigger behind a long, billowing dress.

'Fernando!' María chides, her voice quavering. 'That's a horrid thing to say.'

Joaquín jumps up and, without saying a word, begins to improvise a song about María. I shake my head, both in wonder at the talent of my musical brother and his ability to always charm her childish affections back.

A long time ago, Mother explained to us all, including Joaquín himself, that his papá is not a good man but his mamá is wonderful and kind yet she isn't able to look after him. We all accepted this without asking any questions and Joaquín is treated whole-heartedly as our brother and María's twin.

In hindsight, it's a curious decision Mother made to let us in on this family secret. After all, children are children, and it wouldn't have been surprising for this information to slip out to a grandparent, aunt or cousin, resulting in a huge scandal. Yet it must have been something to do with the way Mother told us; that despite our youth we implicitly understood that it was a secret that must never leave the walls of Carmen de las Estrellas. Instead, we've always guarded it like a valuable treasure, not even discussing it amongst ourselves. It's just the way it is, and we all like the fact we can be trusted.

Besides our lessons which crawl by, Carmen de las Estrellas watches us grow as free and flighty as birds. Being educated at home, we don't really have any friends with the exception of cousins and a few close neighbours. But I don't think any of us feel we are missing out. There's always someone close by to chase around the garden, or to play hide and seek with in one of the secret corners of our rambling house.

One year after Primo de Rivera is sent away, I catch pneumonia. I spend day after day in bed whilst Mother brings me endless cups of elderflower tea she insists will sweat out the toxins. I share a bedroom with María who reads me stories of priceless treasures, maidens locked in towers and valiant princes on horseback. I know my sister isn't genuinely concerned for me; I'm sure the fact Mother lets her miss an hour of classes every day so she can keep me company plays a far greater part.

On certain days of confinement to my bed, I run such a high fever that it distorts my sense of reality. When Fernando rushes into my room one day and announces, 'The king has gone to exile!' because I almost feel delirious, I'm not sure which of us is going mad.

'No silly, you mean gone *into* exile. Exile's not a place,' says Joaquín, who is sitting on the window ledge.

Fernando shrugs. 'Same thing.'

'But what does it mean?' asks María.

'It *means*,' Joaquín declares, 'that Spain's doesn't want a king any more.'

Fernando snorts. 'You don't know what you're talking about, you're just pretending.'

Joaquín shoots Fernando a dark look and hurries out of the room to fetch Mother and Father. They soon come in and, after placing a damp cloth on my forehead, spend a while fiddling around with the wireless to listen to the king's official statement due to be broadcast at midday.

'Who is it?' Fernando whispers as a faint voice starts to come through.

'Shhh!' Mother swats him on the back of his head and we all fall deadly silent as we make out the weak murmur of a solemn voice.

'*After the results of last week's election, I see that I can no longer claim the love and support of my people. It would be possible for me to fight against this turning tide to retain my royal powers; however, I fear this would be futile. It seems that my people are determined to set themselves against one another and I foresee that there is now more than a faint possibility of civil war. My desire is to play no role in this ugly reckoning and thus, until the nation speaks again, I herewith renounce my throne and my crown.'*

With this, the voice dies away and we all look at the faces of Mother and Father who are staring at one another with a mixed expression of shock and excitement. Seconds later, the disbelief in their faces melts away as they break into enormous smiles and fling their arms around one another. Father tunes into a tango on the wireless and Mother hitches up her skirt and they dance around the room as all my siblings hurl themselves onto my bed and bounce up and down. I still find it strange that somebody who once held so much power now has none, but the fact that my parents are so happy is cause enough for celebration.

Later that same night, my fever has dropped sufficiently to allow me to join my family out on the terrace in the spring warmth, enjoying an enormous feast prepared as a special celebration. The sweet fragrance from the fruit tree blossoms combined with the *vino de la costa* Mother gives me a sip of makes me giddy. As we mop up spicy olive oil with thick hunks of bread, María asks from the end of the table what civil war means. Mother looks up from her plate, the cheerful atmosphere momentarily freezing.

'Where did you hear that?'

'It's what the king said.'

'But he's not king any more,' Fernando says at the same time as successfully catapulting a forkful of chicken into the mouth of one of the hovering cats. Mother looks at him grimly and then glances at Father who is coughing nervously. I'm intrigued to know how they'll reply. Moments later, Mother walks over to Father, whispers something in his ear and the two of them walk over to one of the walnut trees in the far corner of the garden.

My youngest brother Alejandro is only small and he's far more interested in playing with his food than worrying about what has happened with the king. But the fact remains that we can hear the cheers in the streets and the fireworks exploding in the sky and my parents know they have to give us at least some kind of explanation as to what is going on beyond the walls of Carmen de las Estrellas. By the time they return to the table, Fernando has miscalculated a further forkful of food meant for the cats and a large amount has landed in María's hair. She's wailing, sauce dripping down onto her shoulders. Mother pulls my sister onto her lap and picks out pieces of chicken from the top of her head before Eduardo clears his throat and begins to talk.

'Children, something very important has happened today. We've had a king for a very long time but the truth is that he hasn't done a very good job of ruling our country. So today he has admitted that he can't rule any longer and he's going to leave Spain.'

'So who's going to take over?' I ask.

Father grins and stands up straight. 'Children, we are living in great times. We have born witness to the second Spanish Republic and you will all grow up in a liberal, egalitarian democracy!'

'*Language*, Edu!' Mother hisses.

Father's cheeks glow and he gives a little cough. '*Sí*. Well, what I mean to say is that everything shall improve from now on. We've moved into the twentieth century, children. We can finally join our European neighbours. And civil war. *Pues*…it's…' Father frowns and scratches beneath his chin.

I watch as Mother reaches out and places her hand on Father's forearm. 'It is when people from the same country fight against one another,' she says.

'But it's not going to happen here,' Father adds hastily. 'Don't worry about what the king said. Things will only get better.'

The evening is warm and smells of blossom and jasmine. The sky is lit up with bright colours as showers cascade down in thousands of tiny sparks. From outside the walls of Carmen de las Estrellas we can hear people joyfully making their way through the streets. I am lighter than air and full of sweet invincibility.

❄ ❄ ❄

In these early days of the Republic, one celebration leads into another. Our family sometimes goes down to the city to join in with the huge street parties and occasionally we're allowed to stay up till the early hours. People of all ages dance and sing in the streets and plazas and I watch my parents' eyes shining with joy and disbelief.

'And who says us Granadinos are straight-laced?' Mother cries as she twirls round in a graceful arc.

We stroll through the sunny streets, stopping occasionally to watch people giving impromptu speeches.
One man talks about the need for higher incomes, another speaks of rights for workers, but the word I remember
above all others is *Freedom! Freedom! Freedom!*

'Freedom from what? Fernando asks. From oppression,
Father replies. From tyranny, Mother says. Freedom. *Libertad.* I can't see personally that we've been oppressed, but
I breathe *libertad* again and again as though this magic
word alone will release the genie from the bottle.

With the Second Republic, Spain has become *la niña
bonita.* Everybody wans to show her off, so men scramble
up lampposts on street corners to attach Republican flags,
the traditional national red-yellow-red flag losing one of
its scarlet stripes and being replaced with a deep purple
band. Purple has become the new colour, and women
come out of their homes in droves wearing fabulous rich
purple dresses in velvets and silks and brocades. I even see
several policemen striding through the streets with their
capes draped over their shoulders, displaying the deep
purple inner lining of their garments.

One afternoon when we are all in the city with Mother, drinking *horchata* in Plaza Bib-Rambla, we see a procession of what must be thousands of peasants from surrounding villages marching through the square in support
of the new democracy, waving banners of progress and
rights against landowners. I feel the beat of wings in my
stomach, a flutter of confusion and excitement.

'Mother,' I ask, not wanting to seem ignorant in front of my younger brothers and sister but needing to understand it better all the same. 'Why are they all here?' To our surprise, Mother responds by banging a fist down on the table, causing our *horchata* to slosh unsteadily in its tall glasses.

'These poor labourers have been suffering under terrible laws for so many generations. They've never had a voice before and they've been kept in poverty for too long. Too long!' Mother's voice has raised to a shrill level I barely recognise and she clenches her right fist in the gesture of support for the Republic. 'You see all these people here.' She waves a hand in the direction of the hordes of *campesinos* passing just metres from our tables. 'This is their chance, *finally*, to be heard and to rise up against their oppressors. Do you understand, Isabel?' she asks, her dark eyes staring at me intently. Do I? Not really, but what I see is that these poor-looking people with their work-darkened faces and shabby clothes are overjoyed as they march and their enthusiasm, as well as Mother's of course, is infectious.

❋ ❋ ❋

One evening, during dinner, my parents make an announcement.

'Children,' Mother says as she exchanges a grin with Father, 'we have some wonderful news for you. You have probably heard that the Republic has been opening up many liberal, non-religious schools.'

I hold my breath. Can it be possible that our stifling classes in the attic are coming to an end?

'Well…' Father says slowly, looking round at our expectant faces. 'We have decided that the time has come to enrol you in El Colegio de la Republica!' Father's words unravel excitedly and we all gasp. The outside world! The thrill I feel is even better than the smell of Mother's fortune cookies, freshly baked; it's even better than being told we are visiting Abuela Aurelia. Finally, *finally* we can escape the sour scent of the attic that slowly roasts us in the summer and freezes our fingers to our pencils in the winter. And not only that, but to me it feels like a great honour; a social experiment of the Republic in which we play the fundamental role.

I have never loved my parents as much as the moment when they give each of us a leather satchel and two new pencils and we walk through the narrow cypress-lined streets from Carmen de las Estrellas, snaking round the bends in single file in age order. 'Look at me!' I want to shout to everyone we pass, '*¡Me voy al colegio!* Of course this is nothing out of the ordinary to the average onlooker of our district who has never held such moral high ground as my parents, but after years of being educated at home by uninspiring tutors, I feel as though I can finally stretch my intellectual limbs.

I take to my classes with an enthusiasm similar to the passion Joaquín has displayed for his guitar and Fernando for his tomfoolery, drinking in the knowledge that flows from our teachers. Going to school doesn't just change my life, it also has a profound effect one way or another on my siblings. As the teachers of our school pride themselves on being cultural pioneers for the new Republic, they bring their love of the arts to the classroom in so many inspiring ways. Joaquín's musical talent is recognised immediately and as well as playing in school concerts and being entered for regional competitions, he begins Saturday classes with a renowned flamenco guitarist.

My parents have always encouraged us in the arts at home, but now we enjoy literature, music, art and theatre in a less lonely and restrictive atmosphere and I'm surprised to discover my siblings' hidden talents. My brother Juan, for example – poor Juan who never says boo to a goose – suddenly becomes fond of acting. He plays important roles in several school productions which we all attend, astonished to see the transformation from painfully shy child to self-assured actor, completely at ease on stage in a way that he can never maintain once he becomes Juan Torres Ramirez again. María realises she has a talent for needlework and begins making clothes for both herself and all of us. Even Fernando feels less inclined to play the fool in class now that he has come into contact with older boys he looks up to. We feel liberated both creatively and academically, and not only that, but we also make friends at our schools who open our eyes in new ways.

Whilst our minds and imaginations are being nurtured at school, our parents' lives are also being steered in a different direction. Both of them start to spend more and more time out of the house whilst we are at school, occasionally not returning till dinner time and leaving Conchi and myself to see to the other children. Mother never goes into details about what she is doing, but I have a hunch she is becoming more politically active. Groups of people often congregate at Carmen de las Estrellas in the evenings and weekends and sit in the conservatory drinking small glasses of *café cortado* and thumbing through sheets of papers on their laps. My brothers and sister and I hover in the doorways before tiring of the adult conversations and running off. As far as I can gather, they're discussing reform of some kind and dreaming of a better future and *libertad, libertad, libertad!*

Father occasionally goes along, but usually he's far too heavily involved in his latest cause to do so. He still practises law, but it's clear that he loathes it. He has four passions in life: Federico García Lorca, writing poetry, Mother and us children. I'd never say that these passions run in this particular order, because I do know that he loves us all, but I always feel that his love for García Lorca borders on something close to obsession. He tries to make his verse comparable to his hero's and devotedly follows his career. Somehow Father even gets wind of the poet's literary *tertulia* gatherings in the Café Alameda in Plaza del Campillo and when he misses dinner, we know that's where he is. I can just imagine him, dear Father, leaning against the bar trying to look relaxed, hoping against hope that he might be invited to join the gathering. So when a job opportunity comes up to be part of a newly formed committee promoting García Lorca's project to take theatre to remote villages, Father of course pounces on it like a wild cat attacking prey.

It is a part-time, voluntary position in which his role is to help design the posters that will be taken out to the rural communities and plastered on the doors of the town hall to encourage all the villagers to attend. One late afternoon, we're all in the garden, lounging on the warm grass, when Father returns home from his voluntary work. He is in such a state of excitement that it takes Mother several minutes to get the story out of him.

'Calm down, Edu, deep breaths. What, *por Dios*, is it?'

Father is pumping his arms up and down like a bird trying to fly, his mouth opening and closing breathlessly, and María and I start to giggle uncontrollably.

'I. Have. Been. Invited,' he gushes, 'to spend an entire weekend with the committee in a small village.' He starts to hop from one leg to the other. 'A six-hour mule journey from here over the mountains! Do you know what this means, *cariños mios*?'

Of course we know what it means; that Father will be spending hours and hours in the company of García Lorca, but we all look at him and smile. Like a child chasing sparrows, he runs round and round a walnut tree, laughing and whooping. Juan jumps up and runs after him and eventually Father stops, ruddy-cheeked and breathless, and catches Juan up in his arms. 'And you, *hijo mío*, are coming with me!' This time it is Juan's turn to give a great shout of excitement and as the two of them continue to scamper around the tree like a couple of schoolboys, I laugh and lie back down in the warm grass and close my eyes, the scent of blossom washing over me.

Many people attend that weekend of theatre to the villages, so it turns out that Father doesn't get the opportunity to directly speak to García Lorca. But that doesn't seem to matter. The fact remains that he's been in close proximity to him, even closer than those *tertulias* he invites himself to in the Café Alameda, and the effect their time away has on both Father and my brother Juan is enormous. When they return late on Sunday evening, they speak excitedly over one another at dinner and I think to myself that Juan speaks more during the next hour than in his whole life up till then.

'The people in the villages, they were so *poor*...' Juan says.

'...but you can't imagine how much pleasure they derived in seeing these plays performed. It was the first time these poor souls had ever seen theatre and you could see their faces quite literally come alive...'

'...and they applauded for hours on end...'

'...not hours, Juan, but I agree, it was a very long time...'

'...it *was* for hours, Papá. When can we go again? Please tell me we can go again?'

'I'm sure Federico will invite us again soon, *hijo mío*. Ah Federico, the talent of that man...'

And so it goes on, all through dinner, whilst the rest of us shoot looks of amusement at one another at Juan's new voice.

❊ ❊ ❊

So the months following the declaration of the Republic are a happy time for everyone. There is an excited buzz as the rooms of Carmen de las Estrellas fill up with new friends and all kinds of interesting associates of Mother's. But even though our lives have become far more active and sociable, Mother is sure not to forget our friends on the other side of the valley. We don't visit Abuela Aurelia and her family as much as I would like, but when we do go I always return with a swing in my stride, a smile on my face – *we* have friends amongst the *gitanos*.

This period of intense joy and opportunity of the new Republic is short-lived, yet to me it feels like a lifetime. A time during which I can taste what it means to live in an exhilarating world. How am I to know that we are sitting on a time bomb that is eating away at the fabric of our society?

One day at school during the mid-morning break, I overhear a cluster of older girls talking in hushed whispers behind me. Something about the urgency of their voices makes me want to hear what they're saying, so I stop eating my crunchy *galleta* and place it in my lap.

'…they're rising up and taking the land by force,' says one girl.

'…and *murdering* their landowners,' hisses another.

'*No digas tonterías*,' says a third girl with a loud, authoritative voice. 'Peasants would never kill their landowners.'

'They would, and they *are*, believe me. My brother told me, and he heard it from a friend whose uncle lives in one of the villages where it's happening.'

'That doesn't sound like a very reliable source to me,' retorts the loud girl. 'Are you sure it's not your brother's friend's uncle's cousin's nephew?' All the girls laugh. 'Anyway, even if it is true, perhaps they deserved it.'

Cold fear rushes down my spine and I realise that my biscuit has crumbled within my grasp. I don't want to hear more and move away from the group across the playground, crumbs scattering the ground. I'm confused – hasn't everything improved for the poor labourers under the Republic? Aren't they being paid more now, and seeing new reforms all the time? Surely they can't *really* be murdering their landowners. Can they? As I walk across the playground, away from the laughing girls, I realise how little I truly understand of what is going on in my country. I feel deeply, achingly ignorant and make a vow to myself to ask my parents to be truthful with me.

It turns out though that I don't need to, as it is around the same time as overhearing this conversation that I become friends with a girl called Sara Rodriguez. Tall, broad and outspoken, with a thick brown plait and chiselled cheekbones, I have seen her many times and we take several classes together. But it isn't until we've been at the *colegio* for several months that we start really talking. Sara is the kind of girl who makes all the boys' heads turn. She doesn't flirt with words but she doesn't need to; it's her body – the way she moves, so supremely confident in her beauty and who she is. I don't think Sara's even particularly interested in boys when we first meet, but it's impossible for me not to notice them staring at her when she walks past, and all it takes is for her to curl her lip up slightly or to raise one of her arched

eyebrows to be adored and longed for. At first I find this
power she holds intimidating. But Sara is so good-natured
and not at all conceited or vain (unlike my sister María) that
it doesn't take long for me to be counted amongst her ad-
mirers. In fact, I enjoy walking alongside Sara, because I've
never been a person to enjoy attention, and I certainly don't
get any when I'm with her. As for my interest in boys, the
truth is I find them, on the whole, childish and silly.

Sara is an only child and she finds our large family and
rambling Carmen in the Albaicín wonderfully exotic and
loves coming home with me after school. After our friendship has been firmly established, both of her parents even
start attending Mother's meetings, which they have heard
about through Sara. Her father is an eminent politician of
the social democrat party and her mother is a doctor, an
unusual profession for a woman. I'm unsure whether Sara
is just influenced by her parents' extreme left-wing ideals
or if she has come to her own conclusions independently,
but she is extremely opinionated and bright and I am fascinated by her. In time, Sara becomes my primary source
of political and practical information, even more so than
my teachers.

Sometimes at the end of lessons we wander back past
a *patissería* and sit in the plaza near our school. On one
particular occasion as we walk past a church, two solemn-
looking men thrust pamphlets into our hands with large
letters sprawled across the front: 'Divorce signals a fall
from the grace of God'. Sara scowls angrily at the men
as she scrunches the paper up in her hands. I glance ner-

vously at her; I am forever stunned by her boldness. Turning the pamphlet over, I read the words aloud.

'If women divorce, remarry or wed in a civil ceremony, they will no longer be permitted the sacrament and in the eyes of the church their children are illegitimate.'

'Nonsense,' chides Sara, once the men are out of earshot. She tosses the pamphlet into a bin and we approach the wall, rolling our white socks down to our ankles. We dangle our legs over the side and unravel the layers of pastry from our *alfajors*, nibbling at the almond and cream filling. Sara begins to chatter animatedly, flicking her fingers about wildly as she talks.

'It doesn't matter how many Republican flags they wave about. The fact of the matter is that nothing's changed. Well, not *really.*'

'But how can you say that? This time last year I was sitting in a stuffy attic room being bored to tears by one tutor after another. And now I have all these opportunities.'

'*Pues sí*, of course *that's* changed.' Sara rolls her eyes in her exaggerated manner as she sucks the remaining cream out of the pastry. 'But what I'm talking about are the fundamentals. The pillars of Spanish society. They haven't changed at all, *para nada!*'

One of the reasons I feel so comfortable with Sara is because if I don't understand something she's talking about, she clarifies without hesitation. And her arguments are so compelling that I can't deny that sometimes I return home and replicate our discussions virtually word for word. In the early days of my ranting my family seem both shocked and impressed. But they realise soon enough that I'm spending a great deal of time with the spirited Sara Rodriguez. The fact is that she completely convinces me and very soon Sara's ideals become my own.

'What pillars,' I ask her slowly, 'do you mean exactly?'

'Well, the upper classes for one. Then there's the god-forsaken army.'

I look around warily. She unnerves me, the way she seems unaware of the volume of her voice. One can never be entirely sure who's listening.

'And not to mention the church!' Dramatically, she flings her arms into the air.

'But the church has so much less influence than it used to.' I pause. 'And surely you don't excuse what's going on at the moment?'

Sara looks at me darkly then turns to stare at the Alhambra in the distance, once the stronghold of the powerful Moors who ruled Spain for years but who were eventually overthrown by the Catholic kings.

'I can't stand the church,' she whispers, suddenly more cautious. 'But no. No, *claro*, I don't excuse it. And you know what I overheard my parents talking about last night? That in Valencia they're lining up monks and forcing them to renounce their vows before shooting them in the head.' She narrows her dark eyes. 'With a single bullet.'

I shudder and feel a flake of the *alfajor* lodging in my throat. Stories. There are so many of them, and who's to say they are true? But who's to say they aren't?

'It wasn't long ago that we were dancing and singing in the streets for *la niña bonita*,' I say despondently. 'And now people are burning down churches. What happened?'

'What happened,' Sara replies, 'is that we've woken up. The problems of this country are far too deep-rooted to smooth over just because a new government comes in. It's a mess, believe me. Listen to this: you know that convent in Madrid that was torched a couple of weeks ago by Republican mobs?'

I nod, not knowing.

'Now, I'm the last person on earth to defend the church,' Sara continues, 'but instead of trying to stop the mobs, the police just stood by and *watched* them do it. Now do you understand why there's all this violence against the church?'

I frown.

'*Because*, Isabel, the police are being utterly passive. They're allowing it to happen. Believe me, it's chaos. A complete mess.'

I stare at my friend in disbelief. How does she know so much, and I know so little? And if she *is* right, why won't it stop? And if she believes everything she is saying, how can she look so cheerful? Sara must see the look of worry on my face because she elbows me playfully in the ribs. 'Don't despair, *amiga*, we're living in exciting times.'

Sara may consider them exciting but I, on the other hand, find many of the stories deeply disturbing. I wish I never heard that every last Jesuit was being expelled from Spain. Or that priests are being marched up church bell towers and pushed to their deaths below. Or that nuns are being locked in their cloisters and brutally gang-raped.

When I return home from school one day, not long after that conversation with Sara, I can tell immediately that my parents are troubled about something. Father is pacing up and down the conservatory. His hands are thrust deep into his pockets and Mother is perched nervously on the side of an armchair. The priest we have known for so long – a kindly, unassuming man who married my parents and christened each of us children has been ambushed after leaving a church in the sierras and murdered. We are all in a state of shock. Nothing seems to make sense any more. As far as I am concerned, nobody deserves this kind of treatment, particularly not Padre Alfonso. But on the other hand, surely the Republicans are the liberators and they know what they are doing?

Soon it isn't just every so often I hear about these things, it is most days. A dark cavern of my mind opens, one that I'd far rather have kept behind lock and key. So these days are bittersweet: there is *libertad* in my learning and my circle of friends is growing rapidly, but black butterflies of fear beat more rapidly against my chest as reports of violence increase. To make matters even more complicated and confusing, new political parties are being created all the time. I suppose this is to try to cover all the different ideologies, but it seems to result in even less unity.

Politics is so chaotic and confused that a year after I am enrolled in the *collegio*, squabbles break out between even previously relaxed schoolmates of mine with their various leftist ideals. I decide I have to know where I stand – not Sara but *me* – and I resolve to finally talk to my parents as a starting point to help me form my own views. One evening, after all my siblings have gone to bed, I go into the conservatory where my parents are reading.

'Which political party do we belong to?'

They look up from their books, eyebrows raised.

'Hmm?' Father takes off his half-moon spectacles.

'I really need to know. Most of the girls in my class belong to one party or another.' I pause. 'Well, at least their *parents* do. I know that we're Republicans. But I don't think I understand what that means any more.'

Mother and Father glance at each other, then Mother beckons me to come and sit next to her.

'Isabel, you know that there have been some troubles for a while now.'

I nod.

'Well, what we need is strong leadership, but nobody seems up to it.' She frowns. 'The prime minister does not have an easy job, but the reforms he is trying to introduce are not effective. He is not being direct enough. And neither is he representing the voice of most Republicans.'

'But that's what I don't understand. Who *are* the Republicans? There are so many different groups and beliefs. Everybody is arguing and whenever I think I know where I stand someone in my class says something that goes against what I believe in. Or what I *thought* I believed in. And I'm not sure I know who I am any more.' The strength of my emotion takes me by surprise. The tension at school has been simmering for weeks and I can feel tears stinging my eyes.

Father sighs deeply, massaging his temple. 'You're a human, Isabel. No matter what happens and whichever way these troubles go, just remember that. You are a human being and so is the peasant from the countryside and so is the monk from the monastery and so is the right-wing politician. We may not agree with certain people but nothing, nothing whatsoever, justifies harming them.'

Mother puts her arm around me. 'Isabel, what is happening is so terribly complicated. The most important thing to remember though is that we are pacifists. Father is right, we do not believe in violence. Not for *any* reason.'

I sniff. 'But we don't belong to the pacifist party, do we? That doesn't exist.'

Mother continues slowly. 'No, it does not exist. You know that we do not like to define ourselves as anything in particular; there is so much confusion amongst all the parties that we prefer to stay separate from it all and simply call ourselves Republicans.'

'But those meetings you have here…you must *call* yourselves something. I know that Sara's parents are social democrats. Isn't that what you are too?'

Now it is Mother's turn to sigh heavily.

'Isabel, the people that come to my meetings are from all kinds of groups. Yes, Sara's parents are social democrats. But there are also those who consider themselves Catalans, or Marxists or Communists or Anarchists.'

'I still don't understand how you all agree.'

'Well, *claro*, we cannot always agree on everything.' Mother stares at me intently. 'But this is the point we are trying to *make* to you, Isabel. That even if we do not agree with one another, that is what makes us human – the ability to discuss and debate and ultimately accept we are all different.'

'In a few months' time there's going to be a general election,' Father adds. 'It's because of the...' he waves his handkerchief around, searching for words, 'of the dissatisfaction people are feeling right now. These elections are very, *very* important.'

'Who do you think is going to win?'

My parents glance at one another again, something – is it fear? – flitting across their faces Father coughs.

'The left must win, but...'

'But what?' I ask, sitting on my hands and leaning forwards.

'But I fear it will not.'

There is a deep silence in the room as I look from Father to Mother, and then back to Father who is frowning deeply. It's clear that they have just opened up to me as an adult, not as a child, and I feel the heady rush of both gratitude and concern. Why should it be so terrible if the left-wing are not in power? Liberal people the world over exist comfortably under non-liberal governments. Don't they? But this is different; I sense it. No, more than that, I *know* it. This will be more than a gentle shifting of power to the right – it will be a deep wound.

Mother takes Father's hand in hers and holds it on her lap as she stares out of the window and strokes over his knuckles absently with her fingers. As I look at my parents and Father's hand in Mother's, I see for the very first time, quite possibly in my entire life, that she loves him. And of course she should – she married him. But so often I have seen the way he looks at her, his green eyes glowing as though he has fever and the way he cranes his neck forwards to listen to her speak. But Mother, returning his love as fiercely? It has never occurred to me.

Of course I love both my parents. But if someone were to draw me to one side and ask 'So Isabel, what do you *really* think of your parents? Do they embarrass you? *Do* they?' I know that I would blush. Mother is everything to me: confidante, counsellor and carer. To confess makes me feel deeply ashamed, but I don't feel the same when it comes to Father. He is the kindest, most open-hearted person I've ever known. He treats us all equally, yet with an astonishing sense of pride that I'm sure surprises even Mother occasionally. And I love him deeply for planting an orange tree in honour of my birth. Yet for all this, he sometimes embarrasses me. I feel humiliated by him. There, I've said it. Perhaps it's because he introduces himself to all the parents of my friends as a poet, when I know that he has only ever published one book of poetry years before and in actual fact he is a lawyer. Perhaps it's because of his absent-mindedness – the times I've been talking to him only to realise at the end he hasn't heard a word I've said – or perhaps it's his obsessive attachment to García Lorca.

I understand that García Lorca is a genius. In fact, as I appreciate poetry more and more, I can share Father's sense of pride that García Lorca comes from our own city. Yet Father takes his admiration a step further and at every opportunity tells people the story of how the poet once asked him a question during one of his readings. Mother never says a word, but I know the story. She once told me that Father, despite having dreamt of that moment for months, clammed up and was so nervous that he never actually answered García Lorca's question. But of course he never mentions *that*, does he.

That being said, the night my parents open up to me is one of the nights in all the years I've lived at Carmen de las Estrellas I treasure the most. I know his words are nothing extraordinary, but what Father says to me about all of us being human suddenly makes so much sense. That underneath all the anger and confusion and layers we've piled on ourselves, we are all just vulnerable souls, trying to find our place in the world. And that both sides, the left and the right and all the parties in the middle, are struggling for ideals with such a passion that it sometimes spills over into a violence I dearly wish I never knew.

CHAPTER THREE
LUISA

Spring 1932

As a young child, I was taken to a bullfight by my grandparents for my birthday. To say this expedition was a calamity would be an understatement, for so horrified was I by the suffering of the bull that I had a severe screaming fit, finally resulting in my grandpapa dragging me from the *plaza de toros* and delivering a sharp slap across my face. A combination of shock and pain terminated my screams, but never, ever have I forgotten the sight of the slow, inevitable, agonised death of the bull. Why was not a soul doing anything to save this proud beast? Why were people clapping and cheering and smiling when there was an animal bleeding to death down in the ring?

When the Republic begins its slow demise, the memory of the bull's death surfaces time and again. For it lingers painfully and, like the bull, staggers to its feet once more and gives me hope, only to be overcome by its inevitable ruin. The votes are rounded up and counted. Then they are counted for a second time and a right-wing Catholic party is declared victorious, just as Eduardo and I feared.

'Intolerable,' Eduardo mutters under his breath at breakfast as he scrutinises the papers. And then, as though really just comprehending the news, he says the word again, this time shouting. 'Intolerable!' I look at all the anxious faces of the children and try to smile cheerfully.

'Children, the election did not go the way we hoped it would. But I do not want you to worry, is that understood? Now, we must get organised for school.'

They all file nervously past me into the courtyard, Isabel passing me last. As she does so, she pauses and looks me directly in the eye. I grasp her hand and kiss her on the cheek, pausing for a moment to smell the scent of youth that still hangs freshly upon her skin. I know that my eldest is suffering terribly; for all her bravado, Isabel is a sensitive soul, more like her father than she realises. With the children out of the house, I hurry back to the kitchen where Eduardo is standing at the head of the table, *El Defensor* spread out in front of him as he hunches over it, hands digging into both corners of the table.

'Edu, *cariño*,' I implore. 'We must make an effort to not agitate ourselves in front of the children. I do not want them to worry unnecessarily.'

'But have you seen the figures for these results, Luisa?' Eduardo cries. 'You know why this has happened, don't you? It is because of those tactics of intimidation they've been using in rural areas, not letting people vote.

It's bullying, that's what it is. No, it's more than that, it's illegal and outrageous and…intolerable!' He slams the paper shut and starts to pace the length of the room. 'What are we going to do? We have to do something. What can we do?'

I catch hold of his arm and hold onto it tightly. 'To begin with, we stay calm. That is what we do.'

'But Luisa—'

'Listen to me, Eduardo Torres. I am equally disgusted by these results. But we must calmly think of our next move. We and every other person in this city that loves the Republic.'

Eduardo sighs deeply and slumps into his seat. 'You're right.' He kicks at the table leg. 'But, *por Dios*, it makes me mad.'

The members of the winning party stand on every stage available and shout loud and clear about how the Republic has failed them. About promises made that have not seen fruition and laws that have enraged the military and the respectable God-fearing populace. In response to this, and to the appalling election results that we have a great deal of difficulty in believing are legitimate, a huge protest meeting is held in the Cármenes sports stadium in the city which we decide we cannot miss, even taking the children with us. A great number of people are there, voicing their fury in a manner I have never before witnessed and demanding a re-election. I question several times whether Edu and I have made a prudent decision in allowing the children to witness this, but for all the anger,

there is also a sense of fierce determination and hopeful-
ness. We buy piping hot *croquetas* from a street vendor
and as we listen to the speeches, and then march along
the main thoroughfares of the city, I truly believe that
with this many voices of dissent, we can change things. At
the end of the march, a protest note is handed over to the
civil governor of Granada, calling for new elections. It is
an exhausting, emotionally charged but peaceful day. Demands are made, but nobody is hurt. So how it leads from
this to the event that occurs two days later, I struggle to
comprehend. Perhaps I have been naïve to hope that human decency would prevail and that all this can be settled
by sitting down together and talking.

Conchi and I are making fortune cookies in the kitch-
en; some of the children are in the garden and the others
scattered around at friends' houses, when Eduardo comes
bursting through the door, causing such a loud bang that
I hurry out, hands covered in flour.

'Where are the children?' he pants, gripping at his
chest.

'Some of them are here, some went to friends' houses
after school, but *por qué*? What? What is it?'

'*Bueno*, first,' he says, straightening up and trying to
control his breathing, 'we need to get the children back
to the house immediately. I've just been in the Café Alameda, waiting to see if Federico would turn up, and
some extreme right-wingers, Falangists I think they were,
opened fire on a peaceful demonstration of workers and
their families in the Plaza del Campillo.'

I hear a gasp from behind me and turn to see Conchi, as pale as her white apron, with her huge hand covering her mouth. 'What happened?' she asks in a voice scarcely louder than a whisper.

'Nobody dead, I don't think, but at least a few women and children were injured.'

'My brother and sister-in-law went to that demonstration,' Conchi says quietly, untying her apron strings as she speaks. '*Señor*, Señora, if you permit me, I should go to my family.'

'*Claro que sí*,' I say.

'Will you manage without me, Señora?'

'Of course we shall.' I look at Conchi's face, visibly shaken. It occurs to me that in all the time I have known her, I have never seen that expression on Conchi's face before. Irritation, certainly, and disapproval on many an occasion, yet never this countenance of fear. As Conchi readies herself to leave, my mind is pulled back to the children.

'Edu,' I say firmly. 'We must go now.'

Eduardo is nodding vigorously and he marches back towards the door. 'You stay here, Luisa. Now tell me who is where and I shall fetch them all and bring them back until everything calms.'

But calm it does not, not that day at any rate. A twenty-four-hour strike is called for by the trade unions and more burning and looting takes place in Granada during this period than at any other time we have known in our normally tranquil city. From right-wing newspaper headquarters to the premises of the Falange party to Café Royal where we have spent each of our children's fifth birthday parties, workers systematically torch every building symbolic of right-wing bourgeoisie they can think of. They then turn their attention to churches as the unthinkable comes to Granada. A convent and church not two hundred metres from our home burns as we hug our children to us, grateful at least to have them all home safely. Despite the terrible incident in Plaza del Campillo, we know that this kind of destruction is provocative and I find myself praying in earnest for the first time in years, imploring the violence to cease. Eduardo is convinced that all of this is the work of right-wing infiltrators, intent on stirring up hatred and violence against the left. I do not know what I think, and I do not care. All I know is that I want it to stop and, until it does, I want my children by my side.

An uneasy tranquillity eventually settles around us. Conchi's family lives in a small village outside Granada; whilst she seldom mentions them, we know that they support the Anarchist cause, looking towards a complete working-class revolution. Her family were not injured that day of the demonstration and Conchi returns to the house shortly after, but she is particularly skittish during the days that follow as we hear more and more about the Anarchist uprisings taking place in villages across Andalucía.

'Conchi, *por favor*, you ought to go home to your family for a while. Just a few days.'

'No, Señora. There is work to be done here.' She juts out her bottom jaw and grimaces, her face strained and tired.

'There may be work to be done,' I implore. 'But we shall manage.' I know that Conchi takes great pride in her work and, as much as I appreciate her loyalty, her face is as long as a mid-summer's day and I know she is worried about her brothers' and father's involvement in the uprisings.

Despite all the unsettling news reaching us and the tense atmosphere we are living in, new elections are called and they are the first elections in my lifetime I am permitted to vote in under the laws of the Republic. This fills me, I must confess, with a new surge of optimism as the bull staggers to its feet once more. I am inflated with pride, an intoxicating nectar that helps me forget, for a short while at least, the realities of drowning Granada. Alongside several friends, we attempt to spread the news as widely as we are able, organising pamphlets and talks and urging women to exercise this new right we have finally been granted. *This* is what the Second Republic is all about, I think as I walk to the polling station with Eduardo, head held high. *Democracía*, how sweet the word sounds. Thus how can I fail to be disappointed when I witness such a tiny proportion of female voters? Nevertheless, I smile warmly at them and they smile back in complicity.

Despite my best efforts, not enough women have been made aware of their rights. Or they have been kept at home. I think of the wife of Miguel, a perfect example, knowing that Miguel would never permit the poor creature to vote. This bigotry is what my friends and I face, but I know the results of the election run far deeper than just that. The Republic is sinking, and we are powerless to keep her afloat. After another crushing defeat at the polls, so it is that reform programmes that the Republic – that *we* – have worked so hard on begin to fall apart at the seams and slowly grind to a halt. And all the while, newly formed left-wing coalitions rally together to protest the undeniable rise of the political right. These are tense days and I keep hoping with all my heart that the Republic can become more united to stand against the right. My friends and I continue to hold our meetings, but we feel as though we are standing on a political earthquake, though none of us know how to put this fear into words, much less to admit it.

One day, we receive an unexpected visit from Aurelia. I have told her about my home, but never imagine she would be able to find it in the warren of narrow lanes that make up the Albaicín – or *desire* to find it, more to the point. She comes with two of her grandchildren, Pablo and Beatriz, and I know as soon as I return from market to find them in the house that something is wrong. Firstly, she is walking much slower than I remember, almost as though the very effort of placing one foot before the other pains her. And though the map of her wonderful face has been drawn with more than her fair share of worries, I have met her enough times now to read that she is absorbing more cares than before.

Whilst the children remain in the garden, Eduardo and I bring Aurelia into the conservatory. I pull up a chair for her but she chooses to stand and I think, for the hundredth time, how noble and proud she looks standing there, even in these surroundings unfamiliar to her and so different from her own.

'Luisa, Eduardo, forgive my intrusion—'

'You couldn't possibly intrude, Aurelia,' I reply. 'We are delighted to see you.'

Aurelia holds her hand up and nods solemnly, bowing slightly.

'Even so. This is not my will.' She sighs very deeply. 'But this is the position I have been forced into. And...' she falters slightly but looks at me directly, 'I have nobody else to turn to.'

Eduardo has, until this point, been perching rather absent-mindedly on the side of the armchair but, upon hearing Aurelia speak these last words, he looks up sharply, concern and compassion etched across his face. He has only ever visited the caves on a couple of occasions over the years, really for my sake more than his own, for I have been eager he should meet the friends whom both the children and I hold in such high esteem. And though he is not close to Aurelia and her family, he recognises how important her friendship has become to me.

I instinctively understand that Aurelia does not want me to probe with questions and we wait, patiently, for her to tell us why she has come. She is silent for a while and then takes a deep inhalation before she resumes speaking.

'I'm afraid I have seen this coming for a long time. But some things one chooses to ignore. Until,' she coughs, 'it is impossible to ignore them any more. I shall not beat around the bush any longer. I am here because I need sanctuary in your home. We all need sanctuary, my family and I.'

I glance at Eduardo who is staring at her, eyes wide. '*Dios*,' he breathes. 'What has happened?'

'My race has been on the receiving end of prejudice for long enough to know that we'd be the first to be marked out with this new wave of...' She waves a hand through the air, searching for words.

'Right-wing fascism,' I offer.

'Call it what you will,' Aurelia sighs and shrugs. 'What I didn't realise, however, was quite how soon or how vigorously we'd be singled out.'

We wait for her to continue.

'We've had to put up with this for years; *ay*, it's never been more than an irritation till now. A few stupid young *chaboró*, fuelled up at night on alcohol, have walked out from the city and painted racist slogans on all the cave doors in our area.'

'That's outrageous!' Eduardo's cheeks have turned pink and the vein high on his forehead is starting to pulsate.

'Outrageous,' Aurelia murmurs. 'Not as outrageous as yelling "*gypsy bastard pigs*", again and again till every single person in the settlement is awake and the children are crying. Then they smash their empty bottles against the cave walls and they leave.'

I shudder. I had no idea my friends have had to deal with this over the years.

'But,' Aurelia says, her face an impenetrable stone mask, 'as I say, they are just stupid, ignorant young men. Of course

I felt angry, of course I did, but as long as my daughter and my grandchildren remained untouched, I could keep my fury locked up. But now…' She falters and her mask slips a fraction, conveying an air of vulnerability I see so seldomly. I urge her with my eyes to continue. 'Now this is happening not just every so often, it's happening a lot.'

'How often?' Eduardo asks, scratching furiously beneath his chin.

'Every second day? Every day? I don't know…' she replies, finally lowering herself into the seat and rubbing her temples.

I want more than anything to go to her and put my arms around her, but I know this is not something she would feel at ease with.

'And the reason I am here,' she continues, 'is because of yesterday. We simply cannot carry on this way. Yesterday afternoon, Mar, Beatriz and I were outside in the yard. I was washing my hair whilst the others were hanging clothes up to dry. Beatriz was the first to notice them, two men standing by the gate watching us. They were dressed in uniform and they had a wild, reckless look about them. I didn't like that look one little bit, and I certainly didn't like the large dirty guns over their shoulders. As soon as I saw them I asked what they wanted. "*Nada*," said one of them, "we're only looking.' The other man laughed in a nasty kind of way and added "And this is a sight that's certainly worth looking at."'

Holding my breath, I listen as Aurelia recounts how she could read the undisguised sweaty lust written all over their faces as they stared at Mar and Beatriz. 'I started to walk towards them and told them "Well, you've had your look. Now be off with you." The younger one, the more conceited of the two, he started snorting. "I don't think I like the way this old *gitana* is talking to me," says he. "What do you think, Javier? Do you think a common gypsy hag should be talking to me like that?"'

I gasp. I can feel my fingers digging into the side of the chair in fury and see that Eduardo has turned so red he looks as though he might explode.

'Before I knew what was happening, the young one had unclasped the latch on the gate and kicked it open with his boot. I shouted at him to stay away from us, but he strode through the gate and rammed his gun into my stomach.'

At this point, Eduardo and I gasp in unison.

'The bastards!' Eduardo spits. 'You describe them to me and I'll…I'll go and find them,' he says very bravely, but I hear the tremor in his voice.

'Aurelia! You must let me look at your stomach,' I cry.

She shakes her head. '*Nada.* There's nothing to see. Nothing that won't heal. That is the least of my worries. Both Mar and Beatriz screamed and their screams brought Pablo and the girls running outside. I yelled at Pablo to get back in, and to take his mother and sisters with him. For one awful second I thought that Pablo was going to try and hit the *cabrón*, he looked so angry when he saw me lying on the ground. But clearly he thought better of it and started to usher everyone into the cave. But the younger soldier had walked over to Mar and was grasping her face with his hand. "You're a pretty one, aren't you?" he says, and Beatriz must have whimpered from the corner of the yard at that point, because then he walked over to her and put his arm around her waist and pulled her to him. Then he said "And you're not bad either, for a *gitana* whore."'

Rage and horror crush against my chest.

'*Pues*, they left after that, *gracias a Dios*, but just before they went, they said "*Adiós*. For now."' And the next morning, we woke up to find our cave painted in red with the words "*Gitano slags, gitano whores. Death to all gitanos.*"'

Aurelia sighs deeply. She looks exhausted to the point of collapse and I move over to her and take her hand.

'Aurelia, *querida* Aurelia. We must waste no time. You must come and live here immediately. You shall all be safe here—'

'I know what I am asking of you, child. I would not request this lightly.'

'I know that, Aurelia. You must all come at once. Must they not, Edu?'

I turn to look at my husband imploringly. Of course I know he will sympathise with her story, but six people coming to live at Carmen de las Estrellas is another matter entirely. But in his face I see nothing but indignation and compassion and he nods vigorously. '*Claro*, you must come at once.' I smile gratefully at him.

Later that evening after Aurelia and her grandchildren have left, something else occurs to me. How ought we to manage the fact that Joaquín's mother shall be living under the same roof as our eldest adopted son? Mar may well feel compelled to reveal her identity to Joaquín. It is doubtful, but we have always operated on a policy of such honesty with our children that it would be unfair to keep the truth from him. And if we *do* decide to tell him, will he be furious with us?

Joaquín has met Mar on so many occasions over the years during our visits to the caves that it is hard to predict how he may react. He is a fiery twelve year old and with his erratic mood swings he can be both reclusive and delightful by turn. And then there is the matter of how the news that a family of *gitanos* are coming to live at Carmen de las Estrellas shall be received, not least by both our parents and siblings, but also by our neighbours and friends.

I have scarcely mentioned my association with our friends to my own family. They certainly know that some connection *has* been made, yet conclude with condescension that it is simply one of my many eccentric liaisons. Had they discerned the depth of friendship that has developed over the years, they would be horrified. Both Eduardo and my own family are extremely conservative and, whilst they would not condone racist attacks, neither would they acknowledge Aurelia's family a worthy enough cause to become so directly involved in. And to bring them into our *house*…this is information that both Eduardo and I far prefer to keep from our parents.

As for our neighbours, they are a sundry group of people. Some of them are similar to ourselves: liberal, free-thinking

Republicans. But there are many more who are nationalists, monarchists or generally right-wing. Though we naturally surround ourselves with like-minded people, ours is
not a broad-minded city. It has long held the reputation
for being home to traditionalists who uphold the values
of church and creed, and I know it will be highly provocative if our already large Torres Ramirez family mysteriously
expands by six people quite suddenly. People have eyes and
people talk. The walls around Carmen de las Estrellas are
high enough to keep out only a certain amount and it will
be a matter of mere days before gossip spreads.

The question also arises that evening of how Eduardo
and I should explain it to the children. Of course they
have picked up on the tense atmosphere: the curfews, the
rules that not so long ago were relaxed but have snapped
back forcefully. I witness how that has wounded them all
in different ways. Naturally, Eduardo and I hope that the
troubles shall soon be over and we can resume our normal
lives but, tensions running high as they are, how can we
possibly predict the length of our houseguests' stay?

CHAPTER FOUR
ISABEL

Summer 1934

The first time my mischievous brother Fernando loses his tongue is on a Sunday afternoon when Abuela Aurelia and her two eldest grandchildren turn up at Carmen de las Estrellas. Fernando is almost twelve years old, his voice swinging high to low and his charms curbed by growing pains and the early onset of manhood. Mother is at the market and Father is watering the plants nestled beside the fragrant myrtle, shirtsleeves rolled up and his curly hair falling over his eyes. María is sitting on top of the garden wall playing marbles (which I had to help her climb – honestly, after all these years she still needs help) and I am seated under a fig tree reading one of Father's books of García Lorca's poetry.

'Visitors!' María pipes shrilly from the wall as she abandons her game and jumps down to the grass before running round to open the door.

Reluctantly, I pull myself away and look up to see Abuela Aurelia, a bright green scarf in her hair, walking through the patio doors with Pablo and Beatriz. It has been a long time since our last visit to the caves and I am overjoyed, jumping up to greet them. Father continues watering, his face creased in serious lines as he moves from one plant to the next. After greeting our guests, I glance back at Father who is lost in his task and clearly unaware of the fact that we have visitors. I walk over to him.

'Father,' I say. He doesn't reply, so I say it again.

'Hmm?' He squints up and I gesture behind me. He immediately leaps up.

'I do apologise,' he mumbles, 'welcome, welcome.' He stands still, looking a little bewildered and then calls up to the open windows of the house to the boys. After a few minutes, the sleepy face of Fernando appears, rubbing his eyes.

'Fernando, *por favor*, can you fetch three glasses of cold *chufa* and take them to the conservatory?' Father calls up.

I show our guests into the house and guide them into the glass-walled conservatory filled with green curling plants and deliciously warmed by the gentle sun. This has always been my favourite room in the house. I love the magnificent, unobstructed view that stretches out across the valley of the brown-slated roofs of the city, proudly presided over by the Alhambra Palace.

Beatriz gasps loudly when she sees the vista in front of her before clamping her hand self-consciously over her mouth, whilst I watch as the eyes of Abuela Aurelia and Pablo grow larger and wider. It is clear that they are all feeling awkward; it is, after all, the first time that any of them have visited our home and most probably the first occasion that they have entered a house such as ours. I try to help them feel comfortable, plumping out cushions for them to sit on. Although Father is happy to see them, the social graces and ease of manner that comes so naturally to Mother certainly don't to him. After several minutes of banal questioning he takes his leave and shuffles off, mumbling something about finishing planting the gladioli. As we sit and wait for Mother to return, Abuela Aurelia smiles her wide, white smile and asks me what I've been doing since she last saw me whilst Pablo and Beatriz perch on the edge of their seats. I tell her about a few of Fernando's latest pranks and how María has just finished making her first dress.

'But what about *you* though, little one?'

I look at her inquisitively.

'How old are you now?'

'Almost Fifteen.'

Abuela Aurelia pauses and fixes her forceful stare on me. 'Well, hasn't the time come for you to start thinking about your future?'

I feel tongue-tied and just sit there staring at her, eventually blurting out 'I like your headscarf, Abuela Aurelia.'

She smiles at me knowingly. 'Green is the colour of hope, little one.'

Before I have a chance to respond to her words, the door is kicked open and Fernando walks in carrying a tray laden with ice-cold *chufa* and a plate of Mother's fortune cookies, his tongue lolling out to the side of his mouth in deep concentration as he fixes his eyes on the teetering glasses. Laying the tray carefully on the table in front of Beatriz, he takes a step back and looks up, about to come out with one of his witty jokes when his eyes fall upon the girl seated before him. They've met before of course; several times in fact. But it has been a while since we've last been to the caves and in this period he seems to be growing, rather painfully, into his rapidly changing body. And Beatriz, with all her natural beauty, has grown a dozen times lovelier. We all watch in amusement as Fernando tries desperately to dislodge the words jammed in his throat, his face contorting in his attempts to look composed. The situation soon turns from comical to painful as he begins spluttering, clearly both delighted and distressed by the effect Beatriz is having on him. I decide it's best to intervene.

'*Ven*, Fernando. I'll do it.' I nudge him aside and take up the task of pouring out glasses of *horchata*. Without taking his eyes from Beatriz, who is now blushing deeply, he edges backwards. He knocks into a table before finding a seat and firmly plants himself on it. This is the only time I've ever witnessed my brother fall completely silent. I'm so used to his constant chattering that I find his sudden speechlessness unnerving. Clearly, Fernando has fallen into a kind of lovesickness and in this new state, I decide it best to leave him there. I try to recover the thread of conversation with Abuela Aurelia, but just one look at Fernando's forlorn, passion-struck face makes it almost impossible to talk normally. Thankfully, Mother soon appears to save us. The moment she enters the conservatory, she takes one look at Fernando, then at the object of his vision and rolls her eyes.

Mother is overjoyed to see our visitors, but it's clear after a few words have passed between her and Abuela Aurelia that this isn't a social call, and shortly the two of them leave the room together before asking me to call Father in. I don't want to put up with Fernando's tongue-tied awkwardness for a moment longer. Jumping to my feet, I grasp my brother roughly by the arm and the plate of fortune cookies by the other.

'Shall we all go and sit in the garden?'

Fernando doesn't say a word and continues to gaze at poor Beatriz till I shake him hard. 'Fernando! Listen to me, shall we all go and sit in the garden?'

'All of us?' he says, with a stupid grin on his face. 'Oh, *por qué no?*'

Abuela Aurelia and my parents are talking for a long time and I set about organising paper and a pencil for Pablo to sketch on. He smiles at me gratefully as I hand it to him and I notice that his eyes are full of a silent intelligence I'd give anything to understand. We all sit on a rug laid out under the fig tree and María immediately runs over and starts to plait Beatriz's hair.

By the time Mother, Father and Abuela Aurelia have returned from inside the house, the sun has lost its warmth and goldfinches are darting in the lengthening shadows of the garden. Fernando is still staring at Beatriz with an idiotic mixture of wonder and boyish wickedness and Pablo is putting the final touches to his sketch. Shyly, he shows it to me and I gasp in delight when I look at the paper. He has drawn my sister María plaiting Beatriz's hair, capturing them both perfectly.

Just before they leave, Fernando snatches up the final fortune cookie that lies on the plate and thrusts it into Beatriz's hand. She gives him a coy smile and then bites into it and crunches on the shell, holding her hand underneath to catch the falling crumbs. Fernando clicks his heels together impatiently and hovers by her side. When she has finished eating, she opens her hand to reveal the tiny paper scroll.

'Are you…are you going to…to…to read it now, Beatriz?' Fernando demands. Beatriz blushes again, which makes her look even more beautiful, and then Fernando is blushing and his behaviour is so excruciating that all of us are blushing. Beatriz lowers her head. At first I think it's the ridiculous anguish in Fernando's voice that has just gone too far, but I realise quickly it's because she can't read. Mother must have realised at the same time because she rushes to Beatriz's side and prises it from her hand, giving it to my brother.

'Why don't *you* read it, Fernando?'

He gulps and, taking it from Mother's outstretched hand, unrolls it with a care I've never seen in him. After taking a deep, prolonged breath and coughing away any frogs that may have lodged themselves in his throat, he opens his mouth.

'As the first rays of spring warm the air, so too does another sweet melody. Be thankful for the love that already exists in your life and, if there is none, perhaps your time has come.'

Beatriz's hand flies to her mouth in an attempt to smother a fit of giggles, similarly to all the rest of us who are trying not to explode with laughter. Fernando is mortified that we all find it so funny but Mother has heard enough.

'I am sure we ought to be letting our visitors get back now,' she announces firmly, grabbing Fernando's shoulders. As soon as they have left, Fernando scampers over to the wall and springs up like a cat as he watches them walk away down the alley. Whether or not Beatriz looks back at him, we'll never know. But what is certain is that Fernando is never quite the same again from that day on.

Long after they have left, I sit under my orange tree in the courtyard listening to Aurelia's words echoing through my head: *Hasn't the time come for you to start thinking about your future?* With a jolt, I realise that Aurelia is talking about more than simple plans of becoming a teacher or a seamstress. Her eyes told me that something will happen in our country and, strange as it is, somehow I understand that it will be my fate to help fight against it.

Those joyful early months of the Republic with its *libertad* and learning feel like a lifetime ago. The corridors at school are filled with whispers and shadows and the teachers can't hide their concern any more. The cultural activities that have worked themselves into our school curriculum and been heralded as such a great success lose their momentum and slow down like the fading warmth of day. Plays and concerts are cancelled, Republican banners are taken down and that invincible sense of optimism that once echoed so freely around our schoolyard falls silent. And then the school closes, just like that, with a sign banged onto the gates reading 'Temporary closure until further notice'. Those of us students who turn up that day stand there for a long time reading the notice, and then reading it again, wondering if we can take another meaning from it before we finally trickle back down the hill towards our homes. Joaquín storms off to his music school, but he finds the same situation there. For my brother, it is more than he can bear and he begins to spend hours upon end in his room, practising his exercises even more diligently than before as we hear the furious echo of scales and melodies down the corridors of Carmen de las Estrellas.

But it isn't just all this that makes me feel jumpy. I realise that the streets aren't safe, not in the way they used to be when I walked to school and down to the city. Buildings of all kinds, not just religious buildings, continue to be damaged and the military lurk on shadowy corners. They appear from nowhere and glare threateningly at anyone who passes them.

And then, one day, I am out at market with Mother and on the way home I see blood flung against the wall, as though somebody had sprayed a paintbrush. I experience the strangest sensation; not fear that the person may have felt pain, but a wash of nausea at the sight of the blood itself, fresh and bright and delicate. Mother notices my reaction and grasps tighter onto my arm. 'Isabel,' she says.

'I'm sure it's nothing. It's probably just from an injured animal.' But it wouldn't have mattered what she said, because I'm stuck in a memory of when I was a small child and I cut my thumb. The blood was flowing fast and I screamed and screamed, not because it hurt, but because the sight of what looked to me like red ink, so fast-flowing and so vital, was more than I could bear. As I stand there with Mother, trapped in the memory of my screams and the sight of fresh blood before me, I realise that I feel faint and quite sick. Mother guides me to a nearby wall to sit on and some time passes before I feel strong enough to move again.

With the closure of our school, we have to stay at home more. And home isn't exactly a fun place to be. Father's voluntary work has been suspended, which has driven him into a black mood, and what with Joaquín's fury, Mother's tiredness (as Conchi is around less to help her) and María pouting and moaning like she's the only person to be affected by all this, I feel horribly stifled.

It's inevitable really when Mother insists that none of us should spend time out of the house.

'But what about—'

'There'll be no more said about it, Fernando.'

'But—'

'The subject is closed.'

Mother turns a bright but strained smile towards us all. 'It hopefully shan't be for long.'

'That's what you said about the college,' says Joaquín as he kicks at the door, 'and that doesn't look like it's re-opening.'

Mother shrugs weakly. 'Everything will be alright, we shall see.'

❊ ❊ ❊

Not long after Abuela Aurelia's visit to Carmen de las Estrellas, Mother and Father gather all of us into the conservatory and announce that they have some very important news. I take a sharp breath. I know intuitively that this is the news I've been waiting for, the news that will somehow change all of our lives. Mother begins by explaining that with all the problems that have been going on, matters have been made more difficult for some than others.

'...and as you all know, Abuela Aurelia came to visit us recently.'

Fernando blushes deeply and starts fiddling with a tassel on the edge of the armchair. Mother sighs, and I can see she is trying desperately to think how she can best break the news to us. Silence fills the room as we all look round at one another with concern, then back at Mother.

'Children, Abuela Aurelia's family are going to come and live here with us for a while.'

A few of us gasp while Father lifts his head up, searching our faces for reactions. Nobody says a word; we simply continue to look at Mother.

'How does that make you all feel?'

Juan eventually breaks the silence with a violent sneeze. As the eldest, I feel I should respond.

'I don't mind.'

Saying these words gives the others strength to add something and all at once they begin to murmur their agreement. A look of relief passes over both Mother and Father's faces and the tense atmosphere of minutes earlier explodes into a steady barrage of questions. *Where will they sleep? Where will we sleep? How long are they coming for? Are they all coming? What has happened to their home?*

'I know this isn't a very normal situation,' Mother says. 'It's something that none of us expected. But we know you'll all help them feel welcome.'

'It probably shan't be for long,' Father adds. 'Just until things have settled down here and...' he coughs, 'everything gets back to normal.' He stares at his hands in his lap. 'We just need to cope as best we can whilst they're here and make a few changes and sacrifices.'

'What kind of sacrifices?' Joaquín asks, one arm wrapped around his guitar.

'Sacrifices with our...' Mother waves a hand around, 'our privacy, that sort of thing. We mayn't have a great deal of that whilst they are all here. And we shall have to be inventive with our cooking and make the ingredients we do have stretch further. Everyone must help with laundry and cleaning, Conchi will need lots of extra hands. Oh Conchi, *Dios*! She probably shan't be back from her village until after they have all arrived, what a shock for her.' Mother's face creases and she shakes her head. 'It shall all be fine, nobody need worry. As Father said, it most probably will not last terribly long.'

'How long?' Fernando asks. Unsurprisingly, he looks overjoyed at the news.

'Fernando,' Father snaps, 'you know very well we don't know the answer to that.' Fernando just grins at him, a big, stupid, lovesick grin and María groans and pushes him. As the others continue asking questions and Mother and Father answer them as best they can, I seem to be the only one amongst us who notices how they're skirting round the subject of *why* they are coming. My siblings are too preoccupied with who is going to sleep where and counting up on their fingers how many people will now be living at Carmen de las Estrellas. But I decide not to ask them there and then. No doubt I'll find out sooner or later. Instead, I put another un-asked question to them: when they will be arriving.

Mother takes a deep breath and stares at me, unblinking, with her olive eyes. '*Mañana.*'

Tomorrow! The murmur starts up once again and as I raise an eyebrow at Mother, she smiles. It's a warm smile, but it's clear to me that it's troubled.

'Mother, what shall we say to the neighbours?' I ask. It sounds pathetic, but everyone seems to be watching everyone else these days and even some close neighbours we've known for years hurry past, no greeting or eye contact.

Mother sighs. 'If anybody pries, you must tell them that they are just relatives who have come to stay.'

'*Pues*, everybody around here knows all our relatives,' Juan points out.

'*Distant* relatives, Juan,' Mother retorts and she fixes him with a stare so fierce that he gulps and nods. 'We shall dispose of all their attire and they shall wear our clothes,' she continues.

Fernando sniggers. 'Whose clothes will Abuela Aurelia possibly fit into?'

Father suddenly bangs his hand on his chair. '*Dios*, Fernando, do you think this is a joking matter? For once, will you please cease with your ridiculous quips.' Fernando reddens and we all stare at Father, both shocked and impressed at his outburst. The room falls silent and I am about to round up my siblings to go to bed when María asks 'But, Mamá, Papá, we can tell the neighbours they are distant relatives, but we can't tell our own relatives that. What about our abuelos for example? What shall we tell them?' She has a good point and I wish I'd thought of it. We rarely see family members from either Mother or Father's side, but it's inconceivable they won't hear eventually about our visitors. Gossip spreads faster than the Río Darro in Granada.

'*Sí*.' Mother crosses one foot over the other and runs her hands over the wrinkles of her skirt. '*Claro*, we have given that some thought too, and your father and I have decided the best thing to say is that they are an impoverished family from the city we have taken in for a short while.'

My eyes widen. 'I know it is an unlikely tale,' she continues, 'but really, when one is in such a situation, what other choice is there?' Mother suddenly looks exhausted

and slumps back into her seat. Father puts his arm around
her shoulders.

'I know you shan't tell a soul,' he says to us. 'You're
such marvellous secret-keepers.' We all know he is talking about Joaquín and I can't help but glance over at my
brother, but his face barely twitches.

'It's late,' Father says, squeezing Mother's shoulders.
'We need some sleep. Tomorrow will be a busy day.'

※ ※ ※

The following morning Fernando spends perched on top
of the wall, eagerly awaiting our houseguests' arrival. He
is so excited that no amount of scolding will remove him
from his lookout station. I can see him from the kitchen,
lying on his belly in the corner closest to the road for
the best vantage point, picking at tufts of moss poking
through the gaps. He is completely oblivious to the whirlwind of activity taking place in our house. Mother, María
and I prepare as impressive a meal as we can from the
ingredients we gather together to welcome the family to
Carmen de las Estrellas. My other brothers are helping
Father change the bedrooms around. Sleeping arrangements have shifted about so much that nobody's room,
with the exception of my parents', remains unchanged.

Fernando must be as numb as ice lying up there on
the wall for close to two hours, but finally we see him
hurl himself down in such a manner that I'm sure he
must have injured himself, but he then sprints towards
the house. We hear him skidding down the freshly waxed

corridor towards us where he flings open the door and stands before us wheezing, trying to speak. Mother is in brisk, efficient mood, her nerves frayed.

'What, *por Dios*, are you trying to tell me? Can you not see I am busy?'

He continues to gasp for breath, one arm flailing around and the other pointing towards the road. It is María who hears Abuela Aurelia's voice first and her eyes light up as she wipes her hands hurriedly on a cloth. 'Mother, they're here!'

Mother raises an eyebrow in the direction of Fernando who is nodding vigorously. '*Sí*,' he pants. 'That's what I was trying to say. They're here!'

Mother rolls her eyes and pushes him through the kitchen door as together we walk out to greet our guests. And there they are, all six of them, making their way slowly into our house: Abuela Aurelia, Mar, Pablo, Beatriz and the two younger girls, Inés and Graciana. As they walk towards us I feel a rush of affection for them. Finally, *finally* we have something else to think about.

CHAPTER FIVE
LUISA

Autumn 1934

'Señora,' Conchi repeats. 'I shall not stay here any longer with these people under the same roof. I simply cannot.'

'*Pero*, Conchi,' I reply firmly, piqued that she should display the same prejudice I expect of my parents or sisters, 'they are my *friends*.'

'Friends or not, Señora, I am employed to assist with you, your husband and children, not with a family of *gitanos*.' The shudder of her shoulders as she utters this last word is unmistakable and my stomach lurches in irritation but also panic. True, Conchi has taken more leave than usual of late, but I cannot recall a time when she has not been present in my life and now I am faced with the very real prospect that I may lose her. I can scarcely imagine running the house without her, particularly with all these extra people.

'Conchi,' I say again. '*Por favor.* I shall give you as much time back at home as you wish, but I beg you to reconsider.'

'Luisa,' she says, hands on her hips as she squares up to me in such a confrontational manner, it looks as though she should like to fight me. I stare, taken aback that she is addressing me by my Christian name. Never, in all the years I have known her, has Conchi called me Luisa.

'I appreciate it's going to be considerable work for you with all your new houseguests.' She scowls and wipes her hands together. 'But it's not just because of them...even though I don't understand at all why a lady brought up proper like you've been should take in that class of people. I have a few of my own troubles at home, you see. I'm needed.' Her dark brown eyes hold my gaze and I notice for the first time the small beige flecks across her cheekbones. It occurs to me that I know pitifully little about Conchi and I feel quite ashamed. True, she has never been a person to willingly share information with me. But neither have I enquired about her family or home life to the extent that I should.

'Oh,' I reply, feeling very young and very ignorant. 'Is there anything that I...I can assist you with?'

'*Gracias*, Señora. But no. I shall work to the end of the week.' Her huge hands drop from her hips and she marches towards the door as I am left to stare helplessly after her.

Life as we know it changes beyond recognition after Aurelia's family arrive at Carmen de las Estrellas. To my great sorrow, I decide that the gatherings I and my companions once derived so much pleasure from must cease. Not only do I find that my time is greatly stretched now, but I also fear that the atmosphere has become too tense; so fraught with distrust is the atmosphere that I concede a group of liberals arriving at our front door should do nothing for our reputation. And though I have so much else on my mind, how I miss and yearn for those meetings; for the camaraderie and debate amongst lively, enquiring minds. On rare occasions, I take the long route back from the market, heaving my basket brimming with potatoes and tomatoes as I go to the house of one of these old companions or another, knock on the door and enter before exchanging a few words of comfort with them in the privacy of their front vestibule or courtyard. Seeing them before me, these intelligent, free-thinking people from my past who still have the bravery to issue forth these laudable, free-thinking opinions, helps me to remember that we are still here. That, in small pockets the length and breadth of this city, we are still living, breathing, believing.

Eduardo and I also have yet to resolve the matter of whether to tell Joaquín about his relationship to Mar. Though he has known from a young age that he is adopted, Eduardo fears that if the truth is revealed, Joaquín may feel deceived for not having been told earlier. I, on the other hand, instinctively believe that in order for us all to live under the same roof harmoniously, we have no other option but to be honest with our son.

As our discussion chases endless circles and we realise we are no closer to nearing a solution, Edu and I concede that the only answer is to ask Mar what *she* should like. And thus, after the family arrives and we share our first meal together, we bring Mar into the conservatory. Eduardo and I agree that under no circumstances may we impose our personal preferences upon her. After I have raised the matter, the question hangs heavily in the air between the three of us, silence bearing down upon our shoulders, our hands turning hot and clammy. Mar eventually speaks.

'I have been thinking about it a great deal.'

She turns her head from Eduardo to me, then back again, her dark curls gently bouncing around her ears and the golden rings in her ears catching the light.

'I know he's my son, but I'm not the one who's brought him up. I owe that to the two of you.'

Eduardo expels an audible breath of air he has kept sucked up inside his mouth, his face a picture of pained relief.

'Yet the more I think about it,' Mar continues, 'the more I feel that we cannot keep from him something as important as this.'

Eduardo winces, trying desperately to maintain a neutral expression.

'*Por favor*, believe me when I tell you I don't want to be a mother to him now. I have my own four to worry about.' Her dark hands twist in her lap. 'I would just like to be his friend.'

Once again, there is silence and I glance at Eduardo, urging him with my eyes to say something. I am sure that it is clear to Mar which position the two of us take and thus feel it is of greater necessity that Eduardo put her at ease. Gulping, he reads my signals and, reaching over, pats Mar's hand awkwardly.

'That is quite alright, my dear. If that is what you should like to do, then we shall support you whole-heartedly.'

Since we are all feeling so emotionally charged anyway, I decide we ought to bring Joaquín directly into the conservatory. He saunters in with his guitar, a pencil stuck haphazardly behind one ear and an amused expression upon his face.

'Sit down, Joaquín,' Eduardo mumbles as he jumps to his feet and makes his way over to the bay windows, furiously scratching beneath his chin. He stares out, his forehead knotted. After a few moments, he turns around to face Joaquín, staring at him fixedly.

'*Hijo*, we have something to tell you.'

Joaquín places his guitar in position and begins to distractedly pluck at a string.

'Let me guess. You want to tell me that Mar is my mother?'

My bottom jaw feels leaden and we all stare at Joaquín who, nonplussed, has started to strum away as he works out a particularly difficult sequence with his fingers. A long time passes before any of us find the wherewithal to speak again.

'H…h…how the devil did you know?' Eduardo asks.

Continuing to play, Joaquín glances up.

'How did I know? Well, how could I not have known? I mean, *look* at us.'

Eduardo and I look from Mar to our son several times, realising in bewilderment that the truth that has stared us in the face all these years has passed far above our heads whilst being astutely picked up by Joaquín. For they are as alike as any mother and son possibly can be, from the arch of their eyebrows to their high cheekbones to the dark curl of their hair.

I have always prided myself on being the kind of person it should be difficult to shock, yet on this occasion I cannot quite believe what I have just heard. 'How long have you known, Joaquín?'

He stops playing and cocks his head on one side, gazing into the distance.

'Hmm…I can't remember *exactly* when I realised. But it was on one of the visits to the cave, maybe when I was about six or seven.'

I shake my head in disbelief as he continues. 'We were all eating lunch one day in the yard and there was that large cracked mirror hanging in one corner. We were sitting next to one another and I caught sight of our reflections in the mirror and I remember thinking to myself "She's my mother."'

I turn to Mar who is staring at our son, her features numb and expressionless. Joaquín picks up his guitar once again and begins picking out a lively tune.

'So you're not angry with me, Joaquín?' Mar murmurs.

'*¡Cómo!*' He looks up, laughing. 'Don't be silly. Anyway, do you lot want to hear this piece I've been working on?'

I shake my head again as Joaquín, as imperturbably as though he has just been told we shall be eating *jamón* for lunch, strikes up an energetic fandango.

The fact that Joaquín has known the identity of his real mother for years leads to the natural question: what of his father? Yet his apparent lack of concern that he and Mar are now living under the same roof suggests that either he has already surmised that part of the equation or that he simply is not interested. And as we listen to him play, the relief we all feel is palpable.

We have other matters to concern ourselves with after all, as the new additions to our household pose several problems. As Eduardo and I have previously agreed, we notify both sets of parents as well as close neighbours that we have taken in a group of insolvent unfortunates, family members of an old colleague of Eduardo's. Both the Torrezes and the Ramirezes are stupefied, asking how on earth we can possibly let our children come into contact with such indigents. However, they thankfully lose interest in the matter fairly promptly, concerning themselves to a far greater degree with the growing sense of unease that is spreading across Granada.

But before any of this, steaming hot baths are run for the six houseguests behind the closed and bolted shutters of Carmen de las Estrellas. After they have all soaked, scrubbed and scoured themselves until their skin is squeaky clean and every last speck of dirt has been expelled from beneath their fingernails, I try as hard as I might to feign indifference as the murky, black water is drained from the tub at the end of the evening.

Finding clothes for them all to wear is not problematic as between all members of our family there are more than enough dresses, trousers and shirts to go around. Only the fuller figure of Aurelia proves more of a quandary, but having given birth to five children, I manage to pull out enough loose-fitting garments to suffice for at least several weeks. As Mar hands their colourful gypsy attire over to me to be washed and put away at the backs of cupboards, she looks pensive.

'When all this nonsense is over, very soon I hope, we shall take your clothes out again. And you can be proud of your heritage.'

Mar stares at me sadly with her huge black eyes. 'Do you really believe that, Luisa?'

'I know that we must remain positive, and hope for the best.'

Mar lowers herself into a chair, her hands fluttering above one of my clean skirts as though she cannot quite bear to touch it. 'You haven't seen these people, what they're like. What they're capable of,' she says quietly, staring down.

'They are ignorant.'

'But it is these ignorant people who are now ruling Granada.'

I sigh deeply. 'We have to believe that life shall return to the way it was. We must. We have no alternative.'

Mar continues staring down and I watch as, with considerable discomfort, she lets her hands rest on the skirt.

❋ ❋ ❋

It is hard for everyone to adjust during the first few weeks. Inés and Graciana cry continually and Graciana even attempts to run away on one occasion. They miss their yard, their friends and the freedom they once enjoyed and even when their mother tries to explain to them that they are far safer at Carmen de las Estrellas, they sob even harder, begging to change back into their normal clothes and return home. Their elder brother and sister take to their new predicament with a far greater degree of calm acceptance. Beatriz marvels at the soft comfort of the eiderdown and the fine splendour of all the objects lying around the house. A number of times I find her in a trance as she stares in wonder at the chandelier throwing diamonds of light across the sunlit floor of the conservatory, or at the detail of the finely engraved handle of a carving knife. Wherever she is, my love-struck son Fernando is always to be found hovering nearby. He gazes at her with his huge saucer eyes from behind a crack in the door, through the posts of the banisters or, more frequently, from his favourite position perched upon the garden wall. For when she is in the garden, he can stare at her to his heart's content.

Beatriz is also fascinated by the piano. Doubtless she has never before seen such an impressive, grand instrument. It belonged to the abuela of Eduardo and though it is used on occasion, this is rarely by any member of our family, but rather by one visitor or another who sits down to play at the spotless ivories. Of all my children, it is María who derives the most pleasure from the forlorn, underused piano when the mood so takes her, and she is more than happy to sit with Beatriz, introduce the notes to her and play a few pieces.

During these musical interludes, Fernando expresses a sudden interest in music and sits on the opposite side of the room, peering over a book he has grabbed carelessly off the shelf and thrusting his head back down into its pages the moment Beatriz looks up, an expression of strained concentration upon his face. He makes such a nuisance of himself that I even hear María, who seldom picks up on such nuances, apologise to Beatriz for her idiotic brother. Beatriz merely blushes and giggles; it is true to say that she does not invite Fernando's unsolicited attention, yet if she is made to feel uncomfortable by it, she never indicates so. For Fernando himself, the fact that tensions have arisen to such a catastrophic level outside the walls of our home brings him nothing but joy.

After the first few days, which Pablo spends nervously jumping and pressing himself up against shadowy walls when he walks, I am relieved when he begins to relax as he becomes aware of the abundance of new subject matter he can draw. He misses numerous meals in order to continue with his detailed studies of a flower, the mountains or one or another of the family as we go about our work. Whenever I raise the subject of Pablo's continued absence at meal times, Mar merely shrugs and remarks that he only ever eats when he is hungry, which is seldom.

But, little by little, new life and energy is breathed into the walls of the house, stagnant with inertia after the children's schools close and they are once more consigned to the attic for their lessons. Everybody is given a new sense of purpose as tasks are assigned and the inflated household numbers and absence of Conchi means that there is always a job to be done and never a dull moment.

Aurelia never fails to astonish me, for just as she had been the mistress of her mountain cave, she silently yet authoritatively assumes this role in our home. I have grown accustomed to my friend's wily ways and fierce obstinacy and admire her for her strength of spirit, yet I never fail to feel slightly cowed in her presence. This is not in a negative sense, for it is clear that I am also the recipient of Aurelia's respect and appreciation. But I cannot possibly deny that the old gypsy knows how to silence the entire room with a single flash of her dark eyes, or entice us with similar intensity with one of her stories late at night. And on the rare occasions that she laughs, we all feel lighter, stronger – clouds lifting from a grey sky.

Even once clad in one of my skirts and blouses, her arms, ears and fingers stripped of their *gitana* adornments, Aurelia looks no less noble, with her long silver hair coiling like a serpent down her back and her high, proud forehead turning this way and that. I often think what it must have cost her to come to seek refuge with us that day. We never discuss it, yet her gratitude is shown in manifest ways. Long before anyone else in the house awakes, Aurelia is scrubbing floors, peeling vegetables and shaking out rugs in the courtyard. No matter how many times I implore her that she is a guest and it is far better for us to all share household chores, Aurelia simply grunts. More often than not, she is joined by Mar and, between the two of them, by the time the birds begin to sing and the floorboards creak, Carmen de las Estrellas is spotless from top to bottom and all the food for the day prepared.

When Aurelia and her family first arrive, I am conscious my own children might suffer, not only because of the reduced amount of food that finds its way onto their plates but also because of the general privations and overcrowded conditions we are now subject to. I am, however, delighted to find that all my children generously and openly adapt to our new living arrangements. If I have anyone to feel concerned about, it is my husband. Although I know he supports my decision to welcome Aurelia's family in, he has become increasingly introspective. Whether it is a direct result of our houseguests' presence or due to external influences, I cannot be entirely sure, but I find myself keeping a close eye upon him.

One evening, after returning from work, Eduardo seems particularly agitated, pacing up and down the conservatory like a trapped animal.

'What is it, Edu?' I ask.

His shoulders are hunched and his hands thrust deeply into his pockets. I stand in his path to cease his pacing.

'I don't know how much longer I can take this for, Luisa.'

I pause. 'Aurelia's family?'

'¿Como?' He pulls his hands from his pockets and grasps my wrists. 'Aurelia's family? No…no. They are fine here, poor souls, quite alright.' He takes a deep breath, tilts his head back and closes his eyes, willing some calm to descend upon him.

'Is it the job? Is it that terrible?' I push him gently.

'Oh yes,' he replies, without a thought. 'But I can accept that. I have always accepted that.' He sinks into an armchair and scratches beneath his chin. 'No, it's the *walk* to work and what I see every day. Every single day. I cannot bear it.'

I can feel myself tense. I am well aware that conditions in Granada are worsening with each passing week. Yet I have immersed myself so fully in the concerns of our expanded family that I have spent far less time outside of Carmen de las Estrellas and silently chide myself for not being more sensitive to my city's plight.

'Do you know how poverty-stricken people have become?' he continues. 'When I used to walk to work, I would be confronted with one, possibly two, beggars asking for money. Now they are on every corner. Elderly people, children, women as thin as rakes asking for money to feed their families.' He opens his palms out on his lap and stares at them, as though willing them to give him a solution. 'It's sickening. This country is sinking.'

'Edu!' I chide. 'We shall not *let* it sink.'

'But what are we doing? We are just surviving, scraping through, trying to stay afloat. And yes, we are managing for now, just about. But Spain is in a terrible, terrible depression and we cannot deny it any longer. The political situation is a disaster, and nobody trusts anyone else and while all the parties try to battle it out, meanwhile people are starving. You know what I saw today on my way home? Hmm? I saw a woman begging on a street corner whilst suckling her baby at her breast. The baby looked barely alive. And not a hundred yards further, I saw a girl not much older than Isabel offering herself, *¡Por Dios!* I want to help them, I want to help them all—'

I kneel at the foot of the armchair and place my hands in his palms.

'Eduardo, I know these are terrible, terrible things you are seeing and this suffering is monstrous but...' I trail off, searching for words and finding none.

Eduardo shakes his head. 'To begin with, I placed a coin in every outstretched hand. But now there's a sea of hands and I just cannot,' he hangs his head and shakes it again, 'I cannot any more and I feel so helpless.'

We sit in silence for a while, listening to the sound of Aurelia scolding Fernando for some misdemeanour. It feels suddenly as though her family have always lived with us and I can scarcely recall a time when our lives felt uncomplicated.

'I told you earlier,' Eduardo says eventually, 'that there is not a problem with work, at least not a new problem. But that's not quite the whole story.'

I wait for him to continue.

'Up until now, none of us at the office have really discussed politics much. We've kept our private lives and political opinions strictly separate from day-to-day office affairs and that's always been a relief to be honest, but...' He sighs.

'This is changing,' I say.

'*Sí*. There's such strong opinion either for or against the Republic, and emotions are running so high it's hardly surprising my colleagues are discussing it. I wouldn't mind so much if I believed I had a single Republican ally amongst them.'

'Perhaps not all of them are as right-wing as you believe.' I take his hands in mine, yet I know my words ring hollow.

Eduardo laughs mirthlessly. 'Staunch nationalists of the most extreme kind, I'm discovering.' He coughs and looks at me nervously. 'The type that are overjoyed at the closure of Republican schools, for example. They have *no* idea that our children went to them.'

'Edu,' I respond, surprised by the firmness of my voice, 'how many people do we know who send their children to non-Republican schools? Have we ever judged them for that? No, we have not. Just remember that we have done nothing wrong.' I feel my hands tightening on the side of the chair. '*Nada*. It may not feel like it, but we are still living in a democracy.'

'Luisa,' he says slowly, shaking his head. 'You can say that all you like. But we are *not* living in a democracy any longer, I tell you. We do not know who we can trust. I loathe being put in this situation. *Dios*, how I hate it. I just nod my head and say "*Sí Señor, no Señor*, I'm sure you're right."' He clenches and unclenches his fist. 'Can you imagine what my colleagues would say if they knew we were playing host to a family of *gitanos*? *¡Por favor!*' He laughs again, but this time it is a shrill, bitter laugh that rings out across the space of the conservatory and I frown, rubbing my hand up and down his leg.

'Edu, come. There is no way they will ever find out. Nobody knows. Even our parents have not doubted our story; why should anyone else?'

He shakes his head. 'Perhaps you're right. But my colleagues are becoming more and more vocal in their opposition to the Republic. They're even joining in with fascist rallies and a few days ago one of them asked me if I wanted to join them in sabotaging a government meeting in the town hall.'

A small, tight knot forms in my throat. 'What did you say?'

'I have always made myself as invisible as possible in that place. Generally, people ignore me, and that's fine. But when somebody asks you a direct question, well that's a different matter. I asked him what they are sabotaging.'

'I know what they are sabotaging,' I say quietly. 'I heard about it on the wireless. Nationwide demonstrations against the Republic continuing to promote state control of education, even if some of the schools *are* closing down.'

'Exactly,' Eduardo replied, first looking surprised that I had known about it and he had not; but then his face crumpling once more into worry. 'He also told me they'll be calling for the return of the Jesuits. I managed to give an excuse but I don't think I fooled him.'

I squeeze his hand. 'Edu,' I say carefully, 'you are right to be cautious, but you must not forget that the government still exerts its authority over the people, the *democratically* elected government.' Eduardo opens his mouth to speak and I hold a hand up to silence him. 'No matter how fragile that seems at the moment, it is still there. And we must hold onto that, and keep our family safe. That is our main priority.'

Eduardo clasps one of my hands between his, brings it up to his mouth and kisses it before laying it against his cheek and staring at me intently with his green-grey eyes.

'You're right, Luisa. *Gracias a Dios* that somebody can keep their head about them whilst all this is going on.' He brings my hand down and laces his fingers through mine. 'I can't stop going to work. It would look too suspicious, but more importantly than that I need an income for us all. But truly it is very, very difficult for me.'

'I know,' I whisper as I stroke my fingers through his hair.

'Stay strong,' he whispers back, 'for both of us?'

❊ ❊ ❊

A great many of the hours that Eduardo spends at home, between snatched moments with myself and our extended family, he can be found hunched over his typewriter in his study. These days, he scarcely permits me to read his poetry, but when he does, I must confess it shocks me. I can understand why more of his verses are infused with the theme of fascism spreading its hand out over Europe, yet his imagery is becoming increasingly morbid. I even wonder at times if he might be suffering from some kind of illness. But then he is the same husband and father with the children and myself as before, if somewhat more distracted and tense than we are accustomed to.

In the evenings, we all gather in the conservatory to listen to the wireless. Eduardo's slight frame sinks into the large armchair as he chews on his nails and scratches beneath his chin whilst the rest of us perch on chairs and lean against walls. Mere days following the conversation with Eduardo in which he opened up to me, after the children have gone to bed, I listen with horror to the nationalist radio reporting on the brutal repression of the armed revolt of the miners in the Asturias by a right-wing general named Francisco Franco. This follows the government's call for a nationwide general strike, which was responded to particularly enthusiastically by a large group of communist-orientated coal miners in the north. Just a couple of nights before we listened to the government report on the success the miners were achieving, only now to realise that General Franco's troops are far more powerful. I would have far preferred to be spared the details of this, yet we are all drawn to the wireless like moths to the light, listening in horrified silence to the trail of murder, rape and torture left in the general's wake, causing even Aurelia to grow pale. As soon as the report ends, I stand up and switch the wireless off and look back at the faces of my husband, Aurelia and Mar.

'It's not going to happen here,' Aurelia says eventually, breaking the silence.

'But it could do,' Mar responds. Aurelia scowls but says nothing. Mar, the enigmatic Mar, so unlike her mother in many ways yet, like Aurelia, she has the capacity to silence a room with a few words. And whilst there are things I shall never quite comprehend about Aurelia, I feel sure I understand her daughter. She is more often silent than not, going about her work in a quiet, determined way. She cares for her children open-heartedly, yet for as long as I have known her there has been an element of de-tachedness from everyone and everything around her. As she pushes out the creases from sheets with a hot iron or hangs dozens of pairs of stockings out to dry in the warm wind, I have always noticed that only half of her is pres-ent. There is something about Mar that makes me want to care for her, for I see that beneath the charcoal glow of her eyes and brisk movements, all she truly wishes for is to be loved and appreciated.

It is clear enough to me that this desire comes in the form of a man: a dashing prince who shall whisk her away from her poverty and her troubles and her cave walls crumbling about her. I also recognise that when Miguel failed her, something died within Mar. I hope more than anything that in the future this can be re-ignited and my friend shall find a man to love and cherish her as she deserves, yet Mar herself has made a vow that her days of futile loving are over. So fierce is her resolve that I am pained to believe it.

We are not similar in character, Mar and I, yet a bond exists between us and we often sit wordlessly side by side in the kitchen kneading bread or make trips together to the market. Of course we converse sometimes; I love to talk, and am proud of myself whenever I manage to coax a smile or a laugh from her. Yet such occasions become scarcer and scarcer as we find less to laugh about these days.

None of us have a notion of how long Aurelia's family shall stay at Carmen de las Estrellas. Initially, the clothes they travelled to the house in were only hidden at the back of cupboards. Yet as we begin to hear threatening, drunken scuffles in the alleyways outside the house, I know I must acknowledge that the breakdown of trust amongst friends and neighbours has become so widespread that it is impossible to know whom one can rely on any longer outside the immediate family. Early one morning before dawn, Aurelia and I take the clothes to a hidden corner of the garden beyond the fig tree and, making a small pile, douse them with paraffin and throw in a lit match. As we stand there, transfixed by the sight of the flames licking their way around the bleeding colours of the garments, we both know that they shall be with us for more than just a few months.

One day ticks interminably into the next and we mirthlessly welcome in a new year, 1935. Aurelia keeps the house impeccable; Mar hangs clothes out to dry, as distant as the clouds; Isabel reads books and dreams, I sense, of life beyond; Eduardo writes poetry; Pablo draws; Joaquín plays the guitar; María pouts; Fernando gazes; Beatriz blushes; Juan frets; Alejandro sits beneath trees staring at the mottled sky through a great canopy of leaves; and Inés and Graciana chase one another round the garden, becoming more restless by the day.

I observe all of this, attempting to create a semblance of normality and as warm a living atmosphere as is possible given the circumstances. I take on the task of tutoring all the children myself in two separate groups, divided up by age. Isabel helps me in this exhausting undertaking, both of us realising that we all need something more productive to occupy our days with than idling in the garden or thumping notes out on the piano. It is an extraordinary set-up, for none of Mar's children are able to read or write, so alongside my own children extending their general knowledge through any book we can get our hands on, we help the new additions to the classroom with forming their letters and, after painstaking months and dozens of wads of blotting paper, they begin to make progress. Only Pablo is exempt from this; he is already seventeen years old and far more content left to his own devices in a corner of the garden working on his artistic creations.

Over a year after Aurelia's family have moved in with us, a new coalition is formed by Azaña, the old Republican President. It is named the Popular Front, though it scarcely merits its self-given title of recognition. For we all know it is a final attempt by Azaña to unite the left-wing. Eduardo and I vote for the coalition the following month, yet we do so heavy-heartedly, for we have nothing else to vote for. The Popular Front's policies are dubious and it has little clarity or vision and we feel like we are voting for a sinking ship rather than a beacon. A new government is hastily formed yet, shortly afterwards, our worst fears are realised.

I am in the kitchen one morning with Aurelia and Mar preparing *almuerzo* when the daily newspaper, *El Defensor*, is delivered. As I hurry to collect it, I remind myself I ought to cancel our subscription. *El Defensor* is notoriously left-wing and its delivery each and every day is as good as hanging a Republican flag outside our home and calling out to the street '*Viva la Republica!*' But this morning, as I take it back to the kitchen, I read the headlines aloud to my friends.

'"*Under Azaña's* Popular Front leadership, *many political prisoners will be released this week. A great many of these men are innocent of the crimes charged to them and the time has come for them to be acquitted and walk free.*"'

Aurelia grunts as she brings her knife down and halves a pumpkin in one swift motion.

'Foolish man,' she says, without looking up, dicing the pumpkin. 'You can be certain that just as many of these so-called innocents are true criminals. It's as good as inviting a fight because the right are certainly looking for any excuse. And now they'll have it. *Qué tontería,*' she mutters and shakes her head. Mar is standing at the sink drying dishes, half turned towards me. She is staring fixedly at the plate in her hand, turning it over and over again and rubbing it vigorously even though it is quite dry.

'Soon,' she murmurs quietly, 'we will pass the point of no return.'

'What do you mean by that?' Aurelia snaps.

'What did your vote for the Popular Front count for, Luisa?' She turns her lovely face towards me. 'Anything at all?'

I frown and ease out the crease in the spine of the newspaper. *Remember to cancel the subscription*, I think again distractedly.

'We always talk about staying positive,' Mar continues, this time a little louder, 'and hoping for the best. But nothing we ever hope for is played out on the streets. Isn't it time to start preparing our children for the worst? At least in that case, if the worst never happens, it will be an improvement on that.'

I think it is the most I have ever heard Mar say at one time and both Aurelia and I stare at her. Perhaps she is right. Instinctively we want to protect our children, but circumstance has already dictated they have learnt something of the brutality of humankind and grown up faster than I should have liked.

Aurelia continues to dice the pumpkin with such speed that I fear for the fate of her fingers. When she has finished, she throws the window open further and spins round to face us, one hand on her hip.

'Listen to that,' she says, her mouth set in grim determination.

Mar and I strain to listen. At first I only hear birdsong but then the loud, shrieking laughter of Inés and Fernando calling instructions for a game.

'That,' Aurelia says fiercely, 'is the sound of playing. *Our* children playing. Let's allow them to play whilst they still can, shall we?' She fixes us both with her black eyes for a few moments more and then resolutely turns her back to us. I glance at Mar and try to smile at her, but she looks away absently and continues to dry the dish.

Life continues in this frightening, agitated no-man's land in which all the members of our household merely exist rather than live, and since the world outside the gates of Carmen de las Estrellas is one we are no longer permitted to freely inhabit, we must keep ourselves amused in any perceivable way. Our confinement seems to aggrieve Joaquín more than any other and at times he scarcely bothers to eat or sleep. Instead, he spends hours in the conservatory, furiously practising his guitar until he wears the skin away from the tops of his fingers and deep red droplets of blood sink into the velvet upholstery.

As trying as the situation is, and despite the horrors I hear each and every night on the wireless once the children are in bed, I always feel certain that our predicament can only improve, not worsen. And so it is to me that everyone comes with their eternal questions: *When will things go back to normal? When can we leave the house? When will our school open again?* All I can do is offer a smile or a hug and tuck a strand of hair behind an ear, saying 'Soon, *cariño*, soon.' Nobody complains, not really, and though the last thing I wish is for my friends to leave, it pains me to notice that the clothes of my children hang more loosely on their bodies than before and that in the mornings I often see dark rings under their eyes from lack of sleep.

Even Eduardo asks the same questions as the children. It has become a game, for he knows how I shall answer, and he also knows that my reply is far from the truth. But perhaps just hearing me say it comforts everyone into believing, for a short while at least, that things shall soon improve.

Thankfully, we are also distracted to a certain extent by a new friendship that has blossomed between María, and a wealthy young American man.

'I've met a boy, Mamá,' María announces to me after lunch one day. I clap my hands together, delighted to be hearing some good news at last, but astonished, needless to say, that this has happened when the children are barely leaving the house.

'What is his name? Where is he from?'

María smiles enigmatically. I am not surprised she has somehow attracted the attention of a male suitor; she looks very similar to my eldest sister, '*la rubia*', with her fair hair, dark eyes and clear complexion and she often turns heads when we are out. I notice how she avoids my questions and responds with her own information.

'He's very kind. A real *caballero*.' She beams and puffs up her shiny hair from underneath. 'We met at Plaza San

Nicolás some time ago, before the schools closed or anything—'

'And you did not think to tell me?'

'I'm telling you now. And we've met a few times since
then.' She enunciates her words carefully and I feel my
brow knitting.

'Would you care to tell me how?'

She laughs lightly. 'It's surprising the conversations one
can have from the top of the garden wall.'

I raise an eyebrow. I must confess that I never would
have supposed any of my children were forging friendships during those hours they spent perched on the wall.

'Have any of the others met him?'

'Joaquín,' she replies, 'but he doesn't like him of course.
And Fernando. He came along with me once or twice to
meet him and Solomon bought us *limonada*.'

'Solomon?' I ask blankly. What kind of a peculiar
name is that?

'Yes, Mamá. He's American. His Spanish is terrible,
but he's trying hard.'

'I was not aware, *cariña*, that you had reached such a
high standard with your English,' I say coolly.

'Oh. You know.' María laughs delicately. 'Languages
never were my strong point.'

I frown; this is absurd and amusing in equal measure…and *American?* I am not entirely sure how I feel
about this, but I sigh and alter my lips into a smile. I have
no reason to believe that he is anything other than a good
person, even if he has not won Joaquín over. But that is

hardly surprising; Joaquín is and always has been fiercely protective of María and their bond as 'twins' has strengthened deeply over the years.

'So when do we get to meet Sol-o-mon?' I say his name slowly, testing it in my mouth but it sounds terribly strange.

Solomon comes the very next day and, rather than conducting their conversations from the unequal levels of street and wall, I insist he be invited into the house for a cold glass of *horchata*. Solomon visits many times in the coming weeks, in between going to the *universidad* where he is studying a course in the history of Spanish art. He appears to be blissfully ignorant and frankly unconcerned by the growing political tensions around him. Though I must confess that rather than being frustrated by his lack of awareness, we welcome his naivety. Because only Solomon has the capacity to allow us to pretend that life is running as smoothly as it ever has done. I rather like him from the first. He is full of jokes and mirth and flattery for María, which of course she adores; María always does love to be admired. I notice that Isabel does not appear taken with him – I think she finds his loud gaiety a little overbearing – but Joaquín and Isabel aside, he is welcomed into our house and we all enjoy the lightness his company provides.

Surprisingly, it is Aurelia who finds him the most entertaining of us all and she hoots and cackles at the terrible jokes Solomon tells in Spanish which, I must say, he takes very gracefully. I am pleased to see Aurelia laugh, for

I fear that in these days of deprivation, she suffers terribly. I wonder if I am the only one to notice her spooning the very smallest portions of food onto her own plate and often barely even eating that, claiming she isn't hungry and distributing it amongst other ravenous mouths.

Yet even the presence of Solomon in our lives can do nothing to fend off the painful but decisive turn matters take two years after Aurelia's family first move in; two long years in which Aurelia hears from her network of *gitanos* in the city that few of the mountain caves have escaped the gangs of looters and many of Aurelia's neighbours have been dragged from their homes and have evaporated into thin air like the fading dew. On countless occasions during these two years, I send out a silent blessing of gratitude that Aurelia came to ask for refuge in our home.

It is a hot, heavy mid-summer day. The air is thick with condensation and I watch in lethargic disgust as fat, buzzing flies hurl themselves against the glass and congregate in dead piles around the windowpanes. It is one of these days on which we resent our inability to leave the grounds even more than normal, for despite the shady trees of the garden and the relative cool of the house's high-ceilinged walls, we would derive a world of benefit to walk down to the city; to dip feet and fingers in the crisp freshness of the fountains and to sit under a wide parasol at a pavement café and sip freshly made *horchata*. There are no more chores to be done, no matter how hard anyone searches,

and the heat is far too severe for anyone to feel like studying. Instead, everyone is scattered around the house and
the garden, listening to Joaquín's moody guitar chords
and the whir of the wooden ceiling fans battling their way
through the cloying air.

It has been a particularly tense week in which a prominent socialist lieutenant was murdered on his way home
by a Falangist gang. As revenge, the following day a group
of his colleagues killed one of the country's most important right-wing political figures with two shots in the
back of his neck. I don't know if I feel more exhausted or
shocked by the news. How can more widespread violence
be avoided now? I sit in the conservatory with Aurelia
and a few of the children, listlessly flicking through old
newspapers as María unmusically hammers out the same
few bars again and again on the piano. I am about to ask
her to play something else when we all hear it, the whim-
pering that starts softly and gradually crescendos until everyone in the room looks up. It comes from upstairs and
Aurelia ceases flicking her fan at the same moment María
stops playing.

'What's that?' Joaquín asks. I stand up from the chair
beside the window and watch as everybody from outside,
clearly having also heard the sound, starts drifting towards
the house. I take the stairs in twos, and then threes. I race
along the corridor and fling open our bedroom door to
find Eduardo sitting on the bed sobbing, his head of curls
in his hands. I realise with a start that in all the time I
have known him I have only ever seen him cry for hap-

piness. I glance back at the sea of concerned faces now congregated behind me in the doorway then approach the bed where I kneel at Eduardo's feet and stretch a hand out to stroke his hair. When he realises that I am here, his sobbing calms a little as a few small, strangled chokes escape his mouth.

'What is it?' I ask quietly.

Eduardo slowly looks up at me, his eyes red and his face as white and starched as his shirt collar. He pulls out a handkerchief and blows his nose violently then, after taking a few more deep breaths, speaks in a calm voice.

'Civil war has just been announced. Spain is in a state of emergency.'

'What does that mean exactly?' Joaquín asks sharply. I turn round to see that everybody has walked into the room and is now standing around the bedposts.

'The government tried to call a general election yesterday…' Eduardo continues slowly, taking care over each word he chooses '…but rebels have risen up against it and the army officers are proclaiming a state of war against the Popular Front.'

'But surely they can't succeed?' Isabel asks, a catch in her throat. 'The Popular Front is the legal government.'

'*Sí*,' Eduardo replies in a small, high voice. '*Sí*, it is.'

'I think,' I say loudly, trying to sound confident although my legs feel numb beneath me, scarcely able to hold the weight of my body, 'I think that it is far too early to say which way the uprising will go. And in the meantime,' I take a deep breath, 'we must sit tight and wait and see.'

'But that's what we've been doing for all these months,' cries Joaquín. A dark lock of his hair has fallen in front of one eye and I think he looks more like Mar at that moment than ever.

'Joaquín,' I say gently, 'I know this is difficult for you. It is trying for us all. But it cannot help by getting angry. *¿Entiendes?* We shall get through this together.'

Joaquín sighs and walks over to the window, leaning heavily against the pane and staring out over the sierras. 'I understand that. But why can't you just be honest and tell us what you really think is going to happen?'

Eduardo has by now fully regained his composure and he stands up from his chair, trying to assume an authoritative voice.

'Your mother is not a fortune-teller. How can any of us possibly predict what's going to happen?'

I find myself glancing over at Aurelia who stares back at me, her mouth set into a tight, grim line.

'All we can do for now is stay together,' Eduardo continues. 'After all, with any luck all this may have blown over in a few days.'

Joaquín scowls. 'But you don't *really* believe that, do you?'

'Listen, Joaquín,' I say. 'As soon as other countries hear about this rebellion against the Republic, countries like France will help us. It will be impossible for them to ignore something as serious as this.'

'But what can France or England or anyone do when the Republic is up against the likes of Germany and Italy's fascist forces? It's a lost cause.'

I turn to Joaquín sharply. '*Por favor*. I do not wish to hear you talk that way.'

He stares back, his dark eyes defiant. Everyone shifts uncomfortably and Aurelia begins to briskly fan herself.

'Well, Father,' he continues, 'you haven't yet answered my question. Do you truly believe this may blow over in a few days. *Truly?*

Eduardo looks directly into the face of his adopted son, full of pained frustration and anger. 'No, Joaquín. No, I'm afraid I do not.'

CHAPTER SIX
ISABEL

Summer 1936

That sense of euphoria we lived and breathed with the Second Republic was so real. Education, jobs, prospects, freedom, women being given the vote, *libertad!* But it has all gone. Everything. This transition happened so quickly it almost feels as though the Republic never existed. Did we imagine it all? For a short while, we let ourselves dream and believe, but it seems that we fell asleep for just one second too long, and in that lost second everything changed beyond recognition.

And in the meantime, people are suffering, and people are starting to disappear; vanish into nothing. Even from my bedroom I've heard screams in the night; we all have, though we don't talk about it. And then there's Conchi. Ever since she left Carmen de las Estrellas, I've missed her. There's something so constant and safe about her presence. She always seemed to be more male than female to me with her square jaw and strong shoulders and the way she effortlessly wrung the neck of a chicken in the yard made me feel rather sick, but I couldn't help admiring her for it. I've always assumed that Conchi would just reappear one day, roll up her sleeves and carry on as normal. But one day, Mother confides in me that Conchi's father and two of her brothers have been murdered and Conchi herself has gone into hiding. I feel sick to the very pit of my stomach, not only because of what Conchi must be enduring, but also because my hopes that she might return to us are finally dashed.

Our city is taken on a sweltering day in July. Not long after the nationalist rebel forces have invaded from North Africa and a state of civil war has been declared, the streets around our house fill up with workers demanding arms to protect themselves from the rebels. All the reports that reach us at the house through Radio Granada are confused – hardly surprising as the situation is changing so rapidly. In these early days, we have to rely on information from the workers who pass up and down outside our house whilst we hang from the top windows, calling out for news.

'The military governor's asking the army to remain loyal to the Republic,' one man calls up whilst the rest hurried on towards the city. 'But the officers have turned against him. They're refusing to hand arms over to us!'

'Where are you going now?' asks Father, his face strained.

'To demand again that we are given arms,' the man shouts, pulling his cap down on his head. '*Viva la Republica!*' he cries before running on.

Father slumps down in front of the window. '*Viva*,' he whispers in a barely audible voice.

We hear later that evening that the military governor has been arrested and after a single shot is fired into the air outside the town hall, the workers are forced to return home, unarmed. Because of all the working-class people who live around our home in the Albaicín, our district holds out bravely for four more days. They are the most terrifying and longest hours of my life. I can't sleep, not even for a moment. My parents barricade the heavy wooden doors that lead into the garden and the courtyard from the street. They place barbed wire along the length of the crumbling brick wall that is our final contact with the outside world. We drag mattresses along corridors so we can all spend the nights together, huddled in just two rooms, and we are allowed to eat our meals (or what little food Mother can find) in the bedrooms.

And then we're paid a visit by my Tío Miguel. It is Mar who first hears the banging on the door and the calling. She rushes into the conservatory where most of us are sitting.

'Miguel is outside!'

'Miguel?' Father's forehead crumples. 'Are you sure?'

'*Sí*. I'm sure.'

'What the devil does he want from us?' His words trail off as Mother shoots him a look and throws her shawl around her shoulders.

'*Vamanos*, let's go and find out, shall we?' Her voice sounds calm but I hear a tremor in it.

Mar sinks into a chair and Abuela Aurelia hands a jersey and ball of wool to her that she is in the middle of darning, a scowl on her face. With all eyes on the two of them, I seize my opportunity to slip out of the conservatory behind my parents. I stay at the back of the courtyard behind a pillar, shocked to hear the volume of Tío Miguel's hammering against the door.

'Luisa! Eduardo!' he shouts in between bangs. 'You must let me in. Immediately. I know you're in there.'

'Miguel!' Mother calls sharply as she hurries to the door and starts to battle with the locks and barricades that she and Father have constructed. 'I'm opening up.'

As Mother heaves open the door and Father stands slightly back, his forehead a tangle of knots and creases, my uncle steps into the courtyard. The first thing I notice about him is how well groomed and healthy he looks. I had imagined that the trials everyone has been going through the past months couldn't fail to have physically touched everyone, even my wealthy uncle. But apparently not.

'Luisa,' he says, his eyes narrowing. 'Eduardo.' He nods briskly to Father who lurks in the shadow behind Mother. 'I'm sure I do not need to explain to you both that Granada is now under the control of the nationalists. Our politics have never...' Tío Miguel stares at my parents with his steely grey eyes and pushes his shoulders back, 'merged, shall we say.'

I hear Father cough and move to the other side of the pillar so I can see his face. His cheeks are burning deep red and I hope he isn't going to shout at Tío Miguel before he's even told them the purpose of his visit. Or he might never tell them and then I might never find out. I know that my uncle is now a prominent member of the Falange party because it came up in conversation one evening in the conservatory when neither Father nor Mar were there. (We are not allowed to talk about Tío Miguel in front of either of them – nobody has ever said this, we just know.) The Falange are becoming more and more popular and Mother says that it represents everything that Tío Miguel stands for: tradition, the Catholic Church, the military and the return of the monarchy. As I stand there and listen to my uncle talk to my parents, I wonder how it is possible to have two such different brothers.

'I am telling you this for your own good,' Tío Miguel is saying in a low voice so that I have to strain to hear him. 'I want you to listen to me very carefully. This little… *fiesta*,' he waves his hand dismissively through the air, 'that the Albaicín is hosting up here is doomed to failure. In two days' time, it will all be over.'

'What do you mean, *over?*' Father practically spits out.

'I mean, Eduardo, that full surrender will be demanded. Or,' he speaks to Father but I can see that he is staring at Mother, 'the consequences will be faced. I have never been more serious.'

He is silent and his cold mask slips slightly. For a moment his face suddenly looks more worried than intimidating, but within seconds he has composed himself once more.

'You are in an extremely dangerous situation here in the Albaicín,' Tío Miguel says, 'and for that reason, I have

placed a safeguard on your house.' I hear myself gasp
and hurriedly hide behind the pillar. But I needn't worry,
because it is probably the same reaction as my parents,
who are staring at him in shock, Mother's hand covering
her mouth. 'But this is under the condition,' my uncle
continues, 'that you remain quiet, do not make a fuss,
that you forget about your *rojo* ideals,' a shudder passes
through him, 'and that you do as I say.'

Father glares at his brother with open hatred and I will
him not to lose his temper and say something he'll regret.

'I am under the orders of General Franco now,' he
adds, 'and so are you. Do I make myself clear?'

Mother hesitates then she nods briefly. Father is leaning back against my orange tree, still as a statue.

'What about our friends, and our neighbours?' Mother
asks quietly.

Tío Miguel laughs bitterly. 'This is not a game, Luisa,
this is a war. You think I can protect every communist
you've dallied with over the years? Or *want* to? I do this
only because your husband, because *you*,' he turns to Father and jabs the air in an accusing way, 'are my brother.'

Father's head suddenly falls forwards and his cheeks
turns crimson as though he has been physically slapped. I
feel my heart beating rapidly and take a step back. We are
trapped and my parents know it. To refuse his help will be
as good as signing our own death warrants, but to accept
it feels like a betrayal of everything our family stands for.
Both my parents remain silent and I try to steady my shallow breathing.

'From today onwards,' Tío Miguel briskly tugs on his shirt sleeves, 'Carmen de las Estrellas will be under a safe-guard. But remember what I have told you, and expect very dire consequences if you do not heed my words.' And with that, he is gone.

I find myself wondering if he has come for Joaquín's sake, or whether he is digging behind all those cold layers to really listen to his heart. Either way, he is true to his word and the Albaicín is soon taken. On the first night of our confinement, two days after my uncle's visit, I am lying on the mattress between Alejandro and Graciana, both nestling into me from either side. The air is stiflingly hot and Graciana is fidgeting, turning over restlessly from one side to the other and swishing her hand through the air at imaginary flies. I comb my fingers through her hair, blowing gently on her hot face to stop the sweat trickling. That's when we hear it, as clearly as though it is coming from the next-door room: the sound of four bullets being steadily fired. We all lie there, paralysed. Then comes the screaming, a thin ribbon of sound that at first sounds like high-pitched operatic notes, but then starts choking as though the ribbon has become snarled in a machine.

Everyone who has fallen asleep is suddenly wide-awake and we listen as the screaming continued. It is joined by separate cries, rising and falling violently through the hot night air and vibrating in our ears. Graciana begins to cry and as I hug her I feel her tears on my burning skin. I don't know how long we are locked in silent terror, listening to the banging of doors, shouting and the clatter of footsteps as people run up and down outside. After what feels like hours, the noises subside and a profound silence sets in. It is so intense that I swear I could hear an insect take flight.

Eventually Mother breaks it by creeping out of bed and slipping out of the bedroom door. I hear voices from the next room where Abuela Aurelia is sleeping with some of the others and footsteps walking down the corridor. Moments later, they both appear with a jug of water and several glasses, followed by everyone from the other room. Mother crouches on the floor to light a candle, and as the orange flame throws long shadows around the room, I look up at her face and notice for the first time the lines around her mouth and forehead and the dark trenches under her eyes. She looks exhausted, and it is no wonder. All these months she has put aside her own fears for our sake, to remain cheerful when really there is very little to be cheerful about. María is crying, huge sobs which make her whole body shake. I can't deny I feel pleased at the sight of her blotchy face and red-rimmed eyes that make her look decidedly ugly.

None of us say a word for a long time. We just sit there and gulp gratefully at the water, trying desperately to take in what we have just heard. After a while, Father speaks.

'Is everyone alright?'

Silence. He runs his fingers through his curls and sighs heavily.

'We're perfectly safe here.'

He is trying to sound calm, but we can all hear the tremor in his voice.

Mother shifted on the bed. 'Your father's right. Now try and get some sleep.'

As I lie there and listen to Alejandro and Graciana's breathing becoming slower and more even, I find that I can't even close my eyes. It is as though they are being physically pinned open. If not for the little ones beside me, I would have hastily climbed into Mother's bed as I used to as a child.

That grim night is only an introduction to the three days that remain before our district finally gives in to the rebels. I don't know how many lives are lost in this time, or how many horrors take place just metres from our house, but I'll always be haunted by the memory of the sounds we hear. Up until this point, I've heard countless stories, yet that is what they remained to be: just stories. When I start to hear life being snatched away in such a brutal and needless way, I am forced to admit to myself that humans can be immensely cruel. Worse, I have to admit that it isn't even a malevolent force from outside that has fought its way into our peaceful community, but that we are killing our own countrymen; our neighbours. We are at civil war.

The following night as we sit huddled in the conservatory, we hear a loudspeaker coming from the streets below the Albaicín.

'*All citizens are instructed to tune into Radio Granada,*' it announces. Father jumps up from his seat and fiddles with the dial before we hear a slow voice, hard as metal, issue a statement.

'*Women and children of the Albaicín district, you must leave your houses immediately and make your way to designated points in the city below. Meanwhile, the men must hang white surrender flags from prominent positions and take all weapons onto the streets and leave them there with hands above your heads. Failure to comply will result in aerial bombardment of the Albaicín. Once again, you must comply at once or face the consequences.*'

This message is repeated again and again and eventually Mother snaps off the wireless. I hear people crying around me, only I don't know who it is and I can't bear to look. Mother whispers something to Mar and they leave the room to start tying a white flag to the balcony.

'This announcement,' Father says, his voice shaking, 'does not apply to us. We are perfectly safe, we have my... my brother's assurance.' He continues to stare at the wireless, as though it can somehow give us something we need. Silently, I stand up and walk to the window where, through a crack in the curtain, I watch as a long line of women and children with small bundles in their hands begin to make their way down through the narrow streets past Carmen de las Estrellas. One small child is screaming with all his might and keeps trying to run back up the hill until eventually his mother shakes him so hard that he stops, in shock more than anything else.

Many of our neighbours do what the rebels ask, yet there are more still who don't. Early the next morning fighter planes begin to fly low and open fire with machine-guns. The second we hear the first shower of bullets, we all rush down to the cellar where we sit in pitch dark-ness amongst vintage bottles of sherry and broken chests of drawers, our hands covering our ears and our hearts pounding against our chests. It seems to last an eternity and many more are forced to surrender during those long hours. It amazes me that we aren't killed. When we finally go upstairs again, we are met with many shattered win-dows and broken ornaments, yet Carmen de las Estrellas has miraculously escaped any structural damage.

When the body and soul of the Albaicín finally falls to the nationalists, I cry out against it from the depths of my soul. But my nerves are so frayed after these days of fight-ing that I can't deny it is almost a relief. For the time being at least, the sound of firearms has fallen silent, apart from the sporadic burst of gunfire. I stay in my room and sleep in fits and starts. One week later, the Republicans begin to bomb the city from the air in futile attempts to reclaim Granada and we start to exist in a living nightmare.

The Albaicín has become a ghost district – once full of the sounds of children playing and fruit and vegetable hawkers calling up to windows, there are almost no signs of life in the streets around our house. People have either been taken or they have been killed. But my uncle hasn't lied – Carmen de las Estrellas has not been raided.

❄   ❄   ❄

'I've decided to come with you.'

'You *have*?' Sara Rodriguez tears the hat from her head and flings it up to the sky. As she catches it, she whirls round to look at me, barely able to contain her joy. 'I knew you'd say yes eventually.'

'You did not.'

'I did. Anyway, it doesn't matter because the fact is we're going!' She throws her arms around me and begins talking in a hurried whisper. 'My parents weren't happy for me to go alone, but now they know you're coming I'm sure they won't mind. They think you're far more sensible than me. Have you told your parents yet?'

I stare back at the exited face of my friend, made even more beautiful by her excitement. The mention of my parents hits me with a jolt. I have absolutely no idea how they'll react. And then there is the other matter of being secretly terrified at the prospect of being a nurse. I know I have to do this – for my own sanity, for the Republic – but the truth is that I'm scared stiff. Looking at Sara's face though, I know I can't share this with her. Besides, staying in Granada wouldn't be any better, because everything we have come to know and understand here has been turned upside down.

'I'll talk to them tonight. When are you thinking of going?'

Sara fixes me with her gaze, hands on hips. 'Tomorrow night.'

'Tomorrow night, *estás loca*? How can we possibly organise ourselves that quickly?'

'What do you need to organise, Isabel? Just throw some clothes in a bag and say *adiós*.'

'But—'

'I know some people who are leaving tomorrow and I want to go with them. I'd feel happier going with a group than making our own way up there, don't you agree?'

As I stare into Sara's sincere face, I feel my stomach lurch.

I have seen Father cry before, but I could never have prepared myself for this. Mother even has to send everyone else out of the room so they don't witness the sight of him on his knees, begging me to stay between sobs. As she closes the door behind her with a bang and leans heavily against it, my eyes flit anxiously back and forth between the two of them.

'But why, Isabel?' Father asks. 'You are sixteen years of age. Sixteen. You're still a child. And that aside, I don't understand *why* you feel the need to leave us and care for men who are fighting for what? For nothing! The Republic is doomed. You're chasing a dream.'

I am horrified. 'You don't believe that! You're worried about me and I understand that but after *everything* you and Mother have taught me, I simply don't believe you mean that.'

I've never argued with Father in my life. From the floor, he shakes his head and heaves himself into a nearby armchair, collapsing into it. Seeing the determination on my face, he tries a different trick.

'You don't know anything about nursing.'

'I'll learn.'

He looks me directly in the eye. 'But you're scared of blood, Isabel.'

'I...' My cheeks burn crimson and I'm furious with him for saying that, and even more furious that he knows. I force myself to reply, my voice small and tight. 'I am *not* scared of blood, Father.'

'You'll learn how to amputate legs? To treat gangrenous wounds? To sew up severed flesh?'

I glance at Mother. She stands there, leaning against the door listening to our exchange and, for once, not commenting. I long for her opinion – to know whether she supports my decision or feels the same as Father – but she remains silent and I can read nothing in her face. I take a deep breath.

'I'll *learn*.'

Father stares at me. Then as he stands up and walks past Mother, I see her catch his hand and give it a gentle squeeze. He stops in his tracks, takes a deep breath and then exchanges a look with Mother. As he opens the door, Fernando falls forwards. Just before Father leaves the room, he turns to me and looks me straight in the eye. 'I hope you know what you're letting yourself in for, Isabel, because I fear you do not.'

I never imagined that Father could wound me like that. I read Mother's silence as acceptance, yet the fact that I am travelling far from home without the blessing of both my parents affects me enormously. As I lie in bed, my bag packed beside me, I feel tears streaming down my face and want nothing more than for Father to come to me; for him to hold me in his arms and tell me he is proud of me.

I suddenly don't feel like I'm a sixteen-year-old girl craving adventure, longing to break free from the restraints of my home and my virtual imprisonment – I am a five year old sitting under my orange tree on my father's knee as he reads me a story; I am a seven-year-old child racing down the snow-covered mountain into his waiting arms; I am a ten-year-old girl reciting my favourite poem to his proud clapping; I am thirteen years old at the coast, skimming the shore for beautiful shells and stones and collecting them in a cap to put in the display cabinet back home. And in all these memories Father is by my side and I find myself crying even more because somehow I have wronged him again and again over the years, loving him but being embarrassed by him; never really accepting him. I regret it deeply and want, more than I've ever wanted anything before, for him to accept my decision now.

I believe that there are certain occasions in our lives when we desire something so passionately that the world can't deny us that wish. And so he comes, pushing open the door quietly and sitting at the foot of my bed. I'm sure he thinks I'm asleep and all he wants to do is sit there and watch me. Even without opening my eyes, I can sense it's Father and through my tears I blindly grope my way into his arms and we sit there for what feels like an eternity, silently crying on one another's shoulders. But from that moment on I know without a shadow of a doubt that he supports me for what I am going to do. And that he is proud of me.

✳ ✳ ✳

It would arouse suspicion if everyone walks through the streets to see me off so eventually, it's agreed that Mother and Joaquín will accompany me to the starting point of the convoy and I'll say goodbye to everyone else at home. I've never had to consider farewells before; not properly, as I've never been away from Carmen de las Estrellas for more than a couple of nights. I find that I'm terrible at it and wonder if my heart might break as I go through my siblings, Mar and her children who have become like family to me, my beloved Abuela Aurelia who says nothing but merely smiles that knowing smile of hers, and Father. I realise for the first time that even with all my noble ideas and the adventure I think I want, now that I'm actually leaving I feel less sure of myself. I know I'm doing the right thing, but many times over the following days I ask myself if I'm really strong enough for all this. Because Father's right of course – the sight of blood makes me feel dreadful. Yet here I am, leaving home to be a nurse. Am I mad?

Mother, Joaquín and I walk through the streets quietly, our heads bowed low so we won't catch anyone's eye. I think about all those hours I've spent in my room, dreaming of a new, free and exciting life for myself. I now ask myself if those dreams were so appealing because of the very fact they were unreal. For a girl with a vivid imagination, is there any more wonderful place than a beautiful big house with winding corridors and hidden nooks and crannies, or a garden filled with trees that have, over the years, become as familiar as friends? Or a view over the sloping roofs of the city and the Alhambra framed by the sierras? I have everything: love, affection, family, learning, encouragement, friends…and if I feel my courage slightly fail me, it is because I suddenly realise that everything I've taken for granted will no longer be within reach.

But the second I spot Sara leaning against a wall, I remember why we are doing this: to hold together all those strands of my life I realise are so important to me, we need to play our role in helping to re-establish democracy.

Just before I climb into the van, Joaquín hugs me for a long time, and standing back, his dark eyes solemnly scan my face. Then Mother says something to me that I'll never forget.

'If I were a bit younger, Isabel, if I did not have everyone to care for, you know I should come with you, don't you?'

As she hugs me, I nod my head, biting my lip to stop myself from crying. I can't identify a time in my life when I've loved my parents as much as I do at that moment and I vow to myself that, no matter what, I will make my family proud of me.

CHAPTER SEVEN
LUISA

Summer 1936

Barcelona
10th August 1936

Dearest Mother and Father,

I am here! I have made it to Barcelona! We've been here two days and leave in another two. We'll be going to a mountain location somewhere outside the city for intensive training before we're divided up and taken to different parts of the Republican zone. I don't mind where I go, I just hope with all my heart that Sara and I aren't separated. I can't tell you how fascinating it is to be in Barcelona and I'll never forget this. I only wish you could see it too. First of all, the architecture is so completely different from anything I've seen in Andalucía. But then once you manage to tear your eyes from the gothic and modernist spires, you see something even more astonishing at ground level. I'd never have believed it if I hadn't seen it for myself, but this city is a thriving model of socialist ideals – it's a living microcosm of Republican Spain!

Do you remember that book we used to have about communist Soviet Union? Well, this is exactly how I imagined it: men and women dressed in overalls, controlling public services and working in collectivised projects; people calling each other 'comrade' rather than using 'usted'; loudspeakers booming out songs of revolution from every street corner and a great many barrel organs playing the 'Internationale'. I tell you, things are functioning still in Barcelona in a way that they certainly aren't back at home. I've seen people playing games of pelota and the theatres and cinemas are generally running.

But alongside all this, I can't deny there are things I find difficult. I'm confused – is this the ultimate aim of socialist living, that there is no such thing as privilege or private ownership? The workers seem to be running the services efficiently and uncomplainingly and the atmosphere is charged with energy, but I keep thinking about our family and how wealthy we are. I believe in the Republic and, yes, I believe in democracy. Yet in the eyes of these workers we'd have to give up the privilege of living in such a luxurious home. There are many things I'm willing to part with in my life, but Carmen de las Estrellas? I must admit I'm both a little fascinated and horri-

fied by this way of life. If I'd been brought up in a working-class family like many of the girls I'm now with, I might be able to accept it more easily.

Also, I've seen a darker side to Barcelona that doesn't sit easily. There may be plenty of victorious slogans of comradeship and egalitarianism painted on walls, but I've also seen people forming queues literally miles long to be handed a single loaf of bread at the end of it. And right alongside collectivised cafés, I've seen a burnt-out church being gutted by a group of workers. I have to say I find the intensity of feeling against the church quite disturbing. Virtually every church has vanished and in their place stands black, smoking, burnt-out shells which the workers have pounced on. I know it's not as though we're practising Catholics, yet surely murdering priests and burning down churches isn't the answer? And what has happened to all the paintings and statues from inside the churches? Clearly they've been looted, but where has everything been taken? One church's front wall has been blown away and is being used as a refugee colony. The thin children huddled under the arches looked terrified. And though I've not seen them, many more I hear are being used to house (and torture?) nationalist prisoners. The very thought of it sends shivers down my spine.

But enough of me. I am fine and healthy and everything I'm seeing here is just fascinating. How is

*everyone at home? I do so miss you all and wish you
could be here with me.*

*With all my love and I'll write again as soon as I
reach the centre,*

Isabel

I sleep with the first letter we receive from Isabel beneath
my pillow, my fingertips resting on the comforting coolness of the paper. Dear Isabel. Though she's been away a
short time, how I feel her absence terribly and know that
her sweet presence would help calm my nerves. Not knowing when I shall next see her tears at my heart, but alongside this, I feel prouder than ever that my eldest child,
with her youth and her fear of blood and injury, has left
the comfort of our home to become a Republican nurse.

But just two days after this first letter arrives, I need her
more than ever. I am awoken early one morning, too early
an hour even for Aurelia, to loud and frenzied knocking
on our front door. Eduardo has not heard it and, sensing
that it is bad news, I leave him sleeping and hurriedly slip
on my linen robe. The tiles of the floor feel cool under
my bare feet as I run along the corridor and slip down the
stairs. Everything is so still and quiet and I feel the silky
coolness of the air before the cloying summer heat wraps
itself around me. It is the kind of morning that should, on
any normal day, be cause for rejoicing.

'Who is it?' I call through the door.

'Vicente.'

The barricade has now come down but it still takes considerable time to unbolt the three locks we have constructed on the front door.

'Luisa,' he says, as he slips through. 'Is Eduardo awake?'

I shake my head. 'No, still sleeping. Vicente, what are you doing in Granada? Are you—'

He takes my arm and steers me through to the kitchen and closes the door behind him.

'Luisa, we're going to leave Spain. We've been staying with my parents for the past few days. They don't think it's necessary, but I do. Things are bad now, but they're going to get worse, *much* worse.' He runs a hand over his unshaven jaw and then grasps onto my wrist and speaks in hushed tones. 'Have you heard the news yet about García Lorca?'

I feel myself stiffen. 'No, what news?'

'A couple of days ago he was taken by the *guardia civil*. Nobody knows where he is for sure, the papers this morning are full of speculation. But Luisa, you need to know that they're all saying he's dead.'

Vicente's hand on my wrist suddenly feels unbearably tight and I shake myself free. 'What?' I say weakly.

'*Muerto*. Some are saying that he died of health problems, even though everyone knows he was fit as a fiddle, only thirty-eight.' I lower myself into a wooden chair, the insistent tick-tock of the conservatory grandfather clock louder than ever. 'Others are saying he had an accident and fell down the stairs. It's lies, all lies.'

'*Dios*,' I breathe quietly. 'Edu…'

'I wanted to come and tell you, and to say goodbye.'

I look up and feel a rush of loathing and gratitude in equal measure for my brother-in-law who has brought such devastating news.

Vicente pulls another chair out from under the table and it scrapes across the floor. He sits down heavily. I stare hard at the table and notice for the first time small initials that my children have etched into its surface. Why have I never noticed these before?

'Are you listening to me, Luisa?'

I nod weakly.

'I advise you to leave, all of you. And take your…your extra family, whoever they are, with you. Do you hear? At the very least, get out of Granada. Go to the Republican zone, to Madrid or Barcelona.'

I look at Vicente and take it all in, the grey shadows, the black stubble on his chin and the fear in his hazel eyes.

'Where will you go?' I whisper.

'I've secured passages to Argentina. We leave in two days' time.'

'Argentina? So far—'

'Please say goodbye to Eduardo for me and convey my…my regret at the news of García Lorca. I know how highly he regarded him.' Vicente pauses. 'I must go.' He pushes his chair back abruptly, stands up and makes his way towards the door.

'Vicente,' I call. He stops, hand on the door. 'Won't you stay and say goodbye to Eduardo yourself?'

He sighs deeply. 'If he is sleeping,' he holds up a hand, 'let him sleep. He can remain in blissful ignorance a few minutes longer. I know Miguel has placed a safeguard on your house. But it won't last, believe me. Either he or someone else will overturn it. Remember how many other right-wing groups there are in Granada, taking the law completely into their own hands.' He looks at me grimly. 'Forget about García Lorca, just get yourselves out of Granada.' And with that, he is gone.

Within another couple of days, Federico García Lorca's death is confirmed, though the details conveyed through the press are still unclear. Eduardo takes the news even worse than I fear. When Vicente leaves the house that morning, I sit at the kitchen table for what feels like an eternity, tracing my fingers over the grooves of childish graffiti that travel like delicate spider webs around the length of the table. I want him to hear it from me, not from the wireless or the papers that fling out a constant stream of contradictory messages. He takes the news quietly, which concerns me a great deal more than if he had flung his arms about and cried; at least then I could try to comfort him. Without even looking at me, or letting me near him, he leaves the kitchen, pushing past Pablo who is standing in the doorway. Pablo stares at me with his huge eyes – eyes that I always feel understand so much – and we listen as the front door bangs loudly and we hear Eduardo's footsteps clatter down the street.

All that day, I am on edge, aware of every sound in the house as I wait for my husband to return. When Eduardo does eventually come back, late that night, he goes straight to our room, ignoring the group of us who have sat up in the kitchen awaiting him. Juan and Joaquín jump up from the table when they see him, but Aurelia mutters something under her breath to them and they slowly sit down again as I rush up the stairs.

As soon as I enter our bedroom, the smell of whisky is overpowering. I close the door behind me and stand for a moment, making out Eduardo's slight frame slumped across the bed.

'Edu,' I say tentatively. He doesn't reply and I reach a hand out and run my fingers over his hot cheek. He murmurs, and turns his face up slightly towards me.

'Luisa,' he whispers.

'Edu, where have you been? We have been so worried about you.'

'Luisa,' he whispers again, his voice slightly stronger. '*Agua*. I need *agua*.'

I hurry round to the bedside table and fill up a large tumbler then return to the bed and help Eduardo to sit up. He drinks the whole glass of water in one, droplets escaping and running down his chin.

'Where have you been?' I ask again.

He hiccups and lets the glass fall limp in his hands. His head drops forwards and dark, sweaty curls fall down over his face.

'I've been out,' he mumbles.

'*Dios*, Eduardo, do not play with me!' I place both of my hands on either side of his face and tilt it backwards so that he is forced to look at me. 'Talk to me. Tell me.'

He is clearly inebriated and finding it difficult to talk, but I am suddenly furious with him. I know he is suffering, but he has made us suffer in turn.

'If you must know,' he replies, trying to focus on me, 'I have been to every single bookshop in Granada.' He hiccups again and removes himself from my grasp, leans unsteadily over to re-fill his tumbler of water and takes small sips. I wait for him to continue.

'But every bookshop told me the same thing: *No, we don't sell García Lorca's works here any more.*' He puffs out his chest and deepens his voice, impersonating the booksellers. I frown. My husband already owns every single book that García Lorca has ever published, some even in several editions, but I know it would help not one bit to mention this to him. I too feel the anger deep in the pit of my stomach that García Lorca, who not so long ago was the celebrated son of Granada and probably one of the greatest poets of our country, has now been murdered and, as though matters cannot be worse, his books are probably all in the process of being destroyed.

I feel so tired all of a sudden. Where has all this hatred come from? True, I have never been as passionate about García Lorca as my husband, but the man was a gifted, gentle artist. I heard the murmurings of his sexual leanings, was *that* his crime? And so what if he did prefer men? García Lorca was a pacifist who believed in truth and beauty and freedom and Granada should feel proud of him, not murder him. I feel my fists clenching and I look at Eduardo who has slumped back against the pillow, his mouth hanging open.

'What did they all say when you asked them what had happened to his books?' I ask quietly.

'Nobody could give me a good reason,' he replies slowly, his jaw slack. 'They just said... that his poetry was... no longer deemed suitable for general reading.' The effort of these final words seems to tip him over the edge and his head hangs heavily forward. At first I think he is crying, but peering down I realise he has fallen fast asleep. I sit there for a while, listening to his heavy, drunken breathing and the hushed footsteps along the corridor outside of everyone making their way to bed. Then I gently remove his shirt and his shoes and pull him down the bed by the ankles before placing a thin sheet over him. Without even having the energy to get undressed myself, I crawl into bed on the other side, pull the sheet up beneath my chin and stare open-eyed at the ceiling.

From the death of García Lorca onwards, one piece of shattering news after another makes its way to the doorstep of Carmen de las Estrellas. I become obsessed, I must confess, with counting the heads of my extended family, checking everyone is present and correct. More stories begin to reach me of the group of friends with whom I held all those lively meetings in the courtyard during the years of the Republic, many of whom I had continued to visit periodically, though far less frequently in recent months. True, they were on the whole far more voluble in their beliefs than I had ever been. Yet they were good, decent people. A few of them simply vanish, normally at night and without a trace, either with or without their children. One charismatic woman whose company I particularly enjoyed witnesses her husband being killed with a single shot to the head and then her eldest son is forced to watch as she is brutally raped before 'Red whore' is painted in large, angry letters on their front door. One month later, she commits suicide. Others I know flee across the border to France or even further afield to Mexico or the Soviet Union, whilst the wife of one of the teachers from the Republican school my children attended is forced into prostitution after her husband is seized and taken to prison.

Such are the chilling tales of the war that engulf our existence, yet they exist on both sides, for revenge becomes as rife as the crimes themselves. Priests continue to be hounded down in their dozens just as stories abound that men of the cloth themselves take part in many a violent reprisal. Anarchic peasants continue to burn down the houses of their landlords and bloodthirsty gangs loot shops and offices as this becomes the chilling normality across towns and villages.

But I take comfort in my family. We are all alive, and we are all well. Ravenously hungry, tired, scared, but well.

We all loathe the way this war is consuming our country, but my daughter María seems to suffer the most. All those days we spend cooped up at Carmen de las Estrellas, one can see the fear that flickers across her eyes every time she hears an unusual noise from outside. María is a girl who needs to be entertained, to try on fine dresses in boutiques and go for her evening *paseo* to admire the latest fashions on the street and to be admired. Solomon, this man who strangely entered our lives, represents my daughter's escape from Spain. He is a wealthy man, and though I should not be cynical when they announce their engagement, I cannot help but feel that María's motivations reach beyond a simple love story.

They do not wait long and when the fragrant blossoms begin to appear on the trees, Solomon and María marry. Part of me rejoices, as I know she shall be granted her passage out of this hell we are trapped in. Yet she is so young, only just sixteen, and I also grieve that another daughter shall be moving far from me. We hold a small ceremony in the chapel near Carmen de las Estrellas and, to my delight, Solomon announces that they are to move to Switzerland which, granted, is still another country, yet not so far as the distant shores of the United States of America. Joaquín's face on their wedding day is as thundery as the threatening black clouds hovering low in the sky and I notice that María can scarcely look him in the eye. There are some things that a mother shall never be a party to or be able to fully understand.

And then Isabel's orange tree, which my dear husband nurtured in our garden since her birth, comes down in a violent thunderstorm that lashes branches and debris against our windows and sends the wind howling down our corridors with deafening shrieks. The force of the storm simply snaps the tree in half. It has been a wet and windy month, but nothing has been experienced like this for years. The hurricane lasts one single night, yet in this short time it blows roofs from houses, shatters the windows of motorcars and the Río Darro even bursts its banks and floods parts of the city.

I am horrified to see the damage to the garden the next day, but it is nothing that cannot be put in order again – with the exception of the orange tree. Eduardo is already in the inner courtyard in his pyjamas, staring in horror at the fallen tree, one hand clasping at his head. I walk up behind him and encircle my arm round his waist and breathe into his neck.

'*Lo siento mucho, cariño*. We shall plant another one. When Isabel gets back, we shall plant another, all together.'

Eduardo remains silent and I look at his pale face in profile, lips clenched tightly together and an expression of pained disbelief contorting his features. I squeeze his waist and kiss his cheek and suddenly hear movement from behind us. Turning, I see Pablo, Fernando and Joaquín approaching, Fernando kicking at a broken plant pot as he walks.

'*Mierda!*' Fernando says. 'Would you look at all this mess?'

'Fernando!' I say sharply. 'Well, this shall keep us all busy for some time, sorting out the garden and this courtyard.'

Joaquín has walked up to Eduardo and touches his arm with surprising tenderness. 'Papá, *estás bien?*'

'Hmm?' Eduardo mumbles as he looks sideways at Joaquín, his eyebrows knitted. 'No. I am not alright. This…' he gestures at the chaos around us and then the tree, 'it's all too much. Perhaps it's a sign.'

I frown. 'What do you mean?'

He continues to look at the tree then after a while speaks again. '*Nada.*'

'I think,' I say slowly, 'that after breakfast we should designate everybody jobs to help tidy up. *Gracias a Dios* the house has escaped the worst of the storm but the courtyard and garden shall take some time to get back to normal. Edu, why don't Pablo and Joaquín chop the tree up for firewood? We're so desperately short anyway.' I sigh. 'And at least this will be one good thing to come from this storm. It has been terribly cold this spring.'

'*¡No!*' Eduardo cries, so forcefully that we all turn to look at him. 'You must not chop this tree up. This tree belongs to Isabel.'

'But Edu,' I say gently, 'otherwise it shall just rot. It cannot be re-planted. You know that.'

'Don't tell me what I know,' he snaps and I look at him, stunned. I know that he is upset – I am too – but it is a voice I have scarcely ever heard.

I shiver involuntarily from the cold and wrap my gown tighter around me. 'I am going to have breakfast. Shall anyone join me?'

The boys and I leave Eduardo standing there in front of his beloved fallen orange tree, his head hanging and the wind whipping around his thin shoulders. As we walk Pablo squeezes my arm and when I look at him, he smiles understandingly at me. It is a small thing, his smile, yet it somehow serves to make our predicament less dreadful. I have not the slightest idea who it is that says something to Eduardo during the course of that day which makes him change his mind; or perhaps his mind changes alone, but by early evening Pablo and Joaquín are out in the courtyard, methodically cutting up the orange tree's carcass whilst Juan and Alejandro make the trips back and forth to the conservatory with its firewood.

That night, we all sit around the fireplace warming our hands and feet with the first prolonged, blazing fire we have enjoyed in months. Perhaps I imagine it, but I am certain the burning wood emits the delicate scent of oranges. I look around at the other faces to gauge whether anybody else has noticed it, but they all seem lost in a happy, glowing warmth and I do not care to spoil this moment with words. Only Eduardo is absent and it is not until the fire has died low in the hearth and I realise how late it is that I peer out to the gloom of the inner courtyard. Eduardo is still there, sitting on the stump, clutching a piece of paper and pencil in his hand, scribbling something. As though sensing I am watching him, he looks up. I raise my hand to wave at him, but perhaps he does not see me, for he looks down again and my hand is left hanging, motionless, in the air.

With two of my children now far from me, I have less heads to obsessively count. This may be a blessing of sorts as in these days of rebel control of Granada it feels like people are watching us each time we leave the house. Perhaps I am being too distrustful, yet I feel it prudent to be cautious, not least because of Miguel's warning to us. One morning, much as it pains me to do so, I comb the house from top to bottom, pulling out anything and everything that could possibly suggest we have ever been supporters of the Republic. I burn old copies of *El Defensor*, notes I made during

my meetings and the children's schoolbooks. In mine and
Eduardo's bedroom, I stand in front of the bookcase which
holds dozens of García Lorca's works of poetry, stories and
plays and hesitate, biting my bottom lip. I know I cannot
add these to the bonfire, yet neither can they remain here.
Eduardo is in the garden and, taking a deep breath, I pull
one book from the end of the shelf and, like dominoes, a
long line of volumes clatter down. I pull them all into a box
and hurriedly arrange them side by side. Crouching down,
I attempt to lift the box but it is too heavy. I push against it
to try to move it across the floor and it shifts a mere inch.

Suddenly, I hear a noise at the door and look up guilt-
ily, expecting to see Eduardo. But it is Fernando. He appears to have just awoken and is rubbing his eyes.

'Fernando,' I whisper, 'help me, *por favor.*'

He walks over to me, peers into the box and, without
saying a word, takes a book out. He looks at the back
cover grimly, the picture of Federico García Lorca smiling
up at him and sighs before placing it back. Even Fernando
cannot make light of this situation and between us we
move the box under a table in the corner of the bedroom.
I fetch a cloth to go over the table and replace the vase of
flowers on top of it. The books are hardly in a secret place
now, but they are, at least, out of sight.

Whenever anybody from our household goes out,
which is fairly rare these days, it is imperative I know
where they are going and what time they shall return. Of
course we still need to buy supplies but I prefer to go
alone or with one or two others accompanying me.

I begin to have nightmares about the *mangas verdes*, the green sleeves, so called because of the green armbands they wear. On my shopping trips to the city I notice more and more people wearing them, along with increasing numbers of civil guards and Falange flags – Miguel's party. But it takes some time for me to realise what the *mangas verdes* signify. *El Defensor de Granada* is long gone, but even if it had been replaced, I know attempting to buy a left-wing newspaper would be nothing short of suicide. We can only listen to nationalist radio, but not a single time have green armbands been mentioned.

So at market one day, as I watch a kilo of unhealthy looking tomatoes being weighed out in front of me, I ask in as neutral a voice I can muster who they are.

'*Las mangas verdes?*' the market seller replies in a low voice. He looks around nervously and leans in a little closer. 'Keep an eye on them. They're under instruction to spy on neighbours and denounce suspicious activities.'

I gulp and nod, feeling too afraid now to even meet his eye. He hands me my bag of tomatoes and I thank him hurriedly and turn away. Suspicious activities? What would be classed as suspicious? Joaquín's guitar playing? Making fortune cookies? Buying tomatoes even? I rush home, pull at the heavy door and then stand with my back against it, sweat trickling down my forehead as I close my eyes. I feel sick with fear. I must tell my family to keep an even lower profile if that is humanly possible. When, when, *when*, I think in exhaustion and fury and dread, when will this all be over?

CHAPTER EIGHT
ISABEL

Spring 1937

Ten months pass before Sara and I are reunited. Ten long months during which I know I have changed beyond recognition. Something in me has ceased to exist, a kind of innocence. Yet at the same time something is born in me: a maturity and confidence of spirit that will see no going back. I can feel myself changing, and as I step out of the skin of adolescence, I wrap my new self-esteem around me and hug it tightly to me until I can relax my grip and it feels natural.

When I manage to find a break, Sara and I go for a walk together, recounting and comparing our experiences. Sara's face looks drawn and tired but we are so delighted to be reunited and, as my arm links comfortably into hers, I feel my whole body relaxing.

'You're too thin, you know, Isabel,' Sara tells me. 'I must say though, apart from that you look very well. Different somehow…'

'I feel different.'

I glance at my friend, her long brown hair piled up boyishly on top of her head and kept in place with a scarf. She inhales deeply on her cigarette and hands it to me. 'Oh Isabel, I'm not cut out to be a nurse. I'm not saying I wish I wasn't here, but *por Dios*, I wish this damned war would end and we could all go home.'

'I'm sure you're a good nurse—'

'No.' She shakes her head forcefully. 'I'm not. But I know they need every pair of available hands, even useless hands like mine. I'm not as cool-headed as you.'

I raise an eyebrow.

'*Venga*, I saw you at the training camp. You were as cool as a cucumber and you know it.'

I smile at her gratefully but feel strange that she only knows half the story and that the reality is that, up till now, I've been a behind-the-scenes nurse. We continue to walk through the long grass, exchanging news from home that has been intermittently reaching us over the months and easily falling back into that familiar companionship we always enjoyed. We are so lost in conversation that when we first hear the siren coming from the direction of the hospital we completely ignore it. After a few moments, the sound begins to register in my consciousness like a dull, familiar pounding. I drop the wild flowers I've been gathering and watch them fall to the long grass as though in slow motion, their petals spiralling as they cascade out around me. Turning, I instinctively grab Sara and we begin running towards the white slats of the corrugated iron building, gleaming in the winter sunshine.

'What does it mean?' Sara calls over the noise.

'*No sé*,' I shout. 'But we need to get back.'

The earth and the air fall silent but for the pounding in my ears as I trample on the flowers I've dropped. I'm scared because I sense that I am about to experience something horrifying and that I can't hide any longer from the pungent scent of blood. Somehow, I know that my life is about to change.

The hospital is in chaos. There are people tearing wildly about, nurses collecting syringes, stretcher bearers shoving past one another in the corridors and wounded soldiers pouring in from every corner. I'm not sure how long it takes to register that the stench filling our nostrils is burnt flesh, but I think Sara realises at the same time as me and I watch her face grow pale as my stomach begins to heave in revolt. We are rooted to the spot in the hospital entrance, dumbstruck, not knowing how we can help. 'Why are you two just standing there?' cries a faceless voice. 'Get yourselves down to ward three immediately.'

I've never seen anything like it in my life, and I don't think any sight will ever equal its horror, for here exists the worst of the battlefield and the extent of human destruction and mutilation. I stand at the door of ward three and take in the small details of the scene unfolding before me: a man with his ear blown off, screaming in agony; another vomiting on the floor before slumping heavily forwards as he passes out; another still calling out for his mother and crossing himself as blood trickles in small rivers out of his mouth and down his chin. I am gripped with a desperate urge to turn and run; I taste bile in my mouth as I try to cross my eyes so that everything falls out of focus. But it doesn't work. Tears are streaming down my cheeks. Mother, I need you. I can't do this. What am I doing here? I cannot be a nurse, not a real nurse.

A senior sister appears at our sides and all of a sudden Sara is no longer there and I am being told to attend to the man in the corner. No more instruction than that. Just 'attend to him'. I feel as though I'm not really there. I feel as though everything I'm witnessing is real but I am no longer resident in my body. Instead, I have detached myself from flesh and bone and am hovering somewhere close by, pushing at my back and whispering in my ear *'Go on, go on.'*

I realise that I'm moving; or rather, not me but my body. I am taking rapid, even steps across the floor whilst everything around me greys and blurs. The other beds and people in the room lose their definition and the screams of pain become one ringing note. The moment I approach the bed and look down into the face of my patient, I know without a shadow of a doubt that this man is going to die, though he seems in a better physical state than many of the soldiers in the room. All his limbs are intact and although he has several lesions on the surface of his body, they don't seem that severe. Yet I know, through an intuition that no amount of medical training can possibly equip you with, that the wounds this man is suffering from have reached the very core of his being. Slowly, painfully slowly, life is leaving him as he bleeds internally to death.

His eyes are flitting across the ceiling in terrified fits and starts and the muscles in his cheeks are heaving in violent spasms. As I stand over him, he manages to focus on me. The force of recognition we read in one another's eyes shocks me, sucking all the air out of my lungs and I lean heavily against the bed. Because in my eyes, he reads that I know he is going to die. And in his eyes, I read him taking this message from me without a single word passing between us. And I read his need for comfort.

I hear the faintest whisper escape from his lips. He is asking for water and, with relief, I fill up a cup from the jug beside his table. Propping myself against the bed, I help him to sit up a little so that he can take a few sips. He leans heavily into the crook of my arm as he does so, his face contorted in both agony and gratitude as the water dribbles down his throat. The pain of this slight action overwhelms him and he gasps for breath, digging his fingers into his thighs so that his knuckles gleam white.

'What's your name?' I ask.

He looks at me, his eyes wide and uncomprehending as a patter of words escape his lips. At first I can't hear what he is saying, but leaning closer I realise he's speaking French. Thankfully, I've always been quite good at the language and, taking a deep breath, I repeat the question. His words abruptly stop and he stares at me, stunned to hear his mother-tongue spoken.

'Jean-Marie,' he whispers hoarsely.

I smile at him as I repeat his name, laying a damp cloth on his forehead. I walk to the foot of the bed and remove the pitifully inadequate rope-soled shoes that have taken him through his life as a soldier. As I come back round and sit on the side of the bed, I take his hand and stroke it very gently as I look into his face. He is a handsome man with fine, fair features and thick yellow hair that now lies in damp, bloodied clumps against his forehead, the sight of which sends a ripple of nausea through me. To my shock, however, the nausea quickly subsides as I concentrate on him as a person, not what he has become. He looks so young, so innocent. Yet here he is lying in a hospital bed after having suffered something I'll never really understand. And now he is dying.

I find myself thinking about the chance nature of our meeting. That same morning I was Isabel Torres Ramirez from Granada, a city where the sun so often shines, even when it is freezing cold, who has a poet for a father and a mother who makes fortune cookies. A girl who has never met a French man in her life and has certainly never watched anyone die. And he was Jean-Marie from France, a young man far from his family, fighting bravely for another country's cause. A man who has probably never had his hand stroked by a Spanish girl and has certainly never known such pain before. We both believe in the Republic, yet our similarities end there. But here we both are in the corner of ward three, looking at one another and communicating with our eyes. For all the power of words, I know that there is a time and a place for them, just as there is a time and a place for silence. After several minutes of sitting like this, he slowly speaks.

'I'm going to die, aren't I?'

During our initial training camp we were told that if we ever found ourselves in a situation in which it was clear that a man was going to die, we must tell them otherwise. We must encourage them with hopeful words for the future and make their last moments as comfortable as possible. At the time, I agreed whole-heartedly. It seemed without a doubt the most humane way to treat a patient. But now here I am, with my arm around a man who is losing strength by the second, and I know with all certainty that I can't lie to him. If I do, somehow I'll be violating him and his trust.

Part of me wants to scream as loudly as I can for somebody to come; that this young man with the yellow hair who has travelled all the way from France to help us fight this war needs help. But I know deep down it would be useless. All I have to do is look around the hospital ward and drag myself back to the reality of the grim medical shortages. Even more importantly, I know Jean-Marie is not going to make it and that I have the greatest responsibility I could ever imagine: of helping him to die peacefully.

I place my arm around his shoulders again and he leans into me. I can feel his laboured breaths rattling painfully in and out.

'*Je m'appelle Isabel*,' I say. 'Jean-Marie, I don't want you to be afraid, because dying is the most natural thing in the world. I want you to tell me about your family; about your home.'

And so, in short, sharp gulps, he describes the rolling hills of his village outside Bordeaux. The fishing boats filled with oysters slowly making their way into shore as the sun comes up. The way his father's nose goes bright red when he is angry. The fullness of his sweetheart's lips.

He tells me all this with his eyes closed and I can see the movement under his eyelids; the journeys that he takes as he describes all these things to me between gasps for air which he swallows like razors. He is smiling ever so slightly as these memories come flooding back to him and I know that he isn't in a hospital room in an obscure Spanish mountain town any more, fighting in an even more obscure war. He is walking along the cliff top as the wind plays with his hair, looking down at the oyster trawlers coming into the bay. He is arguing with his father whose nose grows pinker and pinker before he slaps his son heartily on the back and the pair of them laugh cheerfully. And he is walking his sweetheart home in the warm evening. Her hand is as soft and smooth as velvet and they are shooting each other sideways glances of delight before they arrive at her doorstep. And he is reaching his hands up to both sides of her head and gently pulling her lips to his. That is where I leave Jean-Marie, miles and miles from the hospital bed and the stench and

the screams clamouring around him: in the arms of his
sweetheart.

❊   ❊   ❊

I could never look at life in the same way again after that
experience. And despite the horror of watching the young
man in the bed beside me transformed from Jean-Marie
from Bordeaux to a nameless corpse as he is carried out to
make room for another wounded soldier, I sleep deeper
and sounder that night than I have done in months. Of
course I think about him, wondering if his sweetheart is
still alive and what kind of memorial will be laid for him.
But I realise that something important happens to me that
afternoon. In helping Jean-Marie to die a peaceful death,
I have finally been given a glimpse of the person I really
am and what I can achieve. And like a skin I have shed,
my fear of blood leaves me. Just like that. Yet I know that
if it weren't Jean-Marie, the same thing would have happened to me later with another person. For many more
come after him. Too many.

Does this make me sound callous, the way I feed off
these experiences? I'd give anything to breathe life back
into these men. I would like to give them the opportunity
to sling their packs over their shoulders and stride as confidently out of the doors of the hospital as the day they
signed up to our grotesque war. I do save lives too, it isn't
just about dying. I've become a good nurse, I know that;
better even for the fact that, not so long ago, I couldn't
even look at blood without the world spinning around

me. The training during those first few weeks certainly helped in a way, though at times it was easy to forget why I was really there. Placing an arm back into a plastic skeleton was simple; it was a noiseless task after all and lulled me into a false sense of security. And, more significantly, no blood came from the plastic.

Even so, I experienced a faster learning curve during my training than I could ever have imagined. Materials and resources were poor, but we were taught everything from general first aid to the safest way to amputate a leg. Those days were demanding. Mentally demanding because of the amount we were expected to learn and physically demanding because of the sheer number of hours spent on our feet. But despite all that, I took to nursing in a way that surprised me..

Those hours at the end of the day we used getting to know our companions. After a simple *cena* of soup and bread that we took in turns to prepare, we wandered outside and sank into the long grass with blankets wrapped around us. As we gazed at the stars and compared stories of our homes and families whilst roughly rolled cigarettes were passed around, I tried not to think about how horrified my parents would be if they could see me smoking.

I was and still am fascinated by the backgrounds of my new friends. I've always known I've had an incredibly privileged upbringing: private tutors, a big house with a courtyard and garden, trips to the coast in the summer. But it wasn't until I met several girls with equally large families who were brought up in two-roomed apartments that I really understood the extent of this. I'm not thought of as a conceited rich girl though. We are all comrades here, on an equal footing, and people love hearing stories of my large family.

When I wasn't studying, cleaning or chatting, I used every available moment to write letters home. I knew they might take a long time to reach Granada, if they ever got there at all. But that was even more reason to keep sending them. I filled these letters with cheer, going into great detail about my new friends and everything I was learning. I missed my family terribly, but I didn't miss my old life. Instead, I felt liberated and the fact that I seemed to be absorbing everything so readily gave me a new sense of confidence I'd never experienced before.

As for easing a man's passage from this world to the next, it's the last thing I imagined I'd have a gift for. But it isn't long before it becomes apparent to those working alongside me: the other nurses, the medical personnel, volunteers who work night and day. And so very slowly, but in a direction that gathers a deliberate momentum, my tasks begin to change and I stop being a nurse in the normal sense of the word, but rather someone who can be called upon to sit with a dying man and talk to him. Get him to talk to me. Help him.

My heart breaks a little more each time I see a man hovering on the verge of death. During those first few seconds that I'm called to his bedside, I long to be beside somebody who has a hope of survival – anywhere but there. But something gives me strength – a sense of purpose and drive – and all of a sudden I know precisely what I must do and how I must act though I don't how I know it or where it comes from.

I surprise myself with how cool-headed I can be. Here I am living in a hospital twenty-four hours a day, doing something I never thought I'd do and, more to the point, doing it well. I know it's an unusual talent, but I hold it close to me like a mother nurtures her newborn child. I'm afraid that if I abuse my gift, it might vanish as suddenly as it has become a part of my life.

Sara, of course, immediately picks up on my new self-confidence after our ten-month separation. Our only opportunity to talk is late at night because during the day we can only snatch the briefest of conversations as we hurry past one another. I lose count of the number of nights we lie next to each another in our narrow beds as she sobs, whilst I try desperately to cheer her up. She nearly always says the same thing: that she doesn't know how much more she can take of it and that she is a useless nurse.

'I sometimes wish the bloody fascists would just win and then this god-forsaken war would at least be over.'

'You don't mean that!'

She sighs heavily as she wipes away the tears streaming down her beautiful face, which has grown thin and pale. 'I do. I miss my family. I miss Granada. I want to go home.'

At the mention of family, I am lost in my own thoughts. It has only been a year since I left Granada, but it feels like a great deal longer. So much has happened to me in these months that I almost feel I'll have to get to know each member of my family again on my return. I owe them all so much time; I want to know all about them, all the inconsequential but suddenly significant things I'm not aware of: What is Alejandro's favourite colour? What do Pablo's hands look like – those hands that create small miracles? When Father laughs, what happens to his eyes?

I miss each one of them. I miss Joaquín and the way he gazes at his guitar as though it is the most beautiful thing in the world. I miss Mother, her grace and her good-natured smile. I even miss Juan and his allergies and his enormous blue eyes, so often close to brimming with tears. The letters from home continue to reach me every now and again, making me question how many never arrive.

Carmen de las Estrellas
May 30th, 1937

Dearest Isabel,

This shall be a very short letter, for I should like to catch the afternoon post. I am sitting at the writing table in the conservatory, the window is open and I can hear the most glorious trill of birdsong from outside. I must find out what it is. I suspect it is a shrike of some sort, though I cannot be sure. I can also hear Fernando laughing from somewhere in the house. You shall be pleased to hear that he still laughs a great deal; as mischievous as he can be, his laugh brings me great comfort.

Did you receive my last letter, cariña, *in which I was telling you about how miserable Joaquín has been? He never coped well with being confined to the house, but of late it's been even worse, particularly now that María has gone. But I am relieved to say that he has snapped out of his black mood somewhat since he discovered Inés is a wonderful flamenco dancer. They have cleared a space in the conservatory where the two of them play and dance to their hearts content.*

Father is alright. Perhaps a little distracted. But he sends his love and says that he will write a poem for you when I next write.

Now cariña, *I should have shared this news with you some time ago, but the truth is I was being cowardly for I knew how it should upset you. Your orange tree,* mi amor, *has come down in a storm. We are all terribly sorry about it. I do hope this news shan't affect you too much and we can plant a new one in the same place once you are home.*

I send you all my love. I am so proud of you. You are such a courageous girl, cariña.

Yours,

Mother

I cry for an entire night when I read about my orange tree. I go round in circles, reminding myself that it is only a tree and I must pull myself together because there are men dying every day and here I am crying over a tree. But that only makes me sob even more because that orange tree has always been a part of me; something I have barely noticed until it was gone. It was an old, intimate friend, particularly in the long, hot summer months when I spent countless hours in its shade reading, sleeping and dreaming. Somehow, it doesn't feel like a coincidence that my orange tree has come down not long after Granada falls to the nationalists and, as the weeks pass, my comrades and I hear that Spain is being slowly swallowed by the fascists.

I am seventeen years old and I still believe passionately that honour and goodness will prevail. But when I think of my birthplace, I acknowledge that it was one of the first places to fall to the fascists. With all its conservative traditions and ruthless local governance, it won't revert easily to Republicanism again.

My life continues in a stream of faces and tormented souls; a flow that seems so endless that the memory of these spirits begin to blur. News filters through to us of Guernica, a town in the Basque country that was bombed on market day, and I wonder when it will all end. *If* it will all end. As the end of the year approaches, I am both mentally and physically exhausted. Snow continues to fall thick and fast around the hospital and the bitter temperatures, which often drop well below zero, bring with them more cases of frostbite and hypothermia than we know how to deal with.

Perhaps if we force ourselves to stop running around, trying to find something with which to sterilise filthy needles or look for clean bandages, we will be more honest with one another. And with ourselves. We might say 'This isn't working, is it?' And yet I can never admit defeat or give up hoping; our cause is too noble to fail.

Each morning, even if it is only for five minutes, I like to leave the hospital and walk around outside. It helps to clear my head and better prepare me for whatever lies ahead. On one particular day in December, the small number of patients in the ward encourages me to stay outside for longer than normal. My coat is pulled up around my ears and I gaze out across the white valley, absent of movement and noise but coated in such pure tones of cream and silver that I wonder how so much violence can possibly be taking place beyond those quiet hills.

As I pace briskly around the courtyard, I rub my hands together vigorously and watch the vapour of my breath crystallising. I find myself at the edge of the quad, the point at which I can either turn back towards the hospital, or step into the thick, snowy abyss that covers the thicket and follow the tracks that have been left by wild animals. I stand at the bordered edge, where the paved stones are separated from the wilderness and rock my numb feet over and back, absently humming a tune to myself. Suddenly, I imagine what it would be like for blood to gently seep into the whiteness; for its purity to be slowly stained as, like ink to blotting paper, the blood creeps outwards until each hill and valley is bathed crimson. It is a gruesome image and for the first time in many months, just the thought of it makes me feel giddy. I find that my rocking has stopped, as have my icy breaths as I suck air into my lungs and keep it there, shivering with cold and fear.

'Excuse me, Señorita…'

I have immersed myself so fully in these horrific images that the words I hear are a terrifying intrusion on my thoughts. To my embarrassment, I let out a high-pitched scream. The owner of the voice jumps back. He is clearly as alarmed as I am and he unsteadily lifts a hand up to let me know that he isn't going to approach me. He is on crutches and I realise that he's probably been leaning against the side of the wall the entire time I've been walking around, watching me. I feel colour rushing into my cheeks as he awkwardly teeters about on one leg, steadying himself as a cough rattles through his chest. I rush forward to help him and as I do so, he begins speaking to me in broken Spanish. '*Lo siento mucho*, I didn't mean to scare you.'

'No, *por favor*. It wasn't your fault. I was a little lost in my thoughts, you know…'

My voice breaks off as I look directly at him and see an expression of something between curiosity and amusement on his face. Who is this man? I can't remember having seen him before and realise he must be a member of the International Brigades, the foreigners who have come from around the world to fight alongside us. He has scruffy blond hair that stands up at strange angles on his head, and stubble peppered across his chin. I can feel my cheeks burning and silently curse myself at how easily

I've always blushed. I feel uncomfortable, not to mention chilled to the bone, and I tell him that we should go inside before we both freeze to death.

'Wait!' He grasps my arm. 'Your name's Isabel, isn't it?'

I stare at him in surprise. 'How do you know that?'

He grins and shrugs his shoulders as best he can whilst leaning his weight against his crutches. 'Well, one just knows these things.'

I understand what he is trying to say but his Spanish is fairly muddled and before I can stop myself I have started to laugh. It is his turn to blush and he clears his throat. 'My Spanish is terrible. You must forgive me.'

Worried that I've offended him, I assure him that he speaks very well but as a frosty gust of wind whips up around our faces, I remind him that we really should be getting inside. As I walk towards the door and start to push it open, I am startled to find that he has rapidly hopped around the side of me and as he stands in the doorway he insists that *he* should be holding it open for me. I find myself laughing again that he is being chivalrous at such a time. As I walk through the door, he brings a crutch up so that I am blocked from going any further. I look at him questioningly.

'Don't you want to know what *my* name is?' he asks playfully, his eyes glinting.

'If you'd like to tell me, you're very welcome.'

'Ah, but I shall only tell you if you *ask* me.'

Hands flying to my hips, I stare at him in frustration as I try, unsuccessfully, to edge past his crutch. 'You're letting cold air into the corridor,' I whisper urgently as I notice a stern-looking sister approaching.

'Ask me my name.'

'*Por favor*,' I hiss.

'Ask me my name.'

'Very well. What is your name?'

'Henry. *Me llamo Henry*.' And with that, his crutch clatters to the floor and, after we've walked inside, I pull the door firmly shut behind us.

CHAPTER NINE
LUISA

Autumn 1937

As the people of my country continue to murder one another, the fall of the orange tree awakes in my husband a primal anger that now comes cascading out of him, breathing fire like a dragon. Of course, it is not just the tree that suddenly transforms Eduardo into a more political being, it is the death of García Lorca and it is his sense of injustice and I am certain it must also be his love for all of us; to right the wrongs that good people the length and breadth of our country are suffering. He begins to attend rallies, calling for the return of democracy, and though to begin with he only goes once in a while, it is not long before he is attending as many as possible, as though making up for all these years that he has been politically apathetic.

'This is what Federico would have wanted,' he tells me, his eyes shining bright with feverish excitement, 'do you not see that it's the only way? That if enough of us come together, we can overthrow the fascists?'

I breathe deeply, trying hard not to show him how terrified his words make me. Has he completely forgotten what Miguel said to us? There are eyes and ears all over Granada and people that we love have vanished without trace. But I know how Eduardo feels about Miguel and, in his volatile state, I cannot bear risking his fury by bringing his brother's words to his attention.

So life continues in this troubling way. I write often to Isabel and María and draw comfort from the letters they both write back to me as often as they are able. How different their lives are from one another. My first-born is witnessing the effects of war at its very worst and yet, despite the suffering of those she is nursing, her letters are growing in maturity and I sense, perhaps in the way only a mother is able, that she has found her path in life. María, on the other hand, could not be further from the horrors of war and I feel nothing but relief for her. Dear Solomon is making her happy and they are living high-society life in Geneva, with weekend trips out to a chalet in the mountains Solomon has bought. I shake my head and smile. My daughters could not be more dissimilar; it is small wonder they have never been close.

Eduardo is no longer able to work. Even had this been otherwise, his income would not be much comfort to us, for the price of food from the market has rocketed. I leave the house twice weekly with one or two others to go to the black market districts. It sickens me that I am forced to purchase basic foodstuffs, the right of every human, for such an extortionate price. Yet this is a time of war and, though it does not feel like it, I know we are one of the lucky families.

One night, long after the clicking of Inés's heels and castanets has subsided and Joaquín's guitar has been placed back in its case, I find myself waking with a start. The thin sheet that covers me is soaked in sweat, drying slowly in the slug-like heat of the airless bedroom. Though it is October, the heat has been endless and suffocating this year. Flinging an arm over to Eduardo's side of the bed, it takes several moments of absently patting my hand over the rumpled sheet before I register he is not there. I heave myself upright, flinging my hair back out of my face and smoothing damp strands away from my eyes.

Throwing back the sheet, I grope in the darkness for a glass of water on the bedside table and without pausing for breath, empty its contents hurriedly down my parched throat. Where on earth could Eduardo be at this time of night? Habitually, he sleeps deeply, the kind of person who cannot be woken for all the howling of dogs or even dropping of bombs.

As I push my feet blindly into my bed slippers, I ponder for the hundredth time how dreadfully I miss Isabel. True, there are numerous other people at Carmen de las Estrellas to worry about, as well as Aurelia's family who have become as vital to me as my own. Yet since Isabel left, I feel the absence of my first-born as keenly as a throbbing wound. I know Eduardo feels it too, though we scarcely discuss it.

As I feel my way along the dark corridors, steadying myself against the walls with outstretched hands, I turn my head this way and that in search of a clue to Eduardo's whereabouts. Silently peering around a few of the doors that lead into various bedrooms, everything appears to be in order. Pablo's heavy, guttural breathing. Graciana's inaudible mumbling as she writhes around on the bed, kicking out at Inés who lies obliviously by her side. Concluding that he must have gone to the kitchen to fill his water glass, I am about to set foot on the stair when I hear a noise coming from above. It sounds like the rustling or tearing of paper and, frowning, I feel my way up the narrow staircase to the attic.

Eduardo is sitting at one of the desks, surrounded by several boxes he has dragged from the eaves. He has lit a candle and its hazy light casts shadows across his face, accentuating the dark shadows beneath his eyes. It is oppressively hot in here and as I stand in the doorway I watch as a single drop of sweat crawls down my husband's face like a plump caterpillar. When he sees me, Eduardo looks up, startled. The whites of his eyes shine luminously and he stares through me as though I am a ghost, whilst his fingers continue to agitatedly tear up pieces of paper.

'Eduardo, what are you *doing*?' I whisper, closing the trap door behind me.

He is thoroughly absorbed and I watch in horror as it becomes clear what he is destroying. He has dug out several of his prized boxes, filled to bursting with all the things he has collected and treasured over the years since his boyhood and here he is, systematically destroying it all. Bits of decimated feathers and torn-up scraps of paper lie scattered around the desk and on the floor beneath it, and though my first impulse is to stop him, I can see that it is too late for that and most of the damage has already been done. Eduardo does not answer me; rather he continues to dig his hand into the box nearest him and arbitrarily pull out one object or other, look at it, read it or turn it over before destroying it. I walk round to the front of the desk and crouch down beside it so that my face is opposite his.

'Edu,' I say gently. '*¿Por qué?* Why are you doing this?'

He shakes his head, again and again as he begins to mumble. I feel tears stinging my eyes as I pick up a smooth pebble from the desk and gaze at it in the palm of my hand. It is perfectly round and white and as I hold it closer to the flickering candle I can just see my husband's childlike initials carved into its surface. At least here is something he is unable to destroy.

'Do you remember where you got this?'

'Hmm?' Eduardo stops what he is doing and looks up sharply. Taking the pebble from my outstretched palm, he turns it over gently in his hand, running his finger over its smooth contours. Upon seeing his initials, he draws it closer towards him, scrutinising it as his memory cogs begin to whir.

'Playa Dorada,' he whispers eventually. 'Aged seven. One of my best summers because it was just me and my grandparents.' He continues to stare at it for a few more

moments before tossing it carelessly to one side and resuming his task of assiduously tearing up bits of paper
into miniscule pieces.

I sit and watch him, feeling powerless for the first time in
our lives together to be able to help him. The cold-blooded
murder of García Lorca followed by the fallen orange tree
has sparked an internal riot in Eduardo that no tender
words from me can assuage, shaking him to the very core
of his beliefs. As he continues to work his way through the
boxes, tearing up everything he possibly can and flinging
aside what he cannot on the ground, I dig my hand into a
still unopened box and pull out a small volume of poetry
by Zarate. It is a well-thumbed book, falling lightly open to
the touch and the spine has been worn down considerably.
On the first page in neat pencil I read 'Eduardo Torres,
1907'. I smile to myself ruefully as I run my finger over
the script of my husband as a fourteen-year-old boy. Those
were the days before García Lorca had entered Eduardo's
life and completely altered it; days in which he was a gentle
young boy with a head full of dreams.

I sigh deeply. There is no point romanticising the past;
Eduardo was not happy as a boy just as I too always felt
on the periphery of my own family. No, I think firmly,
however dreadful things have become with the war, the
fact remains that we love one another and have a large,
wonderful family who shall stand by one another, come
what may. I read a short verse to myself about the 'golden
arabesque sands of time' in Egypt. Zarate spent many
years living and travelling abroad and I always believed

part of his appeal as a poet lay in his ability to transport the reader from their living room to far-flung corners of the globe, simply through one or two evocative turns of phrase. Closing my eyes, I am there. I need not imagine the heat, for the airless room provides that already, but there are flecks of sand being churned up as I walk, gently showering my face like a thin veil as my skirt billows out around me. Eduardo is walking beside me and the children are not far behind, crying out in delight as they pad over the dunes. Opening my eyes with a start, I realise that I have never voiced what I truly want.

'Eduardo,' I say in a firm voice. '*Por favor*, let us go away. Let us leave Granada, leave Spain. We shall take the children and Aurelia's family and go somewhere safe; somewhere we can leave the house and not have to count on your brother for our safety.'

Eduardo's eyes look hollow and almost frighteningly devoid of emotion as he stares back unblinkingly at me before shaking his head.

'Eduardo!' I force one of his hands down upon the desk. 'Please talk to me! *Por favor*, tell me what you are thinking. Things cannot continue like this. You are not well—'

'I *am* well. I am perfectly well. In fact, I have never been so well in my life.'

'How can you say that, Edu? You barely eat, you jump at the slightest sound, it is becoming almost impossible to hold a coherent conversation with you and now I find you up here in the attic in the middle of the night destroying all these things you have loved for so long.'

'Yes, but don't you see *why* I'm here?' he hisses aggressively.

Shocked by my husband's tone, I numbly shake my head.

'I'm here, Luisa, because my entire life has been a farce.' He grasps my hands tightly between his.

'What on earth do you mean?'

'I mean that my entire life I have been pushed around and patronised by my brothers, my parents – oh poor little Eduardo, he's not capable of being a lawyer, he's far too weak and delicate for such a hardy profession; he's far more interested in poetry. Must be some defective gene—'

'Edu, you must not talk like that—'

'But it's true! That's what everybody says about me. And then I met you, the most wonderful, beautiful woman in the world and you *accepted* me for who I was…' he shakes my hands vigorously '…but I know that people still say the same things; that they laugh behind my back and call me a failed poet and a dreamer and a pathetic little man and—'

'That is not true!'

Eduardo stands up forcefully, pushing his chair back. It bangs loudly against the wall. '*Sí*, it is true! You know it is, Luisa, don't lie to me!'

I jump up and grasp his arm, whispering in a gentle voice, 'Keep your voice down, *por favor*. You shall wake everyone.'

Exasperated, he slumps back into the chair and runs a hand through his damp, sweaty curls. I watch him as he takes long deep breaths, the irises of his eyes flitting agitatedly about the room as he tries to calm himself. After a few moments, he looks up at me again and speaks in a small, level voice.

'Something must change, *cariña*. Do you not see that? You of all people must see that.'

With the renewed tenderness in his voice, I reach out and put my arm around Eduardo's trembling shoulders as he lays his head against my chest.

'Why do you think I accepted your hand?' I ask. 'Because of who you are. Because I would not want you any other way. Edu, how can this can help you – obliterating the past in this way?'

He continues to breathe deeply into my chest, long hot breaths which rattle wearily as he slowly calms. As he searches for the words to try to explain what it is that is driving him to these actions, I hold him tightly. Eventually, he speaks, his voice a quiet warble.

'I need to be a different person. I don't want to go on in the same way I've lived my life up till now. I know you say that you love me for who I am, but that's because you're a good and kind and dear person. I want to be the kind of man my children can be proud of—'

'They *are* proud of you, Edu.'

'No. I mean *really* proud. I want them to be able to say to their friends "That's my father" and swell up when they say it. All these little things I've collected over the years and stored away in boxes, why have I done it? I need to be firmer and stand up for what I really believe in.'

I draw Eduardo away from me so I am able to look him in the eye.

'It is not safe, you know that. You are starting to shout about the greatness of the Republic and it is danger-ous. Particularly in Granada. Of course you know that I still believe in it. But things have changed. We must not speak our opinions any longer, we must hold them here,' I tap my head, 'and here.' I hold my hand over my heart as my words become stronger. Reaching a hand up to brush away what I assumed was a fly settling on my cheek, I am surprised to find it wet with tears. I have always tried to be so strong, keeping everything going in these vital matters of living and breathing and eating and helping to calm people and maintain belief in a noble future. And now Eduardo, my kind-hearted, forgetful, loveable husband, is so altered that I am unsure how to deal with it.

It is Eduardo's turn to comfort me and he puts his arms around me and brushes his lips all over my face, as my tears fall from beneath my closed lids. 'Luisa, Luisa...' he murmurs. 'Please don't cry, *por favor*, I can't bear it.'

Everything that has been going on around us since the outbreak of the war has weighed heavily upon me, yet Eduardo's unpredictable and peculiar behaviour weighs heaviest of all. I can scarcely remember the last time I cried and it is a peculiar sensation. I know that I am not crying only for my husband, but also for the loss of lives and the pain and suffering that has come about as a re-sult of the war. I am a pacifist through and through; I do not believe that death should be the necessary end of any event, no matter how heinous the crime. Yet each day we listen to the stories filtering into our home on the wireless from around the country of not just death but torture, rape and pillage. Innocent people in their thousands on both sides of the conflict have been ruthlessly murdered without trial and thrown into disused mine shafts, quarries, shallow graves or any pit large enough to house a seething mass of mutilated bodies. We have heard horrific stories of entire families being dragged from their homes simply because they have been associated with people with leftist leanings, or because they read left-wing papers or are in possession of a radio.

Life has become unbearable. Sometimes I would like to close my eyes and block out everything going on around me until it is all over. I would like to walk to the town hall and scream through the loudspeakers that send daily pro-fascist broadcasts out across the city that we are all humans and there is no need for any of this. But more than anything, as I sit here in the attic, crying against Eduardo's chest, I should like to get my family, a few possessions and leave. I want to go somewhere far, far away where we can walk down the street with our heads held high and drink ice-cold *horchata* in a café and express whatever opinion we so desire. And then when this war is over, I should like to return to Carmen de las Estrellas, remove the dustsheets and continue life as normal.

Slowly, I lift my head up and look at Eduardo. His eyes have glazed over and he is very still. He begins to whisper.

'I was so happy once, wasn't I? It was beyond my dreams to hope that one day I'd be a father, or have any poetry published.'

I nod, stroking his arm.

'Eduardo, *cariño*, please could we not go away?' I repeat, trying hard to keep the desperation from my voice. 'What do you think?'

Continuing to stare into the distance, he slowly shakes his head. '*Lo siento*, I can't. I simply cannot. Do you not see? It would be like I have failed again, running away and not standing up for myself and my family.'

'But Eduardo, it has nothing to do with that. What we are talking about is our safety. It—'

'No,' he repeats firmly as his eyes meet mine. 'I have to stay here. I have to do what I believe in.'

I squeeze my eyes shut as I hear the beat of Eduardo's heart beneath his thin cotton shirt. On every other occasion during our life together I have been successful in convincing my husband to make one decision over another. I never felt that I was manipulating him, but that he welcomed my opinion and somehow waited for it. This time, however, I know that I am powerless to change my husband's mind. His decision is final.

CHAPTER TEN

ISABEL

Winter 1937

We try hard to keep our spirits up at New Year, not just for our own sakes, but also for the patients. Some of them simply don't want to join in with the festivities – they bury their heads in their pillows and turn to face the walls as we weakly toast to the coming year. How can I blame them? I can't even begin to imagine the brutal memories crowding their heads. One patient, however, is determined to put a brave face on, organising a talent contest for the evening and a football match for New Year's Day. Henry Stevens is still on crutches but appoints himself as referee and makes sure that every able-bodied person with the slightest inclination towards football joins in. Since our first encounter outside the hospital that snowy December morning, I have spent quite a lot of time talking to Henry. I want to know what it was that made him leave his home in London to travel through France and over the Pyrenees to fight in a war that didn't directly involve him.

'But it *does* involve me, it involves all of us,' Henry says to me as I change the bandage on his injured foot. 'My government's turned the situation into a farce by refusing to intervene and supply arms and troops. Even though it's the democratically elected government for God's sake! And all the while, Germany and Italy are throwing supplies at the fascists like there's no tomorrow.' He winces with pain as I dress his wound.

'It doesn't matter how much we beg our government or how many relief organisations are set up back in England, it's just not enough. Thank God for the Soviet Union.' He shakes his head angrily. 'My government's stand of non-intervention is a farce. Anyone must've had their head buried ten feet deep in sand not to have noticed how things have been changing in England over the past few years. Fascism is spreading all across Europe. If we can beat them *here*, in Spain, then I honestly believe we'll be in a stronger position for the future.'

As I wind the clean bandage round his foot, I glance up at Henry's face. It is as serious and earnest as I've ever seen it. I am fascinated by him, in a similar way I suppose that I was by Jean-Marie, the young Frenchman. But Henry is the first foreigner I've ever had a proper conversation with. There are several things that particularly strike me about him. One is that he is determined to master Spanish. On the first day we met, I noticed that he struggled to form sentences. Although I understood nearly everything he was trying to say, his pronunciation was hard to fathom at times. But over the coming weeks, he improves dramatically. Clearly he isn't fit enough to return to the field after a grenade exploded not far from him, badly damaging his left heel bone. And so, whilst he convalesces, he spends hours on end reading any Spanish book he can possibly get his hands on and practising with everybody.

'How did you get to Spain, Henry?' I ask him one day as we walk round the quad. His injury, I see, is getting better but it is bad enough to prevent him from returning to service, which I know frustrates him.

'Train, ferry crossing, a few more trains through France…and then we had to walk over the Pyrenees. Now *that*, ' he says, eyes sparkling, 'was hard work.' I look at the enthusiasm on Henry's face and can't imagine this man finding anything hard work, somehow.

'It must have taken days.'

He nods vigorously. 'Yes, it did. And it was damned cold and we weren't well prepared for that climb. I had no idea before I reached the Pyrenees just how tall and vast they were; geography never was my strong point. A couple of men even decided at that point to turn back but I knew that I couldn't get that far just to turn back. So we kept going. And made it, obviously.' He turns to me and beams and I notice that his eyes are a shade or two darker than the sky.

'When did you decide you were going to come to Spain?'

'There was this kid at school, see. His name was Joshua and he was Jewish, nice lad. And sometimes we'd walk home together because he didn't live far from me. And one time, we were walking home when this boy came out of nowhere and tripped Joshua up. He fell flat on his face and his nose was bleeding terribly. They started yelling racial abuse at him and I remember yelling back at them to get lost or they'd have me to deal with. They just laughed and said I was no better, standing up for a Jewish pig like him.' Henry frowns and shakes his head, reliving the memory. 'So perhaps that was the start of it, my sense of injustice. But after that it was hard *not* to get involved.' He pauses and bends down to massage his heel. 'You ever heard of the Blackshirts?'

I shake my head.

'They're a fascist organisation, led by the politician Mosley in my country. Anyway, this party started getting bigger and bigger and a couple of years back they tried to march through an area in East London which has a lot of Jewish people. They wanted to scare and intimidate them, you know. I'd already joined the Communist Party by then and we'd heard about the planned march so a huge group of us headed down there to stop it.'

'What did you do?' I ask, wide-eyed.

'We set up barricades and they certainly hadn't expected so many anti-fascist demonstrators because both the police and the Blackshirts were taken by surprise. No matter how hard they tried to get through, we wouldn't let them. My kid brother Stan threw a bucket of rotten apples at one of the Blackshirts.' Henry grins. 'The police couldn't do anything, there were too many of us. Eventually the march was called off. So it worked, you see. And that, I suppose, is why I'm here: because if enough people come together to protest something they know is wrong, they can create change. Change for the better.' Henry sits down on a bench and stretches his foot out in front of him. He pulls a packet of tobacco out of his pocket. 'Smoke?'

I shake my head. '*No, gracias.*' I come and sit down beside him. The sun is warm and I close my eyes for a moment, losing myself in its gentle heat. When I open my eyes again, I turn to see that Henry is staring at me, smiling.

'So where is he now?' I ask.

'Who, Mosley?'

'No,' I laugh. 'Your kid brother, Stan.'

The smile fades from his face and he turns from me, placing his cigarette in his mouth and striking a match. He inhales and then replies, without looking at me, 'He's dead.'

I don't say anything for a while. I can tell Henry doesn't want to talk about it and quietly tell him I'm sorry.

Henry looks down and shrugs. 'Not your fault. How about you?' He turns back to me, a pained smile on his face.

'What about me?'

'Tell me about your family. Why you're here nursing.'

I know we're back on safe ground, and I chat to him about my extended family. Over the coming weeks, as I get to know Henry better, I assume that he might want to share the pain of his loss with me in some way, though I'd never dream of pressing the matter. Yet he only refers to him in passing every so often, calling him 'Stan, my kid brother'. It's clear that he's suffering enormously; that he and Stan were very close and the lack of emotion I read in his eyes is simply a front.

I respect him for the way he copes with it. It seems to me very English. Although it probably isn't healthy to keep it all inside like that, by then I understand that it takes people different amounts of time and different ways to deal with such immense loss. When I meet Henry Stevens, I quickly learn that he is just as likely to be charismatic and charming as he is thoughtful and withdrawn. To begin with, I find it hard that the man who chats so easily with me one minute can shortly afterwards sit silently by the window, staring out across the hills. But I learn that when he retreats to another world, I should leave him there.

❄ ❄ ❄

Looking for Sara one afternoon, I find her taking a nap in the dormitory before the next shift begins. As I quietly sit on the bed next to her, I look at my friend long and hard. She isn't well – that much is clear to anyone. But I know more than most. Sara has been suffering terrible nightmares and I recognise that engulfing dread in her when she is called on to treat a gangrene wound or a case of frostbite.

I'm sure that if anyone who had met the two of us before we'd left Granada would have said with little hesitation that Sara was better suited to nursing. I *certainly* would have said that with my fear of blood. Yet looking at her now as she sleeps, I see the dark shadows under her eyes and her pale skin and I know that there isn't much more of this she can take.

She was always the centre of attention when we were younger, the boys included. They all jostled around her at the school gates, vying for her attention, and I couldn't fail to notice the sideways glances my brothers threw in her direction whenever she came to the house. So when Henry Stevens starts to pay me so much attention, I'm sure I read an element of surprise in Sara's eyes. Yet her good nature doesn't allow the green-eyed monster to surface for long. Shortly after she first begins noticing it, her envy transforms itself into a mild form of teasing.

One afternoon, we are changing the bed sheets in the ward whilst Henry sits on the other side of the room, smiling as he watches.

'My, you *do* have an admirer, young lady.'

'He's a friend, Sara. Nothing more,' I whisper as I fling the sheets into a laundry basket.

She grins at me and shrugs. 'Whatever you say.'

I feel myself blushing and turn my head a little to prove to myself that he isn't really looking at me. But there he is, his eyes firmly upon me and as he nods his head ever so slightly in my direction, I quickly look away again and continue with my task. I can't work out how I really feel about Henry. A lot of the time, I convince myself that he is, as I said to Sara, just a friend. But I can't deny he's paying me a great deal of attention. Nor can I deny the tinge of disappointment I feel if I ever tell myself that this attention is no greater than he pays to the next girl. I think I know, deep down, that I'm not just 'any girl' to him. But I am inexperienced in these matters and have no idea of what I can do other than wait for him to say something. Or even, I think in my bed late at night, kiss me – the thought of which brings me out in such a deep, hot blush that I am relieved it's pitch black and nobody in the dormitory can see my face. I chide myself for such idiocies, but this gentle flirtation with Henry Stevens does make these days easier to bear and helps take my mind off the nagging concern I feel for my family in occupied Granada.

❋ ❋ ❋

The year drags on and Henry's injury continues to improve. He still has to use a walking stick and is level-headed enough to recognise that he'll be a fairly ineffective soldier in his condition. Instead, he begins to work as an ambulance driver, shuttling wounded soldiers back and forth between the battlefields and hospital. It is absurd really that he is even doing this work, considering how much pain his foot still gives him, but he needs to feel as though he is being useful. That is why, after all, he has come to Spain in the first place and I can understand that.

Not long after he starts this work, the lights of the ambulance break and, as there are no replacements available, Henry and his companion have to drive through the dark hills at night- time in the pitch black. This terrifies me, and I find myself staying awake whenever he goes out at night and loitering in the wards, checking and re-checking on the patients until I know he is safely back. As soon as I see him – the limp, the sand-coloured hair, his blue eyes and ruddy cheeks – the wash of relief that floods through me makes me feel physically sick.

And my dear friend Sara, I knew it was only a matter of time before she would eventually decide she couldn't remain at the hospital any longer. As she sobs into my neck, she tells me that she feels like a failure; that by leaving she is going back on everything she believes in. I assure her that's not the case and that she's risked a great deal by coming here in the first place.

'Besides,' I add, 'think how long you have dedicated yourself to a job as difficult as this.' My words seem to cheer her a little, but I know that she is almost equally terrified of leaving. There is no knowing what she'll find in Granada and whether she will have to go back to a state of virtual self-imprisonment in order to survive from one day to the next. Yet leaving is a better prospect than remaining at the hospital with the demons that haunt her dreams at night and the horror she feels each new day at what she might witness. As I wave her goodbye, a part of me wants more than anything to go with her, yet whilst there is still work to be done here, my conscience simply won't allow it, and she promises to write with news as soon as she is home.

So much is happening here and events are moving rapidly. I know that the Soviet Union, and France and Mexico to a lesser extent, are still supplying the struggling Popular Front with arms and money. Even so, the

Republicans are losing the war. I know that. And the truth is that I stay here not only for the work and the strength it gives me. I also stay for Henry. Something is growing between us by the day; feelings that we can't articulate. But the smiles that linger a fraction of a second longer than normal and the small excuses we find to be in one another's company speak far more to us than any words could. And as the Republicans lose more and more territory, I always feel his presence, near me. Comforting me somehow.

Then the Republican stronghold of Catalonia is taken. This comes as a hard blow and the chief of staff starts trying to restore contact between Catalonia and the rest of the rapidly diminishing Republican zone, but this is far from simple. The nationalist forces are moving closer and closer to the capital, so in order to keep them as far away as possible, a decision is made. The Republicans will launch an assault over the fast-flowing Ebro River. Strategically, it will be a nightmare. Long before it has even begun, the logistics are being planned down to the tiniest detail. Whilst the troops are being prepared, we brace ourselves for an influx of casualties. The truth is that it isn't until I become aware of the scale of what is being planned that I acknowledge my feelings for Henry Stevens run far deeper than I've ever admitted to myself. I realise with a pang that, even with his injury, there is every possibility that Henry will be leaving for the front.

I needn't have worried. The decision is made that, with his marked limp, it isn't wise for him to fight. I can see how disappointed he is, particularly as this is such a significant battle. Yet eventually he accepts that he can be of greater use in other ways, namely in continuing to drive ambulances.

Taking part in the siege of the Ebro feels to me not far off signing the Republic's death warrant. The troops succeed in crossing the river at night on pontoons and newly built boats and reach an important target point on the other side. But the might of the fascist forces is more than can possibly be dealt with. Fascist reinforcements pour into the area. Not only that, but for the next four swelteringly hot months, the Republican side is pounded with aerial and artillery bombardments by the nationalists. They prove to be far more effective, not least because of the number of Nazi planes they can count on their side.

Whilst all this is taking place, we travel eastwards and are re-based just a short distance from the Ebro, bringing everything we can find from the hospital that may be of some help to the all-too predictably high number of casualties. We load up dozens of rickety ambulances and trucks and drive in close convoy to our new hospital base which, I am horrified to discover, is little more than a cave. It is a huge cave but, even so, I can barely believe that we are planning to treat wounded men in such conditions.

These days are a blurred whirlwind. I don't have time to question anything that is going on, nor to eat a decent meal. And I certainly don't have time to feel fear. We set up over one hundred beds and wait breathlessly as we hear the steady bombardment of the pontoon bridges each day by the fascist forces and the hurried repair work carried out through the night by the Republican fortification units. The war has been brought to me on previous occasions, but never have I been brought to the war, not so closely.

The beds fill up almost immediately as wounded men pour in. We are completely overwhelmed, not only in terms of medical supplies and ambulances but also in terms of the sheer numbers arriving day and night. We cope as best as we can, but we're painfully aware of our shortages.

Rumours also start circulating that there are dozens more wounded on the other side of the river that need urgent attendance and, whilst some of us have to stay at the makeshift cave hospital, several of us are picked at random to cross the river and given less than an hour to collect everything up and start moving. Up until now, I've always known where Henry is. For several days, we've barely had a chance to talk to one another yet we've always known where the other is and snatched the odd opportunity to squeeze each other's hand encouragingly or force out an exhausted smile. Yet when I cross the Ebro, he remains on the other side. This terrifies me. A smile from Henry, a few words or a squeeze of my hand, no matter how sporadic, always propels me, gives me purpose. Yet I am not afforded the luxury of dwelling on this for long, for shortly after being told I must cross the Ebro, we are making preparations to leave.

I am thrown together with several other nurses and medical staff who have been transferred from other hospitals, much like myself. Whilst most are Spaniards, these days are a rush of introductions, foreign voices and curious Spanish accents from the furthest-flung corners of the country. We leave early in the morning over the newly repaired pontoon bridge but no sooner have we safely reached the other side than a large number of huge bomber planes loom overhead and begin to pound the riverbanks with missiles. Thankfully, we manage to hide ourselves in the safety of an overgrown olive grove while this continues for half an hour or so, before they circle a few more times and then leave. I shall never forget it as long as I live: lying frozen under a bush, my head buried deep into the prickly reeds along the riverbank as I breathe in their sweet, watery smell and try to imagine that the gunfire above is simply the erratic beating of my heart. An Australian nurse lies beside me, clutching the hand I've offered her with so much force that I can't feel it any more.

As I lie there on the ground, barely breathing with my head in the reeds and listening to the whirr of the bombers overhead, I try to detach myself from my body and watch the scene from above, telling myself I can't be harmed.

'*This is just part of it,*' I say to myself. '*It's not something you bargained for, but you're going to get through it. Nobody ever said it would be easy. Your father warned you of that, didn't he?*' Yes, he did. Father, where are you? What are you doing? '*Think of the rest of your life you must live. Think of Henry. Think of your future.*' Isabel…Isabel…I hear my name being whispered as softly as the rushes and when I feel my sleeve being tugged at I turn my head. It is the Australian nurse, pulling at my arm. 'Isabel, come. The planes have gone. We must continue.'

I jump up and join the group on the hillside trail as we start to walk through the heat and swarms of flies with our heavy packs. It is a gruelling journey. The sun is suffocating despite the early hour, but we also have to walk past wounded and dying men on the track. We've been hurriedly briefed before we left that we are to set up hospital a little way on at a large white hermitage and then return for the men we can still help. When there are this many injured men lying on both sides of you, without dropping to your knees and giving each one of them the time they deserve, it's impossible to say whether they have a chance of survival.

It's not the same as it was with Jean-Marie, for I was instructed to tend to him and him only. I gave him my full attention and it was only by doing so that I could grant him as gentle a passage into death as was possible under those circumstances. Yet here I am, walking through a deathscape of contorted figures, writhing in silent agony, not able to tend to a single one of them. For this is what strikes me most about the scene: the silence. Many men have long since died, but those who are still hanging onto life are not screaming in pain; rather I see their lips moving in noiseless agony as I walk alongside them, a layer of thin mist glazed over their eyes. *Put one foot in front of the other, Isabel. Keep walking, keep breathing, that's right. You'll come back for these men very soon.*

We reach the hermitage and we do indeed return to the banks of the Ebro to help as many men as we can. Could we have saved more? It's a question I fear will always return to haunt me. Weeks later, rumours circulate about the number of lives lost during the siege of the Ebro, the hardest fought battle of the entire war. It is well into four figures, with thousands more wounded or taken prisoner. And was it worth it? That battle has finally destroyed the Republican Army as an effective fighting force. So I think it's fair to say that it was the beginning of the end for us. Yet if any man or woman loses their life whilst fighting for something they believe in from the core of their soul, I can hold my head up high and say without flinching: Yes, it was worth it.

✳ ✳ ✳

As the dreadful realisation of what the failure of this battle really means begins to set in, we are given news to further dampen our spirits. A meeting is called in which we are informed that the International Brigades are to be sent back to their own countries. It seems that their presence in Spain can't be justified any longer and we can only assume the worst from this news. I feel ill at the thought of it, what it means for our cause. And what it means for Henry.

It isn't until the Battle of the Ebro comes to its violent close that I see him again. At first, I barely recognise him. He is painfully thin and drawn and has grown a thick beard and moustache. I suppose it's his eyes that give him away – those unfailingly kind blue eyes which hold in them so much warmth but now, even more pain and disappointment. I spot him before he sees me and I catch my breath, leaning against the wall to steady myself as I watch him unload equipment from the ambulance. But then I can't hold back any longer and at the same moment, he sees me. As our eyes meet, he stares at me – a stare that is long and deep and hard and truthful – and we move towards each other and I feel his thin arms around me and his tears on my neck and I hold him close and never want to let go.

That same evening, he suggests we go for a walk. We make our way slowly up the steep pine-clad hill beyond the huge white hermitage, stopping every few minutes so that he can rest his foot. Eventually, we reach the top and sit, panting on the shrub as we gaze down to the hospital and the fertile valley. I draw my breath in. It is so beautiful – so utterly unlike the south of the country during the summer months where the land is scorched dry and brown by the fierce sun. Digging my fingers into the warm pine needles I close my eyes and take long, deep breaths. I imagine that I am there as a traveller. That I haven't witnessed the death of countless men and that my country is at peace.

'What are you thinking?' Henry sits beside me, so close that I can feel his breath on my cheek, light as a feather. I smile and lean back so that I am propped up by my elbows and continue to look out across the valley.

'How beautiful it is here, and how peaceful.'

I look back towards Henry, who has pulled his good leg up towards him and placed his chin on top of it as he stares out across the landscape. Suddenly, before I am able to control myself, I open my mouth and a torrent of words tumble out that have been building up since our reunion earlier that day.

'Henry, now that the International Brigades are being disbanded, does that mean that you're going straight home?'

He looks away from me and his expression clouds as he begins to fumble in his pocket before drawing out a packet of tobacco. 'Yes,' he says slowly as he begins to roll a cigarette. 'Yes, it does. Do you want one?'

I shake my head and notice that his hands are trembling as he lights it. 'I haven't told my parents yet about Stan,' he says quietly. 'They have a right to know,' he continues, very softly so that his words are almost inaudible. 'I know that you do too, Isabel. I've not told you a thing.' He takes a deep breath. 'Talking about it makes it more real, I suppose, and the truth is that I partly blame myself. Stan wouldn't have come out here if it weren't for me. He always wanted to do what I did and we were fairly inseparable and…well, it's not fair that he's dead and I'm not. It's not bloody fair.' Henry's head falls forwards and he clasps at a clump of grass and digs his fingers deeply into it, closing his eyes. 'He was shot at the Battle of Jarama, the same battle I got my injury. Clean through the heart.' I hear his voice catch. 'At least he didn't suffer.'

I reach a hand out and place it over his and after a while, with his eyes still closed, he brings his other hand on top of mine. It feels warm and calloused. 'It's been so long since I've contacted them, my poor parents probably think that the pair of us are dead. Isabel…' he stops and opens his eyes and stares at me, eyes wide with an expression of fear '…how do I tell my parents that their son is dead?'

I return his steady gaze and instinctively reach out to stroke his hair. 'You've lost a brother too, Henry,' I murmur. His head drops onto my shoulder and the tears that have been holding themselves back for all those months spill out as his body is racked with sobs. We sit there for a long time as the sun starts to dip and the birdsong becomes more frenzied in the golden light. Quite some time after his cries have subsided, I feel his breaths become more even on my shoulder and think that he has fallen asleep. I draw my head down slightly and see that his eyes are still open. He is just leaning against me in contentment, his eyes scanning the horizon.

'Yes,' I say. 'You must go home and tell them. They need to see you.'

Henry lifts his head off my shoulder and looks me deep in the eye. 'I know. I'm going to spend some time with them. But then I'm coming back here. Back to Spain.'

'What do you mean?'

He takes a deep breath and inches a little closer, gazing at me with an intensity I've never seen. 'I mean that since we've been separated I've not been able to get you out of my head. I mean I can't imagine my life without you in it.

I mean that you're the most wonderful woman I've ever met. I mean that I love you. I love you, Isabel.'

I can't say anything. I continue to look at him as I search his eyes; search my soul for the words I so desperately want him to hear. But at that moment I am too shocked and too deliriously happy to be able to utter a single thing.

'Oh Isabel, please don't look at me like that.' He turns away and drops his head into his hands. 'If I've said the wrong thing…if I've offended you or assumed something I should never have done then you only need to say the word and I swear, I shall never bother you again. You must only—'

'Henry…' He looks up to meet my eyes, and as he does so, something in the deepest, most secret corners of our souls reach out for one another. Something that travels far beyond words. When I look into Henry's eyes I see something there I've never experienced and know will only happen once. Beyond my tiny reflection bathed in the light of the sinking sun, I see my past, my present and my future all coming together and winding their strands of time around his. I know that he is experiencing it too and as his lips softly close on mine I am aware, without the slightest shadow of a doubt, that I have transformed from *I* to *we*, and that there is no going back.

❋ ❋ ❋

I have no idea how many people turn out that day in Barcelona to bid farewell to the International Brigades. I'm

sure we must number in our thousands. It is an unusually
warm November afternoon and I crane my neck above
the sea of heads to try to catch a glimpse of Henry who is
marching with his comrades in the parade.

The atmosphere is electric. A band plays the *Internationale* as the soldiers stride down the wide street lined with
plane trees and people are waving red handkerchiefs and
calling '*No pasarán! No pasarán!*' These words, 'They shall
not pass', have been printed on banners and painted on
walls in every Republican stronghold and are the common
refrain of the left. It is impossible to hear the words without joining in and before I know it my right fist is raised
in the air and I am shouting '*No pasarán*', again and again.

Looking around at the faces of the crowd, charged with
emotion, I allow myself to imagine, for just an instant,
how much greater the joy would be if the war were over
and we had won it. And how much greater my happiness
would be if Henry weren't leaving by ship the following
day. I force myself to push those thoughts aside and concentrate on the scene before me. I can see both the Republican President and the Prime Minister on the stage as
well as billboards of Communist leaders from the Soviet
Union displayed around the plaza where the procession
ends. People are throwing flowers onto the marching soldiers and the scent of wild rose petals is overwhelming.

After the Republican leaders have finished expressing
thanks to the International Brigades, I watch as a small-
framed woman makes her way slowly onto the platform.
The atmosphere changes immediately as the entire crowd

falls silent. Everything is so still I barely want to breathe. This is *'La Pasionaria'*, the passionflower, and she has earned her name through her ability to evoke emotion in the most hard-hearted of listeners. I have longed to see this woman in person. Not only has she broken the acceptable mould by becoming an important political figure in a male-dominated government, but she's also spent the good part of her life campaigning for social justice, particularly for women and the underprivileged. She is dressed entirely in black and her hair is pulled back from her face in a tight bun, but she looks elegant rather than severe and her face is noble.

I'll never forget her words. Though they aren't addressed to me, I don't think a single person present that day is left unaffected. She tells the Brigades that they must be proud of the role they have played in Spain and that they are history; they are legend. At the end of her speech, she invites them to come back once democracy has returned to our land and a roar like the swell of waves rises up from the crowds as fists punch the air. I see men openly weeping, some of them falling to their knees on the hard ground as they sob into their hands.

By that point, the brigades have left the plaza and rejoined the crowd and I look around for Henry. Yet he finds me first and as I feel his arms wrapping themselves around my waist, I squeeze my eyes tightly shut to stop the flood of tears welling up inside me. 'I love you, I love you, I love you,' he is breathing again and again with his lips against my ear and I hold him tightly against me.

Later that afternoon we book into a cheap *pensión* near the city centre. The window shutters are broken and it smells musty, probably because of the scrawny chickens that the landlady keeps on the balconies. The same evening, whilst I bathe as best I can behind a screen with a jug of tepid water and a bar of soap, Henry tells me he needs to go out for a short while. He returns an hour or so later, grinning from ear to ear like a schoolboy as he grasps a bottle of wine. I have hurriedly dressed but my hair is dripping wet and I leave a trail of water gleaming behind me as I walk across the dusty wooden floorboards towards him.

'Where did you get that from?' I laugh, prising the bottle from his hands and turning it over as though it is a precious gem.

'Ah, well I *know* people, you see,' he replies with a wink as he produces a corkscrew and two metal tumblers from his bag. He has thought of everything. As he hands one of the tumblers to me he shrugs. 'Not very romantic, I'm sorry, but it was all I could find.'

I shake my head in disagreement, watching as he expertly works the corkscrew. We both know what the other is thinking: that after tonight, we have no idea when we shall see one another again. But neither of us can bring ourselves to discuss it. It is better that way. We are both still feeling energised from the parade and as we sip the wine and let it slip slowly down our throats, I recognise that words would only spoil the moment.

I've never lived a sensation so intensely in all my life, for I feel both desperately miserable and happy at the same time. I know what it is to be in love, and how it feels now that the man sitting in front of me with his kind, intelligent eyes has, quite literally, turned my world on its head. Yet tomorrow morning he'll be gone. I don't doubt for an instant the integrity of his promise that he'll return, but I know realistically that it won't be in just a few months.

I never want to forget this night; the small details: watching him shave in front of the lopsided mirror, the pale hair on his long fingers catching the fading light from the open window; the way he props himself up against the wooden bedpost with a pillow, his top button undone as he cradles the wine in his large, warm hands; the way he reaches out and touches the damp strands of my hair; how he empties the last drops of wine into my tumbler before leaning back and smiling at me. How I should like to bottle that smile, the blueness of his irises almost vanishing as his eyes turn into fine slits and the fullness of his lips, stained a deeper red in one secret corner by the rioja.

The wine goes straight to my head. I know my cheeks are flushed and when he asks me if I'd like to dance, I smile at him and drain my glass. He rises from the bed and puts his hand out to me, smiling playfully. As he takes me in his arms, we dance around the wooden floorboards to an imaginary tune as the evening light streams in through the broken shutters. I lay my head on his shoulder and close my eyes. We are not in Barcelona. We are not in the middle of a war. We are in London, dancing at a ball in a grand hotel on a fine summer's evening. My hair is curled

and I am wearing a little rouge on my cheeks and I have a
silk stole around my shoulders and…

'Isabel…'

Abruptly, I am pulled out of my dream. Opening my
eyes, I look directly at Henry. He appears nervous and
as we stop dancing he clasps my hands and smiles awkwardly. I continue to gaze at him questioningly, and as I
do so he reaches into his pocket and pulls something out,
mumbling as he does so.

'Believe me, I tried searching in so many different places but I can't tell you how difficult this kind of thing is to
come by these days. I even went out to—'

'Henry.' I put my finger to his lips. 'What are you talking about?'

Before I know what is happening, he reaches down
and lightly clasps the ring finger of my left hand as he
silently winds a single length of purple thread around it
and ties a firm knot.

'Isabel, will you marry me?'

My eyes flicker between the purple thread and his blue
eyes, barely able to grasp what is happening. Henry Stevens is proposing to me. He is asking me to marry him. I
don't think I even say the word 'yes', I just fling my arms
around his neck and hold him. But I don't need to – he
knows my answer. As he draws me away from him, he
places both hands gently on either side of my face and
gazes at me hard. How can someone I've known for such
a short time seem so familiar? I place my hands on his
forearms.

'I love you,' he says slowly, not taking his eyes from me.

'*Te quiero*,' I whisper back and he brings his lips to mine and kisses me with a deep strength. Is it possible to taste love? If so, I taste his love for me in that kiss, and I never want it to end. My hands come up behind his head and play with the golden roughness of his hair; the hair that I will never stop marvelling at. It is thick and un-kempt and I even find myself wondering, if we have children together, will they have this hair, the colour of sand?

Henry's lips travel down my neck, slow, soft kisses that feel like the wings of butterflies beating against my skin. His fingers tremble as he unbuttons my blouse and pushes it back off my shoulders. A shadow of self-consciousness darts through me but it doesn't last long. For I want this. I am eighteen years old. This is my first real taste of a man beyond the briefest of kisses I've shared with Henry. But I don't want it to end here. I want everything. Henry removes his shirt and I see for the first time the freckles on his chest, the light hair around his navel, the small scar on his right shoulder.

'How did you get that?' I whisper as I run my fingers over it.

'Stan pushed me out of a tree when we were small. He was fed up with me always telling him how much stronger I was.' When he mentions his brother this time, there is no pain in his eyes. This time I know that I am the only person he is thinking about.

The light is fading in the room and he holds a hand out and leads me to the bed. We kick off our shoes and I unzip my skirt and let it fall to a loose heap on the floor. Henry kisses me again and, our bodies closer together, I feel something stirring in me that I've never really felt before, the unmistakable stirring of desire.

Before I know it, we are crawling backwards up the length of the bed, and his hands are pulling up my camisole. I stretch my arms above my head and let him tug it free over my body and fling it to the floor. I turn my head slightly and look at the creamy material against the dark wooden floorboards and I think *Is this me? Is it me this is happening to?* I turn back and look at Henry, his eyes boring into me. Without taking his eyes from mine, he begins to gently stroke my arm, my belly and my inner thigh, slow deliberate movements that send tiny ripples of delight shooting through my body. I can feel my toes curling in pleasure and as his hands stop on my underwear, working their way with gentle pressure in small circles, my back arches.

'Henry…' I breathe, and my hand tightens around his arm as I pull him towards me. Fumbling, I take off my underwear and tug at the shorts he is wearing. He is smiling, I think I am smiling too, laughing even though I don't know why but I feel so happy to be in love and to be able to feel his body against mine and to be able to speak to one another in this way without words. Finally free of clothes, he pulls back and strokes my cheek. 'God, you're beautiful.'

Nobody has ever said that to me before. I have never thought of myself as beautiful. María, my sister, now she is beautiful. And Sara is beautiful. But me? Well, I am just me.

'Are you nervous?' Henry's eyes gleam in that same charming, mischievous way they did on the day I first spoke to him outside the hospital.

'No,' I answer truthfully.

He smiles at me tenderly and then runs his fingers over my breasts, caressing my nipples and making me stir again with longing. I pull his head down towards mine and we kiss deeply whilst Henry moves on top of me and I feel a burning, pulsing, exhilarating sensation between my legs. My hands push down on his buttocks as he arches his back up and straightens his elbows on either side of my body.

'Are you alright?' he manages to say, and I nod, urging him on, wanting him more. I pull him down to my body, needing the closeness of him against me and he moans softly as he buries his face in my hair. Our bodies sway together, slowly at first, and then faster. I can hear myself gasping with pain and with pleasure at the same time until finally, Henry pulls me into him with one gentle but strong movement and we cling to one another as he breathes and whispers into my neck.

I don't know how long we stay like that for, but darkness has fallen and I slip from the bed and clean myself in the bathroom. When I come back, Henry is sleeping and, suddenly cold, I nestle in behind him and pull a blanket over us both. I squeeze my eyes tightly shut and cannot stop the smile that has spread out across my face. Henry, Henry, Henry, I say to myself, over and over again, and his name is suddenly the most beautiful word I have ever heard.

The next morning at dawn, as he slips quietly from the bed and dresses, I watch him in the dimness of the dusty room. I know that he is leaving now, and there is nothing more we can say to one another that can help. When he is ready, he sits by the bed as he holds my hand in his and pushes away the hair from my eyes.

'I'll come back as soon as I can,' he whispers before bending down and kissing me slowly on my lips. Standing up, he slings his khaki backpack on and walks to the door. He turns briefly, murmurs that he loves me and, with that, he is gone. I close my eyes as I listen to his footsteps clattering down the staircase and the thud of the front door as he leaves the *pensión*. It is morning, a new day. I am eighteen years old with my whole life stretching ahead of me, but how am I to live my life now, now that the man to whom I have given my heart and soul has gone?

I have never been the type to feel weak with pessimism or lethargy, but I find the days that follow almost impossible to bear. I feel too despondent to even call my parents to share with them the happy news of my engagement. Instead, I find myself wandering the streets of Barcelona, staring at the destruction of the buildings and the glaring poverty that screams out at me from every side.

The city has changed so much since my last time here. Many of the gothic buildings that spiral majestically skywards have been damaged by bomb blasts and it seems that almost half of the shops and public buildings have been boarded up. Huge convents have been converted into refugee colonies and I gaze up as pigeons swoop in and out of the towering arches. I even go to the zoo two days after Henry's departure, as I am so astonished to discover it still open. As soon as I've been there a mere fifteen minutes, however, I leave, wishing I'd never gone, for the only animals I see are a desperate, emaciated polar bear and a pained-looking kangaroo munching on dead leaves.

After the first few days I start to wonder if I should go home as Henry's absence makes me ache for the company of my family. I am still staying in that desolate *pensión* run by an expressionless middle-aged woman who walks about with a dirty, runny-nosed child that hides in the folds of her skirt. I think about going somewhere a little more cheerful as I still have some money left. Yet I stay, for this is where Henry and I have been together.

A steady rain has set in for the day and I walk through it towards a street-corner bakery that I know will have bread if I get there early enough. Half-dead-looking chickens scratch about on window balconies above me and the mild November sunshine we welcomed just the week before at the parade almost feels like a figment of my imagination. It is truly wintry and I pull my collar up around my ears and hurry over the slippery cobblestones.

A hard-faced man serves a line of customers from behind the counter. He stretches out his clammy palm and scrutinises the coins placed into it. He is so suspicious and I suddenly can't remember a time before everybody was so guarded. Before reaching the front of the queue, I suddenly hear the high-pitched whine of a siren. Back at the hospital, this means that wounded soldiers are being brought in, whereas in the city it signals an air raid. It all happens so quickly – one second I am rushing out of the bakery and my eyes are drawn skywards like a magnet as distant black aircrafts dart through the misty drizzle. The next thing I remember is somebody grabbing me roughly by the arm and pulling me down into a doorway whilst the siren continues ringing in my ears. As I cover my face with my hands I hear a distant thud and tremble. Separating two fingers that cover my face, I peer through them to see thick lines of grey smoke rising from above the tops of buildings. As I take a deep breath, I look around to see who the owner of the hand is that had dragged me down to ground level. It is a middle-aged man and, without glancing at me further, he brushes the dirt from his coat, tilts his hat back on his head and vanishes round the corner.

An elderly lady who was in the bread queue ahead of me has dropped a few coins in the street and I watch as two filthy children wearing little more than rags descend on the money like hungry beasts before sprinting off, leaving the old lady screaming after them. I notice that nobody is paying any attention to her. She just stands in the street, her face contorted with fury and pain as she cries after them to come back. Others have resumed their places in the queue whilst still more continue on their way as though they've witnessed nothing more than a passing rain shower.

Sitting there on the side of the street, taking all of this in, I become aware that, despite all this deprivation and food shortages and constant air raids, people are still going about their daily lives. They have lived through two years of this and grown accustomed to it, as I realise that I have too. I don't feel fear, only a dull sensation in my chest that murmurs weakly *'Not again, please not again.'* But even that is drowned out by the acknowledgement that I've lost my place in the line and I don't have the desire or energy to wait again.

I remain sitting on the doorstep with my knees huddled into my chest. I catch the stench of decaying fish and, turning, see that I've been crouching on discarded fish bones and vegetable peelings. Gagging slightly, I heave myself up and lean heavily against the wall. It amazes me – just a few minutes previously the inhabitants of Barcelona suffered yet another air raid, yet, watching the plaza filling up before me, it is virtually impossible to believe. A group of small schoolchildren begin to snake their way through a side street, their teacher constantly turning and calling to them to stay together. They walk in pairs, their small hands grasping one another and I feel profoundly moved as I stare at them. Several of them look unhealthy and underfed, yet they are clean and tidy, and as they walk under a giant propaganda poster, my eyes flit upwards. Fascism is represented by Walt Disney's big bad wolf and I watch as the two last little boys in the line hang back from the group and stare up at the poster. Their eyes are wide and it's impossible to mistake the fear in them before they hurry to catch up with the others.

It strikes me clearly at that moment that I can't go home, because this is why I've come in the first place – for these children and for future generations, so they don't *have* to live in fear. And this is something I can do – no, *more* than just do. It is something I am good at, very good at. The idea comes to me, for the first time, that when this war is over, I can continue working with people in this way. Don't places even exist where people go to die? Yes, I find myself smiling. It's an unusual gift, but it's a gift all the same and it would be wrong to not use it. I take a deep breath and make the decision to continue with my work as a volunteer nurse.

CHAPTER ELEVEN
LUISA

Winter 1938

There is a bitter chill in the air this morning and I am kneading dough in the kitchen whilst Aurelia prepares our *almuerzo*. I am idly listening to the wireless, contemplating switching it off as it is unusual to encounter anything that is not pure nationalist propaganda, when I hear the name 'García Lorca'. Rushing to turn it up, covering the dial with flour, I lean my entire body into the wireless and listen.

'We are pleased to announce the publication of a new edition of Federico García Lorca's gypsy ballad poetry, *Romancero Gitano*, available in all good bookstores as from today.'

I gasp in delight. García Lorca's works have been prohibited for two years now since his death but this means, surely, that the grip of censorship is loosening and that our lives are to improve? Hurriedly, I tug at my apron strings and Aurelia wordlessly comes toward me and brushes my

hands away so she can untie them. She quickly prepares a
bowl of soapy water for me to wash my hands in and nods
at me briskly, for she has no need to ascertain my purpose.

The streets are alive with birdsong and chatter and as
I run down the slopes I feel, for the first time in months,
full of optimism and hope. Life is to improve. Life is to
get better! Perhaps nothing is so dreadful as we all imagined and Isabel shall be home soon and darling Eduardo
shall smile more and life shall continue as it did before.
The bookseller in *Librería Los Molinos* smiles at me warmly as he hands the book over the counter in a crisp paper
bag, and I smile back, even though I do not recognise
him, and it is not the bookseller who worked there for so
many years – what was his name? – yet at this moment it
does not matter, for the sun is shining through the win-
tery frost and the book is warm in my hands. As I steal
a look at it on the way back up, I see Federico's dignified
face smiling up at me and I think I may burst with joy, for
all is suddenly well.

Despite the chill, Eduardo is on the patio drinking coffee, shrunken into his winter coat. I stand for a little while
at the door, hugging the book to my chest and watching
as he takes small sips of the coffee, swills it around in his
mouth, crinkles his nose in disgust and adds another couple of teaspoons of sugar. Good coffee is almost impossible to come by these days, but sugar is dear and Eduardo
is certainly not acting as though he knows that each gran-
ule must be used wisely, particularly when he then repeats

his tasting charade three times. I push my irritation aside, take a deep breath and walk down the steps towards him, pulling out a chair and sitting down.

'*Hola, cariño*,' I say. 'Any coffee for me?'

Eduardo flips the lid of the coffee pot open and grimaces. 'All gone, I'm afraid. Damned revolting stuff anyway.' He jabs his finger into the remaining sugar crystals scattered around his glass and places them in his mouth before glancing up at me. 'Are you alright, Luisa? You look a little flushed.'

I beam at him and hug the book to me once more before placing the package on the table and sliding it towards him. 'I have something for you.'

Eduardo raises an eyebrow before tentatively lifting the paper bag and running his hand gently over the top of it before pulling the book out. He looks at the front of it, then at the back, and then at me.

'*Romancero Gitano*,' he murmurs, and I smile, feeling like a schoolchild eager to please their teacher.

'You just bought this?'

I nod.

'But this is…'

I nod again.

'*Dios!*' he exclaims, as his fingers hungrily tear open the book and he busies himself in the pages. I watch as the irises of his green-grey eyes flick up and down, up and down and I settle back into my chair, lean my head back and half close my eyes, scanning parts of the garden. The winter pansies are out and their deep purple blooms look striking against the whitewashed walls. Further out in the garden, the gnarled old walnut tree appears to need a little attention and I think to myself to ask Pablo to do some pruning.

A sharp slam gives me a fright and makes me sit upright. Eduardo has closed the book and is now pushing it roughly back across the table to me. Deep lines run across his forehead and the vein in his forehead is pulsating.

'I need a cigarette. Do you have a cigarette?'

I frown deeply. I can hardly bring myself to reply to him, for he knows that I have never smoked. And I am aware that he has smoked a little in previous years, but had no idea he had taken it up again.

'What is the matter, Edu?'

'Have you read this, Luisa? Did you actually open the book?'

I bite my bottom lip, not wanting to hear what he shall say, but knowing that I must. 'No,' I reply quietly.

'This is *not* García Lorca,' he says, emphasising his words by bringing the palm of one hand firmly down upon the table.

'What do you m—'

'It's not, I tell you. I barely recognise these poems!' His eyes shine with fury and, as the reality of what I have just bought begins to sink in, I lower my head into my hands.

'The censors have gone through,' he continues, his voice becoming more agitated, 'line by line, poem by poem and desecrated Federico's art beyond all recognition.'

'But they cannot do that,' I interject weakly.

'They cannot, but they have done.' Eduardo pushes his chair back noisily from the table. 'As if the *fascists,*' he spits the word out, 'haven't already pissed on his name enough. *Gracias*, Luisa, for thinking of me. But here's what I think of this fucking book.' Hands trembling, he opens it again and goes methodically through each page, ripping it down the middle as swords of pain and sorrow tear through me. When he has finished he walks into the house without even looking at me, the patio doors banging behind him as torn pages flutter across the garden like small white doves.

❉ ❉ ❉

One month following my husband's destruction of García Lorca's violated book, Pablo disappears. He goes alone to the market down in the city, but by nightfall, he has not returned. Mar paces endlessly around the conservatory, not in the fast, agitated way that most people pace, but like a lioness, slowly and stealthily, ready to pounce on anyone that might bring her news. Eventually, I succeed in coaxing her into an armchair and bring her tea but she scarcely touches it, merely staring at it, open-eyed.

Pablo does not return that night, nor the next. By the following day, we have all joined Mar in her pacing. Eduardo smokes one cigarette after another and even Aurelia flits nervously around, her customary repose shaken. By the evening, after we have eaten a small meal in silence, nobody having the heart to speak, we all file miserably into the conservatory and begin to absently flick through books or stare into the distance. I notice that Eduardo has not joined us and walk back through to the kitchen where he remains seated. His fingers are drumming rapidly on the table and he is lost in thought but as I enter the room, my footsteps jarring on the cold stone floor, he looks up.

'Luisa,' he says. I realise, with a jolt, that this is the first word he has spoken to me in a day or two.

I sit down beside him and he grasps my hand. 'Luisa. I'm going to go and look for Pablo.'

'What? Eduardo, *por favor!* Pablo will come back, I know he shall.'

'Luisa,' he says again firmly. 'I shan't be long. I shall go and make some enquiries. Maybe even try and ask Miguel.' He swallows and looks away from me. 'I must bring him back safely.' Eduardo stands up and I follow him out to the hall where he puts on his overcoat and gloves.

Something is building up inside me, a desperation that I cannot let him out of my sight, and I clutch his forearm.

'Edu, *por favor! No te vayas.* I know your intentions are honourable, but it's not safe. *Por favor*, for me, stay here.'

'And what about Pablo?'

He looks me directly in the eye and I realise that I have not seen him so poised in months. Yet every fibre of my body rejects his decision. He makes to leave, but I continue holding his forearm.

'Let me *go*,' he says sharply, shaking his arm. I tighten my grasp.

'*Por favor*,' I beg him, tears streaming down my face.

'Luisa,' he says, this time more gently. 'Please let me go.'

Defeated, I drop his arm and hang my head as tears burn my cheeks. Eduardo takes me in his arms, holds me for a moment, then kisses me on the cheek.

'I'll be back soon,' he says, 'I promise.'

CHAPTER TWELVE
ISABEL

Winter 1938

I am surprised that Juan answers the telephone. As his voice crackles over the line, I try desperately to make out what he is saying. Slamming down the receiver, I push the door of the booth open.

'I need another line, *por favor*. I can't hear a thing.'

The man behind the desk glares at me beneath his puffy eyelids and sighs as he tries the number again. He nods his head over in my direction, motioning me to pick up the receiver. I dart back into the booth and snap it up impatiently as Juan's voice rings out clearer. I know that Juan more often than not sounds nervous when he speaks to people – that is just who he is _ but as soon as he starts talking I know that something is wrong.

'Juan…Juan, it's Isabel.'

'Isabel, Isabel…'

He keeps saying my voice over and over again, fighting for breath.

'Juan, *qué pasa*, what's wrong?'

Suddenly, I realise that he is crying. Between his gasps for breath, I keep hearing him say 'Pablo' and I try to interrupt his garbled flow to get him to speak clearly.

'Juan, *bueno*. Take a few deep breaths and tell me what's happened.'

I hear him breathing heavily down the phone as I envisage him on the other end, white knuckles gripping the receiver and pale cheeks soaked with tears. I bury my head into my collar to hear him better as the story reaches me in fits and starts.

'Pablo…two days ago, he went missing. He went to the market and never came back. Then yesterday night Father…he went to look for him and now he's gone too… nobody has seen him…'

I feel my heart start to thud loudly against my ribcage. I lift my head to breathe air into my lungs as perspiration gathers at my neck and damp droplets work their way down my back.

'Juan,' I say weakly. 'Is Mother there? Can I speak to her?'

The line crackles and hisses and I think I can make out his voice at the other end, shouting back at me. But then it goes dead and I push open the glass door once more and tell the man I need to be connected again.

'Have you got enough money for this?'

'I have more money back at my pensión…I'll go back and get it—'

'How do I know that you'll come back?'

'I'll come back! You have my word. I need to—'

'No.' He shakes his head.

'*¡Por favor!*' I beg. 'I just need a couple more minutes.'

The man shrugs and picks up his newspaper. 'What do you want? For *me* to pay?'

I can see that it's useless and slam all the money in my pocket down on the counter and run outside, a rising sense of panic building up from the pit of my stomach. I run towards the *pensión*, all thoughts of staying and continuing my much-needed work as a nurse gone in an instant. There is only one thing I have to do and that is to get home as quickly as possible.

By the time I reach the station, I've missed the last train to Madrid. I have to sit in the waiting room for five hours until the early morning departure, watching as the clock hands tick round, agonisingly slowly. I am trying to stay calm, trying to tell myself that they are both fine. Pablo has wandered off to do some sketching and Father has bumped into an old friend and is sitting in a cosy bar somewhere drinking wine, unaware how long he's been gone. I stare round the waiting room, seeing everything – the people, the suitcases, the screaming infant, the emaciated mother – but taking nothing in. None of it means a thing to me. All I can think of is getting home. Pablo and Father will have reappeared by then and, with any luck, I can get on a train back north a few days later.

Eventually, five hours pass and the train arrives. I fall into a deep, dreamless sleep the moment I sit down and have to be prodded awake by the passenger in the next seat.

'Madrid,' he growls at me through yellowed teeth. I pull my bag down from the rack and rush out onto the platform. Frustratingly, there is another long wait until a train leaves for Granada. I fiddle with the thread on my finger, though Henry himself isn't on my mind at all.

By the time I reach my hometown, I am mentally and physically exhausted. I wait impatiently at the station for a bus, but after half an hour I rummage in my purse to see how much money I have left. It is just enough for a cab and I wave my arm desperately in the air to flag one down.

It should have been my great homecoming. It has been almost two years since I hugged my family and walked away from Carmen de las Estrellas. So much has changed: I have trained as a front-line nurse and I have grown up in so many ways. And I have fallen in love. Yet as we speed through the streets, none of that matters. The city I've grown up in has lost its *alegría*, that lightness of spirit that I've always loved Granada for so much. True, even when I left all those months before, it was occupied by the fascists. But as I press my nose against the window and stare at the red and gold flags flying from the sides of buildings that have replaced the Republican flag and the civil guard hovering on street corners, it's clear that life in Granada as I once knew it has altered beyond recognition.

Walking through the front door I feel weak with fear and lack of energy. I pull it shut behind me and lean heavily against it, clutching my bag. I try to take long, deep breaths as I stare around the inner courtyard, immaculate as ever with its neatly potted plants and trellises of honeysuckle weaving their way along the latticed balconies. From the creak of the heavy wooden door to the cracked, sapphire flowerpot in the corner to the stars dotted around the floor, everything seems the same, save of course the gaping hole in the centre where my orange tree once stood, which I try hard not to look at. I know I must put one foot in front of the other, to make my way beyond the courtyard, but every time I almost move, my legs begin to shake uncontrollably; I feel certain that if I manage to take a step, they will give way beneath me.

I close my eyes and inhale deeply. As I do so, I hear someone approaching me. Half-opening my eyes, I see a blurred figure surrounded by full skirts coming closer and as I open my eyes fully, I find myself face to face with Abuela Aurelia. I drop my bag and throw my arms around her, laying my head against her ample bosom as she clasps me and strokes my hair.

'*Gracias a Dios*, you're finally home, little one.' She lets my head rest there for a while and then, pulling me away, she looks me up and down. 'But you're as skinny as a sparrow! Let's get you down to the kitchen and find you something to eat.'

'But Father…Pablo…Where's Mother?'

'Food now, talk later. Your mother's asleep.'

I hesitate as my eyes search the higher level of the house.

'Come, little one.'

The kitchen is warm and comforting. I sit down at the head of the table and watch Abuela Aurelia heating up a pot of stew on the stove for me. She's right, I probably have lost weight, yet looking at Abuela Aurelia, who's always been so robust and healthy, even from beneath the folds of her clothing I can see that they don't fit as snugly as before. Her skin, which always reminded me of polished brass, had also lost its sheen.

The stew is simple but delicious and warming and as I gratefully eat Abuela Aurelia sits beside me at the table. Her eyes never leave me for one second as she urges me to finish it and ladles out more. It is strangely comforting, a way to prolong the unspoken questions and answers that hang in the air between us. But once I have eaten my fill and lean back into the chair, we both know we can't avoid the conversation any longer. As she gazes at me with her dark eyes, I feel my heartbeat quicken.

'You spoke to Juan?'

I nod.

'And he told you that your father and Pablo have gone missing?'

I nod again as I begin to tap my fingers on the table's surface.

'They still haven't come back, little one. It's been three days since Pablo went and almost two since your father, the complete fool, went out to search for him.'

I feel tears stinging my eyes and I pick up the glass of water in front of me and take a large gulp. It trickles painfully down my throat.

'Where do you think they are?'

Aurelia continues to stare at me, her eyes giving nothing away as I search her face for a clue.

'Where do I think they are?' she echoes, taking my hands in hers and grasping them tightly. '*No lo sé.*'

I search her face imploringly as I feel tears falling down my face. Aurelia reaches into her pocket for a handkerchief. With one hand, she grasps my chin and with the other she firmly presses away the tears in the same way she used to do with her grandchildren when they were little.

'Isabel…' She brings her face very close to mine. 'You must be strong, *entiendes*? I know this is a hard time for everyone, but the only way we can get through it is to be strong.'

I nod under her grasp. I feel something shifting within me – that firm resolve as I slip out of my body and hover above the scene, staring down at my trembling bottom lip and Aurelia's silver plait, coiled round and round her head like a sleeping serpent. It is just as well that I can take on this role of observer rather than participant, because in the days that follow I need this strength more than any other time. More than when I closed Jean-Marie's eyelids. More than when a man's leg was amputated, the stench of rotting flesh overwhelming me. More than when I watched Henry turn in the dim room and weakly smile at me before closing the door behind him and clattering down the stairs. No, during these days I need an entirely different strength. Were it not for the hardships of the past months, I'm not sure I would have known how to bear it.

❄ ❄ ❄

It is almost impossible for me to imagine how my family has coped, for during all this time I've been away they have remained virtual prisoners in our home. True, it is a large home and in our privileged position we are fortunate in comparison with so many others in their cramped living conditions. But they rarely leave the house. It simply isn't safe. I find myself having to re-adapt to this stifling atmosphere, made all the more tense by the absence of Father and Pablo.

Mother has stopped talking. She was always the one to know what to say and when to say it, no matter what the situation. But this is different – it is as though the world has caved in around her and she doesn't know how to cope with the demons of 'what if'. There is no way of knowing whether they are dead or alive, imprisoned or tortured. Just thinking about it makes me feel sick with fear and all those naïve hopes I entertained on the journey here quickly fade. But Aurelia is right: I have to be strong, for all our sakes. So as Mother sits in the conservatory, staring out across the sierras without eating or talking, I attempt to keep everyone occupied.

They all know what I'm trying to do. I organise little concerts and poetry readings and make up a cooking and cleaning rota so at least there is some variation to the long days. I think they appreciate it in their own ways, for it brings some activity and sound into the otherwise silent house. I am still convinced though that Father and Pablo will reappear at any minute and the horror of the past few days will fade away like a dimly remembered nightmare.

It is during these days, however, that the truth of Father's recent state of mind hits me with a clarity that was always diluted in Mother's letters. Juan might tell me a small story, or Joaquín might be reluctant to answer the questions I put to him, and little by little, I piece together what has been going on here. I also spend time walking around the garden and the inner courtyard, looking at the miserable stump where my orange tree once stood. This upsets me hugely. It isn't only because it's no longer here, but also because Fernando tells me that it was after the tree came down that Father started to behave so strangely.

It is a bitterly cold December, but on my third morning at home I wrap myself up in a warm coat, walk out to the courtyard and sit on the tree stump, tears uselessly escaping from my eyes. *Father, where are you? We need you here. Pablo, come back to Carmen de las Estrellas and draw the moon shining on the silver boughs, the dreaming towers of the Alhambra.* As I listen to the church bells rising from the city, I turn Pablo's drawings over in my head. I've just spent the past couple of hours looking through them: Alejandro showed me where he kept them stashed under his bed in the room they shared with Fernando. Ever since I was small I longed to be able to draw. I made a great effort, but I had little talent, while drawing came to Pablo as naturally as walking or sleeping. I think he put all the energy that others invested in talking into the relationship between his pencils and the paper. I find all the sheets in chronological order – I never knew what a perfectionist Pablo was. When I look through those pictures, I realise that they are like reading a diary of events that have passed since I've been away. It is clear that when I suddenly stop featuring in any of the group scenes, this indicates my departure.

In his pictures I see Mar and Mother hanging the washing up with endless sheets blowing in the breeze. I see Aurelia telling Graciana off for some misdemeanour as she stares sulkily back at her grandmother. I see Joaquín and Fernando constructing football goalposts at the far end of the garden. And I see the boys chopping up the orange tree whilst Father stands to one side, watching them. This is the drawing that stays with me the most. In his expression and body language, Father's pain jumps out from the paper. Pablo has clearly spent far more time on him than any of my brothers, because though I can make out who everyone is, only in the figure of Father can I read something of his emotional state of mind. His hands are drawn up to the back of his head where they are awkwardly resting and the tenseness of his body is captured in Pablo's precise strokes. But it is the expression on his face that I can't get out of my mind. Somehow, from the hollow look of his eyes to the rigid muscles in his cheekbones, he has combined grief with a deep anger.

The cold air has snowflakes in it and, as I sit there, I want to be submerged in white more than anything else in the world. I want to be covered in a layer so thick that it will engulf me. It will continue to snow until Carmen de las Estrellas is covered and we'll all be frozen in body and in mind. Then when this nightmare is over, the spring sunshine will come out and the icicles will thaw and we can carry on with our lives. Father and Pablo will have re-appeared, the war will be over, we will live in a democracy and Henry will be by my side.

Henry. I've been so preoccupied that I've barely thought of him since returning home. He'll be back in London and will have been reunited with his parents and shared the news of his brother's death. Perhaps he'll have told them about me too.

It suddenly feels as though Henry is a figment of my imagination. Everything that has happened since he left Barcelona weighs far too heavily on my mind to leave room for Henry. When he returned to England, the pain I experienced was overwhelming. But this has been replaced by a pain that I can't express because it's so inconclusive. I still love him with all my heart. But to share him with any of my family right now feels completely wrong. I decide that all I can do is wait until we are reunited with Father and Pablo before breaking the news of my engagement.

❄ ❄ ❄

Christmas Eve is unbearable. It has always been a tradi-tion to prepare an enormous feast and then spend hours around the dining room table. By then, five days have passed since my return and there is still no news. Mother hasn't risen from her gloom either. She sits at the head of the table, silently handing round plates of fried potatoes and beans whilst I rack my brains to think of something to say that might cheer everyone up. Looking down into my plate of food, it occurs to me how extravagant we normally are at this time of year. Our dinner usually consists of turkey and goose and all kinds of seafood and shellfish, caught only that morning. For dessert we eat marzipan or *turrón* made from honey and almonds and it is washed down liberally with *chufa* or strong wine from the coast. Just thinking about it makes me feel quite weak with hunger as I prod at a shrivelled-looking bean.

'So, Isabel…'

Looking up from my plate, I see that Mother is addressing me with a strained smile. The fact that she is talking at all fills me with something I can't exactly describe as relief, but gratitude perhaps. 'What is Barcelona like?'

Barcelona? I swallow and feel the single bean ramming its way down my throat. Which part about Barcelona should I tell them: that I've never seen such poor or desolate people after months of having their city pounded? Or should I tell them about the beautiful architecture that is almost impossible to appreciate through all the smoking rubble? Or the sight of so many desperately ill children with scabies and rickets?

'Barcelona…' Every pair of eyes around the table is fixed on me. I suppose everyone is relieved that some form of conversation, no matter how strained, is finally filling the tense air. 'Well, I didn't spend very long there, just a few days before I started my training and a few days at the end. It's very grand – much bigger than Granada and there are some amazing buildings there. And the workers, as you know, are running the city now. Everything has been collectivised and I think, on the whole,' I play with my food, 'it's working quite well.'

I try to keep the flow up. I want to say something, *anything*. 'And there's a part of the city called Las Ramblas – have you heard of it? It's a boulevard that runs down a large area but there are all kinds of smaller streets and plazas that come off it, filled with shops and restaurants and that kind of thing. There are lots of artists and musicians there too, except now there aren't because of all the problems, but I did see one man there playing an accordion. I think he was French, but then I only say that because he was playing a French tune. He could just as well have been a Spaniard playing a French tune, but...' I frown, breaking off. I know that I am rambling and stare down at the purple thread around my finger and start to pick at it. 'But...I don't know.'

Nobody offers any more questions on the subject of Barcelona and the room falls silent again. I listen to knives scraping against plates and the movement of chair legs scratching across the floor.

'What's an accordion?' Juan eventually asks.

'You know what an accordion is!' Fernando retorts.

This is the type of conversation I am used to, Fernando riling somebody.

'I *don't* know what an accordion is. That's why I'm asking Isabel.'

'There was a man who used to play one all the time in Plaza Nueva. Don't you remember?' Fernando's voice is scornful.

'Of course not. Otherwise I wouldn't be asking, would I?'

'It's...' I try unsuccessfully to offer an explanation to Juan before Fernando, now on a tirade, cuts in.

'You know *exactly* what an accordion looks like, Juan. You're just playing dumb.'

Beatriz, who has spent the entire meal picking at her food and staring out of the window, flashes a quick look at my brother.

'Fernando, *párate*. You're being cruel.'

And that's it, he stops. Just like that. Nobody else seems to take any notice, but I stare at Beatriz in astonishment. Of course, I haven't forgotten the crush Fernando had on Abuela Aurelia's beautiful granddaughter. In the past Fernando would be reduced to a stuttering fool in her presence but in my absence it seems that a significant rapport has developed between them.

The damage for Juan, however, is already done. I watch as first his bottom lip begins to quiver and then he sniffs as large tears fall down his cheeks and splash into his food.

'Oh, come on, Juan. There's no need to be so sensitive about it. I didn't mean—'

'Fernando, just shut up! Yes, you're right, I *do* know what an accordion is. I'm just sick to death of silence. And I...I...'

Whatever Juan is trying to say is clearly costing him a great deal as his head hangs miserably down and his entire body is shaking.

'I…just want to know when they're coming back, that's all.'

With that, he pushes back his chair and walks out of the dining room. We hear the patter of feet running up the stairs two at a time and the distant slam of a door as we stare wretchedly at each other. Mother sighs deeply.

'Juan is right,' she says quietly. 'We cannot continue in this way. We need to know what has happened to them.' She looks up and glances around the table. 'Now, I know that I have always said to all of you it is not safe to go too far from the house, but this situation is unlike any other. So after we have finished this meal I shall go and make some enquiries and get to the bottom of this.'

Abuela Aurelia looks sharply at her whilst I grasp the sides of my chair with both hands.

'I'll come with you.'

'No, Isabel. You must stay here.'

'But Mother—'

'*No.*' She looks at me and shakes her head. 'It will be safer if I go alone. Now, *por el amor de Dios*, let us finish this meal.'

CHAPTER THIRTEEN
LUISA

Winter 1938

I scarcely recall when or how Isabel returns. She looks and seems so different, and I long to talk to her about all that she has experienced, but I find I am unable to converse at all. Not until Eduardo has returned. And Pablo, of course, dear Pablo. Having Isabel in the house once more appears to cheer the others a little; I have no idea what she is doing but I gather that she is somehow organising everyone.

On Christmas Eve, a day normally filled with food and laughter and music and merriment, we all sit at the table trying to eat and make the slightest scratchings of conversation. It is, though, a paltry attempt. We are all struggling, and we know it. Nothing, save Eduardo and Pablo joining us for that meal, could possibly lift our spirits. Aurelia, as always, has barely touched her food and she is waiting for her little scavenger granddaughters, Inés and Graciana, at her elbows to hungrily tear into her plate.

Dios, I think, as I squeeze my eyes shut, at what stage does a person begin to starve to death?

Alejandro is sitting beside me and he must be concerned that my eyes are closed for he squeezes my arm gently. I open my eyes and look at the face of my son, my baby, just eleven years old, at his earnest little face and the spattering of freckles over his nose, and my heart breaks a little to think how no child should be living through this.

It is not a pre-meditated decision, but perhaps it is enough to look into the eyes of my husband's son to know that I must find Eduardo, no matter what it takes. Nobody wants me to go; doubtless they fear that I too shall be swallowed by some vast black hole of the disappeared. But I leave as quickly as I am able, pulling on my shawl and hurrying through the dark streets. My footsteps sound louder than I have ever heard them as they slap against the cobbles and as I go, I see candles flickering in windows with muted festive celebrations taking place inside.

I have not brought adequate clothing with me and by the time I reach the house of Eduardo's parents some half an hour later, I am shivering with cold and nerves.

'*Dios*, Luisa!' Señora Torres exclaims as she bundles me inside. 'You're frozen through. Hurry, let's get you into the *salón* where there's a nice warm fire. What is it, child? Whatever is the matter?' I have started to cry again. I think all I am capable of doing proficiently right now is crying.

'Is Señor Torres here?' I choke.

'Yes, yes he's in the *salón*. Come.'

I allow myself to be led through like a small child and when Señor Torres sees me, seated in his armchair and smoking a pipe, he frowns. He knows instantly that I am not paying them a social visit.

Señora Torres pulls a chair up close to the fire and pushes me down in it. I stare at the flames for a moment, marvelling at the strength of the fire and how they must have a great deal of firewood to produce such a hearty blaze. Looking back, I see my parents-in-law staring at me expectantly, both of them frowning now.

I take a few deep breaths, trying to steady my voice. 'Eduardo went out two days ago. He has not come back. I need to find him. I need to know he is safe. But I do not know where to look.'

Señora Torres gasps and clutches the sides of her chair. 'He is safe, he must be. He must have met some friends and…and gone to share a *tapa* with them.'

'Two days ago,' I repeat slowly. I turn to face Señor Torres who looks ashen. 'Help me, *por favor*. We must find him.'

He places down his pipe and unsteadily heaves himself to his feet, leaning against his walking stick. 'I am going to telephone Miguel. You ladies remain here, please.'

And so we do. We remain there for what feels like hours, days, with the roaring fire burning down to nothing; although there is a pile of logs there, neither of us have the heart to attend to it. We exchange not a single word, both locked in our own nightmares of possible scenarios, and I must eventually fall asleep, because I

wake with a start to the sounds of a door banging and
two pairs of footsteps and a walking stick making their
way to the *salón*. I jump up, pulling my shawl around
me as my heart starts beating furiously. It is Eduardo, it
must be – Señor Torres has found him and this hell shall
be over.

But when the door opens, Señor Torres stands beside
Miguel, not Eduardo. You look, I think weakly as I stare
at my husband's brother in bitter disappointment, as
though you are dressed to go to a *corrida* or the opera.
How can you be so well groomed in the middle of this
god-forsaken war? Before Miguel has even opened his
mouth to speak, his mother has collapsed on him sobbing, clawing at his lapels.

'Oh Migé! Tell me he's alright! Tell me he's alive!'

My eyes flit from Señor Torres who is staring at the
ground, back to Miguel, who stands awkwardly with one
arm trying to restrain his mother. But he never takes his
eyes from me.

'I'm sorry,' he says quietly.

I hear a scream, and think for one moment it is my
own, but then I realise it is Señora Torres who has collapsed sobbing onto the floor and is now being attended
to by her husband. Miguel is shaking his head and remains rooted to the same spot.

'I tried,' he says, his voice dark and tight. 'I did everything I could, but I warned him, did I not? This was
beyond my control. I warned him that the only way to
stay safe was to remain quiet.'

Miguel continues to talk but I can hear nothing and all I can see are his lips moving rapidly beneath his black pencil moustache. The room caves in on me; bricks, wood, fire, books, paintings, ceiling and floor, light and dark, everything comes down around me as I feel myself falling and then the whole world turns black.

CHAPTER FOURTEEN
ISABEL

Winter 1938

When I first enter Mother's room, I can't see her and think that maybe I am mistaken and she isn't there at all. But then I realise that the shapeless form huddled in the corner of the room is not a shadow at all.

I creep up in the darkness and, crouching down, sit beside her. Slowly I feel her arm creeping round me and I lay my head on her shoulder as her fingers start to gently untangle the knots in my hair. She doesn't look at me, but continues to gaze out of the window down to the garden, painted in a silver glow.

'Do you know the moon is full tonight?' she whispers, continuing to stare out of the window. I shake my head. 'It is. It is full moon.'

Something about the way she enunciates her words sounds to me as though she is smiling as she speaks. I lift my head slightly off her shoulder and sure enough her lips are curling upwards. I've never seen such a look on

Mother's face before: she is smiling but it is not the full, generous smile I am used to. Her eyes are full of pain and I bury my head back into her shoulder and pull my knees tightly up against my chest. We sit there like that for a long time without saying a word and I gaze at the mysterious shadows that the moonlight is throwing onto various objects in the room. I remember, as a child, the way the moon shone in through my bedroom window and how, at certain points of the night, its light would fall onto my pillow. I used to imagine that by sleeping with my head directly in the light of the moon I would be filled with secret powers as I slept.

I am about to drop off to sleep when I hear Mother start to murmur beside me. 'Did I ever tell you how we met?'

'Hmm?' Sleepily, I turn my head slightly towards her so that I am looking up at her face, profiled against the moonlight.

'How we met, your father and I?'

She tugs absently at a knot in my hair.

'I heard about one of García Lorca's poetry readings over at Sacromonte. I had recently become more familiar with his work and thought it marvellous so made sure I got myself there early. But they were only accepting the first fifty people because it was a terribly small place and I was the very first person they turned away. I pleaded and pleaded with the man on the door, trying to charm him and tell him that, after all, I was ever so thin and I should take up no room at all!'

She laughs lightly.

'The man sighed and kept looking back over his shoulder and I am sure he was just about to relent when one of his superiors turned up and told him that was it and he must shut the door. Well, I pouted and begged but that was the end of it and before I knew it, the door had closed. I was frustrated but it was the most beautiful evening, clear and bright, and I could see all the stars stretching out across the valley. It was so warm, I remember, and I had no desire to rush home even though I knew it was a risk to stay out. I had succeeded in convincing Conchi to not chaperone me that evening...*Dios*, Conchi, where is she? How I need her.'

Mother pauses for a second and takes a deep breath as I watch the shadow of the clouds glide across her eyes. I am enraptured. Although I've heard very briefly how my parents met, it has never been brought to life in such detail.

'*Pues*...I was sitting on the wall looking at the Alhambra – oh, how divine it was! Then I remember hearing a commotion behind me. And there was Eduardo, banging on the door like a man possessed. I turned round and watched the scene – it was terribly entertaining. At first nobody answered but he persisted and after a few minutes the same man that had turned me away appeared at the door and Eduardo tried the same as me, begging as though his life depended on it. Well, I knew immediately that he would have no hope of getting in and so whilst I sat on the wall I watched him ranting and raving, but of course, nothing worked. Truly, I do not think I had ever seen a person so furious before. His curls were flying and he was waving his hands around wildly but eventually they just closed the door in his face. When he turned round he looked devastated and my heart went out to him.

'I think it must have been around that same moment that I realised where I had seen him before – it was at a poetry gathering of García Lorca's a few months previously. García Lorca asked Eduardo a question, but the poor darling was so nervous that he completely clammed up and could scarcely get a word out. I thought it was ever so sweet and amusing, but of course he was crushed. I did not help matters either, because before I could stop myself I laughed a little and from the way he flinched, I am certain he must have heard me. It was ever so cruel, but really, I could not help myself.

'Anyway, when his face came into the light I realised who it was and of course I was not at all surprised because he was clearly a devoted admirer of García Lorca's, judging by the scene he had just made at the door. I decided to go and talk to him but he was a little flustered when I introduced myself. But when he asked how I knew who he was and I told him I had sat behind him at the reading, he clearly remembered that I had laughed and then he looked mortified. But for me it only brought back amusing memories and I found myself laughing again.'

Mother breaks her flow and begins to laugh a little and I find myself smiling too.

'I do not know *what* he made of me! He had turned as red as a *pimiento* and could not make any eye contact with me whatsoever. First he stared at my nose, then at my feet and then he fixed his eyes quite firmly on my chest! Well, I told him who I was and tried to make a little conversation as the darling man was struggling – you know how Eduardo gets all tongue-tied sometimes. Eventually, after some encouragement from me, it must be said, he offered to escort me home.'

Mother laughs again, bringing her hand to her mouth. 'I even remember the way he said it. He said "M…may I escort you safely home, Señorita Ramirez Castillo, since your ch…chaperone is otherwise engaged?"' I laugh along with her as I hug my knees into me. I can clearly imagine Father saying those exact words.

'I must say that after he walked me home I thought he was a terribly poor conversationalist. I kept trying to draw information out of him but he found it difficult to keep it up. He was such a bundle of nerves and I did find it a little frustrating. But when we parted company he managed to stammer out a question and it clearly cost him so much to ask me that I could not help but be impressed by his courage.'

'What did he ask?'

Mother's head jerks sharply round to look at me. She's been so lost in her flow of memories, I think she's forgotten I am even here.

'What did he ask? He asked if he could call on me again. And I smiled at him and said "If you wish, Señor Torres" and that was that. At first I kept seeing him just to irritate my parents. But do you know when it was that I realised that I actually had feelings for him? When he could not come and meet me.' She smiles ruefully. 'All those times that he visited me at my house and I thought I might tire of him and those love sonnets he wrote for me. But then he couldn't come, and my disappointment shocked me. So I knew, you see, I knew it was something more.'

I stay silent as I look expectantly up into her face.

'And then we married and moved into Carmen de las Estrellas and then *you* came along, Isabel.'

For the first time in Mother's long monologue, she says my name. Turning her head, she gazes at me and as I look back at her I am sure that I can see shadows of memories dancing across the dark irises of her eyes.

'Eduardo fell in love with you the second he set eyes on you. He just could not stop sobbing when he saw you and I remember I was longing to hold you but it was almost impossible to get him to hand you over. In the end, the midwife had to gently prise you out of his arms. Besides, he was soaking you with his tears and I do not know who was howling louder, you or him. Of course he was proud as any father is when the others were born but not in the way when you were born, Isabel. You were the first and afterwards he told me he thought that his heart and soul might burst with pride. Two days later he took all his clothes off and ran around the garden naked, laughing with joy. He was like a small child. So excited and happy.'

Mother is softly laughing at the memory but as I look at her, I see tears begin to slowly stream down her face and suddenly the expression on her face becomes unrecognisable as it clenches up in agony. Through her closed eyes, the tears continue to pour down her cheeks as she crosses her arms and hugs herself, rocking slowly back and forth.

'Oh, Eduardo, Eduardo…' she sobs. '*¿Por qué? ¿Por qué?*'

I have been as lost in the past as Mother and I would gladly have stayed there longer; heard stories about the early days of their relationship or life at Carmen de las Estrellas as we grew up. I would like to hear more about those love sonnets; how he asked her to marry him; when he first told her he loved her; the moment he planted my orange tree and the naming ceremony the three of us shared; the first trip to Abuela Aurelia's cave together. I'd like to hear heard more about these things. But I know it is too late for that and though I fight against it with all my might, I can't prevent the words from coming. I try to step out of myself, to employ that safeguarding technique which has helped me on all those other occasions, but this time it doesn't work. It is as real as the pain of a sharp knife twisting in my side and as Mother grasps my hands between hers, I close my eyes.

'He is dead, Isabel. *Muerto.* They shot him against the cemetery wall. He is gone.'

❊   ❊   ❊

I remember little of the days and weeks following the death of my father. Mother never tells us how she learned of his fate, and we never ask. It is a painful fact that we all have to accept in our own ways.

Pablo returns three months after he disappeared. When he first pounds on the door of Carmen de las Estrellas and collapses in the street outside, we don't recognise the painfully emaciated, gaunt figure with a layer of grey skin hanging loosely over his body. Beatriz is the one to open the door and, upon seeing the man slumped in the street with his face in the cobbles, she runs back into the house and screams to her mother to come quickly. Mar rushes through the courtyard out onto the street and between the two of them, they turn over the motionless figure and stare into the hollow eyes of Pablo. Not in a thousand years have any of us dared allow ourselves to hope he was still alive. As Mar cradles the limp body of her son in the street and Beatriz openly weeps, my mother and I watch the scene from an upstairs window with conflicting sensations of relief and pain.

Of course, he can never tell anyone what happened to him. But he doesn't need to. For below his hairline on the left side of his head, where his ear once was, there now only sits a raw, jagged scar – angry and purple and twisted. Pablo can never tell us who cut his ear off or why they did it. He can never tell us why he was released. But mere days after he turns up on the doorstep of Carmen de las Estrellas, he is drawing again. Whilst we all hover around him, hoping that his pictures may provide some clue to his whereabouts over the past three months, or even something connected with Father, instead he draws the pulse of life as it is continues in the house: me reading a book; Mother sitting in the garden; Joaquín playing the guitar; the mountains.

Two months after Pablo returns, Mother and I are in the conservatory one night, the last two still awake. We are about to turn the lights off when we hear a noise coming from the partially opened door. I turn and see a pair of dark eyes observing us solemnly through the crack.

'Pablo? Is that you?' Mother calls.

The door is pushed open and he shuffles in, a hat pulled down over his head to hide the scar.

'What do you have there?'

In his hand, Pablo holds a piece of paper and he walks towards Mother and hands it to her. No sooner has she glanced at it than her eyes cloud over and her hand flies to her mouth. I walk towards them and look over Mother's shoulder. For the first time, I see Father, not through my own eyes, but through Mother's. For there he is, her darling Eduardo, immortalised in the delicate strokes of Pablo's hand. He is planting bulbs in the garden and there is something so accurate captured in this simple sketch that it has taken Mother's breath away. The stubborn set of his jaw; the loose curls that haphazardly hang over one eye; the gentle respect he holds for the bulb as he tenderly pats down the soil around it.

'Oh Pablo, Pablo,' Mother murmurs, tears streaming down her face. She lays the picture gently on the sideboard and takes him in her arms, hugging him tightly as she runs her hands over the flatness on the side of his head, rocking him from side to side. Remembering me, she extends one arm outwards and pulls me in and the three of us stand there, locked in a silent embrace.

✹ ✹ ✹

It is all ending. All of it. It's not long before Barcelona and indeed all of Catalonia, the Republic's stronghold, falls to the nationalists. It is impossible for me to imagine that great city of Barcelona without the ringing sound of the '*Internationale*' from the barrel organs or the anti-Fascism posters on every street corner. This is the city where I began my nursing journey, the greatest adventure of my life. Over the coming months, my mind turns time and again to the thought of working in a hospice back here in Granada. But, I concede, how could I, when this is considered the work of the priest, not of a young, inexperienced female nurse?

When Azaña resigns, his voice is broadcast across the airwaves declaring that the war is lost and he wants no more Spaniards making useless sacrifices. Eventually, the final piece of the nationalist puzzle slots into place as the fascists take Madrid. How many families are affected by our war? The question is obsolete, because, more to the point, how many families aren't? We personally cannot pinpoint a single one. Alongside the countless loss of life on both sides of our conflict, something in Spain dies in April 1939 when the last Republican armies surrender and we know – finally, intolerably, gratefully – it is over.

As for Henry, slowly, very slowly, my thoughts return to him as my fingers again begin to stroke the purple thread around my finger. At times, the physical need I feel for him overwhelms me and I find myself doubled over, clutching myself with my arms and tightly gathering folds of material within my fists. The first letter I receive from him I take to my room and sit on the bed and read it over and over, terrified but grateful that he has taken the risk of writing to me. I know he has left a great deal out for fear of it being intercepted. But just as with Mother's letters whilst I was nursing, I have long since learnt to read the unwritten; those invisible words that dance amongst the blank spaces of the page.

London
15ᵗʰ October, 1939

My darling Isabel,

I trust that this letter reaches you safe and well. I think of you each and every day and wait impatiently for the day we shall be reunited. How I long to return to you and to Spain. I assure you, Isabel, that I shall think of a way. How are your family? And life in Granada? I hope that you are all finding a way to press forwards through these dark days and are seeking comfort from one another.

It is autumn here and the shades of Regent's Park, a large green space near my home, are beautiful. I have been walking there a great deal with my parents and also friends I've been reunited with. Sadly these reunions with many friends have been short-

lived, however, as now that Germany has invaded Poland and war has been declared, a great number of them are being called up for service.

I can't deny it hasn't been easy since being back in England. Breaking the news of Stan to my parents was harder than I could ever have imagined. Somehow the loss I feel at his death is greatly enhanced when it comes to my parents as it goes, of course, against the natural order of things. Though I fear that a great many more shall lose their sons and daughters in the months to come.

I'm sure you're wondering whether I too will be going off to war once again. The doctors have told me my limp is too pronounced to serve effectively as a soldier, so at least there's no chance of me being killed fighting. London's not exactly safe either, as bombs are being dropped most days so maybe I shall be killed here instead. But still, I do think I have a better chance of survival this way!

I love you, darling Isabel, and think of little else than the day I can once more hold you in my arms.

Yours,

Henry

Oh, how I cry when I read the last paragraph of Henry's letter. I know he is just being dry in his British way and he probably means to make me laugh, but the thought of a bomb dropping out of the sky directly onto his house terrifies me. Meanwhile, we are being kept out of the war sweeping across Europe. It is clear that Franco supports Germany and Italy, and due to the weak infrastructure of our country after having taken such a terrible pounding, mobilisation for war is made virtually impossible.

Spanish products begin to be boycotted across democratic nations because our country is recognised as a fascist power. Hypocrisy, my soul screams. Just because the allies are winning the war and you didn't care to help us retain democracy with all your high ideals of non-intervention. And now you let us starve! I don't know how many thousands of Spaniards die of hunger in the years following our civil war, but just because someone has made it through the civil strife, this certainly doesn't guarantee future survival – as we are now learning.

All I can do is pray to a God I have no idea if I believe in, dream of a day when I can nurse again, and wait for Henry. I never remove that length of purple thread from around my finger and it isn't until a whole year after Father's death that my family learn of my engagement. One morning at breakfast, I am particularly despondent, feeling the aching absence of both Father and Henry. I pick at my food, staring out of the window, unaware even that the fingers of my right hand have crept up to play with the thread on my ring finger.

'Isabel,' Mother says suddenly. Her tone in that single word takes me by surprise, for it is a voice I have not heard in a long time: clear and strong.

I look up at her, not saying a word.

'Isabel,' she says again, this time a little quieter. Everybody is staring at her expectantly. 'What is that? That thing around your finger?'

I look down, realising I must have been fiddling with it. I feel tears filling my eyes and prod desperately at the breadcrumbs on my plate, willing them to stay away. But it's all too much and I push my plate away, place my elbows on the table and let my head fall into my hands as the tears come.

I feel a hand on my left shoulder, gently resting there in such an expression of silent, tender support, that as soon as I realise it's Fernando, I cry even more. All I can think is, it shouldn't be Fernando. He should be joking and quipping and teasing, not doing this. When did he suddenly grow up?

Nobody says a word, they just wait for me to stop crying before I look up to find something to wipe my eyes with. Alejandro pushes a napkin across the table towards me and I smile at him gratefully. It is a couple of minutes more before I can bring myself to speak.

'While I was away, nursing, something happened,' I say quietly. I glance upwards and Mother encourages me with her eyes to continue. 'You see, I met someone. His name is Enrique. Henry. He's English. I…I got to know him quite well.'

I pause again, searching for the right words. All I need to do is say it. Tell them I fell in love. Tell them he asked me to marry him. Tell them that I am engaged. Yet somehow these words catch in my throat. They should be cause for such celebration, but all I feel at this moment is a deep, stretching sadness. Looking up at Mother, I search her eyes and realise with certainty that she understands; that she knows. As she stares at me, her dark eyes full of mirth and sorrow, she wills me to share the news with everyone and I have to use every last ounce of strength I possess not to cry again.

'Tell us, Isabel.' Mar, who is sitting to the right of me, places her hand over mine and smiles.

I take a deep breath. 'He asked me to marry him.'

I hear someone gasp. I'm not sure who it was but I look back at Mother and wait, so glad that she noticed the thread around my finger, so glad that I didn't have to search for the right time to tell them all.

'*Enhorabuena, cariña,*' Mother says quietly as she rises from her seat and comes over to hug me. *Enhorabuena, Isabel,* I hear all around me. Perhaps it is the relief at having finally told everyone which unlock more tears that spill down my face.

'I'm sorry,' I say as I sink into a chair. 'I just don't know when I'm going to see him again.' Everybody fusses around me as Abuela Aurelia hands me a clean handkerchief and I am smothered in more embraces. When I have stopped crying, the inevitable barrage of questions begins: *Where did you meet him? When is he coming to Spain? What is he like?* I feel much calmer, but still heavy-hearted that Henry is not here with me to share our news.

Abuela Aurelia immediately sets about organising a celebration. It's lovely – we eat spicy lentils and she even manages to find a few hunks of chorizo from heaven only knows where and Joaquín plays the guitar. Yet it is only a half-hearted celebration because we all feel Father's absence. And of course none of us know when Henry and I will be reunited.

But he does return, just as I knew he would, almost two years after we last saw each other. It is a risky journey for him, not only because of the dangers he encounters on his way through France but also in Spain. If anyone knew he was a former member of an International Brigade who fought on the defeated Republican side, I'm sure he'd immediately be denounced as a 'red' and marched off to jail or worse. So he wisely primes himself in pro-Franco speak and, I don't know how he manages it, but he passes himself off as a British archaeologist who believes that General Franco is the best thing that has ever happened to Spain.

It is early one morning when he returns to me. I am in the kitchen washing up after breakfast when Alejandro walks in and quietly says, 'Isabel, I think you should go to the courtyard.' I look at him questioningly but he simply smiles in return, that honest, unassuming smile I have always loved him for. Mar and Abuela Aurelia stare at me and I silently dry my hands and make my way along the corridor. When Henry and I see each other, we just stand, apart, for some time. I can't find the right words; I have dreamt of this moment for so long. And whilst his lips don't smile, his eyes dance as we scan one another's faces and bodies, almost unable to believe that we are seeing one another in flesh and bone. He looks different, somehow both older and younger at the same time but achingly familiar. And when, eventually, he draws me into his arms and I sob quietly into his chest, I vow to myself that we shall never be separated again.

❄ ❄ ❄

Little by little, Henry and I fill one another in on this missing section from one another's lives. I tell him of the loss of Father, showing him Pablo's pictures which come closer to revealing his character than any words are able; I introduce him to each of my extended family members, never letting go of his hand for fear I may lose him again, and we take long walks through Granada. And Henry tells me of the repatriation fee he was forced to pay upon his return to England for enlisting in a foreign army; of the depth of his parents' despair upon learning of Stan's death; and the resignation of his comrades whom he fought alongside in Spain at being called up to fight another war they had all tried to avert.

Abuela Aurelia behaves with Henry in a similar way she did with Solomon, María's husband. She teases him and laughs at and with him, often turning to me mid-cackle and exclaiming 'Where did you get this *chaboró* from?' I am always happy to see Abuela Aurelia laugh, because I know how selfless she has been over the years; each and every action and movement is for the benefit of another. And she is barely recognisable as the person who came to Carmen de las Estrellas to ask for help; she is a thin, old woman now who could even fit into my clothes. But she also seems to have shrunk in height, so that whatever she wears trails along the ground. Looking at her now, there is barely a physical trace of *gitana* about her whereas Mar's gypsy roots are stamped indelibly upon her features, no matter what she wears.

Despite all this, Abuela Aurelia's spirit remains unchanged. She is a rock – for me, for my mother, for Mar, for each and every one of us and we need her as much as we need the air to breathe. One day she asks Henry and I to take her for a walk up to Plaza de San Nicolas as she would like to see the mountains. I am about to say that there is a wonderful view from our own garden but Henry catches my eye and I think better of it. Besides, it is a beautiful day, clear and crisp, and Abuela Aurelia now rarely leaves the house.

We walk on either side of her and it occurs to me that I have no idea what age my formidable old friend is. She, like her daughter and grandchildren, has never celebrated a birthday but now, walking alongside her at painstakingly slow speed, I realise that she must be in her eighties at least.

There are just a handful of boys in the plaza playing marbles with skinny legs and too-short shorts, all of whom completely ignore our presence. Abuela Aurelia is breathing heavily and she clutches onto Henry's arms as he leads her towards a seat.

'You must sit down, Aurelia,' Henry says. 'There's a good view of the mountains from here.'

'Ay, *chaboró*, I don't know what has happened to my strength,' she wheezes as she allows herself to be lowered onto the bench. We sit either side of her and she takes my hand in hers.

'Look at that view,' she pants, motioning with her chin across the valley. 'Who could imagine that *Dios* would give us such a beautiful world, only for us to destroy it and each other. *Tssk.*' She shakes her head and pats my hand. Henry and I stare at the view. I haven't been up here for some time, and though we can see the sierras from our garden, the plaza is higher and gives us a wider vista of the brown-slated roofs, cloud-white houses and the Alhambra Palace beneath a wide arc of blue sky. It is breathtaking.

'I wanted to come up here,' Abuela Aurelia says, 'because it is the last time I shall leave the house.'

I frown and tighten her hand in mine as I stare at her. '*Como—*'

She holds up a hand to silence me. 'We don't like talking about death, us humans, do we? After all this time and still, we have no idea how to talk about it. Even if it has surrounded us these past years.'

The small group of boys cheer from the other side of the plaza and we all look at them.

'Are you feeling unwell, Abuela?' I say, my heart pounding as I turn back to face her.

'*No.*' She shakes her head. 'But there are some things I know. I don't know why I know them, but I do. And I know that my time is soon up and...' she pauses and turns to face Henry, grasping his chin between her thumb and forefinger and shaking it '...I'm glad I don't have to look after you any more little one, because you have this

guapo to care for you. Your mother on the other hand…'
She breaks off and sighs. 'I know you will take care of her.
Now, let us sit and enjoy the view a little longer and then
I want to go home. I'm tired.'

I lean back into the bench, a myriad of emotions
crowding at my chest. She can't die, it isn't possible. She's
always been here and Mother needs her. *I* need her. I have
never doubted anything that Abuela Aurelia has said. Every word she speaks with such deliberate force and truth
and as I've grown up she's been like a compass for me, just
a few words from her pointing me in the right direction.

My thoughts are interrupted by two of the young boys
running up to us. One pushes the other forward, encouraging him to say something.

'If we dance for you,' he says, skinny arms thrust into
his pockets as he rocks back and forth, 'will you give us
money?'

Henry laughs, leaning back and crossing his arms.
None of us have any money with us and, even if we had,
it wouldn't be possible to give enough to all these boys.

'No,' Abuela Aurelia says. 'Will you dance for us anyway?'

I smile, not imagining for a second he will say yes, but
the child expels an inevitable sigh before grinning and
beckoning the group over. '*Bueno.*'

And as we sit there in the Plaza de San Nicolas overlooking what must surely be the most beautiful view in
the world, six small boys fumble their way through a
few Sevillanas, laughing and chattering whilst we watch
and clap.

✳ ✳ ✳

If you drive in a southerly direction from Granada through the mountains and then turn west along the coastal road, there is an easily missed track that leads down to the ocean. There's a tiny village there that has hardly changed over the years. It's surprising, considering the ugly development that has taken place in so many of the neighbouring coastal towns. Uncle Vicente, my father's eldest brother, lived just outside this village for a number of years before he left for Argentina during the civil war. He went partly through growing alarm, but Father always said he had a head for business and a nose that could smell a deal a thousand miles off.

I never knew Vicente well. But what I *do* know is that he left Spain in a hurry, so fast in fact that he didn't even bother selling his house or sorting out the belongings inside it, saying he'd come back for everything one day. I don't know whether it's fear or new business opportunities that makes him stay away, but the same year we lay my beloved Abuela Aurelia to rest, scattering her ashes on a westerly wind to carry them towards her cave and birthplace, Henry and I spend our honeymoon in Tío Vicente's deserted home by the sea. At the time it never occurs to me that an abandoned villa is an unusual place to celebrate; we are far too excited by the fact that we are able to escape together at all to Villa Golondrina.

Both Henry and I would have preferred a civil ceremony but things have changed by then. It is a marriage sanctioned by the Roman Catholic Church or no marriage at all. We also have to conform to the new society in ways that go against everything I've been brought up to believe in. Yet we must play the game; we know the possible consequences only too well if we don't. I've asked myself so many times why we didn't follow the example of Tío Vicente or my sister María and move abroad to a safer and more tolerant world when we had the chance. Why *did* we choose to stay in one of the most dangerous places in the country for anyone with left-wing associations after the civil war? A place that has witnessed our family being ripped apart at the seams?

As much as I love Granada and Carmen de las Estrellas, I would still leave. But Mother? I know that the comfort she takes in immersing herself in the memories that our home provides her is too great to forsake. And I know with the same strength that I love Henry and hate fascism that I could never, ever leave her.

Henry and I have a small wedding ceremony in a church near the house. I've never held any grandiose ideas for this day, so the modest service and small number of guests doesn't trouble me. Besides, in light of everything that has happened and the fact that my family are trying to keep a low profile, anything showier would be foolish. Ever since the fascist government has taken control, the status of women in Spain has plummeted to a lower level than before the Second Republic, further dashing my hopes of being able to work. We are expected to quietly submit to the will of our husbands and dutifully bring up children and tend to the home. This is reflected in the words that are read out to us by the priest on our wedding day. I am told that as a new wife, I must agree to be subject to my husband in every aspect. I should keep the home clean and tidy and only leave the house if my husband permits it. Of course Henry believes in none of this, and though I find it galling to have to repeat what the priest says, they are 'just words, empty words', as Henry murmurs into my ear later that evening.

The absence of certain people pains me that day. I know that Henry feels his own sorrow. England is at war and there is no possibility of any member of his family taking the journey to Spain at such a time. We could have waited to marry, I know that. We could have waited until the guns have fallen silent and some kind of fragile peace and stability has returned to war-torn Europe. But we have no way of guessing how long we'd have to wait. If history and our own experiences have taught us anything, it is that we must act quickly on what we believe.

Abuela Aurelia has been gone for only three months and I miss her terribly, yet I am grateful that at least she had the opportunity to meet Henry. I thought that perhaps, since she had told us her end was near, I might share that with her, particularly as I'd told her about my unusual experiences of nursing. But Abuela Aurelia needs no help, slipping away painlessly one night. I think of her each and every day and imagine I always shall.

A girl needs her family around her on such an important day – it's natural, of course. I suppose it eases the opening of such an important new chapter in her life. A girl needs her parents there. Particularly her father. As Joaquín walks me down the aisle, I feel him grasp my arm in a way that isn't only to help steady *me*, it is also because he needs support and strength to deal with his own emotions. It must be difficult for him too, for he knows that it should have been Father's role to give me away. I feel his presence on the other side of me, an invisible strength gently holding my arm and whispering in my ear '*Go to him; go to your husband, Isabel. He's waiting for you.*' I probably imagine it, but it is as real as the image of Henry at the end of the aisle. Without it, I don't know how I should have got through the day.

The day we arrive in the village is swelteringly hot and as the motorcar leaves us at the side of the road, it covers us in a thick layer of scorched dust before zooming off. We peer towards the sea in the distance, shimmering like a mirage. Since returning to Carmen de las Estrellas from the north, this is the first time I've left Granada and, although the pounding heat makes me feel faint, I'll never forget this feeling of exhilaration. Here I am at the coast, standing next to the man I've just pledged to spend the rest of my life with. We are young. We are in love. And even more importantly, we are alive.

After finding the *dueño* of the village bar who has the key to the villa, we make our way down the narrow track beneath the blistering sun before collapsing in the low-roofed shade of the house. That night, neither of us can sleep. We lie with our faces a hair's breadth from one another, talking about our childhoods and my dreams of a hospice before eventually deciding to go for a walk. A half moon hangs in the sky, lighting the steep path that leads to the sea. The further down we walk, the breeze picks up, cooling my damp, mosquito-bitten skin. As we approach the end of the track that leads into a curved bay, I spot a ramshackle old fisherman's hut and suggest we take a look. I don't imagine the door will be open, but after barely touching it, it falls right off its hinges and clatters noisily to the ground. Henry takes my hand and we step over the rotten piece of wood into the humid interior. We've brought a candle with us and Henry lights it and slowly moves it from one side of the hut to the other, our eyes taking in everything around us. There are some out-dated fishing contraptions, a box of decaying newspapers and a cracked tin mug. The wooden boards that serve as walls are slowly being eaten away with the passage of time and neglect, and although it is claustrophobic and musty in here, something about the hut makes me want to linger. I can almost conjure up a solitary old fisherman who spends hours in silence at the ocean's edge before making his way back to the hut, flicking through a newspaper and drinking a steaming brew to warm his chilled bones.

Henry's face is very close and as I feel his warm breath against my skin I marvel for the hundredth time how this man with kind blue eyes and hair the colour of sand loves me so openly and generously. He gently presses his lips to mine and then pulls away.

'Señora Stevens.' His eyes glint and crease into a smile. 'I can't believe you're my wife! Señora Stevens! I'm sorry, it doesn't sound quite as glamorous as Isabel Torres Ramirez, does it?'

I squeeze him tightly. '*Sí*, it does. I love it.'

He pulls me to him and kisses me deeply before we step over the battered door and walk down towards the sea.

❋ ❋ ❋

Late one evening, not long after Henry and I are married, Mar, Pablo, Beatriz, Inés and Graciana come to the conservatory together to talk to us and mother. I know within an instant that they are going to tell us something important as they have never trooped in like this with such serious faces.

Mother stares inquisitively at them, patting the seat beside her. Mar looks nervous and remains standing, shifting from one foot to the other whilst Pablo leans back against the door, black hat pulled down and his arms crossed.

'Luisa,' Mar says. 'We have come to tell you something.'

At that moment, it's clear what she is going to say, but I wish and hope I'm wrong. Mother, of course, knows as well and I can almost feel her preparing herself emotionally. After a while, she nods for Mar to continue.

'We have to leave now. We've stayed here for such a long time…we never imagined it could be this long. We…' Mar gulps as she looks down, her fingers interlacing and twisting.

Inés, now a striking young woman, clears her throat. 'You are our family, and you always will be, but it's time to go.'

'*Donde?*' Mother asks quietly. 'Where will you go?'

'They are building new *pueblos* outside the city,' Inés says. 'The rent is cheap, we've heard.'

'But how do you know you shall be safe?'

'We'll be safe, Luisa,' Mar says simply. 'I will make sure of this. But…as Inés says, you will always be our family.'

I feel tears stinging my eyes as one by one they approach us and put their arms around us for a long time. Mother dabs the corners of her eyes with her handkerchief. 'Is there nothing I can say to make you change your mind?'

Mar shakes her head, her black curls dancing. She is still so beautiful, Mar, but so tortured. I feel as though I have never really understood her, not in the way Mother does.

'I hope you realise that if you ever need anything, or if you should need to come back for any reason, Carmen de las Estrellas is your home as well.'

Now it is Mar's turn to wipe a tear away from her eye. She turns to me and strokes my cheek. 'You must take care of your *madre*, Isabel. And this one.' And suddenly, she lays a hand against my belly. My eyes widen. It has never occurred to me that Abuela Aurelia might have passed her gift as soothsayer onto her daughter. Sure enough, I realise the following week that I have missed my period. Henry and I stand in the bedroom, his hands spread out over my belly, and both of us laugh in disbelief and joy.

The timing couldn't be better. Mother is too proud to say as much, but I know she is distraught that Mar and the others have decided to leave and I must confess the house seems quiet and empty without them. Fernando bangs around the house moodily and often disappears. Nobody asks him where he is going and he never offers an explanation but he is a grown man now with stubble on his chin and a confident swagger and we can hardly make demands of him.

As for me, I'm unsure what to make of being pregnant – I swing from being deliriously happy, thinking it the most precious gift imaginable, to feeling horrified by the nausea and the shock of the little punches from inside me, so powerful that I sometimes double over.

'If it's a boy, shall we call him Eduardo?' I whisper to Henry one night.

Henry swivels round to face me. 'Eduardo? How do you think your mother would feel about that?'

'*No sé*. Perhaps it's too soon.'

'Perhaps. Let's see how we feel when the baby arrives.' He reaches out and gently pushes hair away from my eyes. 'Isabel, do you think your mother's alright?'

I pause. She isn't alright of course, but I am no good at admitting it to myself, let alone anyone else. 'What do you mean?'

'I know I didn't know her when…when your father was still around, but I wish there was some way I could help her, that *we* could help her.'

I sigh. Mother's moods are completely unpredictable. Like the sun coming out from behind a cloud, occasionally a glimpse of the old Mother returns. During these times, she talks about Father openly and lovingly, almost as though he is in another room and we can practically feel his presence. When she looks beyond Franco and shares her hopes for a freer, more liberal Spain, she also regains that glimmer in her eye I remember so well from my childhood, that glimmer of playfulness and energy and optimism. I love it when she talks like that and I am taken back to those days of the Republic when I hid behind a pillar and listened to Mother and her friends' animated discussions, attempting to unravel the impossibly grown-up but delicious web of words unfurling around the courtyard. But then her eyes cloud again and, once more, we are all left to play guessing games.

'What kind of things did she use to like doing for herself?' Henry continues.

'Spending time with friends. Making fortune cookies. Walking…but she still does all these things, sometimes. Henry, it can take years and years to grieve. You know that.'

He brings my hand up to his mouth and kisses my fingertips. 'Yes, I do.'

'Perhaps having a new baby in the house will help,' I say.

I wrap an arm around Henry and pull him in tight and a memory suddenly comes back to me of the last time I saw my parents together. I had just told them I would be leaving for Barcelona and Father had begged me not to go. I don't remember exactly what he said to me, but what I do remember is Mother reaching her arm up as Father left the room and squeezing his hand. And the effect of that small gesture was instantaneous; he was calmer and stronger. I don't think I'll ever be able to understand the depth and breadth of Mother's loss but Henry is right: we must help her in any way we know how.

❋ ❋ ❋

Our daughter is born in 1943 in the very same room in which I came into the world. She has a thick tuft of jet-black hair that stands on end like Henry's as well as her papá's sea-blue eyes and enormous feet which look incongruous against the rest of her dainty features. Because of my difficult pregnancy, I assume my labour will also be hard but I am lucky; as painful as it is, she comes quickly and quietly. It isn't until several hours later, when Mother cradles the baby in a white blanket in her arms, her tiny perfect mouth opening and closing like a little bird's, that I feel a wave of relief that we won't have to decide whether or not to call her Eduardo. As if reading my thoughts, Mother looks at me. The expression I see on her face makes me catch my breath for I realise immediately that this is the best thing that could have happened: for me to lay a baby in my mother's arms and for new life to be breathed into the walls of Carmen de las Estrellas, heaving with memories and ghosts. This is the first time since before Father's death that her eyes are clear and bright; that they are free of the pain that shines through them even when she is smiling.

'What are you calling her?' Mother whispers.

Henry crouches down beside the chair Mother sits on. He has barely taken his eyes from our daughter since she has been born but now he turns to me, his eyes lost in the creases of his smile.

'We'll christen her Carmen,' I say, 'because officially we must give her the name of a saint. But her name is Paloma. *Se llama* Paloma. Henry, what's the word for that in English again?'

'Dove,' Henry whispers. He bends down and tenderly kisses our daughter's forehead. 'Symbol of peace.'

CHAPTER FIFTEEN
PALOMA

Spring 1958

Semana Santa, Holy Week. Probably the most important event in the Catholic church's calendar and, as
such, we have to 'be seen' attending. It gives me the creeps,
the long black gowns and pointy hoods on the heads of
the *penitentes,* walking solemnly along the streets; many
people even walk with no shoes to make their journey of
repentance more severe.

'We'll go if we must,' grumbles Papá in the safety of
our home, 'but I'll be damned if I allow my children to
scratch their feet up.' Mamá whole-heartedly agrees and
shoes, much to my relief, stay on. But we do carry small
candles that flicker amongst the thousands of others as we
wind agonisingly slowly along the Paseo del Darro, the
river rushing alongside us.

Everybody comes to Semana Santa. And I mean everybody. Even elderly people who are too ill or wheelchair-
bound are carried. On this occasion, I'm stuck with my

family behind a particularly gruesome, bloodied statue of Christ carried on a float on dozens of shoulders. The procession seems to be moving even slower than I remember on previous years, probably because a number of people keep breaking off to hurl themselves to the ground, begging forgiveness from *Christo y los santos*.

I am feeling claustrophobic and the constant bugle calls from the army trumpeters are giving me a headache. No more, *por favor*, no more, I think after one showy demonstration of an elderly woman hurling herself to her knees and wailing a never-ending prayer of repentance. I'm right behind the woman and am forced to stop and watch but the crowd to my right are carried forward in the surge, taking with it my entire family. I crane my neck upwards to catch sight of them, only to see Papá waving at me and mouthing 'See you back at home!' before he's swallowed and disappears from sight. Great, I think. Now I'm stuck behind this wailing woman who's clearly begging forgiveness for every minor misdemeanour in her life and there's no sign of escape.

And right at this moment, I hear a sigh of impatience coming from beside me. I turn to see a boy of around the same age as me with thick brown hair, dressed in black. He's glaring at the old woman, his mouth clenched grimly and I know, instantly, that I've found an accomplice. He doesn't want to be here any more than I do and he too is being pulled along in this Semana Santa charade under the watchful eye of civil guards, mayors, Falangists, bishops and priests.

As the old woman arthritically pulls herself to her feet, the boy looks at me and, in much the same way that I make an instant judgement of him, he does the same. He reads 'friend' in my eyes and grins. I smile back and at that moment the crowd behind the woman starts to move again. As we're carried forwards, I suddenly care a little less about the snail's pace the procession is moving as I become more aware than I ever have been in my life of the male presence beside me. Just five minutes later, the old woman repeats her theatrical performance in front of us and perhaps it's the volume of her cries that gives the boy the confidence to lean in ever so slightly towards me and whisper through one side of his mouth, '*¿Como te llamas?*'

I glance nervously around me but every other noise is drowned out by the call of the bugle and, grabbing my chance, I attempt his method of speaking through the side of the mouth whilst barely moving my lips.

'Paloma,' I whisper as I lean close.

'*Yo soy Antonio.*'

With that, the bugle stops and as the woman drags herself up once again I notice in horror that blood is pouring from one of her knees, spraying the cobbles beneath us. I glance at Antonio but he just shakes his head slightly. As we start to move again around a particularly narrow section of the street, a surge of people push from behind like the swell of a wave and I'm thrown against Antonio's side. It all happens so quickly, but as I am pushed against him, he catches my hand in his. I don't even look at him. I know if I did, we'd draw attention from behind. As my cheeks burn, I stare unblinkingly ahead of me, more grateful at that moment than any other that I'm wearing long sleeves that cover my hands.

His hand is warm and smooth and as we walk, thankfully all crammed in together as the narrow stretch of road continues, I feel giddy with happiness. And something else. This is a boy, the opposite sex. I've never been interested in a boy before but this unexpected warmth and contact makes me feel weak with something I instantly recognise as desire. I long to drop the candle I'm holding in my left hand, turn to this stranger and run my fingers through his thick hair and kiss him hard on the lips. I want the road to never widen again so that we can stay pressed up together like this, my hand in his, forever. I don't know if his family are beside him and he doesn't care or whether, like me, he's become separated from them. But as we continue our slow and steady pace I feel my hand tingling and burning.

Incredible, really, that up until this point and unlike many of my friends, I haven't even been curious about what it's like to hold a boy's hand or to kiss him. I've always felt there are far more interesting and important things to think about. There was the cinema incident, not long ago, when a boy from the school across the street from ours asked a girl in my class to go with him. This, of course, isn't the done thing, particularly not for impressionable teenagers. Either my friend had to be chaperoned by a parent who'd sit in the middle of the two of them, or she had to go with a group of friends and he'd sit on the opposite side of the cinema. The boy in question opted for the latter, poor soul, having to pay for a gaggle of school-girls' cinema entrances whilst he could only sit and cast the occasional glance over in my friend's direction. Although this was nothing to do with me and I was uninterested in the mechanics of the secret longing that must have passed between the two of them, the experience left me horri-bly frustrated. What I really wanted was to beckon the boy over to sit with us beside my pretty friend and if they wanted to hold hands or steal a kiss, well, so what?

But now, suddenly, because of a chance encounter with a boy walking beside me at Semana Santa, I want it all. I want to kiss him, to stroke him, to feel him in my arms and to peel his clothes off so I can see what his body is like under them. And suddenly the hushed moans from my parents' room next door come into focus and make sense and I want it; I want to discover what it's all about and what makes a person make sounds like that.

I wonder if Antonio is feeling even a fraction of what I am. I can't know for sure, but I sense that he might be. Something is passing through our hands, a kind of cur-rent, travelling along every nerve ending into our bodies. As the procession continues, I know that any minute the road will widen once more and that will be it, we must drop hands. As though he's thinking the same thing, An-tonio gives my hand a slight squeeze and then, seconds later, I hear a collective exhale, almost like the loosening of a belt after a heavy meal, as people spread out more comfortably along the street.

At the moment his hand drops, the flame of my candle blows out. My hand feels cold without the warmth of his and I stretch out my fingers that have been still for so long. Antonio reaches in towards me with the candle he holds in his right hand and, as the flame ignites the wick, his eyes catch mine for just a moment. But in this moment I see a few things: I see that he has a small mole directly above one eyelid and I see that he has a few freckles scattered across his cheeks. But more importantly, I see the desire that is stamped, without question, across his face.

And that is it. I hear the man on the other side of him say something and realise it's probably his father and stare straight ahead as Antonio vanishes with the fading bugle calls and I'm left alone to continue my agonisingly slow journey home.

Over the following weeks, I can't stop thinking about Antonio. Actually, the truth is, I can't stop thinking about sex. What does it feel like? Does it hurt? How often do my parents do it? Do my friends think about it much? I'm consumed with a sexually charged curiosity and in the privacy and dark of my own bedroom at night, I begin to creep my fingers further and further down between my legs.

It must be a couple of months after Semana Santa that I see him again. I'm out with my father and brothers on one of our customary trips to the city. Papá has had his shave at the barber's, we've bought some fruit from the market and now we're making our way back home. It's a beautiful day so we decide to go home the long way by the river. When I see a group of boys sitting on the wall chatting, I know immediately that the one closest is Antonio. As I walk past, I stare hard at him, willing him to turn and look. And as he turns, he does a small double-take. I don't look back but hear the murmur of voices and the sound of feet against cobbles and I know that he's following me.

Every so often, but not enough to raise my father and brothers' suspicion, I glance back and sure enough, there he is, about a hundred yards behind, hands in pockets as he whistles to himself. My heart beats furiously and several times I think how absurd this all is and that I should just tell Papá I've seen a friend. At least that would be a legitimate way to get him into the house, as no doubt Papá would invite him in for a drink. But I purse my lips; I know that my brothers would tease me horribly for having a male friend and it's the last thing I feel like at this moment.

When we reach Carmen de las Estrellas, Papá fumbles for his key in his pocket, which gives me an opportunity.

'Papá,' I say, before I've barely had the chance to think. 'My hair clip has fallen out.' I am already walking away from them. 'I think it dropped just round the corner.'

Papá looks at me, his blue eyes surprised but trusting, and I feel the slightest pang of guilt. 'Alright,' he calls. 'I'll leave the door open,' and with that, he and my brothers vanish into the courtyard.

As I hurry round the corner, Antonio is there. He catches my hands in his, quickly looks around and then murmurs in a low voice, 'Can I come to you tonight?'

'Tonight?' I repeat as I feel my stomach flipping. I feel my head move up and down and my cheeks burn. 'Come at one o'clock. My parents will definitely be asleep by then.'

'*Bueno*,' he says, and as I turn to move, he catches my arm and hurriedly pulls me back and kisses me deeply on my lips, the kind of kiss I so longed to give him at Semana Santa. I pull away and run back to my house, not looking back.

We are unspeakably foolish to take such a risk; every step of our meeting that night is hazardous, from Antonio avoiding the *guardia civil* or other prying eyes as he makes the journey through the streets up to the Albaicín late at night, to not awaking my parents, grandmother or brothers. And of course there is the question of who he really is and if it is safe to be with him – I know nothing about him. But instinct plays its hand and, even more than that, desire. Risky as it is, I know I have to see it through.

Long after my family are asleep, I tiptoe down the stairs, avoiding the single step with the creak (I've been testing them that afternoon) and then standing with my back against the door, waiting and hardly breathing. Moments after I hear the grandfather clock from the conservatory strike one, there is a gentle tap on the door and slowly, very slowly, I open it. We stand there and look at one another as I scan his open face that, somehow, I implicitly trust. Without a word, I take Antonio's hand, pull him through and, after closing the door behind him, lead him through the courtyard and house to the garden. I know that there is one tiny corner of the garden out of sight of all the upstairs bedrooms and I lead Antonio to this corner where the lone fig tree stands, as the warm summer night breeze floats through my hair.

Romantic it isn't. It's lust of the purest kind and as we grope and fumble under a mercifully slender crescent moon, I remember the small mole above his eyelid as he moves over me and a searing pain, mingled with something far more pleasurable than I've ever experienced on those dark nights alone in my room. But more than any of that, as he lies next to me when it's all over, his breath heavy and irregular and we stare up at the canopy of leaves, I feel triumphant. Not that I've lost my virginity, but that we've done something unthinkable in the strait-laced world we live in. And as I pull my skirt back on and listen to Antonio's breathing regulate beside me whilst my family sleep just metres away, I grin up into the star-streaked sky.

I don't discuss anything that's going through my head with Antonio. It's strange, but I don't want to know what he's thinking, because that would make us closer. And I don't want to be close to him, not in that way. I do believe that we've used each other but somehow, without words, we implicitly understand that our relationship won't go anywhere. We are two creatures trapped in the system's undergrowth but we have managed to break through to the surface together, for just a short while. Which proves to us that the system isn't without cracks.

Over the following days, I veer between a crippling fear – *What if I get pregnant? Did somebody see him come to my house? What was I thinking?* – and an elation which leaves me breathless in its wake. When my period comes, I stand in the bathroom at home and laugh and laugh.

'Paloma?' Mamá calls from outside. '*Estás bien?*'

'I'm fine,' I call back. 'I'm just remembering a funny joke from today.'

She doesn't, of course, suspect a thing. And I never tell a soul about my encounter with the boy from Semana Santa. A short while later, the nuns run a door-to-door campaign across the city, asking girls to avoid dresses with short sleeves. As I open the door and listen to what the nuns have to say, I smile sweetly and nod my head, all the while thinking *if you only knew.*

The Granada of my childhood is not a beautiful place. It is full of neglect (not of me, of my city which is poor, damp and dusty), suspicion and cinema. From a young age, I'd catch the tram with Mamá from Plaza Nueva to Cine Doré for our fortnightly reality escape. I was so excited, I thought I might be sick. We'd hand over our precious *pesetas* (we sacrificed a sack of wheat every other week for our cinema experience but I tell you, it was worth it) and squeezed into the narrow seats. From there, we watched images of glamorous women, cowboys and pirates flit across the screen. I didn't listen to the words much as the storylines had been censored and dubbed but I couldn't care less. I wasn't even bothered that the *policia armada* lurked in the aisles each and every show. I was in heaven and I could sit there forever, breathing in the smell of burnt popcorn and cigarette smoke.

One time, the film stopped in the middle. Just like that. A large notice flashed across the screen saying there were two people in row J who were indulging in immoral behaviour. I knew that we were sitting in that row and I prodded Mamá.

'Is it us?' I whispered.

She frowned and shook her head and, as I looked to the right of me, I saw a couple blushing as red as the screen curtains, staring ahead with stony faces. Their hands were planted firmly in their laps and they looked the same kind of age as my parents. What could they possibly be doing that was so terrible? Another message flashed up, this time telling us that if these people continued, their seat numbers would be pointed out and they'd be ejected from the cinema. I stared at the woman beside me who blushed an even deeper shade of red and shifted in her seat. And then back at Mamá, who gave nothing away. It wasn't till much later, when we were back home, that I asked her what she thought they were doing.

'They were probably just holding hands,' Mamá replied, shrugging her shoulders.

'Holding hands,' I repeated blankly. Surely not. 'But what's wrong with holding hands, Mamá?' I pushed her.

She sighed and shook her head. '*Nada*. There's nothing wrong with holding hands. Nothing at all. This is just the way we must live.'

This is just the way we must live. I was only eight years old at that time, but I knew very well that this wasn't how Mamá wanted to live. Nor Papá. And I certainly didn't want to live in a world in which a husband and wife can't go to the cinema and hold hands. Every bone of my eight-year-old body tightened in indignation and at that very moment I thought to myself: this isn't how it will be. This is *not* how it will be when I am a grown-up.

Am I spoilt growing up? A little, perhaps: being the only daughter, I'm looked up to by my younger brother Eduardo, indulged by my middle brother Dani and watched over lovingly by both my parents. But I need this kind of cushioning from within my family, because growing up in 1950s Granada is oppressive to say the very least. My family has to conform, just like everybody else's. As soon as I can talk I implicitly understand that the things we discuss at home stay at home. There are eyes and ears everywhere and in many ways I don't trust anybody outside my own family. Not even the girls at school I call my friends.

But the truth is I don't have many friends. I enjoy my own company more than anyone else's. I love cinema and books above all else and the friends I do have are those who don't expect me to make conversation or tell jokes or entertain them. In other words, people who expect nothing from me because that way they won't feel let down. I've always preferred quieter people, because it's what's left unsaid that's fascinating to me.

Mamá and Papá do just about everything they can think of to remain outside the scrutiny of those hovering in the wings, waiting for them to slip up. Papá has converted to Catholicism and each and every Sunday we troop to duller-than-dull mass, backs straight as rods as we shift about on the hard wooden pews. Oh, and you couldn't find a stricter Catholic school in Granada if you tried. It's run by monks and nuns and each morning, we have to sing a hideous song at the top of our lungs: '*Franco, Franco, que cara más simpatico!*' I sing this hymn to our dictator with mock force, imagining myself to be acting in a play. Honestly, it's the only way I can get through it, because as a little girl, I even take *myself* by surprise, so strong is my loathing for the general. All I really want to do is shout out above the throng of voices, 'Franco, Franco, how I hate your face!' and one time, the desire to do this is so strong that I have to bite on my hand so hard I draw blood. Does Franco know that our entire city is often plunged into darkness for hours on end? Does he know that his people sit huddled around one of their few rationed candles, waiting for light to return? Probably not, and even if he did, I can guarantee he wouldn't have cared less.

No, the Granada of my childhood isn't a happy place. It's decaying and poverty-stricken and even when the sun shines, everything somehow seems grey. Mamá buys wheat and olive oil on the black market, there is little music and even less dancing. I long to learn how to dance. But dancing, of course, is ungodly. I am often cold, even more often hungry. Thick layers of dust cover everything, there are peeling notices on unpainted walls and the street lamps rarely shine. Winter's the hardest time, and our only source of heating is the *brasero*, a metal pan which my brothers and I take out to the street and heap with the powdery dried pulp of olives after the oil has been extracted, bought at great expense. We pile kindling wood on top, set it alight and fan it till the powder smoulders, then rush inside and slide it under the dining room table into a special fitting. A woollen cover is draped over the table and round our legs so that at least our legs are toasty warm while we eat our meals, even though the rest of our bodies are freezing.

As I get older, I see how much my poor papá hates how we have to live with such double standards. He is an ex-International Brigader, after all. Yet the face he presents to the world, or to our corner of Granada at least, is that of respectable, middle-class *caballero*. It's important he has a well-tailored suit; that he parades down the street before lunch on Sundays wearing his well-shined shoes and smoking a foreign cigar. It's a grotesque charade for Papá, but I dread to think what might happen to him should he act otherwise and, God forbid, people find out what brought him to Spain in the first place. What it must cost my father, the socialist, to maintain this culture of *fachada* – keeping up appearances – makes me realise just how deep his love for my mother runs.

What with the light problems and the hot water problems, Granada's barbers run a roaring trade and once a week Papá takes Dani, Eduardo and I down to the city where we watch him being shaved by a thick-set man with a cleft in his chin, black hair sprouting from his ears and

only four fingers on each hand. Despite this, he's a wizard
with the shaving knife and Papá will go to no other. We
all long to ask what happened to his fingers, but Papá
strictly forbids it.

After Papá's been shaved, we walk back through Plaza
Nueva, passing the water sellers who lead their donkeys
through the streets, covered in bright woollen blankets
and little brass bells. I always feel sorry for the poor beasts,
struggling under the weight of the metal canisters filled
with water, but any time they slow down, their owners
slap them on the rump and call out to passers-by '*¡Agua!*
¡Agua! ¡Fresca como la nieve!'

Occasionally we buy water from them on summer
days, or hot potatoes that are sold in used jam tins in
the winter. Holes are punched round the tin with a nail
and we wrap handkerchiefs round them, discovering
that this way the tins make fabulous hand-warmers all
the way home before we then devour the potatoes. More
often than the water or potatoes though, Papá buys us
chumbo from the *gitanos*, sweet cacti fruit which we suck
noisily through our teeth. I love stopping to buy from
the gypsies, and it always makes me wish we could see
more of Mar and her family. Whenever we do get the
chance to visit them in their *pueblo* in the suburbs, I'm
always amazed that they once lived at Carmen de las Estrellas; that my grandmother was brave enough to take
such a risk, even with her own family to consider and at
a time when food shortages were even more severe than
they are now.

Sometimes, to escape from the heavy heat of the summer days, my family take the train out of the city to the beach, though I must say I never enjoy these excursions. Because of the strict segregation at the beaches, Mamá and I have to sit on the other side of a high barrier from Papá and my brothers. Despite this separation, we must still bathe with all our clothes on and I loathe that sensation of my dress growing heavier and heavier and winding round my ankles as I flap uselessly about in the water. The only part of this trip I look forward to is buying a *granizada de limón* – a tall glass with crushed ice, lemon and lashings of sugar – from the station café before boarding the train back to Granada where Abuela waits for us at the station.

My wonderful abuela. When I'm growing up, we often sit together in the kitchen listening to soap operas on the radio, awful though they are with their thinly veiled trumpeting of traditional values and pathetic tales of love and longing. Of course my abuela is intelligent enough to recognise this too, but it's a harmless pleasure and they sometimes make her laugh. Watching Abuela's face crease in amusement is like seeing Granada's *salida del sol*, the sunrise that spreads its gentle glow over the valley. But just as I only occasionally witness the sunrise, so too is the smile of my abuela a gift. I learnt from a young age that, infuriating though these soap operas may be, I'd have a better chance of basking in the ripples of her happiness there in the kitchen than anywhere else. Sometimes we just sit at the table together, listening to the dramas unwind and other times we make cookies. Mamá tells me that when she was young, Abuela would write fortunes and place them inside the shells. When I was very small, I asked her on one of her far-away days if we could do that and she looked at me strangely, almost as though she couldn't quite place me. *One day*, she told me. And then I wished I'd never asked her, because the last thing I wanted was to make my abuela sad. But then, many weeks later, she suddenly brought it up again with no prompting from me. She had tied an apron around her waist, plaited her hair and coiled it onto her head and beckoned me from the doorway of the kitchen. 'Paloma,' she said with her sunrise smile, 'shall we make fortune cookies?'

I know, of course, that my abuelo died and that he shouldn't have. There is a single photograph of him in Carmen de las Estrellas, on the mantelpiece in the conservatory, taken on the day of his marriage to Abuela. He is handsome with thick curly hair and shining eyes and looks like an older version of my middle brother, Dani. But strangely, more than the photograph, faded with time, I like to look at the framed drawings of him that Pablo made many years ago. There are several dotted about the house and many times when I've looked closely at them over the years, I've found the clouded imprint of fingertips against glass and don't doubt for a minute it is Abuela's hand pressing against her husband, willing him back to life.

As for Antonio, the boy from Semana Santa, I see him a few more times before he vanishes from my life completely.

That first night that he comes to my house, before he leaves, he wordlessly stuffs a scrunched-up piece of paper into my hand before slipping through the heavy wooden doors. When I open it, I read a single line: the name of his school and the street it's on. I am well aware of what is at stake here; that the reputation of my family and my own name for that matter could be stained forever should I be found out. But I have that reckless confidence of a fifteen-year-old girl and, despite the risks, I'm willing to see how far I can push the boundaries of the system.

I always walk straight home after school, but one day, head low, I hurry to Antonio's school. I know exactly where it is because my parents considered that school for my brothers. I linger at a distance, ignoring the surprised looks of the boys who flood from the gates. Antonio spots me first and moves towards me slowly but stealthily, with the hint of a smile on his face to suggest he's been expecting me. We don't say a word but, glancing around to check that nobody is watching, I raise the palm of one hand towards him on which I have inked the words *donde* and *cuando*. Where and when. I watch as Antonio's black eyebrows knit in fierce concentration before he murmurs, in a barely audible voice, *same place, tonight*, before walking past me into the throng of boys.

This time he brings a condom with him, a thick, rubbery thing that is agonising to put on. I have no idea where he's managed to get it from and don't ask, but it's a huge relief that I don't have to worry about getting pregnant. Though we say so little to one another, I feel that I know this person; that in many ways, he is just like me – my male shadow. As we cling to one another beneath the canopy of the fig tree, we're both smiling, emboldened by our bravery. Nothing else matters apart from that moment, that tingling pleasure of feeling his body against mine and the knowledge that, yet again, we have got away with it.

And so the pattern is set in motion: I go to his school and with a signal or whisper our plan is made. But then comes the long summer vacation and I have no idea how to find him. When Antonio doesn't come to my house, I assume that his family must have left Granada for the season. But when term starts again and I arrive once more at his school gates, he isn't there. I go another two or three times before acknowledging that he's not coming back. I'm surprised how unemotional I feel about this. After all, I've been closer to Antonio than anyone else before and risked so much to be with him. But instead, I feel a deep sense of acceptance that this is the end of our story and that what we achieved together would only have worked with him and no other. I do still think about him now and again – wonder where he is and if he's happy, and if we'd talked more, what we'd have talked about. But then rather than being left with a sense of regret, I feel only gratitude that his hand met mine on that candlelit evening from within the stifling folds of the Semana Santa crowd.

CHAPTER SIXTEEN
ISABEL

Autumn 1958

At the age of sixty-four, to me Mother is still the most beautiful woman in the world. She wears her hair, now streaked liberally with silver, with a thin plait as a top layer and her dark eyes are wide and shrewd. In the years following Father's death, I found myself in a perpetual state of something close to mourning for the confidante Mother had been. But as the years went on and the rawness of the pain slowly lessened, the Mother of old would increasingly appear once more. There are certain people in her life who manage to rekindle that old spark in such a way that I can almost believe she is the same person. Paloma's presence, for example, instantly draws her out of a trough of memories into which she sometimes retreats and I see so much of them in one another. And then there is Mar, who continues to play a significant role in her life – the beautiful, unfathomable Mar who at the age of thirty-three declared to my mother that she never wanted to involve herself with another man for the rest of her life. Up until now she has, as far as I know, been true to her word.

Every so often Mar turns up at the house unannounced. She's never been a talkative person herself and she and Mother slip back into that easy camaraderie that never fails to move or surprise me as they wordlessly take up a task together which can last for hours. Mar tells us little about her apartment on the outskirts of Granada and she has only invited us to visit them two or three times over the years. I think she is ashamed of her home; ashamed of this suburb where fields and orchards have been bulldozed to make way for low-cost housing that sprouts up from gaps in the pavement like grey weeds. This apartment is as far from her roots as it is possible to travel with its cardboard-flimsy walls and filthy streets with children scavenging for scraps of food in the gutter like animals.

Sometimes I think it's better that Abuela Aurelia didn't live to see the day that her family left Carmen de las Estrellas. She was so fiercely proud of her *gitana* traditions that to have returned anywhere other than her cave dwelling would have been unbearable for her. It was hard enough to change their lifestyle so dramatically from living far from the city in a rural community to a comparatively luxurious house in the Albaicín. But when the war ended and Mar insisted it was time for her family to leave, she was wise enough to realise that, no matter how much she longed for it, to have returned to the cave would have been nothing short of suicide. By then, they had all been burnt out by a terrifying group known as the Black Squad. After destroying the dwellings beyond recognition, they hunted down any *gitanos* that still lurked in the city and murdered them. We heard stories about gypsies on the run in the early days of the conflict coming face to face with men in uniform and then, after looking at their badge to see which side they were on, saluting and declaring either 'Franco is my father!' or 'Stalin is my father!' whilst of course, they couldn't have cared less about either man. One particular story runs of a poor short-sighted *gitano* who thought he saw the opposite emblem declaring allegiance to Stalin and being shot on the spot. It was, of course, just a story, but true or not, Mar was wise to not attempt to return to her old life.

To this day, I realise how lucky we were that Abuela Aurelia swallowed her pride sufficiently to ask my mother for protection. Vast numbers of their friends and kin didn't survive the war. But there were even more who perished in the following years. I think that there are two main reasons why Mar's family has managed to escape a similar fate. First of all, ever since the military rising against the Republic, Granadinos have been afraid not to be thought of as good Catholics and wear badges on their lapels known as '*santos*'. These represent their loyalty to the faith and, whilst they aren't an absolute guarantee of safety, they certainly help. It must cost Mar, a confirmed atheist, a great deal to sport a *santo* on her clothes and insist that her children do the same. Particularly Pablo, after everything he's been through. But she can be very persuasive when she wants and every time they come to visit us, they look every bit the devout yet impoverished Catholic family.

The other reason they aren't sniffed out by informers, I'm certain, is due to my Tío Miguel. I have no proof of this, but I feel sure that for all my uncle's faults, he continues to act as something of a guardian angel over both our family and Mar's. We never see him, but we know that he's risen to prominent heights in the Falange and that he holds great authority. When he came to our house that time to warn us of what was on the horizon, he said that he could ensure our protection up to a point. Whilst it was through no love of any of us, I think he felt some convoluted sense of duty that the child he fathered was now living at Carmen de las Estrellas. I honestly believe that, for all his unpleasantness, Miguel has a conscience. Perhaps I'm naïve, but I believe that if he could have stopped Father's murder, he would have done.

I know that he never loved Mar – what he felt for her, I'm sure, was far closer to lust. But he certainly never wanted her dead either, and my uncle exercises a great deal of control on the goings on in Granada. We are living in frightening times in which the end of the war was certainly not the end of fear. If anything, it just began in a far more sinister form. As well as the Black Squad, both the civil government and the military are responsible for compiling lists of citizens whom, in their eyes, have strayed from the straight and narrow or are known to have left-wing leanings. These unfortunate people are

arrested, often tortured and then shot without trial. Our
family hardly has a clear record: it would be easy enough
to do some digging and discover two Republican parents,
a daughter who nursed on the Republican side and her
husband the former International Brigader, not to mention what my brother Fernando has been involved in, and
I maintain that both our family and Mar's have escaped
reprisals largely due to Tío Miguel.

When he died of a heart attack last year, I went to
the funeral with Mar. Mother refused to go, I suppose
out of loyalty to Father. It was incredible, for despite the
years that had passed and the way he had treated Mar,
I couldn't help noticing the tears that silently streamed
down her cheeks beneath her black veil as she sat beside
me. I also watched his wife sitting in the front row of the
church and I'm almost certain she had a very small yet
perceptible smile on her face.

It breaks my heart to see Mar and her family living
in such poverty. We save as much food for them as we
can muster together, yet we barely have enough for ourselves. But in these dark days, a gentle ray of optimism
filters through to us, infecting us all. Fernando and Alejandro are the only two amongst my siblings who have
remained living with us at Carmen de las Estrellas and
we all watched the blossoming friendship between Fernando and Beatriz and chuckled at my brother's tongue-
tied stammering around this lovely young girl whilst they
lived with us. But we didn't imagine for a single moment
that his feelings for her might be reciprocated.

The day that Mar's family left our home and we waved sadly goodbye to them, I must admit that I noticed the look that passed between Beatriz and my brother. It was a long, mournful gaze that lasted longer than was necessary. I forgot about it instantly, but when the two of them announced just a few months later that they were passionately in love, that look suddenly came back to me. Fernando was only a boy when he'd first fallen for Beatriz but a man when she left. We never did find out at exactly what stage she started to return his affection, but it's clear now that it was going on for a long time, right under our noses.

I believe that if it weren't for the sweet persuasiveness of Beatriz that my brother might not be alive today. In his late teens and early twenties, partly in memory of Father but also through his own genuine conviction, Fernando became far more politically motivated. He was furious about the way that the victors of the civil war were treating the defeated. 'The fascists have won, haven't they?' I heard him say bitterly on more than one occasion. 'What more do they want?'

Fernando heard about a guerrilla band in Granada led by four revolutionary brothers, the sons of our one-time local butcher. He knew that they'd succeeded in kidnapping a prominent fascist Granadino as well as carrying out various robberies and gunfights with the civil guard. Word had it that they were so fierce that even the police were frightened to go near them. Fernando started to spend more and more time with the brothers and was evasive when we questioned him on his return. He wouldn't listen to any of us if we begged him to be more cautious; he was far too stubborn. Yet Beatriz managed to convince him that the activities of the brothers were doomed and that if he continued to work alongside them, he'd end up like his father. I'm certain that she was right, for after the brothers' period of keeping the civil guard at arm's length, eventually their hiding place was dynamited, killing two of them. Over the next couple of years the remaining two as well as many of their followers were either shot or took their own lives.

It's always very touching to watch Beatriz and Fernando together, for my brother has never lost his mischievous air. But you only have to take one look at him when he's talking to Beatriz to notice the calm in his normally forceful voice and also Beatriz's coy smile when he speaks to her. Over the years, they've discussed marriage many times, but always come to the same conclusion that until the day arrives in which they can marry freely in the traditional *gitano* fashion, they will simply live together.

Pablo has moved to the suburbs close to his family but in a different apartment. I remember that Abuela Aurelia always said that Pablo didn't talk not because he couldn't, but rather that he wouldn't. I was never sure about her theory, but I suppose she knew her grandson better than I. I was always very fond of Pablo, right from those early days when Mother took us to the cave and my brothers and sister ran around with Mar's children playing tag. I loved watching him transform a blank sheet of paper into such a real and touching representation of the scene before us. Drawing was, for him, everything. Or even more than everything; the sole thing to keep him sane after he was tortured and finally returned to us.

As for Joaquín, I often questioned whether I was biased with regards to his talent. But it came as no surprise to any of us when he moved away from Carmen de las Estrellas and started to play with more and more prestigious musicians, though how he managed to do this whilst keeping a low profile remains a mystery because music in those days, particularly flamenco music, was frowned upon in the extreme. As for Joaquín's relationship with Mar, as the years have passed they have become very close and he often visits them in their *pueblo*. At the same time, he has remained loyal to Mother as her eldest son, something that Mar has never seemed concerned by.

The house of Sara Rodriguez, my dear friend I shared so much with, was boarded up when I returned to Granada to discover the fate of Father. For months I made enquiries as the whereabouts of her family, but nobody could help me. It wasn't until five years later that I received a letter from her. Her family had fled from Granada and headed northwards, making the gruelling journey over the Pyrenees into France. They remained in a makeshift camp on the coast in appalling conditions alongside thousands of others, being treated more like criminals than refugees. Sara lost two of her grandparents, a nephew and her youngest sister in that camp. Eventually, her remaining family were amongst the lucky ones who escaped from that living hell on a boat bound for Mexico City where the socialist government received them warmly.

❋ ❋ ❋

Living in fascist-controlled Spain has become less stifling as the years have passed, but it is never, ever easy. We have to keep our heads down and lie through our teeth to prevent attracting unwanted attention. Despite being the most patient man I've ever known, life for Henry is particularly hard for many reasons. Every ninety days, he has to traipse to the *Comisaría* to renew his visa because no matter how long he's lived in Spain, he remains a foreigner and people are extremely suspicious of *extranjeros*. He is known as '*el inglés*', many people uttering it with contempt. I think I feel more offended than my husband, who accepts his name with his typical good-humoured grace. But besides our hushed conversations at home, Henry has little outlet for what is really going through his mind. He is rarely able to visit his parents in England and because we know that letters are often intercepted and read, he can't even use these as a means to talk about his true feelings.

Work is hard to come by but Henry managed to find a job several years after the end of the civil war. One of the regime's myths is that Spanish is such a rich language that it is completely impossible for *extranjeros* to master it, particularly if their native tongue is English. Henry finds this amusing and whilst it is obvious to all that he is a *guiri* with his fair hair and blue eyes, over the years his talent at speaking Spanish, even the intricacies of thick Andaluz, is undeniable. The steady trickle of tourists visiting Spain is slowly increasing and the fact that he can also speak fairly good French enables him to work as a tour guide at the Alhambra Palace. He comes home one day telling me that a stony-faced British colonel asked Henry if, now that he has made Spain his home, he supports Spain's attempt to regain control of British-occupied Gibraltar. For things are heating up in this department.

A year after Queen Elizabeth's coronation in England, a visit to Gibraltar is planned and the Spanish press goes wild during this time, requesting the British government to cancel the visit as it is supposedly an insult to the people of Spain. But no cancellation comes, and just ahead of the event, poor Henry gets caught up in some of the demonstrations on his way back from work. One day, when he returns home, two hours late, he looks shocked and unsettled and Mother and I gasp as we notice that his shirt is torn near the collar.

'What happened, Henry?' Mother asks.

'It was like a witch-hunt, Luisa. People were marching through the streets yelling "*¡Gibraltar Español! ¡Viva Franco! ¡Viva España!*" Then they were yelling for the downfall of England and death to Winston Churchill—'

'*¡Dios!*'

'Honestly. Lots of them were wearing Falangista uniforms and carrying Spanish flags and red and black banners – they were just kids, half of them – but pretty threatening, I can tell you.'

'And they saw you?' I ask.

'Yes.' Henry frowns and runs a hand through his hair. 'I was frantically searching around on the ground to see if anyone had dropped a cap to hide this damned hair colour of mine, but I ran out of time and a group of them came towards me, yelling "Where are you from?" Well, there was hardly any point trying to make out I was Spanish, so I just told them as calmly as I could that I was English, but I lived in Granada.'

'And then?'

'And then one of the louts at the front started to spit and jab at me.'

Anger wells up inside me as I shake my head in disbelief, glancing beside me to see Mother's features etched into a deep frown.

'He was calling me every name under the sun, quite a ring-leader, I should say. I truly thought he was going to physically harm me, he was in such a frenzy. He was puffing out his chest and then snarled at me and then...'

I hold my breath and nod.

'...then somebody next to him whispered in his ear and they both nodded and then he said to me "Kiss the Spanish flag"!'

'*Como?*' Mother cries, with such force that we both look at her in surprise. 'They made you kiss the flag?'

Henry nods grimly. '*Sí.*' Reflexively, he looks around him and adds quietly, 'Pathetic, isn't it?'

I frown and hug him tightly. 'At least they didn't hurt you, *cariño.*'

He pulls away and smiles at us both, though I can see he is still shaken. 'When they decided they'd had enough fun with me, they all headed off in the direction of the

British Consul, no doubt to see what fun could be had up there. I hope Davenport's faring alright, poor bugger.'

Henry goes off to make coffee and Mother and I sit down. Anger is bubbling up inside me and I know Mother feels it too. When I look at her, I see that look of defiance of old on her face and though I'm horrified at the treatment my husband has experienced, I can't deny I feel a surge of gladness at her indignation.

Henry, I know, doesn't dislike his work. For a long time, however, he cannot shake the feeling of discomfort that as a man, he should be permitted to work whereas in my case, it is close to impossible, a source of great frustration for me. It has been many years now that I've dreamt of my hospice; of caring for people who are dying in a loving, humanitarian environment. But I simply am not allowed to work. Furthermore, this potentially provocative work lies outside a religious context and I know that I would be hounded down by fierce Catholic groups and severely punished if I should be caught. However, though it's perhaps a foolish step, it's a risk I am prepared to take as I am filled with energy and ideas and very slowly and cautiously, people begin to hear about me.

Though a vast number of left-wing Granadinos have either not survived the civil war or have fled, there are of course those who have remained. People who, like us, have to vocally compromise their beliefs yet whose true ideals burn brighter than ever before. It is to these kinds of people that my services have become known.

To this day I'm amazed how far my reputation has spread whilst managing to keep it in check and preventing my work being found out by the numerous *mangas verdes* and other informers that creep around Granada. A message is posted through the letterbox of Carmen de las Estrellas (the door is *never* knocked at), and as one or another of us are often passing through the courtyard, someone always lays eyes on it and brings it to me. I wait a short while and then go to the address given on the note. There, I enter the house of the person in question and sit with them. Talk to them. If possible, be with them in their final moments. People often ask me how it makes sense that I should take precedence over the dying person's closest family members. Yet I always explain that I am by no means more important than the people they know and love. Rather, it is less difficult for a person on the outside to deal with the death of someone they care for so much. I only serve to lessen the strain of that time and help them, as much as I possibly can, to not feel afraid but rather at peace.

It must hit a chord somehow, for rarely a week passes during which I'm not called upon. Naturally no money is exchanged and I draw hope and energy from these encounters, meeting wonderful and wise and brave people. There was the head teacher of the Republican school my siblings and I attended who was tortured during the war and finally succumbs to his wounds and his nightmares; and the first female professor of medicine who had her title stripped but held her pride very much intact. I even go to the cousin of Federico García Lorca who, from his deathbed, whispers stories of his wonderful cousin. And all the while, I long to open a hospice and create it in my head down to the finest detail. It's ironic really, that all these years of going to confession and inventing 'sins' for the priest to atone, what I really want to say is 'Father, I am helping left-wing Republicans to die. But I'm not repenting, I'm very proud of it.'

But of course, thoughts and deeds are a bridgeless chasm in these days and we all carry on as best we can, given the circumstances. Not a day passes that I don't feel a surge of protective love for my husband, my children and my mother and I know that, even if it takes everything I possess, I must keep my family quiet and close and safe.

CHAPTER SEVENTEEN
LUISA

Summer 1959

Loneliness is a curious thing, for it can overtake a person when one is the least alone physically speaking. Some years I have borne it better than others, but this summer, even with family and friends constantly flitting in and out of the house, I feel more alone than ever. It matters not how many years have passed – the breeze that travels across the *vega* still carries a song of sorrow and the traces of Eduardo. When my husband died, something in me also ceased to exist and no matter how hard I try to grasp that contentment I once took so much for granted, it eludes me too often, slipping through my fingers like sunbeams. If Eduardo had lived, I often wonder what would this have done to him, this necessity to exist under General Franco. It pains me to dwell upon this, for I know it should have destroyed him, just as I believe on my darker days that it is slowly destroying me, each bone of my body, each emotion, each fibre.

In the first few years following Eduardo's death, I coped with my loss in the only way I knew how, by devoting myself entirely to the innumerable tasks around the house and obsessively caring for the garden as though it were a small child. I sought comfort in my children, though how much I ever let them be a party to my sorrows, I cannot say. My dear friends Aurelia and Mar were a great comfort to me through the grim nightmare of those years and helped me to understand that Eduardo should never return. To add insult to injury, in the eyes of Franco's state, as a widow of a murdered Republican, I was not recognised as a widow but an abandoned wife. I was not permitted to grieve openly, yet my desire to leave the house those days at any rate was limited. When I did resume a life beyond the walls of Carmen de las Estrellas once more, mostly trips to the market, I paid no heed to the looks people gave me and locked myself into a solitary silence.

One by one my children have grown up, fallen in love, married and moved from the house with the exception of Isabel who, I am relieved to say, has chosen to remain with me at Carmen de las Estrellas. There is, of course, also Conchi. More than twenty years after she left she simply turned up one day at Carmen de las Estrellas. I answered the door and it took a while to recognise that the slight and frail person before me was the same woman from my memory, broad and strong as a bull. I welcomed her with open arms and, without even discussing it, returned her rightful job to her. She never told us what had happened to her during the war, but she did not need to. Suffering was pencilled into every line on her face and though she may have lost much of her physical strength in her body, her hands could still pummel dough in a way I have never seen in any other.

When Pablo first returned to us, I found it painful to look at him. This was not because I blamed him of course, but more that he was a reminder of how much I blamed myself for not being firmer that night with Eduardo. Should I have prevented him from going out to search for Pablo, how differently everything may have turned out. Yet with the passing of the years, the stabbing grief I experience when I look into Pablo's eyes has dulled. Moreover, I have gradually admitted to myself that if Pablo's disappearance had not served as the catalyst for Eduardo leaving the house, then something else would have done.

I cannot say why, but in the past few years I have been thinking of those meetings I once held in the conservatory during the days of the Republic when we discussed reform and even philosophy. I should like to transport myself back to one of those meetings, to a time when none of us knew how to live any other way than optimistically. Surprised as I am to admit this to myself, I have been thinking that perhaps, just perhaps, it is time to reconvene them. Of course, I should have to begin again as my old companions are no more or scattered to the wind. Yet whilst I once imagined every free-thinking liberal to have been wiped from Granada, now I believe, I *know*, that many of us are still here. We are here, living these lives of oppression beneath a dictator and a system that wrongs us, each and every day of our lives. When my mind runs in this direction, these are the days when my spirit feels lighter and I can approach life with more vigour, yet in recent months I have felt, far too often, weak and despondent.

But then, the unthinkable happens. Alejandro is spending the day with me, a day of thick, cloying heat; my youngest, in whose calm, quiet presence I cannot help but feel safe. I am dozing in my chair, when we both hear a knock at the door. Alejandro answers it and brings Pablo into the conservatory. He has his black woollen hat pulled low over his head, despite the heat; a hat that he is never seen without as it hides the jagged scar where his ear once sat. He walks to me, places his arms gently about my neck, kissing me on both cheeks. Then he sits on the floor at my feet and removes a satchel from his shoulder, not meeting my eye as he opens it and draws out several sheets of paper. And then, only then, does Pablo look at me. The papers remain in his grasp but as his eyes fix themselves upon mine, I realise that what he is about to show me will somehow change everything. Pablo's inability to talk has, I have always known, heightened his adeptness to express himself in other ways. Never have I known eyes to hold so many words; for the air around a person to hang so weightily with unspoken meaning. For when he looks at me, I feel myself swallowing hard, something catching in my throat before he nods almost imperceptibly and hands the papers to me. And this is what I see as I slowly turn the sheets.

Eduardo. Alone. Sitting on a bench with his head in his hands. His feet are bare, illuminated by a slender stream of light that trickles through the barred windows from the half-moon.

Eduardo. Standing in a dark courtyard opposite a guard in uniform. He is shouting. One arm is raised, a finger pointing skywards in anger, his cheekbones clenched in defiance.

A group of men, all in the same striped work-clothes. Faces gaunt with hunger and exhaustion. They look ahead of them with the empty eyes of the defeated. But towards the end of the line stands Eduardo, head askance. He is looking out at something beyond, something more.

Eduardo and Pablo. Sharing a thin gruel from one bowl. With one spoon. They sit against a cracked wall, shoulders touching and there is the faintest glimmer of a smile upon Eduardo's mouth, drawing strength from his nearness to Pablo.

Eduardo and Pablo. Eduardo's face is happier still. He is standing at one end of the room, reciting something, one hand raised in a theatrical flourish. Pablo sits and listens from an upturned crate, both hands beneath his chin.

A group of men, slumped against walls and broken chairs. Pablo in the middle of the room, looking up at Eduardo who stands, his face expressionless. From the door, a guard stands, beckoning to Eduardo.

Pablo. Alone. Weeping as he stares up at the high, barred window. There is no moon. There is no light.

Eduardo. At Carmen de las Estrellas. Sitting in the shade of the orange tree. A book held tenderly in his hands and a smile of contentment playing upon his lips. The smile that I so loved him for, and shall always do so.

CHAPTER EIGHTEEN
PALOMA

Summer 1961

It's been a long time coming but slowly, very slowly, things are changing. For the better. Unlike the long, hungry days of my childhood, there's now nearly always enough food to go around and people are starting to live more freely. Mamá and I continue to go to the cinema each fortnight like crazy fanatics and although the films are still censored, we now even see kisses on the big screen – imagine!

I can feel this change all around me. At first I just catch a subtle scent of its perfume on the restless breeze. But then it grows stronger and bolder. More than anything else in the world, I want to be part of these changes. I owe it to my family, you see, to pick up that thread of reform that was cast off so long ago. I know how much my parents want me to stay and study in Granada, but when I reach eighteen there's no stopping me. After dinner one evening, as we're sitting round the table peeling *naranjas*, I clear my throat.

'I want to make an announcement,' I say. My parents, brothers and grandmother all look at me in surprise. Clearly they aren't used to me making announcements.

'*Pues*,' I say slowly. 'I have decided to go to Barcelona to study modern languages.'

After a short pause, Dani speaks. 'You know they have a very good modern languages department at the University of Granada, Paloma.'

'*Sí, muchas gracias*, Dani,' I snap. 'I did know that.'

Papá looks at me, his head on one side. 'Your brother's right though, Paloma. Need you go so far?'

'Barcelona's not that far, Papá,' interjects Eduardo and I grin gratefully at my younger brother.

'But you're a little young to be going off on your own for such a long period,' Papá continues.

'Oh Henry,' Mamá says. 'You know full well that I was even younger than Paloma when I first went away from home.'

'*Sí*, but that was different.'

'Different in what way?'

Papá pauses and taps his middle finger on the table. 'But really, what's wrong with the university here? It has a marvellous reputation and…and…' his eyes flit desperately around the room '…think of the money you'd be saving.'

I smile at Papá. Of course he's saying this just because he'll miss me. And I him. I'll miss all my family, but it's something I need to do. One day, I'm certain of it, I'll find my path. And Franco or no Franco, I'll work and earn a living. How can I possibly not?

I glance up at the head of the table where Abuela, who has remained silent till now, sits busily peeling her orange and removing the pith.

'What do you think, Abuela?'

'I think,' Abuela answers, 'no, I *know*, that you must go to whichever university you wish and study whatever you should desire.' She extracts a couple of pips from her mouth and sucks on the peel. 'And my final word on the matter is that it shall be a sorry day indeed in our family when a woman is prevented from holding their own alongside the men. It has never been like that amongst us and it never shall be.' She gives her mouth a sharp wipe with her napkin and pushes her chair back, signalling the end of the conversation.

One morning as I sit in the kitchen with Mamá and Abuela, Mamá rushes in with the newspaper. She stands behind a chair, grasping the paper in her hands. Her dark eyes are burning with emotion.

'What is it, Mamá?' I ask, reaching out to turn down the volume.

'Look!' she replies, thrusting the paper into my hands and jabbing her finger at something half way down a page. I look from Mamá's flushed face to the paper and read the words. I have to read them again before they really sink in. '*Women are being urged to join the workforce,*' it reads. I knit my eyebrows together. This is a right-wing, pro-Franco paper. The only paper, in fact, that we can get our hands on. Can I really be reading this?

I scan the announcement beneath the headline and then look back at my mother in shock as I hand the paper to Abuela.

'This is just the start, Paloma, you'll see,' Mamá says, grasping my shoulder. 'The economy's in tatters. The only way out of the mess this country's in is to let us contribute. They're going to open up nurseries and care homes and I'll even be *permitted* to go out to work. I'm sure of it.'

I look at Abuela. Both of her eyebrows are raised in surprise, then she turns to me. I notice the faintest quiver in the corner of her mouth, but it's her eyes that are shining like polished brass. I grin at her, my mind starting to race with the opportunities I myself might be presented with in the years to come. And I feel wildly, absurdly, ferociously happy.

✻ ✻ ✻

And so it is that I leave Carmen de las Estrellas on my first extended trip alone. As I travel north the days become shorter and cooler and the dialect changes so much that in some areas I wonder what on earth's being said. I often think of Mamá in these early days in Barcelona, imagining her own brave journey here thirty years back and where she'd stayed, what she'd seen. She's told me various stories of her time here, but I'm certain the city I see has completely changed. For in the passing years, new roads have been paved, railway lines re-built and any vestiges of war swept under the carpet and heavily padded down.

When I get to the Universidad de Barcelona, it doesn't take me long to look around and realise a painful truth:

where are all the girls? To say that we're in the minority is a huge understatement. But after the initial stab of sharp disappointment, I remind myself that ten years ago there would have been virtually no women studying at all. And in another ten years our numbers will multiply. I quickly find a soul mate in the equally quiet, industrious Ana from Galicia who is studying biological sciences and is the single girl on her course. We share university accommodation and connect immediately.

One evening as Ana and I walk through Plaza Catalunya after a full day of lectures, she confides in me how the attitudes towards her are mixed.

'Most of the other students don't worry about the fact I'm the only female. They treat me just the same. But there are a few who...' she wrinkles her nose up, 'well, they're just *ignorantes*. If I worry about them, I give them strength.'

'What do they say?' I ask.

'It's not so much what they say, it's what they do. The looks they give me, like I'm scum of the earth because I'm a woman. I know they think I should be at home.' She quickly glances around her and lowers her voice. 'Ignorant *Franquistas*. They're not worth my energy, I know. But still...' she trails off.

'It hurts,' I say and she gives a brief, brisk nod. 'If only there were more of us,' I continue. 'I know there are so many like-minded girls out there craving for knowledge. But why aren't they being braver and coming to study?'

Ana's brow knits. 'It's not lack of interest, Paloma, that's for sure. People are scared. You realise what we're risking by coming here?'

I stop walking. I've never really thought of it like that before. Of course I know that the step I've taken is unusual. But risky? There's no law saying women can't study. I'm keeping my head down and getting on with my work, but at the same time, so much is changing and my friend has good reason to be paranoid. Several of her extended family members were killed during the civil war and many of her remaining family have left Spain.

Ana stares at me, her dark eyes intense under the glare of the streetlamp. 'There are so many ghosts, Paloma. They're sitting here,' she taps both shoulders, 'and each time a family thinks about sending their young women to university, families like ours, so that they can grow and learn and live, their ghosts start to whisper "But don't you remember what happened last time you spoke out like that? You really want that to happen again?"'

I shudder.

'And so,' Ana continues, 'it's not that people want to listen to them, but they can't help it. They push aside their sense-speaking consciousness and give into these... these...' she waves her hand through the air, searching for a word, 'malevolent spirits. And that's why there are so few of us here.'

'You're right. I know you are. But you have to believe that things are changing, Ana.' I take a deep breath and look around me, but there's nobody there. 'Franco can't live forever. And these wounds, I know they're deep and they're painful. But they will heal eventually.'

Ana frowns at me. 'Paloma, aren't you afraid of anything?'

I laugh gently, trying to lighten the tone. 'Of course I am. Of many, many things.'

She looks at me for a while longer in that intense way of hers. '*No te creo*. I don't believe you are. I wish I had your courage.'

'Oh Ana.' I smile at her and link my arm through hers as we start walking again. 'You're one of the bravest people I know. *Venga*, it's chilly out here.'

We walk in pensive silence and then Ana asks me quietly, 'Do you think about your abuelo often?'

I hold my breath slightly. '*Sí*,' I reply. 'I…I feel his presence in our house.' I've never said this to anybody before. Somehow it's a relief to now be talking about it.

'What do you feel?' Ana whispers.

'I feel…I feel, *mierda*, it's hard to explain. I think it's this idea of him I've pieced together over the years from photographs and Pablo's drawings and so many people say my elder brother Dani looks just like him. And then there's all the stories my mother has told me, and also my abuela.'

'Does your abuela talk about him much?'

'*No mucho*,' I sigh. 'She's like a clam. She'll open up and inside she's a wealth of riches and stories but then her shell closes again and it can stay like that for months. But she's amazing. And this presence I feel of my abuelo, it's like he creeps up on me when I'm least expecting it. I might be walking down the corridor or in the garden and suddenly he's just…there.'

Ana's eyes widen. 'Isn't it creepy?' she asks.

I shake my head. 'No. Not creepy. His presence is gentle.' I shrug and run a hand through my hair. 'I know it sounds mad…'

'Not mad. As I said,' Ana replies knowingly, 'there are ghosts everywhere. But unlike *you*,' she smiles at me sadly, 'they scare me so much, I sometimes can't sleep at night.'

I squeeze my friend's arm and we round the corner into the street we live on.

❆ ❆ ❆

Life at university continues in a whirlwind of lectures and learning and conversation, though I am happy to keep my friendship circle small. By my second year of studies, I feel confident enough not only to watch one of the frequent student demonstrations that surge through Barcelona's thoroughfares, but also take part in one. The feeling of empowerment and liberation it gives me is unlike anything I've experienced and I know I must share my exhilaration with my family, rushing home to pull out paper and pen the minute it's over.

Barcelona
14th April, 1962

Dear everyone,

I'm too excited to keep this to myself and I want to tell you about my very first demonstration I attended!

Now, first of all, please don't worry. It was all very law-abiding and peaceful. Ana came along too, though initially she wasn't eager to. But she's re-alising, as I am, that freedom of speech is real and powerful. I honestly believe, with my head as well as my heart that, despite Franco's propaganda, his regime is starting to unravel. I did feel nervous go-ing, I must admit. Ana and I made banners read-ing 'Nosotras también somos ciudadanas – dan-os tu voto!' – 'We are equal citizens, give us the vote.' And I felt so proud holding it, I can't tell you. As I stepped into the moving crowd of women from the side of the road and began to be pulled along with them, I instantly felt as though I was part of a living, breathing organism: all of us working together for social good. The only other procession I've been in is Semana Santa, year after year. But we all know how oppressive and false that feels. Quite the opposite of this, which makes me feel like a flower turning its face towards the sunlight for the first time.

During this particular demonstration, we were call-ing for female franchise, religious tolerance, a free press and a greater openness to foreign investment, and we could do it with our heads held high! Of course there are those, both citizens of Barcelona and fellow stu-dents, who loathe what we're doing. But they also know that they can't stop us expressing our opinions.

Ten years ago this would have landed us in jail, but not any more. I never doubt for a minute that there's a collective point to our actions; that if enough people demonstrate in enough places throughout the country the government will have to eventually acknowledge the strengthening call for reform.

Even last year I wouldn't have had the courage to write this letter, but I don't believe anything will happen now. I believe I can write it and send it and you can read it and I am doing NOTHING WRONG and nobody can say otherwise!

I love you all,

Paloma

Of course I choose not to include my liaisons with men in my letters home. There have been a few, but nothing serious. The truth is that ever since my rebellious encounter with Antonio, the Semana Santa boy, I lose interest a little. I do have male friends and whilst I know that some of them want more, I'm far too fired up by the demonstrations and everything else going on around me to leave much room for romance. This intensifies when I become involved in a movement calling for equal rights for women. I join the youth branch of the university and help organise meetings, debates and social events. During my time with this group I learn so much about female legal and social discrimination and I even write a couple of small articles for the movement's magazine.

During my final year at university, Franco and his supporters organise a huge celebration to commemorate twenty-five years since the nationalist victory. 'Twenty-five years of peace!' they cry from every platform available. Cities, towns and villages the length and breadth of the country are festooned with Francoist posters, but in my little student corner of Barcelona, the poster I see time and again declares '1939–1964: A glorious achievement of righteousness over Spain's godless atheists'. *Mierda*, it makes me crazy to see these propaganda posters hanging on the walls in Barcelona. After all, I know from my parents' stories that this is a city that held out for so long against the insurgents. Ana and I see students tearing the posters angrily down, ripping them to pieces and burning them in the streets.

I'm afraid for these students, but here's the thing: nothing ever happens to them and I'm sure that's what makes me bolder still. As I watch the flames flickering upwards into the reddening sky, I try to imagine the sights that my parents witnessed in this same city. They *didn't* go through all that for nothing, not a chance. I can hear Mamá's voice echoing gently in my ears as I watch General Franco's jubilant declarations curl and blaze before me into a heap of ashes: '...*the time will come, Paloma. I'm sure of it*'. Smiling to myself, I kick at the smouldering words before pulling my coat closer around my shoulders and stepping over them into the dusky evening.

Around the same time as all of this, one day I see a photo of Jackie Kennedy in a magazine I buy on the black market. She's wearing something I've never seen before. The magazine describes this garment as taking the world of female fashion by storm and I feel both horror and excitement coursing through my body just looking at it. It's a skirt that actually shows the knees, a mini-skirt! The question is though: do I have the courage to wear one? I spend the next few days mulling it over but once the idea has been planted, that's it. I know about all the black markets in Barcelona where you can buy banned books and even marijuana or other drugs if you're prepared to pay for them. I can't be sure they'll have mini-skirts but one Friday afternoon, when lectures have finished, I go alone. And sure enough, there are a couple.

The one I buy is black leather. It hugs my buttocks and thighs and feels very, very strange. As I stand in front of the mirror and look at the length of my legs, I think to myself *Dios, can I really wear this?* As though my reflection has a life of its own, I see the girl in the mirror with the long dark hair smile confidently back. I'm not yet brave enough to wear it out in public, but I put it on for one of the youth movement meetings and when I walk into the room, everybody gasps in shock (and maybe admiration?) and I can't help but feel a surge of pride: this is me, Paloma. This is who I am.

❄ ❄ ❄

On the night before our graduation, Ana and I sit up in my room with a few candles scattered around and a bottle of wine, too excited to go to bed. The following day we'll be celebrating our academic achievement, but so much more than that.

'You were right,' Ana says to me, legs crossed on my bed as she rolls a thin cigarette.

'Right about what?'

'About things changing, that we don't have to be afraid any more.' Ana lights the cigarette, takes a small inhale and then offers it to me. 'It took me such a long time to really believe that. But you're partly to thank for that. You *helped* me believe. If you'd told me when I first met you Franco would pass this constitution, I'd have just laughed. Or cried. But now look where we are.'

She stretches her legs out and then hugs them into her body, her face young and beautiful and full of hope.

I nod. 'Franco knows,' I say, 'that he has to give concessions now. *Bueno*, so he might not like the fact that new parties are forming all the time, but he can't stop them. And he can't stop people practising religion in the way they want to. Even if you're not Catholic, or don't *practise* Catholicism, you're still human.'

'I hope with all my heart that by the time we have children they don't have to be educated by the church,' Ana says, her nostrils flaring.

I smiled. '*Paciencia*. It will come.'

'Well, you have more of that than I do, that's for sure. And of course it's important that people can choose religion as they wish, but imagine this: no more press censorship! It's incredible! Do you know what that means, Paloma?'

I grin at Ana; her enthusiasm is infectious.

'It *means*,' I reply, 'that we can say what we want, when we want and how we want. That I can wear a mini-skirt if I choose, because it's my *right* to do so.'

Ana giggles nervously. 'We're not all as brave as you are, Paloma. But I suppose it helps me in a way by making me think that your abuelo, and my abuelo, and all the others who didn't conform, that the Spain they dreamt of is finally being built. Finally.' It's late and we've drunk two bottles of wine between us and are feeling heady and tired and emotional, and I watch as suddenly her laughter turns to tears. They escape from Ana's dark eyes and steal down her cheeks. I stub out the cigarette and sit beside her on the bed, embracing my friend.

'We're so lucky,' I whisper, 'to be alive now. We've escaped the hell that our parents and grandparents went through, and we have so much to look forward to.' I can feel Ana nodding on my shoulder as her tears continue to flow. 'And Ana, when we fall in love and decide to marry, we can vote, actually vote! *Vale*, we all know that single women should be given the vote as well, but it's a start. We'll get there, Ana.'

'I know,' my friend replies quietly and then, her face brightening as she wipes away the tears on her cheek, 'What are you going to do this summer?'

I grin at her. 'I haven't worked out the details yet, but I think I'll go to Morocco.'

She stares at me, wide-eyed. *'Morocco? Estás loca?'*

'Why?' I laugh. 'What's the problem?'

'Now I'm all for women's liberation but girls,' she intones, '*don't* travel in Morocco alone.'

I shrug. 'This girl does.'

Ana kisses me on the cheek. 'And that's why I love you, Paloma. Not scared of a thing.'

'I guess that means you won't come with me?' I light another cigarette and take a deep inhale.

'I'd love to, *amiga*, but I've promised my parents I'll help in the shop over the summer. Maybe another year?'

'OK,' I reply, 'I'm going to hold you to that, Ana,' I say, as we both lie back on the bed, candlelight flickering around the room. 'I'm so excited, for you, for me. For our futures.' She squeezes my hand, and I long for this night to go on and on.

❇ ❇ ❇

Three months later, the sun is sinking behind the dome of the Koutoubia Mosque and I sit perched in front of it, sketching the intricate minaret and eating roasted cashews. My sketchpad is filling up quickly and I flick through it, smiling at the memories of Tangiers and Chefchaouen and Fez and other places with equally magical names. I've always considered myself terrible at drawing, but as I flick critically through the pages, I decide there are a few I rather like, such as the Moroccan tea pot and glass of mint tea and the pyramid of spices at a market stall.

Never mind Ana, my family were *horrified* when I told them I was going to Morocco. And even more shocked to learn I planned to travel alone. But on all my previous jaunts through Spain, this was the way I'd enjoyed travelling. *Bueno*, so North Africa may throw up a few extra challenges than I'm accustomed to, but I know that Ana would never really have agreed to come, and that I'd learn a great deal from travelling alone.

The call to prayer begins. It drifts over the heads of men hurrying to and fro through the mosque's arched gateway. I watch as large white storks with black-tipped wings are disturbed from nearby and swoop over my head, powerful wings pounding, before settling on the wall near to me. The air is still warm but I've been sitting for a long time and decide that a stroll will do me some good to pump circulation back round my body. I replace everything into my bag, jump off the wall and start to walk. I love this city: the brightness of the souks filled with sparkling slippers, curling lampshades and teapots. The pungent smells of sweetmeats and freshly tanned leather. Spices filling my nostrils. But more than anything else, I love the Jemaa-I-Fna, Marrakech's town square serving as outdoor restaurant, night-time circus and meeting place. It is alive in a way I've never imagined possible before: all the colours and textures and sounds and smells melded and fused so powerfully that the square is like a magnet, pulling me back again and again.

This evening it's filled with dancing monkeys, fortunetellers and long-haired hippies with glazed grins etched on their faces. I've been walking around for a while when I stop at a large crowd gathered around one elderly man and a young boy. Though I can't understand a word, I'm intrigued by the crowd they've drawn and the hold they posses over everyone watching. Dozens of people, both young and old, sit enthralled by the tales they spin as they expertly take up the story from one another. They allow for plenty of pauses, both for dramatic licence and suspense and for the boy to nip round the crowd with an upturned hat.

I'm about to move on when a man in the crowd catches my eye. He looks just like one of the many hippies who've set up home in Marrakech, with his long tousled hair and bearded face. But his eyes have a sharpness that I haven't really seen in the usual band of pleasure seekers. He's squatting on his haunches, engaged in intense debate with a local man wearing a *jalabi* next to him. I'm curious. I edge round the back of the throng until I'm standing behind them and try to pick up on their conversation through the din of the crowd. They're conversing in French and although I speak the language well now following my years at university, the noise around me is too loud. The man has a camera slung round his neck and after a while he rises and calls something out to the storytellers that makes them laugh. After placing a coin into the hat, he takes several photos as the pair pose and bow. As he turns to move away, our eyes meet for an instant before he smiles broadly at me and vanishes into the crowd.

I keep an eye out for him around Marrakech in the souks and the fragrant palace gardens. I don't quite understand why I want to see this person again that I haven't even spoken to. After a few days, I tell myself that he's probably moved on; either that, or even if he is here, it'll be virtually impossible to single him out again in the crowds. But four nights after the evening in the square, my wish to see the stranger again is granted. I'm sitting at a pavement café drinking fresh mint tea, absorbed in my diary writing, when I realise that somebody has sat opposite me at the table. Startled, I look up and am even more surprised to be greeted by the sight of the man with the kind brown eyes in the souk. He is smiling at me and I feel my stomach violently flip with nerves and excitement but manage to smile back.

'*Bonsoir*,' he says.

'*Bonsoir*.'

'May I join you?'

I want to say that he's already done so, but just grin inanely back and say 'Sure.'

There is a pause. I feel completely tongue-tied and have no idea what to say to this man. But he seems perfectly at ease, which I don't know whether to feel grateful for or annoyed by. He raises a hand and orders another mint tea and cakes from a passing waiter and then looks back at me and gives me that same boyish grin he gave me in the square. He's wearing a blue T-shirt and red flares over scuffed leather sandals and his arms and face are deeply tanned. Dark brown hair sticks up at haphazard angles on his head; it is the kind of hair that I normally hate because I can never understand why people don't take more care with their appearance. But I have to admit that the tousled look suits him. And then there are those eyes –

deep brown, depthless eyes that somehow make me feel I can instinctively trust him.

'*Oyé*, you're Spanish, aren't you?' he asks, swapping languages.

'*Sí*,' I reply. 'How did you know?' ·

'The Spanish accent's a hard one to disguise. I should know. I'm Alberto.' He stretches a long arm across the table and we shake hands. 'Where are you from?'

'Granada,' I reply. 'And you?'

Alberto leans back in his chair and laughs. 'Otivar.'

'Really?'

'Really.' He looks straight at me and smiles and my stomach lurches again. Otivar is a small town in Granada province, not that far from my own home. I've been travelling in Morocco now for almost three weeks and have met various foreigners from around Europe, America and Canada but, surprisingly, not a single Spaniard. And certainly not a Spaniard whose home is so close to my own.

'You haven't told me your name,' Alberto says.

'Oh,' I say, flustered and then, immediately annoyed with myself, tug at my ponytail. 'Paloma. *Soy* Paloma.'

'Paloma,' he repeats quietly, looking suddenly serious, as though weighing up my name. I watch as he stirs two teaspoons of sugar into his tea and then he looks up at me and grins again, the friendliest smile I've ever seen. And, in spite of myself, I feel myself relaxing.

Alberto and I sit there for two hours, talking and ordering one tea after another until my teeth and mouth are tingling with all the sugar. A self-employed photographer, he's spent the past year travelling around North Africa, compiling a portfolio of images depicting all the peoples and landscapes of these nations and eking out a living by selling the black and white prints in market places back home. He doesn't make much money, but it's money all the same he says, and he has to be grateful for anything.

When I eventually motion to leave, saying that it's getting chilly, Alberto jumps up, unties the jumper from around his waist and places it around my shoulders.

I laugh. 'Very chivalrous, *gracias*. But I should be getting back.'

'Why should you?' There is a twinkle in his eye.

I sigh. There's no reason, really. But I've created a little routine for myself back at the tiny riad I'm staying in: tea with the owner's wife in the courtyard, and then writing my diary from the roof of the building, listening to all the sounds rising from the city beneath me.

'I just should,' I say stubbornly.

I stand up and motion for the waiter. I go to hand back Alberto's jumper but he holds his hand out and says 'Keep it till tomorrow.'

'What's happening tomorrow?'

'You're going to meet me if…' he suddenly falters, 'if you'd like to?'

I bite my bottom lip and give him a small smile. 'Well. *Bueno*. Where shall we meet?'

❉   ❉   ❉

The following morning, I wake up to mottled shafts of bright sunlight streaming through the cracks in the wooden shutter and warming my forehead. Vivid shapes and patterns dance beneath my closed eyelids as, still half-asleep, I listen to the shrill chatter of women scrubbing the courtyard outside my room and the slosh of water upon tiles. I drift in and out of sleep, threads of half-remembered dreams edging their way back into my mind and leading me through a waltz of distant voices and scenes.

Suddenly, I sit bolt upright and throw the cover violently away from me. I catch sight of myself in the mirror at the far end of the room and stare at my reflection. Ruffled hair, the imprint of the pillow against my cheek. *Deep breaths, deep breaths. Where am I? Morocco.* My reflection smiles, a grin of pure delight at the realisation that I'm in Africa.

I fling my legs over the edge of the bed. *What time is it?* I pull open the bedside drawer and bus ticket stubs and my hairbrush go flying as I search for my watch. Normally I'm meticulously organised and know exactly where everything is. But now I start to panic as I remember the way I felt the day before. The lightness of my step as I'd walked back to the riad from the café after Alberto and I had chatted – for how long? – over tea and delicious cakes made from almonds and sesame seeds. Eventually, finding my watch, I feel calmer. I still have another hour and a half until our meeting. I begin to look through all my clothes, deciding what to wear till eventually I make a face at myself in the mirror at the absurdity of it all and pick the first thing from the top of my pile.

Alberto is half an hour late. We arranged to meet at the Menara gardens beside the pavilion and I sit happily at first by the lakeside, watching the water gently changing colour in the delicate morning light and people strolling along the pathways with a calm, steady pace I haven't yet witnessed in Morocco. But then I start to wonder whether he's really going to show up and feel annoyed with myself for being quite so eager and trusting. Every thirty seconds or so I glance at my watch until I become thoroughly frustrated and take it off, stuffing it to the bottom of my bag. When half an hour comes and goes, I jump off the wall and, slinging my knapsack on my back, spin round and start walking back towards the garden entrance.

'You're not leaving, are you? I've only just got here.'

I look up to see Alberto standing directly in front of me, smiling at me through his beard, his dark eyes glinting in the sunlight.

'Oh...*hola*.'

I feel awkward and frown. Alberto leans forward and kisses me on both cheeks then walks back towards the wall I've just left and sits down.

'Isn't it beautiful here?'

I smile. I can't stand it when people are late. But he's right. It *is* beautiful. Alberto has a brown paper bag in his hand and he brings out warm cinnamon rolls, small ginger cakes and almond filo pastries and lays them out.

He looks up at me and his eyes smile. How can eyes smile like that? 'Sorry I'm late. I went to buy some breakfast. I hope you haven't eaten yet.'

I walk back towards the wall slowly, feeling my stomach lurch with delight and nerves. *Why is it*, I think to myself, *that this man I barely know is having this effect on me?*

After eating breakfast, we spend the entire day together, wandering through the city, bartering at the bazaars and trying delicacies from silver trays piled mountain high in the souks. Towards the end of the day, Alberto and I wander around the Jemaa-I-Fna together, dodging whirling fire sticks and acrobats. I know I don't have to leave. And I know I'm attracted to this man. But I'd planned to leave the following morning and when it comes to my itinerary, I'm fairly bloody-minded in sticking to it. There's part of me that wants more than anything to stay, but strangely I don't know how to. I don't know a way to break free from the rigid schedule I've bound myself to.

We stand in front of great shanks of meat roasting on spits, listening to them fizz and hiss and I turn to Alberto.

'I'm leaving for Essaouira tomorrow.'

He doesn't react and again, I feel annoyed with myself that I've let myself believe that this could be something more.

'Ah,' he eventually says and shrugs, his kind brown eyes not leaving mine. 'I suppose this is *adiós* then.'

It hurts to hear him say that. But I'm the one leaving after all. '*Sí*,' I reply.

'*Adiós*, Paloma.' He leans towards me and kisses me on both cheeks and he smells of smoke and earth. He is smiling a questioning smile at me and I don't know how to respond to it so feel myself going into automatic brisk and efficient Paloma-mode.

'*Adiós*, Alberto.' I turn to leave, but he catches me gently by the crook of one arm and pulls me back. His smile has faded.

'Why don't you stay?' he asks quietly.

He's staring at me intently and as I gaze back into his eyes I think of how much has happened in a single day. Before I've had a chance to even mull over his offer, I hear myself say 'Why don't you come?'

Our lips curl upwards simultaneously, both lost for words. Because I know he'll come. I can read it in his eyes. And he knows that I know. He plants another kiss on my cheek, this time lingering as he does so. His beard brushes against me and he whispers into my ear '*Hasta mañana.*'

And so the following day, laden down with brightly coloured trinkets I bought from the market, I board a bus bound for the western coastal town of Essaouira. But I'm not travelling alone. I'm with a wild-haired, dark-eyed man whom a few days previously was a stranger to me. We sit at the back of a crowded bus filled with men in long, thickly woven capes with pointed hoods. Wide-eyed children press their mouths and noses to the windows and blow hot moons into the glass. Then suddenly we are picking our way over old mossy cannons behind the

sea wall with a fierce wind, specs of sand whipping up
in our faces, tawny eagles soaring overhead, glints of the
dipping sun catching on the tips of their wings. Suddenly
we are staying up for hours on end in cafés and restaurants, discussing our families and our pasts and what it
is that attracted us to Morocco. And suddenly we shock
ourselves and each other to find we have fallen irrevoca-
bly, profoundly in love.

I am the first to say the words; a girl who has just spent
weeks on her own and has never felt the need to be in the
company of another person for long periods of time, particularly not a man. With Alberto, I don't feel the need to
talk. Nor to impress or intrigue. I can continue being the
person I've always been and he doesn't ask for anything
else from me. Making love to Alberto is not the fumbling lust I experienced as a teenager. Nor is it the indif-
ferent acceptance that took place at university more out
of mild interest than passion. No. Feeling my skin against
Alberto's – the cadence, scent and beat of his body makes
more sense to me than anything I've ever known. I never
imagined I could fall in love so hard or so quickly but it
is what it is. Within weeks, I love everything about him: I
love the slight flare of his nostrils when he's talking about
something important to him. I love the dark hairs on his
strong arms that makes me feel both safe and needed. I
love his quiet lilting voice and unassuming manner. And
I love that he loves me.

Even when Alberto takes my photograph, he doesn't
disturb me or ask me to look his way as I sit on the beach

sketching, searching for shells or plaiting my hair. And so I grow accustomed to the moments when he lovingly draws his heavy Olympus camera out of its case and plays around with the aperture and exposure until I hear that tiny click.

We spend more time discussing the civil war than anything else; how it's affected our families as well as our mutual longing for democracy in Spain. Alberto comes from a small family in comparison to mine, yet one that has suffered enormously at the hands of the fascists.

'The war ended so long ago,' Alberto says as we sit on the beach and stare out to sea, 'but still, *still* it hangs over us like a big black rain cloud.' I lay my head on his shoulder and gaze at the colourful fishing boats being tossed about on the Atlantic.

'We do seem to spend a lot of time talking about it,' I agree. 'It's because we both know that as long as *el cabrón* Franco lives and Spain exists under a dictatorship, our families can't really move on from the war. Or its legacy.'

'Yes,' Alberto murmurs. 'That's it.'

I shiver as a cool gust of wind buffets around us and Alberto pulls me closer to him. 'I had friends at university who shared my ideals, but with you…' I break off and frown slightly '…with you, it's so strange, but it feels like I'm holding a mirror up to what I believe in.' Alberto turns his head and kisses me on the forehead, keeping his lips there.

'It sounds like we were doing exactly the same thing at university, campaigning on the streets with hordes of other disaffected students.' He pulls away and gazes at me. 'I wish we'd met earlier.'

'We wouldn't have been ready for each other,' I reply.

Alberto laughs quietly. 'You're probably right.'

We lie back on the sand and I nestle into his side, listening as the call to prayer begins and floats over the beach towards the waves. 'When Spain's a democracy again,' I say as I run my hand up and down his brown T-shirt, 'when that happens, I'm going to open up a café in Granada.'

Alberto takes my hand in his and kisses my fingertips. 'You never told me that.'

I grin. 'There's a lot I haven't told you yet.'

Alberto pauses. 'What will you call it?'

I push my head back and stare up into his face as I smile at him. '*No lo sé*. What do you think?'

Alberto knits his eyebrows together in concentration as he lifts a hand up and twirls a few strands of my hair around his finger. 'What about something you've always longed for over the years? Something you've hoped for?'

'Maybe that's it! Maybe that's what I should call it…'

'What?'

'Hope.'

'Hope,' Alberto repeats quietly. 'I like that.' He places his head back into the sand and breathes it quietly, whispering the word again and again, '*Esperanza, Esperanza*', until it sounds at one with the waves and is carried gently away on the wind. And as the breeze catches the word, it plays with it and carries it like a torch of peace and optimism to a land over the seas.

❋ ❋ ❋

One month later, I am sitting in the garden of Carmen de las Estrellas with Papá and Abuela, lying on my front as I sort through my sketches from Morocco into chronological order. I've been back in Spain for a whole fortnight, but for some reason can't bring myself to tell my family about Alberto. As we parted, Alberto promised me that the minute he was back in Spain, he'd come straight to see me. 'You believe me, don't you?' I had nodded vigorously, trying desperately to keep the tears from spilling down my cheeks. I believed him more than I'd ever believed anyone, but I was suddenly terrified at the prospect of him leaving. I wanted to fling my arms around his neck and never let him go.

And as I lie on the grass, squinting through the sunlight, I wish I could turn to Papá and Abuela, hand them the sketch and say 'Look. Here is the man I'm in love with.' It's silly, but there's a part of me that's afraid that if I share him with anyone, he'll evaporate like the morning dew. That if I open my heart and express I've met the man I believe I'll be spending the rest of my life with, I'll be tempting fate and something disastrous will happen to him in Algeria where he travelled to after I left. That the plug will be pulled away from his very being. That the texture and colour of his soul will drain slowly from him until he becomes a shapeless mass, a figment of my imagination.

I turn over onto my back and close my eyes. I feel sleep clawing at me as my senses become more attuned to the sounds around me: birdsong, a distant knocking at a door, the shuffle of feet, Papá clearing his throat and a tap dripping from somewhere, as steadily as a metronome. Alberto's face from the sketch flashes beneath my closed eyelids. The sun distorts his memory into sepia negative images, transforming his thick dark hair into a white mass and his eyes into an eerie reflection as they stare strangely at me in their waxen transparency. I have no idea for how long I've dozed off, but moments later I feel an insect crawl over my hand and absently flick it off. It persists, creeping slowly up my wrist and further along my arm. Opening one eye, I notice a shadow bending over me and with a start open the other eye to see Abuela sitting beside me. She is working a thin blade of grass up and down my arm whilst her other hand clasps the sketch of Alberto. Groggily, I pull myself up on the rug.

'So, are you ready to tell us about him yet, young lady?'

From his deckchair behind Abuela, I notice Papá lowering his newspaper ever so slightly. I sigh heavily and frown, scratching behind my ear.

'He's just someone I met in Morocco. Nobody special...' My voice trails off weakly as Abuela gazes at me.

'Nobody special, hmm?'

Abuela stands up and walks back to sit down again in the deckchair besides Papá.

'Well, would you be so kind as to tell us what your not-very-special friend is doing standing at our front door right now?'

Thinking I've misheard her, I jerk my head up and stare at Abuela wide-eyed. '*¿Qué dices?*'

Papá has completely lowered his newspaper. He's taken off his sunglasses and is looking in bewilderment at both of us.

'You heard me,' Abuela continues as she gestures with her head towards the courtyard. '*Tu amigo.* He is standing on our doorstep.'

I spring to my feet and tear across the grass towards the garden wall. Heaving myself up, I steady myself on the uneven, mossy surface and call out to Alberto. His face, dark from the sun, pokes out from beside the studded wooden door. Lowering myself down, I fling myself joyfully into his waiting arms. He holds my face gently on either side and kisses me deeply on my lips.

'What are you doing here? I wasn't expecting to see you for at least another few weeks!'

Alberto hugs me tightly and lowers his mouth to kiss my neck. 'I haven't been able to stop thinking about you. I tried to see out the time I'd intended in Algeria but… I failed miserably!'

I cling to him, breathing in his comforting, earthy scent and running my fingers through his long, unruly hair. After a few moments, Alberto takes hold of my arms and gently draws me away from him, holding both of my shoulders. 'Is that your abuela who answered the door?' I nod.

'You haven't told any of your family about me, have you?' My smile fades and, biting my lip, I start to explain that I wanted to but didn't know where to begin or how I could do him justice. Hugging me again, Alberto breathes into my hair. '*No te preoccupes*, my family don't know about you yet, either. I think we've both got a lot of introducing to do.'

The following week is blissful and I feel I may burst with joy at any moment. Alberto and I stroll along the Paseo de Los Tristes and over the old stone bridges. We explore the gardens and tiled courtyards of the Alhambra. And we sit in Moroccan tea-houses, sipping at mint tea from tiny painted glasses. Not only is Alberto introduced to all of my family members, who adore him straight away, but I also go to Otivar where I meet his elder sister and grandfather, the only members of his family who have survived the wave of post-war violence directed against left-wing supporters.

Whilst in Morocco, Alberto told me about the fate that had befallen his staunchly Republican family, so I feel I'm prepared to meet them. I've learnt to deal with my own family's loss because I've grown up with it. But to walk into a house in which memories and the absence of loved ones audibly echoes around the photograph-lined walls is more than I can take. I feel the warm, calloused hands of Alberto's grandfather draw around my face and bring me closer to him as he gazes short-sightedly at me. He kisses me tenderly on both cheeks and tells me I should sit at his wife's seat at the table. I have to muster every last ounce of strength I possess not to break down and cry. Just as my family whole-heartedly accept Alberto, I rapidly feel at ease with Alberto's grandfather and sister who fuss over me as though I'm a long lost daughter.

In the cellar downstairs is Alberto's dark room and during the few days that I spend in his home, I'm introduced to the wonder of fixing and setting and the magical apparition of images on contact sheets as they swirl about in the solution. Alberto has shot endless rolls of film and randomly, he chooses just a couple to show me what can be done with them. 'Incredible,' I murmur as before my eyes a close-up image appears of myself sitting on the beach, examining some pebbles I've just collected. As we develop print after print and I peg them up on the line at the back of the cellar to dry, I come to a picture taken at the start of the film. It's of Alberto's grandfather, sitting in his chair outside the house staring wistfully into the distance, cradling a pipe in his hand.

'This is a sad photo,' I whisper.

Alberto walks round beside me and studies it as it hangs loosely from the cord, wet blotches slowly drying in the corners.

'He's still in mourning. Even after all this time. He lost his wife, his brother, his son and his daughter-in-law. He knows they're never coming back, but even so, I've always felt that deep down he's never quite given up that hope. If it weren't for the fact that he'd been away that night, he definitely wouldn't be around today either.'

Alberto runs a hand through his hair as he blows gently on the drying photo.

'But...but where were you and your sister when this happened?'

Alberto shrugs. 'We were locked up in the house. We were only tiny, they didn't want us. The next day, when it was all over, a neighbour banged the door down and we waited for our grandfather to get back. It was left up to him to explain to us what had happened.'

I feel myself choking as the tears I've tried to suppress during my days in Otivar finally work their way free and I reach out for Alberto and cling to him, burying my face deep into his chest. 'You've never told me that.'

His hands stroke my hair as slowly, quietly he responds. 'Paloma, my heart and soul are yours. But there are some things that will take longer than others to tell you. We still have a great deal to learn about one another.'

I nod into his chest and I suddenly understand that it's down in the dark depths of the basement he's chosen to tell me this most traumatic event of his past. For we are in a place where the sunlight can't fall on his tears and where they can drop noiselessly, anonymously. As I feel the dampness against his cheek, I clasp him tighter and murmur again and again, 'I'm sorry. *Lo siento mucho.*'

This same afternoon we leave the village and drive to the coast for the afternoon before returning to Carmen de las Estrellas where we plan to have dinner. It's one of the rare occasions that Tío Joaquín will be there and I'm desperate for Alberto to meet him. I haven't told Alberto that my uncle is a celebrated musician, *the* Joaquín Torres Ramirez, and I can't wait to surprise him this evening.

'Any preferences for where we stop?' Alberto asks as he hands the road map to me. I'm busy fiddling with the radio dial as fits and starts of heated interviews, flamenco music and news reports burst across the airwaves. Finding some relaxing music, I settle back into the seat, open the map and study the winding lines and clustered towns and villages before me.

'The coast around here is too developed.'

Alberto nods in agreement.

'Actually, there is a place I'd like to go to.' I bring the map closer as I scrutinise the area further along the coast.

'Where is it?'

'I'm just trying to remember the name. My mother once told me about a house she went to a few times – I think it belonged to a cousin or brother of my grandfather. Oh, what was the name...'

I frown, place the road map down in my lap and gaze out of the window as we whiz past jacaranda trees and cacti bathed in the golden afternoon sunshine.

'Mamá's mentioned it to me a couple of times...I think Papá might have done once as well. A tiny little bay, somewhere not far from the turn-off up to Granada.'

'We've got a while till then. Let's just keep going and we may spot it.'

I nod and sink back in my seat as I half-close my eyes and look outside. Spring sunshine – there is nothing like it. Nor any light as intensely beautiful as the evening sun. During the years I was away, I always missed the quality of light I swear is more beautiful in my native Andalucía than anywhere else.

'Paloma...Paloma, wake up.'

Alberto is shaking my elbow, gently nudging me out of my slumber.

'I've passed the sierra turn-off. I kept looking out for a road to take us down to the sea but they were all quite major turnings leading to resorts so I'm carrying on a bit.'

I heave myself up in my seat. 'Wherever they were talking about could have changed a lot since the last time they went there, but let's keep going a little further and if we don't find anything, we can turn back.'

Alberto's stomach rumbles violently and he turns and winks at me as the landscape around us becomes wilder with lemon groves and olive trees dotting the hills.

'I think that's a village over there.' I point to a white spire gleaming in the distance with the deep blue of the sea beyond it. Alberto continues driving until we reach the centre of the tiny *pueblo*, a palm-tree flanked plaza where old men sit in groups sharing stories and small children chase one another round and splash each other with water from the fountain.

'Excuse me,' calls Alberto, leaning out of the car window. 'Is there a road that drives us down to the coast from here?'

'*Solo hay un camino estrecho,*' one old man calls back, nodding with his head in the direction of what looks like a small track, possible only to follow on foot.

'Is it far?' I ask.

'*Media hora, más o menos,*' he replies before turning back to his companions and resuming his animated debate. Alberto and I look at each other and grin. We both know exactly what 'more or less' signifies; that it could just as likely be a ten-minute stroll as an entire hour.

We park the car off the plaza and when we reach the cove forty-five minutes later, there are a few families there. A young boy is paddling in the shallow white sea-foam and an old woman crouches on the sand, barbecuing fish as the smoke carries its mouth-watering smell around the bay.

'Do you think this is the beach your parents were talking about?'

I shrug as I look around me, shielding my eyes from the low sun. 'I don't know, possibly. I seem to remember that the house they were talking about was set back from the coast. I can't see a house, though.'

We wander slowly over to an outcrop of rocks that give us good views of the crescent-shaped bay, the sea and the sun that has started its gentle descent into the horizon. Alberto has brought some bread and *queso manchego* and we sit and eat in silence. We listen to the steady swell of the waves against the shore and the call of the gulls mingled with the laugh of the young boy as he gleefully runs back and forth. The moon has come out and I gaze up at it, trying to imagine those invisible lines that dance between it and the powerful pull of the tide.

After finishing the food, we stare out across the sea and I take Alberto's hand in mine, gently stroking it. So much has happened since I've met him and I've never been so sure about anything else that our lives are entwined. What he told me this morning is just the beginning, I know. I turn to look at him, at his proud profile staring at the ocean. He has the kindest face I've ever seen. I don't know how it's possible to read such kindness in the features of a face but it is there, unmistakably, from the loyalty of his brown eyes to the set of his brow. And I feel, at that moment, like so many moments since our worlds collided in Marrakech, that I am the luckiest woman alive.

It's starting to get cold and, as he stands up, Alberto points towards the far end of the cove. 'What's that over there?'

I follow his outstretched hand towards the corner of the beach where I try to make out the heap of wood that lies piled there. 'I don't know. Let's go and have a quick look.'

The beach is deserted now and we walk across the sand that sinks under our feet and see what used to be an old hut. One side of it is still partially standing whilst the rest has rotted away with the years and is covered in grains of sand and pebbles. I walk round to the far end and run my hand over the fragile wood, gnarled with age and the dampness of the sea air and a plank falls away under my touch. I bring my hand away sharply and peer under to try to see what is lying beneath the collapsed structure.

'I think this used to be a fisherman's hut,' calls Alberto who is busy setting his tripod up. 'There are a couple of old rods down there.' As I crouch down to have a look at them, I start to hear the comforting click of Alberto's camera. Sure enough, there are a few rods, rendered useless with the passage of time and modern equipment. My imagination starts to run wild with questions. I wonder what the story of this hut is. Who used to come here, what kind of fish did they catch, where did they live, what was their story?

'Everything has a story, doesn't it?'

'Hmm?' Alberto murmurs as he adjusts the height of his camera.

I smile as I smooth hair away from my face which keeps curling round my eyes in the breeze. 'Nothing. *Nada*, I was just thinking.'

The sun has reached the level of the ocean, a great ball of crimson fire that turns all the streaked clouds pink. And as it continues to slowly sink, the gulls screech and swoop and scavenge as a cool gust of wind makes me shiver. I dig my hands deep into my jeans.

'Paloma...' Alberto says. I look up at him, unsuspecting, into his waiting camera as I hear a faint click. Then he walks towards me and hugs me to him. 'You look frozen.'

I nod and he tilts my chin up towards him. 'I love this place,' he says as he kisses me deeply. 'And I love you.' I gaze at him, light dancing and playing with the colour of his eyes and I say the words back to him, knowing that my heart will be his forever.

CHAPTER NINETEEN
ISABEL

20th November 1975

Early in the morning, as I pull the curtains back in my bedroom, a small greenfinch appears on the other side of the window. It is picking delicately at some foliage and I freeze, not wanting to scare it away, transfixed by the beauty of its green and yellow plumage. I don't know how long I stand there for, two lives separated by glass, but however long it is, I know it is a gift. The bird eventually hurtles off through the garden, a tiny bullet of startled green. I can never look at the colour green without thinking of Abuela Aurelia, for green was always her colour of choice. '*It's the colour of hope, little one,*' I remember her saying to me. I can still hear her voice now, as clear as ever.

Over the past few years, Franco has been growing frailer and Juan Carlos of the royal family has sworn loyalty to the head of state and the principles of the movement. For years, Franco has been preparing him as his heir but there is something in those intelligent brown eyes of that young man that I instinctively trust. Of course he has to pay lip service to Franco, but the will of the people is moving away from Francoism, and he knows it. When the general's closest ally, prime minister Carrero Blanco, was assassinated by ETA a couple of years ago, we all held our breath. What was coming next? Murder can never be the answer to anything, but it was as though the Basques were pinning a label to their actions, shouting '*This is for Guernica, this is for your repression of our people. No more.*'

By this time, Paloma and Alberto had been married for a few years and were still living with us at Carmen de las Estrellas. Their wedding was a small affair attended by family and a few close friends with the ceremony in Iglesia San Nicolás and then a celebration back at our home where we drank *vino de la costa* and danced until late into the night. I could barely take my eyes from my daughter all day – she had wound jasmine into her hair and I shall always remember the sight of her and Alberto standing on the patio beneath the wisteria, his arm wound round her waist and their fingers interlaced. Never had Paloma looked so beautiful or contented. There was a look of Mother about her, the mother of my childhood with her long dark hair and natural grace, and I felt more proud than I ever had done in my life.

Henry, I know, was experiencing much the same as me as his eyes were lost into the creases of his face when he smiled. His grey-blond hair, no matter how much water I put on it in the morning to smooth it down neatly, had still worked its way skywards again. Over the course of the day, he took my hand in his many, many times and squeezed it, equally wordless with happiness.

Paloma and Alberto decided to continue living at Carmen de las Estrellas, which I am glad of as there is more than enough room for us all in the house. A morning routine has long been established without ever having to discuss it. Alberto is always up first and he goes out to buy the paper and a long *barra* of bread. By the time he is home, I have made *café* for everyone, strong with hot milk. Henry prepares the table for *desayuno* and Paloma pounds fresh tomato to top the bread, mixed with olive oil, salt and garlic. By the time breakfast is ready and the tomato pulp spread thickly onto the *tostada* I wake Mother with a cup of chamomile tea and sooner or later she joins us at the breakfast table.

And so, this morning when I come downstairs after seeing the greenfinch, everything seems just the same. We all eat breakfast and the newspaper is pushed back and forth between us and nobody speaks; none of us like to talk much at breakfast. Henry leaves for work, Alberto goes down to the darkroom in the cellar, Paloma helps me tidy away and Mother drifts through the patio doors, as she does most mornings to inspect the garden and the mountains.

And then. Do I imagine this or is everything suddenly quiet? Henry returns from work just two hours after leaving and when he comes through the doors and I look round in surprise from the kitchen, I read it instantly in his eyes that something has happened. He reaches for my hands and he stares at me long and hard and he breathes the words *'Franco ha muerto'*. Franco has died. Franco has died.

And like moths straining towards the light, everybody in the house gravitates to the courtyard and we all reach out towards one another, a silence bearing down upon us so weighty and so wordless that our only means of communication become small gestures: the nod of a head, eyelids squeezing tightly closed, and mouths opening and closing – words forming in our heads but incapable of transferring to our tongues. It is all too much – it all means too much and how can we say anything with this weightless, soundless pressure bearing against us from all sides?

The death of a single man, arguably, can make no tangible difference to any of our lives. But perhaps this day means so much to us all because we know, in our hearts, that Francoism eventually *will* die with Franco; that our lives *will* improve. *Democracia, democracia*, whispers the wind and for the first time since the Second Republic has been pulled out from beneath our feet all those years before, we can believe it may be returned to us within our lifetimes.

The following days are a blur and tangle. I know that Juan Carlos is crowned king and I know that an enormous memorial service is held for *el Generalissimo* and he is interned at El Valle de los Caidos along with the other victims of the civil war who were lucky enough to have their deaths commemorated. But the details are hazy. What I remember above all else is the voice that comes on the radio at ten o'clock on the morning of his death; Franco's will being read out to the nation. I hear those words so many times over the following days that they have been forever stamped upon my memory. '*I beg forgiveness of everyone,*' the will reads, '*just as with all my heart I forgive those who declared themselves my enemies even though I never thought of them as such. I believe that I had no enemies other than the enemies of Spain.*'

The first time I hear those words, a strange buzzing sensation overcomes me, almost like a jolt of electricity surging through me, because just by hearing these words, a realisation hits me for the very first time through all this lunacy: Franco actually thought he was doing the right thing. Yes, I still believe he was a cruel dictator and yes, I believe the suffering he caused over decades was immeasurable. But despite this, Franco never doubted his own ideals and if it weren't him, it would have been someone else. So did I have any right to continue hating him? He killed my father; true, he may not have been the one to pull the trigger himself but my father's death came about as a result of extremism; of fascism; of the suppression of free speech. For the first time ever, I realise that the time will come when I will have to forgive the murderer of my father. Because through the joy and the pain of those following weeks, all I keep thinking of is that small greenfinch and the song of hope it carries on its wings as it flies away from me. Franco, I think to myself, you are wrong that I am an enemy of Spain. I love my country and I love the promise of what it can become. But it can only become this now that you are gone.

CHAPTER TWENTY
PALOMA

Autumn 1976

What's your perfect idea of happiness, somebody in Barcelona once asked me. And I answered quickly. I didn't have to think about it. It was to have all the people I loved most in the world in the same room as me. And now, it's a Friday evening, late September. I sit in the conservatory of Carmen de las Estrellas looking around me, feeling almost giddy with contentment, knowing that I now have this. Alberto is here, as well as my parents, brothers, grandmother and Tío Joaquín, my favourite uncle, though I probably shouldn't admit it. We've just finished eating dinner and have now come together to drink *manzanilla*. My uncle being as busy as he is, I feel the warm glow of gratitude that he's here, just for me. For tomorrow's an important day: I will open my new café, *Esperanza*, conceived as a dream but now a reality. Tío Joaquín sits beside me as he lays down his glass of sherry and tunes up his guitar.

'Paloma,' he says. 'If you agree, this is the piece I want to play tomorrow night.' The lights twinkle behind him from the city below, beyond the conservatory and I smile at him. I know that anything he plays will be well received. I'm fully aware that my decision to rely on my famous uncle's support for my opening night has already been mocked by various people. That it'll be his fame rather than the café's merit that will potentially attract customers to *Esperanza*. But I don't care. I'm close to my uncle and after the initial excitement has died down following his appearance, it'll soon become clear whether my café really has a chance of success.

After he's finished tuning the guitar, I watch as he begins to play. His long fingers expertly master the strings and produce the sound for which he's renowned. After a few minutes, to my left I can hear the very subtle but discernible sound of my abuela weeping, something that often happens when Tío Joaquín plays.

We sit there for ages, long after even Tío Joaquín has stopped playing and I hear the breathing of my grandmother become slower. I look over to her and can see her eyes have closed and she's fighting sleep. I feel a sudden sharp stab of love for her. For her frail white hands and the thinness of her legs under her dress. For her oversized feet and her long grey hair, still soft to the touch. I know I'll never really be able to understand the pain she experienced. But to me she'll always be one of the most beautiful and inspiring women I know.

The following afternoon, I unlock the wooden door with my key before pushing it slowly open and walking tentatively inside. Inhaling sharply, the realisation hits me afresh that I've been waiting for this day for many years. Without turning on the light, I look around, my eyes slowly becoming accustomed to the cave's dim light. I take it all in: low wooden tables covered in candles. Intricately designed metallic chairs. A beautifully painted and lined bookshelf. A record player with a neat stack of vinyl placed next to it. A piano with its white keys grinning up at me. Moroccan rugs covering the floor. Walls filled with paintings and black and white photographs hung on the fossilised rock and mud walls of *Esperanza*. I've placed the largest print over the bar – it features the proud, smiling faces of a young Moroccan peasant boy and his grandfather surrounded by an applauding crowd. Yes, everything is here. Everything is exactly as it should be. I sink back against the wall and close my eyes. The door is slightly ajar and a thin trickle of sunlight filters in and paints the cave's interior with a wan glow.

'It's too remote up here,' my brother Dani tells me when he first sees it. 'You'll never attract enough of a crowd to make a success of this.' I listen to his advice, searching high and low around the city for a suitable location. But I keep dreaming about the cave that has stoked my imagination and made my mother and grandmother's colourful stories of visiting the *gitano* cave almost feel like my own. This particular one sat empty and neglected, beckoning me from its dark, mysterious interior. A few other possibilities came up, but I'd backed down on all of them at the last minute. Either the location lacked the charm I wanted, or the setting was fine but the building itself was too small, too cramped, too damp, too soulless. So, amidst the warnings of my brother and against my own sense of reason, I made the decision. This was a risk I had to take.

I want to draw a diverse crowd of people in from all corners of Granada to my café. I'm an introvert by nature, but at the same time, I've always been fascinated by people: their contradictory nature, the nuances of relationships and above all the interaction between people from different segments of society. I envisage a café not just as a place to relax over a steaming cup of peppermint tea or flick through a book, but also as somewhere that can play host to the meeting of minds. A place that can attentively watch the evolution from first contact to potential discussion and friendship. For this reason, I've created an intimate setting, with minimal space between the tables.

I sit now at one of the tables and try to stop my mind from racing. What if too many people come? Or what if *nobody* comes? I hear noises from outside and stand up and walk to the window. I can see several people starting to appear, walking alongside the pomegranate bushes that line the path. I gulp and open the door.

'*Buenas tardes,*' I say. 'There are two hours left until the official opening.'

One young man gives me a huge smile. 'Joaquín Torres Ramirez is definitely worth waiting for!' I smile back and shrug before closing the door again and standing with my back against it. *Mierda*, have I underestimated Tío Joaquín's popularity? I know he's considered one of the greatest flamenco guitarists in the region, the country even. But he's just my *tío*, my uncle, and sometimes I don't grasp the full truth of that. Have I made a mistake in asking him to play at the opening ceremony? I look around the cosy interior of the cave and feel my stomach churning with both nerves and hunger. The café is poorly equipped to accommodate hordes of enthusiastic fans. Realising that I'll just have to cope with it one way or another I start to busy myself. I put the final touches to the *tapas*, dropping a few remaining olives from the jar into my mouth as I begin a final clean of surfaces. Alberto soon arrives and as I dash around, he sits at the bar and pours two large *cañas* of beer. Gratefully, I take the glass from his outstretched hand and hold it close, taking small sips. Alberto reaches out and runs a cool finger down my hot, flushed cheek.

'You've done it, Paloma.'

'Not yet I haven't. I want it to be—'

'It will be,' Alberto says resolutely. 'It will be perfect.'

The opening night of *Esperanza* proves more successful than I could have dreamed. So many people turn up, they even sit on the roof and seem to hang from the narrowest corners of the cave like bats. It's a warm night and I can hear laughter and the electric buzz of voices filling the night air. People sit around drinking chilled glasses of *tinto de verano* and beer and children chase each other around the pomegranate bushes. Before he plays, Tío Joaquín clears his throat to talk and the effect is instantaneous. A hush falls upon the lively gathering and a domino effect of gradual silence reaches all the way to the person sitting furthest away on the grassy verge outside.

'I am honoured to have been invited here this evening by my niece, Paloma, to help her open this café, *Esperanza*. Not only is tonight the culmination of many years of dreams and ideas and hard work, but as the café's name suggests, it will serve as hope and inspiration. Even through the darkest days, Paloma, I have the most profound respect for you and this dream you have turned into a reality and I have no doubt that through your determination and spirit you will make it succeed.' He pauses to take a sip of water and I look around at the expectant faces, hanging off his every word. At that moment, I watch as two people make their way through the crowd assembled at the door. I'm overjoyed to see that it's Mar and Pablo. Mar moves slowly with the help of a stick and Pablo walks beside her, her arm through his. I beckon for them to come and sit with us and, as seats are cleared for them, Tío Joaquín acknowledges them, smiling deeply in their direction.

'It is interesting to note my niece's choice in deciding to house her café in this historic cave. I'm sure that I don't need to remind anyone present of what happened to the original inhabitants of these *gitano* dwellings forty years ago.' A sympathetic murmur reverberates around the walls of the cave. Tío Joaquín pauses again, gazing intently around. 'What happened here amongst my people was simply a catalyst for what went on to take place in this city and across the country. It hasn't left any of us unscarred.' A tomb-like silence has fallen upon the crowd. He has bowed his head slightly, a lock of dark hair falling over his face, and I'm sure I can see the slightest tear forming in the corner of his eye. Strange that I've never thought of it before, but I realise that my uncle uses his guitar as a channel for showing emotion. Without his guitar in his arms, he looks far more vulnerable than I've ever seen him. I look around at the sea of faces before me. Young and old alike are locked in silence, those above a certain age probably reeling in their own memories. Looking up, Tío Joaquín continues. 'We are here tonight to respect and learn from the past. But above all, we have come together to celebrate a most welcome addition to Granada's cultural and culinary scene.' He smiles warmly at the crowd as the tense hush erupts into hearty clapping.

Raising his glass of red wine, he tips it in the direction of all those in front of him before taking a slow, appreciative sip. 'I'll now play a ballad I particularly love. I dedicate it to all those who lost their lives during the conflict; to our country's new democracy; to all of you, my friends.' Turning to face me, he takes my hand. 'And I dedicate it to you, Paloma. For your strength and your courage. To *Esperanza*.'

'*¡Esperanza!*' The crowd raise their glasses and call out, listening in delight as the throaty acoustics of the cave swallow their words and bounce from the walls. I hand

my uncle his guitar. Unhurriedly, he tunes it and then
enters another world, another existence where he plays of
love, of longing and of liberation.

※ ※ ※

It is half two in the morning and I've only just managed
to coax the remaining revellers out. I close the door with
a relieved but deeply satisfied thud. The interior of *Esperanza* looks like it's spent far longer than one evening
in the throes of merry-making. Strewn around the tables
and shelves are a huge number of empty glasses and left-
over morsels of food. Books have been taken down from
the shelves and thumbed through and I can still feel the
air of pleasure that lingers long after the last candle has
burnt out. As a vinyl soothingly whirrs, Alberto sweeps
the floor, whistling along to the tune. The only others
still here are the two late-comers. Pablo stands at the sink
washing glasses and dishes, as always a black woollen hat
pulled low over his head despite the heat. I walk slowly
around the café with Mar, admiring Alberto's photographs and Pablo's framed drawings. She stops in front of
one of my grandfather planting bulbs in the garden, his
face a picture of concentration with curls flopping down
over one eye.

'How perfectly Pablo has captured Eduardo's look,'
Mar murmurs before she continues walking. I remain
where I am, staring at the picture. I would love so much
to have met him. Even just spent a day in his company. I
turn to look at Mar who is scrutinising other photos and

drawings, a knowing smile on her lips. She must have been so beautiful. She is *still* so beautiful. Her face is lined but pride is etched into each and every one of those lines and her dark eyes have a haunted but knowing look about them. I never feel I can hold Mar's gaze for too long. Almost as if she keeps looking at me, she'll discover something I don't want her to know, though I have no idea what this could be.

Pausing at another sketch, Mar carefully lowers it down from its hanging place on the wall. I know she's seen this picture many times before. In fact, *she* gave it to me for the very purpose of hanging it in *Esperanza*. But seeing it now so beautifully framed and placed on the cave's wall, it must have taken on a new, moving significance, stirring long-forgotten memories. I walk up behind her and look at it over her shoulder. Pablo drew this picture when he was just a young boy. It's of his mother, sweeping the yard of the cave they used to live in.

'Do you remember when Pablo sketched this?'

Mar laughs a deep, raspy chuckle. 'Oh, he was always drawing. *Siempre*. But this one in particular?' She squints her eyes and cocks her head on one side in such a girlish way that I can barely see the difference between the woman in the picture and the woman she is now.

'*No*,' she sighs. 'I can't say that I do. But every day I swept, and stoked fires, and strung peppers up to dry, and washed clothes. Beatriz was always there with her tattered rag doll, what was her name? And Graciana and Inés would have been small babies at this time, probably lying in their cots I put under the tamarisk tree. And Pablo, drawing,' she casts a proud sideways glance at her son, 'always drawing. He used to perch on the roof of the cave watching us, ay, so serious!'

Mar breaks off and shakes her head. 'My mother was always trying to make him laugh, but it rarely worked.'

She turns to look at me, her black eyes unnervingly large and bold. 'You know, Paloma, my mother was not much older than I am now when she died.'

I pause as I try to hold her gaze. 'I didn't know that.'

'I still miss her, *sabes*. I don't think you ever really get over the death of your mother. Even if it *is* their time to go.' She sighs. 'Paloma, *estoy cansada*, fetch a chair for me, *por favor*.'

I rush to pull a chair down from where it's been stacked. 'Why don't I walk you back?'

'No, no,' she says. 'I just need to take the weight off my feet; have a small drink perhaps.'

'I'll join you, I was going to light the stove again anyway and we can have some tea. Are you cold?'

'No,' she replies and smiles at me. 'You look like your mother, you know.'

'Do I? Most people say I'm more like Papá.'

'*Qué dices*, you have far more of the Spaniard about you, *guapo* though your papá is. And I always was susceptible to a handsome man, as everybody knows.' Mar raises an eyebrow, almost challengingly. I sense she wants to talk about something I've never discussed with her before. At least not with Mar directly.

'Miguel.'

'Miguel,' she repeats, and shakes her head. 'He was a rogue. But…' she spreads her hands and sighs, 'I loved him. I don't know why, but I loved him. And look at the wonderful son he helped me produce. Who would have thought Joaquín would be such a prodigy?'

'Did…did he ever show any interest in being part of Tío Joaquín's life?'

'*¡Qué va!* Did he ever. No. That man thought only of himself.'

'Except…' I hesitate. This isn't my story. I wasn't there and I don't want to speak out of turn. But I know what Mamá told me about the safeguard that my abuelo's brother put on Carmen de las Estrellas all those years ago.

'Except what?'

'Except maybe his way of repenting,' I reply slowly, 'was by trying to keep our family safe. And his son.'

I don't know how she'll react. But I'm relieved when she pats my hand and says 'You're right, *cariña*. There are so many things we'll never be sure of. But one thing is certain, and that is that there's no such thing as black and white.'

We fall silent and after a while I remember the tea and ask Pablo to stoke up the fire. He gives me his dignified, quiet smile and nods his head. I turn back to Mar, a woman who's intrigued me for so long and who now seems to be taking me into her confidence.

'You know,' she continues, twisting her mouth into a tight smile, 'after Miguel rejected me, after I realised there was absolutely no hope for us, I left for a long time. You must think me terribly irresponsible when I had children to care for.'

I open my mouth to say something, but she quickly adds 'You would be right to think this. It *was* irresponsibility, pure and simple.'

'Where did you go?'

'I was never a strong person, not like my mother. I simply could not deal with the fact that I knew Miguel and I would never be together and if it could not work, then I didn't want to be mother to his child either.' Her forehead creases up and she looks up at me with those haunted eyes. 'Terrible, isn't it? *Claro*, I love Joaquín, but in a different way. It is your grandmother who is his mother, not me.' She shrugs. 'I travelled west along the coast and took various jobs and spent so many lonely weeks and months on my own. I think I was determined to return only once I felt liberated from that bond of love, futile, rotten love that it was. I *know* it was weak to leave my family. But I am a weak person, Paloma.' She smiles at me brightly, as if she has just told me some wonderful news. Confused, I search her face questioningly. I know she doesn't want me to say anything and so I don't. Pablo draws up at that minute with cups and a *tetera* of tea that he pours out and then disappears back into the shadows of the cave. How is it that Pablo has that uncanny knack of always camouflaging himself with his surroundings?

'Anyway,' Mar continues. 'The point is that I knew my heart would call me back when the time was right.'

'How old were you?'

'Thirty-three, thirty-four or thereabouts. When I got back, I was refreshed in mind and spirit and I made a vow to myself that I needed nothing from a man from that day forwards beyond friendship.'

I stare at her in surprise and, as though reading my mind, she adds 'And yes, I have been true to my vow.' She stifles a yawn. '*Ahora*, I really am tired. And so are you, Paloma. Perhaps we should all go back.'

I smile at her, grateful that she has opened up to me. She has permitted me a small slice of Mar from long ago, knowing that the words she's shared have been spoken little over the years. 'You're right,' I answer, squeezing her hand. 'I can always finish cleaning up tomorrow with Alberto.'

Pablo joins us at the table and we finish drinking our tea in silence. Before leaving *Esperanza*, I take one final look around. My heart skips a beat with pride and happiness. As the moon shines down on us, I pull the door tightly shut and turn the key in the lock.

CHAPTER TWENTY-ONE
ISABEL

1978

The year after those longed-for elections is an important anniversary of Father's death. We've never been able to retrace his last steps, but somehow, with Pablo's drawings, this need has diminished. All we know is that his name appeared on a list of people who were shot against the walls of Granada cemetery on that frosty morning of December 1938. Forty years to the day after father was executed we make a pilgrimage. The entire Torres Ramirez clan are there as well as Mar's family. Despite Mother and Mar's age, they insist on walking all the way. We rise silently before dawn and wrap ourselves up in several layers to keep the biting chill of the wind out.

As I walk down the stairs, a glimmer of glass catches my eye. I turn to face the picture hanging on the wall and move closer to it. It is Father and I, immortalised in pencil by Pablo, sitting beneath my orange tree. I am lying on a rug, staring up at the leaves whilst Father reads to me from a book. I remember that afternoon. I remember it well, because it was the only time when I have been the subject of Pablo's drawing that I noticed him drawing me. Drawing us. I caught him in the act. And I remember that smile of complicity that passed between us. I pause for a moment longer, marvelling as I always do at the uncanny likeness he has caught in those carefully constructed lines, before I continue my descent.

Silently, we congregate in the courtyard of Carmen de las Estrellas. Mother steps forwards, clutching an orange tree seedling in her hands as with infinite care she plants it in a pot and pats the mound of earth down around it. The seedling will receive everything it needs there for it is open to the elements – rain and sun, air and earth and the warmth of the family around it – and I send a prayer up to somewhere and something that this tree will thrive.

We make our way down through the narrow, winding paths of the Albaicín. It is barely light and we can still see a spattering of stars across the sky against the lilac-tinged dawn, the clear night making the intensity of the cold even greater. None of us say a word as we walk along, arms linked for warmth and for strength. Mother leads the procession and I marvel at the spring she has in her step still and the determination set in the lines on her face.

By the time we reach the cemetery, dawn is breaking. A light mist is rising from the frosty ground and gradually the outline of the sierra becomes more pronounced. None of us will ever know the exact spot against the cemetery wall where my father breathed his last breath. Nor shall we know the thoughts that would have been racing through his mind. But as we all stand in silence with our eyes fixed on the wall and the frost-covered moss and ferns covering the ground, we all have our own interpretations.

As I stand there with Mother on one side of me and Paloma on the other, I feel the echo of the gunshot from all those years past searing through my body and the heavy thud of Father's body as his knees crumple beneath him. I have this idea that his eyes would have remained open for a few minutes as he lay with his head against the cold, hard ground of the cemetery, feeling his life slowly ebbing away from him. And in that time he wouldn't have thought about the fact that death had stretched its hand out to him. He would have thought about the tears of joy he shed when I was placed in his arms as a newborn baby; the pride he felt at seeing his work in print; the thrill of García Lorca's presence in his life; those large family meals on the terrace, discussing poetry and music and the quest for a higher truth. But more than anything, I'm certain that he would have thought about Mother; about Luisa, the great love of his life.

After a while, we all notice that Mother has reached into her pockets. She is pulling out pebbles and feathers and is scattering them lightly across the pale ground. I don't know what they signify, but they clearly have an important connection with Father. She is smiling gently, lost in a world of tender memories of her beloved Eduardo and when there is nothing left, she takes a deep breath and says in a firm voice 'It is better to be the widows of heroes than the wives of cowards.' I feel myself choked with emotion – these were the words of *La Pasionaria*, that captivating, inspirational woman whom I heard speaking all those years ago in Barcelona addressing the courage of the International Brigades. How right she is. Her words are so perfectly apt, and no more so than right at this moment. And finally, *finally*, after all those years of being forbidden to openly mourn, my mother can call herself a widow with her head held high.

I squeeze the arm of Mother and Paloma on either side of me. After several more minutes of silence and contemplation, we take one last look at the walls of the cemetery, listening to the comforting birdsong that is breaking out and feeling the first rays of weak sunshine filtering through the swaying poplars and warming our skin.

As we make our way back down the side of the valley, I break off a little from the group and stand at the foot of a partially wooded slope, gazing up at it. It was the exact spot where, as children, Father brought us to toboggan down the snowy hill on Mother's skillet pans. I have thought about that time on several occasions but as I stand there, rooted to the spot, the memory comes back to me with a clarity I've never experienced before. María, Joaquín and I are standing at the top of the slope, trying to entice one another to be the first to go down the hill. They tell me that I am the eldest and therefore I *have* to go first, and though I'm unconvinced by their logic, I am far too excited to wait much longer.

Carefully, I pat down a small mound of snow beneath my mittens and arrange the pan on top of it. With my legs dangling out at awkward angles from either side, I crouch down and Joaquín gives me an almighty push from behind. I whiz down the hill, the wind whistling in my ears and whipping against my cheeks and stinging my eyes and I can barely breathe, I am going so fast. And there he is, my father, waving his arms excitably over his head and hopping about from one foot to the other. As I reach him and ground to a halt, he lifts me high up in the air and laughs as he twirls me round and round and round.

EPILOGUE

1979

My hospice is in a small building in Campo del Principe, about a fifteen-minute walk from Carmen de las Estrellas. I would like it to be bigger, and I would like to help more people, but the fact remains: I have a hospice. I am able to work with my head held high. The truth is that I probably could have opened it earlier since Franco's grasp on the country was becoming weaker and weaker in the years preceding his death. But something prevented me from doing so until he was no more. Besides, I'd been thinking about it for so many years that once that time came, I was given a free rein and people were astounded at how quickly I set it up. I'm proud of what I've achieved; proud of what the hospice has become. For I truly believe that it's a place that people can come to and die in peace and dignity. And people do come; they come in their dozens. Many are survivors of the years of terror and the stories I have heard and continue to hear are horrifying and astonishing. The slow erosion of fear takes more than years, it takes generations. But now that people are starting to talk about those years – the executions, torture and repression – many people, particularly those denounced as 'reds', want to quite literally dig up the past and uncover the remains of the bodies of their loved ones who lie in mass shallow graves across the length and breadth of our country. It's only been since democracy has returned to Spain that Republican victims of the war have been honoured. For some, this comes in the form of people who fled Spain slowly trickling back in and holding memorial services. For others, it means erecting plaques or memorials. And then there are those I mentioned who want to dig up graves to identify victims. I understand the need people have for this – their desire to honour the deaths of their loved ones in a more fitting way and to give them a dignified burial, yet Mother is adamant that we should let Father's bones lie undisturbed. 'So what if we find his skull or one of his vertebrae?' she once remarked dryly. 'That has nothing to do with his soul. It is not the way I should like to remember him.'

And me, how do I feel about it? I know that people grieve differently, just as people deal with the pain that surrounds death in numerous ways. Yet when we are speaking of my own father, my own flesh and blood, for me it's not his body that's important. Instead, I like to keep his memory alive through his poetry, Pablo's drawings and through stories that will be passed down about the gentle character of Eduardo Torres to future generations.

I shall never forget the first time Mother comes to visit the hospice. She stands on the threshold, her hair snaking down her back, and she sighs, the kind of sigh that is depthless. How desperately I want her approval, I realise. Just as I always have done. She says nothing, simply walking around the hall, each step purposeful. She looks at the pictures hanging on the walls, runs her fingers lightly over the deep red petals of a potted geranium and then turns to me.

'*Me gustaría ver un paciente.*' I would like to see a patient.

At that time, as it is the early days of my hospice, there are only three. I hesitate. Whom should I take her to? After pausing for several moments, I lead her down the light, airy corridor, flanked with plants and paintings to the room at the end, take a deep breath and then walk in with Mother following me.

A tiny, frail woman lies in the bed, her head on one side and her mouth open. As she sleeps, her brow furrows in the middle, two thick grey eyebrows touching and a web of veins criss-crossing her face. Very quietly and gently, Mother pulls a chair up to her bedside and looks long and hard at the woman.

'Tell me,' Mother says in a whisper, unable to pull her eyes away.

'Her name is Elvira. She has cancer,' I reply. 'Gastric cancer.'

'And nothing…' she trails off.

I pause. 'Of course I always hope for a miracle, Mother. I'll never stop hoping for that.'

Mother nods. She tears her eyes from Elvira and looks around the small room. There are flowers and cards and a large bay window overlooking the plaza. 'What a lovely room,' she says, and then turns her attention back to the bed. Very gently, she reaches her hand out and places it on top of Elvira's. The old lady starts, opening her eyes in surprise and grunting. She turns her head to the other side of the pillow, watery grey-brown eyes staring at Mother for an instant, before she closes them again and continues to sleep.

'This lady,' my mother says slowly. 'She lost her husband. Just like me. Am I correct?'

I look at her in astonishment. 'Yes. But how did you—'

'*No lo sé*,' Mother murmurs. 'I don't know. I just see it. Actually, I do not see it. I feel it.' She purses her lips together and draws her hand slowly away, folding them in her lap. I stand beside her for several moments longer as we both watch the uneven rise and fall of Elvira's fragile chest. Then Mother turns her head to me. One stout tear has formed in the corner of her eye and, impatiently, she raises a knuckle to wipe it away.

'*Bien hecho, cariña*,' she whispers. 'Well done.'

❋ ❋ ❋

As for my own dear mother, she needs no help in dying. Independent to the end, she takes her last breath at the age of eighty-four and I lose a true soul mate. I find her in the conservatory in the straight-backed wooden chair with the evening sunlight catching the silver threads of her hair and her face serene and accepting. I sense that she has gone before I witness it; a gentle shift from within the earth and wood of Carmen de las Estrellas, the home that has held and protected us all these years. When I stand in the doorway, arms outstretched towards the frame to steady myself, I know there is no need to feel my mother's pulse or hope I may be mistaken. And as I stare at her, this beautiful, courageous spirit, I breathe in the echo of secrets, of sorrow and of laughter that press into me from all sides, inhabiting the space around me and around Luisa: mother, grandmother, friend and wife of a poet.

Letter from Rebecca

A huge thank you for reading *The Poet's Wife* and I do hope that you enjoyed reading about the lives of the Torres Ramirez family in Granada.

I would love to know what you thought about the book and would be so grateful if you could leave a review. This can also help other readers discover *The Poet's Wife* for themselves.

If you'd like to keep up to date with my latest book news, please sign up at:

rebeccastonehill.com/email

Thank you for your support and I look forward to sharing my next novel with you.

Rebecca

PS. You can also follow me on twitter: @bexstonehill

What first drew you to writing a novel set in Granada during the Spanish Civil war?

The setting came before the story. I lived in Granada many years ago teaching English and was mesmerised by the beauty of this place: the mountains that encircle the city, the whispcr of the rivers, the cypress trees, the light, the people. It wasn't until I'd left Granada that I started writing a story set there. I knew I wanted it to be in the past as have always been drawn to historical settings and as soon as I started delving into the Spanish civil war and talking to people, I knew I had a story there. I think coming from England where people generally know very little about what happened in the civil war or Franco's dictatorship (despite more Brits visiting Spain as tourists than from any other nation), I wanted to write a fictionalised account of one family's experiences to introduce readers to this appalling but fascinating slice of modern European history.

All three women, Luisa, Isabel and Paloma are strong in spirit and true to their beliefs. When researching for the novel, were there any real life figures or particular accounts that inspired you to write these three women?

I read a lot of Paul Preston's books, a British historian who is an expert on the Spanish civil war. One of his books is

Doves of War: Four Women of Spain. I was very inspired by this, particularly his account of the communist Nan Green who felt so strongly compelled to fight fascism in Spain that she left her children in England for a while so she could work with the International Brigades.

I was also fascinated by Dolores Ibárruri, also known as La Pasionaria (the passionflower) whom I mention briefly in the novel giving the farewell speech to the International Brigades in Barcelona. She was a tiny woman physically but her electric oratory skills became a rallying cry for the Left. I'd like to have brought her into the narrative more but there didn't feel a natural opening for this. I would, however, encourage anyone to read the full transcript of her farewell address as it's incredibly moving: http://www.english.illinois.edu/maps/scw/farewell.htm

Your writing has a beautiful, lyrical quality to it and poetry is a theme that ripples throughout the novel. Eduardo is a huge fan of the real life Spanish poet Federico García Lorca. Can you tell us a little more about him and why you wanted to weave him into your novel?

It's impossible to live in Granada without noticing how important García Lorca is to the city's inhabitants, a man whose life was cruelly snatched away at the age of thirty eight and whose memory lives on in his poetry, plays, art and music. Whilst not overtly political, he was associated with the libertarian movement and this, coupled with his thinly veiled homosexuality, made him a target for the fascist forces. I once acted in his play *Bodas de sangre* (Blood Wedding) at university which was the first time he'd really entered my consciousness but since then, I found myself drawn to this highly talented, enigmatic but shadowy figure from Spain's past.

The family home, Carmen de las Estrellas feels like such an important part of the novel. It's the anchor and bedrock of stability for its inhabitants, particularly in such unsettling times. Is it based on a real villa that you have visited?

In Granada I visited several Carmen's which never failed to amaze me as from outside the wooden doors, you'd never imagine them to be hiding a large, open courtyard with all the rooms backing off from it. Whilst the details of Carmen de las Estrellas (which translates to Carmen of the stars) comes from my imagination, that sense of the house being personified as a central family member comes from two places close to my heart. Firstly, my grandparents house in a Cambridgeshire village. I come from a large family with many aunts, uncles and cousins and we would often get together in my grandparents beautiful house. It is long gone but I'll never forget it: the smell of the books, the feel of the wallpaper, the drafts of cold air from beneath the doors and how it held so many family secrets. Secondly, my father lived in Switzerland and as a child and teenager I'd spend a lot of time in this chalet – it became as familiar to me as an old friend. Memories of our pasts being inextricably bound up in a home is so significant to me.

434   REBECCA STONEHILL

The friendships and love between Luisa and Aurelia is incredibly moving. Was it important to you to tell the story of the Gypsies during this particular historical period in Spain?

Like Luisa, I was also fascinated by the *gitanos* whilst living in Granada and used to love walking out to the cave areas where many used to live and some still do. García Lorca wrote many ballads and poems inspired by the *gitanos* whom he held a deep respect for. Just as he was singled out and hunted down by the fascist forces, so too were the gypsies and I was interested in all those who didn't conform or fit the mould of 'good Spanish citizens' that General Franco had created. The gypsies of Andalucía have been romanticised and eulogised in so many artistic forms over the years but, after reading what happened to them during the civil war and the following years, this fit perfectly with my intention to portray a darker side of their narrative.

When did you first realise you wanted to be a writer?

As a young child, I was fairly anti-social and would spend hours reading and writing stories and poems. I think I always knew I wanted to be a writer but it was probably reading Harriet the spy by Louisa Fitzhugh that confirmed it for me. She used to hide in cupboards and up trees spying on people and making notes about them and I duly followed suit, filling countless notebooks with my observations.

Can you talk us through your publishing story?

It was lengthy! I spent a long time seeking traditional representation from agents and whilst I managed to attract the attention of a few agents, none of them were prepared to take my novel on. I then sent it off to an authors' advisory service who gave the structure a big overhaul. After spending a lot more time editing, I did a final read through of the manuscript (reading it out loud which was very helpful) before I finally sent it to Bookouture.

Do you have any advice for aspiring novelists?

There was a period of ten years between first starting to write this novel and being taken on by Bookouture. Whilst I never imagined I'd still be working on it after all that time, I wholeheartedly agree with American writer and artist Debbie Millman who once said 'Expect anything worthwhile to take a long time.' So what I'd say to aspiring writers is don't give up. If you really believe in what you've written, if you truly believe it's good (because if you don't, nobody else will), then keep going. Don't do it on your own – get a variety of people to critique it and consider paying for a professional advisory service as nine times out of ten, a writer is too close to their own work to be truly objective.

What are you writing next?

As I'm currently living in Nairobi, I'm setting my next novel in Kenya. It's another historical setting in the ear-

ly twentieth century when Nairobi first became a colo-
nial settlement and also the Mau Mau emergency of the
1950's. It will be centred around a young Englishwoman
who goes to Kenya against her will to marry a man she
has never met and the unexpected direction her life moves
in once there.

What / who are your top influences as a writer? (authors / specific books you've read / people you've met in life who have inspired you)

I started writing *The Poet's Wife* shortly after reading Isabel Allende's The House of the Spirits. For a long time, I
loved reading the magic realism masters Allende, Salman
Rushdie and Gabriel García Márquez and when I first
started writing my own novel, I wrote in a magical realism
style that I later moved away from.

It would be difficult for me to pinpoint specific people
as there have been so, so many people I've met over the
years who have inspired me and informed my writing in
some way. I've dedicated this book to my father who's
no longer alive, but I feel he needs special mention as he
was instrumental in helping instil in me that sense of self-
belief; that anything is possible if you really open yourself
up to it and persevere.

ACKNOWLEDGEMENTS

There are so many people I want to thank for helping turn this book into a reality:

Oliver Rhodes, who first believed in my story and Claire Bord, whose insightful and sensitive editing of my manuscript has done it justice a hundred times over.

Hilary Johnson from the Authors' Advisory Service, who gave my manuscript a very necessary shake up and helped me to mould it into its final cast.

For reading the first section of my novel and providing invaluable feedback: Louisa Burns, Jane Cacouris, Caroline Thompson, Sarah & Pete Woods, Betsy Braden and a special thank you to Shirley Read-Jahn whose scrupulous eye for detail didn't miss a thing.

The late Bob Doyle, an Irish member of the International Brigades, who shared his time and memories with me to gain a greater insight into what it was really like to fight against fascism on Spanish soil.

Jenny Becker, the most inspiring English teacher a child could ever hope for, who recognised a writer in the young Rebecca and encouraged this throughout primary school.

Lucia Espiniella Sánchez, for those countless *desayunos* and ironing out some of my less than perfect Spanish phrases.

My mother, Elizabeth Stonehill, who bought me countless notebooks whilst I was growing up to fill with my ideas and stories and who always believed I could do it. My mother in law, Liz Narracott for all her support, particularly with the children.

My brother and sister, Sam and Louisa, for forming the backdrop of my childhood, the inspiration for many stories and being the stars on either side of Orion's Belt, plus my extended family and web of wonderful friends, too numerous to name individually, for all your support and belief.

And last but certainly not least, thank you to my amazing husband, Andy Narracott, for his love and support throughout and my three children, Maya, Lily and Benjamin for putting up with their Mama when her head was hundreds of miles away in Spain.

CPSIA information can be obtained
at www.ICGtesting.com
Printed in the USA
FSHW02n2016310518
48923FS

9 781909 490512